GIL'S GRIMOIRE, VOL. 1:

THE ZEROS AND THE MAN WHO COULD NOT DIE

BY ERIC BONKOWSKI

COPYRIGHT

DEDICATION & GRATITUDE

For Kathleen, as always. With love.

&

Special thanks to Dean Kotz for another beautiful cover.

ALSO BY THE AUTHOR:

Two Zeros and The Library of Doom!

The Zeros and The Man Who Could Not Die

The Zeros and The Empirical Evidence of Stars (forthcoming)

Brick Brannigan is Knee-Deep in Peril!

Brick Brannigan is Buried Alive in the Faroe Islands! (forthcoming)

A NOTE TO THE READER:

The Zeros and The Man Who Could Not Die is the first full-length novel of the Zeros. Be sure to check out *Two Zeros and The Library of Doom!*, a free ebook that takes place after this novel. Available now!

Visit http://www.gilsgrimoire.com for more information.

GIL'S GRIMOIRE, VOL. 1:

THE ZEROS AND THE MAN WHO COULD NOT DIE

"If you think this universe is bad,
you should see some of the others."
- Philip K. Dick

CHAPTER 1. THE ZEROS

The battle was over–my first with the team, definitely not my last–and Finch was speaking in his mind-numbing ninety-five year old college professor monotone, complete with the barest hint of an English accent. Ironic in this case, considering he looked like one of those twenty-something hipster kids from Brooklyn.

"Oftentimes, it is the lack of any truly conclusive evidence that will perpetuate natural earthborn doubt. That doubt–along with fear and a hint of stubbornness–is enough to keep even the most inquisitive minds at ease when faced with the seemingly impossible. However, when confronted with irrefutable physical evidence, even the most skeptical mind cannot ignore fact, regardless of how inexplicable. I call this the 'evidentiary silver bullet.' I think this evening was your silver bullet, Dylan."

Gil was giggling. "Got that right!" he said. "Our boy's got hard physical evidence splattered all over him!"

Gil Abercrombie. Eccentric billionaire, monster hunter, and exuberant manchild. Aficionado of pipes, scale science fiction models, and Hawaiian shirts. Alistair Finch. Know-it-all boy-genius, monster hunter, and deep well of cold pragmatism. Enjoys frowning, fine Scotch whiskey, and indecipherable foreign films. Together they're friends to the lonesome and desperate; villains to the undead and malicious.

To backtrack a little, either one of these guys could have dropped a few hints in their original job offer so that I could've had some hint at how my life was about to turn into a crazy circus funhouse. I mean, that just seems like courtesy, really. Unfortunately, they hadn't.

That morning I'd found a note tied to my newspaper. It read: The Docks. Midnight. Come armed.

1

Cryptic, minimalist, and dramatic. Eventually I'd learn that Gil liked drama; he found it funny. No job description, but the certified check included helped me forget those questions for the moment. If it hadn't been a *certified* check, I would have torn it up and thrown it out along with that day's credit card bills and take-out menus. If it hadn't been certified, I would've taken it as a joke. That check had more numbers than the note did words. So yeah, I decided to give the note the benefit of the doubt. You have to admit, a couple of zeros can be pretty persuasive.

I'd been laid off four days earlier from the private security firm where I'd been working for the past six years. It wasn't bad money, but I had to wear a suit with a logo on the breast and spend ten hours a day checking IDs and putting up wet floor signs when it rained. Maybe getting canned was a blessing in disguise. I'd spent my handful of unemployed days watching daytime television and reading murder mysteries (I've got a soft-spot for cozies; don't judge). Daytime television is a nice reminder that being at work isn't so bad.

I took my time in getting to the riverfront, bringing nothing but my old snub-nosed .38 Special, the only surviving relic of my days on the force. Despite having spent time as a soldier and a cop, I don't really like guns; that being said, I have to admit that the heavy piece helped keep me calm in situations like this.

I may have taken my time, but I still arrived at the dock early, taking a cab east from the Broad Street line's last subway stop. In Philadelphia, the harbor overlooked the Delaware River, a churning snake of black water that had once been a busy import/export route. Now, it was pretty much deserted. These days the only things you'd likely find in the Delaware would be bags of trash and maybe a few stray jumpers from the Walt Whitman Bridge. Yeah, welcome to Philadelphia. In the pale moonlight, huge bodies of empty ships rose and fell along the water's edge as the tide lapped at their rusty hulls. Behind me, a long line of warehouses stood against the dock and the shoreline, most of them abandoned. In the distance I could hear the low foghorn of a passing tanker. I felt like an extra in a shitty film noire.

A deep rumbling of music cut through the cool April evening and announced my new employer's arrival. I turned away from the Delaware to see a brown mammoth of a car circa 1955 roll up, clouds of exhaust burping up into the starry night sky. Inside, what sounded like epic power metal wailed, rattling the car's windows. I would have liked it when I was sixteen. From inside, I could hear a screeching guitar solo and some high, operatic vocals. Through the windshield, I could see the driver bobbing his head in time. After a moment, the engine sputtered to a halt.

The driver's side door opened and a tall lanky man emerged. I suppressed the urge to squint on seeing his yellow, purple, orange, and green Tiki shirt–complete with girls in grass skirts and palm trees. Shaggy jeans and a pair of huge white orthopedic sneakers completed the ensemble. Salt and pepper hair hung down to his shoulders; a thick bushy mustache half-covered his mouth.

"Hey there, brother bear, you must be Dylan," he said to me, grinning. "You look like you could rip a phonebook in half, my man."

He's right. I'm big, and I mean damn big. I never really work out anymore, but I'm still pretty ripped. People assume I'm either a linebacker or bouncer when they meet me. They also usually assume I have the IQ of a microwave oven.

"You must be Mr. Abercrombie," I said, extending my hand.

He shook it enthusiastically. I'd eventually learn that my boss did nearly everything enthusiastically. "Call me Gil, big D. If somebody calls me Mr. Abercrombie then I figure they either want me to make a donation to their university or become a Scientologist."

"All right, Gil," I said. "Is this your partner?"

He turned and laid his hand across the battered car's roof. "No way, this is my *baby*," he said. "We call 'er *the Tank*. A real classic. 1960 Mercedes 190B. Vintage collector's car here. This puppy is worth a fair chunk of change, lemme tell you. It's not everyday you find an antique in this primo condition." I noted the rust stains blooming from the wheel wells, the missing hubcaps, and the dents that covered the car like polka dots.

"Nice," I said. "How about your other associate? Is that your... son?" I pointed to the slim kid stepping from the open passenger's side door. He was a tad under six foot and skinny as a rail, dressed head to toe in black, making his red hair all the more glaring. His face was pale and freckled just under his eyes, which were dark and deep. I assumed he was the artist of the group.

"Oh, that's awkward," he laughed. "No, this is neither my associate nor my son, this is my true blue *partner*," Gil said. "Finch, come say hello."

3

"Hello," Finch said with a nod as he rounded the Tank and opened the trunk.

"He's very serious," Gil said with a wink. "I mean we *are* on a mission. Protectin' the innocent, defeatin' evil monsters, savin' damsels in distress, etc, etc." He shrugged, grinning. "We're a big deal. After this we're probably gonna get some Mexican food or somethin'."

My eyebrows rose. "Monsters, huh?" *Yeah, okay.*

"That's why I included the check, big man."

"So, uh, what kind of work do you guys actually–"

"Wait, wait! Hold on there, pardner!" Gil interrupted. "I didn't do the job interview yet. We don't take just any ol' slouch. You ready?"

"Sure?"

"Number one: Can you drive?"

"Yeah, of course I–"

"Okay, nice. Now hold your ponies, we're almost done. Number two, and this one's the real doozy, okay?" He licked his lips. "Can you... cook?"

"As a matter of fact, I love to–"

"Hey, hey, boffo! Here's what I like: Spaghetti-os, tacos, sloppy joes, grilled cheese, hot pockets, nachos, fried chicken, mac and cheese, hot dogs, that pink wine that comes in boxes..."

"Am I your butler?"

"What? No. I mean, not really. Wait, no. No. You're an equal partner, just like Finch here, of course. See, I'm here for morale, Finch is obviously for the laughs, and you, my large new friend, you can be the cook, and every now and then you can smash something. But come on, the fact that you cook is pretty friggin' stupendous."

"What exactly are you paying me to do? Cook and clean?"

"Well, there's driving too–" Gil started.

"–but what is it you guys do again?" I continued. "I mean, really?"

Gil smiled. For a long moment the only sound was the Delaware River lapping against the pier. "I didn't say," he admitted. "See, this is that really awkward moment on the first job where you ask a bunch of totally fair questions because you're beginning to wonder what you got yourself into, and I try to answer them without scaring you away. You know, the whole what's goin' on here, what do you do here, blah, blah, blah thing. Why don't we just skip it, eh?"

Oh boy.

He nodded. "I see that look on your face, and it's completely understandable. You definitely deserve to know what's up. I get it, big man. And you're right. But I picked you because I hear you're tough and you're discreet." Gil rounded the Tank and stood at Finch's side in front of the open trunk. "So trust me when I say this isn't the first time I've trained somebody this way, and this way is much easier. Just roll with it, okay?"

"Roll with it?"

"Yeah," he smiled. "You know, roll with it." He pulled a flashlight and a thick weathered tome from the trunk and dropped them into a duffel bag Finch was holding open. Across the book's leather jacket, the words **GIL'S GRIMOIRE** were stamped crookedly.

"If you start to get spooked or you lose your nerve, just keep that check in mind. Remember that one that had all those zeros on it? You'll be getting one of those puppies every month."

"Every *month*?"

"You got that right, big man. It's worth it for us heroes!" He set his jaw and struck an honest-to-God Superman pose.

"Zeros is more like it," Finch said. His voice was bitter in the cool night air. "Worth nothing to no one, we are." He smiled coolly at me.

Gil smacked Finch's arm like a disapproving grandmother. "Stop being a downer. This is supposed to be fun, remember?" I saw the glint of moonlight on metal as he pulled something from the trunk.

"Hey, is that a sword...?"

Gil either didn't hear what I said or just ignored me. He chattered on as he slid another long, impeccable blade free and dropped it nonchalantly into Finch's bag. "Gotta admit, it's gonna be pretty awesome dukin' it out with some revenants. Really clears the palate, you know? Remember, if we get done early enough, the burritos are on me. Burritos and nachos and some guac..." He looked up at me; I must've had shock in my eyes. Really, can you blame me?

"Just some swords, dude. Relax. Haven't you ever dressed up for a ren faire? Anyway, this is gonna be a cakewalk. Didn't you hear me say 'revenants'?"

The last thing he pulled from the trunk was a weathered skull covered in crooked runes. Gil rubbed his hand across the surface like a Magic 8 Ball. "Do us proud tonight, old buddy," he said before dropping the skull into Finch's duffel. Finch shouldered the bag and leaned into the trunk, pulling out one more longsword and leaving the leather sheath behind. Gil reached in and pulled a double-sided battle ax free with a cackle.

He looked up at me. "Oh, damn, I'm sorry. Where are my manners?" From the duffle on Finch's shoulder, he dug out a blade, shorter than the others, and the only weapon with noticeable nicks cut into the edge. He held it out to me, hilt first. "Short sword?"

CHAPTER 2. JUST ROLL WITH IT, REALLY

We were walking towards one big mother of a warehouse.

"Mr. Abercrombie? What exactly is a revenant?"

He looked over his shoulder at me and smiled. "Call me Gil, please," he said. He lifted his leg with a grunt and kicked, meeting the warehouse's utility door just below the deadbolt. The frame splintered with a satisfying crack and the door fell open into impenetrable darkness. Beside me, Finch clicked on the flashlight. A long beam of light sliced through the gloom like a scalpel, illuminating a barren concrete landscape broken only by steel support beams than ran upwards and disappeared into the blackness of the high, peaked roof. Above us, I could make out long tracks that ran the length of the building, twenty feet or so off the floor, tracks made for suspending and moving heavy freight to and from ships. They were empty now, but I could hear the occasional tinkling of chains moving in a faint breeze that felt disturbingly similar to a warm breath of air.

"Okay, Gil…revenants?" I asked again. My voice wavered more than I would have liked.

Gil lifted his ax and took a step into the warehouse, his white sneakers squeaking as he walked over the felled door. From a coat pocket, he pulled a pair of welder's goggles and slipped them over his head. "Finch, revenants?"

"Revenant: A ghost or other incarnation of the dead re-corporialized into one of various states of being, none of which should be mistaken with living. Perhaps also to be described as a reanimated corpse or the possessed dead."

I took a minute, chewing over the *reanimated corpse* bit, trying to decide how literal he was being. Finally, I said, "What?"

"You'll see," Gil said. "We get a lot of trouble from revs down here on the waterfront. Revenants are like Dark Magic 102, so we find ourselves dealing with this kind of BS a lot. Some of the broader-minded constituents at City Hall hire us out for things the cops don't have the resources or wherewithal to handle themselves. With revs, it's usually a bunch of jackass kids, but we'll see what tonight holds."

"Magic. Okay, like when you pull a quarter out of somebody's ear or saw a lady in half. Got it. But dark magic? That's a new one on me. And did you say 'reanimated corpse'?"

Gil laughed. "Yep."

"Reanimated corpse like zombie reanimated corpse?"

"No, no, this is Dark Magic 102, remember? Zombies are Dark Magic 101. This is one step past that. Revenants are a little... meaner. And a little smarter."

"Okay, great. And Dark Magic 101, Dark Magic 102... I take it there's a Magic University or something?"

"What do you think this is, Harry Potter? Jeez, it's just an expression, man. Hey Finch, pass me Yorick, eh?"

From the duffel, Finch pulled the rune-carved skull free, its two empty eye sockets glowing with a misty red light. Gil took it with a smile and extended his arm, holding it before him like a flashlight. The red light began to grow and pulse, spreading wild patterns across the expanse of the warehouse. Shadows seemed to grow from nothing, casting twisted and unnatural shapes across the cracked concrete flooring. That freaky feeling of hot breath grew wetter against my skin, making the hairs on the back of my neck stand on end.

Finch spoke up. "I believe this is a nasty one, Boss."

Gil nodded. "Uh huh. This kid ain't messing around." He cleared his throat and began to speak in a strange mishmash of what sounded like Latin and French; 99% of the words meant nothing to me. After a few sentences, I caught one I definitely knew: morte. *Dead.*

The shadows in front of us began to flicker and strange forms began to take shape, hard silhouettes slowly appearing where once stood nothing. I squinted into the darkness–not trusting my eyes–and curled my free hand around the butt of my pistol. In Finch's hand the flashlight flickered, firing uneven blasts of white light into the darkness, the only other light being the faint red glow from Yorick the skull. With each snapshot of pure light, the shapes in the dark began to take more concrete form. A final strobe illuminated the space before Finch's light went out completely.

My eyes adjusted to the darkness. I could hear breathing, deep and throaty, and not from one of us. Finally, I saw something in the dim red light.

Pale green skin, knotted and inhuman, stretched across a wide bony ribcage covered with winding black tattoos. Long, muscular arms extended out from a barrel-chested body and dragged on the ground alongside short but massively thick legs. There were no fingers, only ragged claws capped off by dagger-like talons sharp enough to flay a man. At the top of the crooked shape was a wide head with deeply-set eye sockets over the hole where a nose could have been. A gaping maw filled with jagged black teeth opened and the monster unleashed a wail strong enough to rattle my bones.

There was that hot, wet breath I'd felt earlier. I knew I wasn't imagining it.

The dead flashlight clattered to the floor. I pried my eyes off the beast's long enough to realize the thing wasn't alone. In the faint red light shining from Yorick's eye sockets, slow bodies were moving, feet dragging, the crimson glow offering glimpses of little more than profiles.

"Oh... oh my," Gil mumbled. "All right, okie doke, um step on back, gents. Finch, stay with Dylan, this sure isn't what I expected." He took a deep breath, and when he spoke, his voice was little more than a strained whisper. "This ain't just some damn kid."

I felt Finch's hand close over my arm and pull me backwards. In the dark, I could still make out the faint outline of the green-skinned monster. I heard a wet thud as the thing took a step towards us. Half a dozen paces from Gil, it screamed again.

Gil's shout broke through the monster's shriek, "*Mortuus exsisto silens. Nex absum!*" He raised the skull in his fingertips as he spoke and the skull's red light was replaced by beams of yellow that shot from the eye sockets like sunshine.

The creature screamed. Fully illuminated, I saw its eyes open wide– two monstrous black eyes recessed deep into its skull.

With a bellow, the beast turned away as green flames rose from the floor, engulfing its body in smokeless fire, casting a light so intense I had to cover my eyes. Gil raised his ax and charged, swinging wildly at the heart of the inferno. The blade passed through nothing but air as the green conflagration disappeared, leaving only darkness in its wake. His ax clattered to the floor. Despite the light, I'd felt no heat. I took a knee, rubbing my blinded eyes and blinking into the darkness.

"Dammit!" Gil shouted into the new silence.

Finch spoke up. "It's gone, I take it?"

"You got that right. We didn't have the chance to do a thing. Bad tip. Revenants my foot, Yorick was useless. Here, take 'im," Gil said.

Still blinded, I heard the zipper of the duffel open and close. I opened my eyes, but still saw only faint traces of the green light. "What the hell happened?" I asked. "And what in the holy hell was that?"

"That wasn't a revenant. And this wasn't some punk kid, either. It was a djinn, and it was *pissed*," Gil said. "Sorry about that, man. A little scarier than average for a first day. I wouldn't have brought you if I'd known that thing was down here. I figured we'd squash some undead thingies and then go get some nachos. This wasn't any kind of first contact for you."

"A djinn, huh? So *very literal* about the monsters, then?" I said. I shook my head, feeling dazed. In the dark, a new scent had arisen, heavy and cloying like the smell of spoiled meat.

"It's complicated," Gil said. "Everything is. I'll have Finch explain later. I'm hungry."

I opened my mouth to speak when a cold, wet hand closed over my throat. Overgrown fingernails dug into my skin as unnatural strength yanked me away from the group. A second hand closed on a fistful of my hair, and I struggled to scream–or breathe for that matter. The rubber soles of my shoes flailed against the floor. I may have managed a gurgle on the way. A manly gurgle.

"Abrrrcrrrmmm…"

The flashlight had returned to life, and I saw the blade of light slashing through the air in my direction. I dropped the short sword to the floor with a clatter and closed my hands over the fingers on my throat. With desperation I grabbed a slimy index finger and twisted, hoping to free my airway enough for one gasp of air. With a crisp crack, the finger snapped off in my hand. I tossed the finger to the floor in disgust as stars began to cloud my vision. Other than being one finger poorer, the hand seemed unbothered.

"Hey, hey," Gil shouted, "Now *that's* a revenant! Finch, cut the big man loose!"

I heard the clang of metal and the splintering of bone. A second later, the hearty splashing of fluids on concrete followed. Around me, dark figures rose from the concrete floor and began to close in with a single-minded purpose a la George Romero. Another crunch of sword on bone heralded the grip on my throat easing, and I dropped to the floor in a circle of wet bodies. I took a few deep breaths and the stars disappeared from my field of vision. *Big mistake.* The breath filled my lungs with nothing but the deep stench of decay. I dry-heaved and pulled my pistol from my belt. On the ground at my feet lay the revenant who'd grabbed me. It was a woman in a dirt-smeared business suit. Her face was ravaged by death. A hive of others just as gruesome and heartbreaking stepped over her body and lumbered towards me.

"Dylan, get down!"

I ducked as Finch's sword tore through one of the revenant's midsections, slicing him into two messy segments and spraying me with a cool liquid I imagined was blood. Hands closed on me and I responded by firing my pistol into the nearest cold body–a man in paisley pajamas with sallow skin and red eyes–I hit him but didn't slow him down. Instead he opened his mouth and leaned towards my face, baring his blood-soaked teeth.

His head left his body at the edge of Finch's sword. I took a step back and pulled his doubly lifeless hand from my shirt. My shoes were squishing in puddles of gore on the floor. Finch grabbed my hand and pulled me back from the swirling mass of undead, leading me stumbling towards Gil. On the way, I snatched up the short sword from where I'd dropped it and pocketed my useless revolver.

"Let's try this again," Gil said, handing me the flashlight as he pulled the skull Yorick from the black duffel and began speaking. Like me, he was soaked in blood, but unlike me, he looked like he was enjoying himself.

Red light returned to the eye sockets and runes as Gil spoke his gibberish one more time. The three of us stood back to back to back, facing the approaching mass of revenants that had risen from the deepest corners of the warehouse. I traced the light over the lifeless eyes and reaching hands as they staggered towards us, closer and closer.

Gil continued chanting as Finch stepped away from us. I felt droplets of blood raining down on me and could hear the sickening *thwack* of a sharp edge on rotting meat. I lashed out awkwardly with my sword at the approaching form of a stumbling woman when the floor beneath me lit up in a wash of green, cascading flames. I waited for the heat, but felt nothing but the cold clutch of the djinn's hand as it closed over my arm. I spun away as the slippery talons tore my sleeve to shreds. As I twisted free, I put a few revenants to the floor with the short sword before turning to face the djinn. The monster loomed over me, at least seven feet tall and rippling with muscle. It opened its black-toothed mouth and shrieked at me, spattering me with thick, hot strands of drool.

"Gil!" I shouted as I ducked and rolled backwards, barely avoiding the djinn's massive claw that passed like a 747 through the air where I'd just been standing. Behind the creature, Gil continued chanting, the red light pouring from the skull slowly morphing to a sour mustard yellow. The djinn's green flames continued spinning in webs across the concrete floor, mixing with the yellowing light to fill the warehouse with a dizzying array of unnatural color. Gil's attention was focused on the endless waves of revenants that rose from the darkness, his back to the djinn as he continued speaking.

The beast turned and raised a clawed hand over Gil's head, leveling its talons for a killing blow. From my position prone on the floor, I did the only thing I could: I lifted the sword and threw it end over end towards the djinn.

The short blade impacted the monster in the center of its back, burying itself to the hilt between the creature's shoulder blades. An angry rumble filled the air like a thunderbolt as the djinn turned to face me. Stumbling to my feet, I pulled the useless pistol from my pocket and raised it. The monster took a step towards me, the impact of its footstep sending a tremor through my body. Revenants appeared on either side of me, dead eyes finding mine and glowing with mindless hunger.

Gil continued chanting, the crazy kaleidoscope of colors reflecting off the welder's goggles on his face. The light from the skull kept changing, moving through what seemed like the entire color spectrum before finally becoming a clear, silver light that emanated outward in wide, halo-like rings.

The djinn's black eyes locked on me as it opened its mouth unnaturally wide—in this case, wide enough to swallow a man whole. I could see bits of flesh tangled in the shot glass-sized molars. It took a step closer and lowered its head, inhaling deeply, the sucking breath pulling me towards its mouth. I felt myself slide across the concrete, pulled by the strength of the beast's lungs.

A revenant interrupted my slide-o-death as it grabbed my throat and pulled me to my feet, turning my body to face it and leaning in to take a bite from my face. I pushed the muzzle of my pistol flush to his chest and pulled the trigger.

The gunshot was lost amidst the djinn's roaring, but the revenant released me. In its stumbling, it came between me and the djinn. I watched in shock as it was pulled into the djinn's mouth and disappeared with a wet *crunch*, like a bird into a turbine engine. I smiled before realizing my bullet had nothing to do with weakening the rev. The halos emanating from the Yorick were literally burning up the bodies of the revenants, working their way outward from Gil and leaving nothing but gore in their wake.

With a burst of hot breath, the djinn's huge mouth snapped shut as it turned its attention back to Gil. Howling, the djinn cast bolts of its green fire out to the far reaches of the warehouse, wide arcs of light that passed beneath the remaining revenants who screamed in protest as the flames engulfed them. For a moment the entire room was filled with overwhelming green flickering light. Then, like falling dominoes, the fire began to swallow itself, receding like a roaring freight train back towards the djinn in the center of the room before finally swallowing the beast in an explosion that blew me off my feet. The creature made one final swipe with its claw at me before it was gone, one long talon cutting across my cheek just deep enough to draw blood. I felt a sharp, lancing pain like a jolt of electricity lance through my body just as the green fire extinguished itself and disappeared with a *whooof.*

I landed on my back and felt bits and pieces of nastiness raining down on me. The pistol was still in my hand, and I could feel myself pulling the trigger but heard only the hollow clicks of the firing pin slamming against spent shells. On the concrete a few feet from me, the flashlight returned to life without even a flicker, sending a strong beam of light straight across the length of the warehouse floor. It illuminated a twisted maze of limbs and shredded remains. The djinn was gone.

I picked up the flashlight and passed the beam around the room. Amidst the ruins, I saw the skull Yorick, the duffel, Gil's sword, and the charred and bloodied shape of my own short sword. I felt sure I was the only one alive until I heard a chuckle. A moment later, Gil said:

"That. Was. So. *Awesome.*"

I felt myself smile in agreement.

CHAPTER 3. GETTING TO KNOW THE GANG

"You did all right, my man." Gil stood on the dock smiling, reveling in the spray cast up by the rush of the river against the pilings. He was covered in blood. I was disgusted and a little disturbed, although maybe not as much as I should have been.

I surveyed the goo that covered me. Not human in origin, I realized. "I need a shower," I said. "*As soon as possible.*" I'm not OCD or anything, but damn.

Gil laughed. "You look great, big man. And you were great in there. And sweet move on that djinn. I mean, throwin' a sword? Where'd you learn that, like Xena Warrior Princess school or something?" He pulled a blob from his tangled hair and tossed it into the water.

"You did very well," Finch said with a tip of his freshly-donned newsboy cap–also black. He stood at the Tank's trunk, stripping off his soiled shirt and mopping up long strands of what may or may not have been entrails with a towel.

"Yeah I don't know where I picked up that sword thing. I'd never exactly fought with one before today, let alone thrown one at a demon."

"A djinn's not really a demon," Gil said as he pulled a pipe from his pocket and slipped it between his teeth. "But don't worry, you'll learn." A match lit and disappeared momentarily into the bell of the pipe. Smoke rose in a twisting cloud, smelling remarkably foul.

"Yeah, maybe you can explain it to me later. Like I said Mr. Abercrombie, I need a shower."

"Listen," he said with a sigh, "we've fought evil side by side, so

14

please call me Gil."

"Okay. Gil. Listen. I need a shower. My hands are coated with something that yesterday I would have sworn didn't exist, but more importantly, my hands are sticky. Really sticky. I need a shower."

He laughed and tossed me the car keys. "You got it, brother. You're drivin'. We'll go to my place."

It took a few tries to get the Tank started. Once we got rolling, Gil switched the radio back on, which seemed to pick up right where it left off. Epic power metal once more filled the cab—I caught enough lyrics to pick up on the fantasy motif. It seemed to make Gil pretty happy. Finch and I didn't enjoy it quite as much, but the drive was short.

Gil directed me to a large apartment building within sight of the Art Museum. The apartment rose endlessly into the night sky. A weathered stone facade bore ornate sculpted molding, and I guessed that rent in the building's janitorial closet was probably more than my split-level's mortgage. An alley beside the building led down from street level to a subterranean parking facility. It was the prettiest parking garage I'd ever seen, decorated by wide swatches of brightly-painted wall segments and a few strategically placed carpets. A carpeted parking garage? Even the alleyway above had been decorated with potted palms. Beside the elevator bank were fresh flowers sitting on honest-to-God oak furniture. Surreal. Gil had a reserved parking space with his name stenciled on the wall within ten feet of the elevator's golden doors. I didn't notice at first that one of the elevators was key-operated.

Lavishly decorated and equipped with one button only—it said **P**—the elevator was beautiful, and the trip was just long enough to really appreciate it as we rode straight to the top. Gil sat on a plush red velvet bench for the duration of the short ride, smiling the whole way. The elevator doors opened to reveal a penthouse apartment large enough to make Donald Trump salivate. Impeccable wood floors stretched endlessly to large windows that showed the Art Museum and Logan Square, both colorfully illuminated at night. Huge framed works of art covered the walls. To the right, a wide staircase rose, leading up to a second floor mezzanine and beyond. Finch, carrying the duffel and an armful of bloody weapons, pulled open a door and disappeared down a long corridor, whistling a jaunty tune.

"All right, big man, this way to the clean-up room," Gil said. "It's not on this floor, though, so we're gonna have to walk on up. I should fire my architect for that, right? It's like putting the mudroom in the master bedroom. But I been thinking about getting one of those moving sidewalk things they have at the airport." Gil spoke as he led me through the penthouse, making our way for the stairs. We passed an autographed *Star Wars* poster. It hung next to a framed painting.

"Is that Gauguin?" I said with a nod towards the painting. "That's fantastic."

"Yeah, I think so? Not positive. It was a gift from a client. He said it was from his time in the tropics or something? I dunno, whatever." He offered a nonplussed shrug. "I was gonna hang it in the bathroom, but the guy gave me some bunkum about irreparable steam damage, so I had to put it out here next to my *real* pride and joy." He walked over to the *Star Wars* poster and patted its gilded frame lovingly. "This was a gift from George after I settled that little curse problem he had."

I didn't even have time to comment on the original Gauguin. "Curse problem?"

"Yeah, but we'll wait 'til we hear the reviews for his next flick to see if he actually got his money's worth. Anyway, the shower's this way." He turned away from the art and led me up the long flight of steps. I stepped lightly across thick carpeting, fearful of getting entrails on the thousand-dollar upholstery.

The stunning penthouse had kept me nice and distracted, but as we walked my mind began to wander. Considering what we'd just been through at the docks, I felt all right. Monsters, magic, and the walking dead. Gil had said to "just roll with it," and I had. Rather than fear or confusion, I felt a certain satisfaction grow in light of the fact that what we had done felt like *real good*. I hadn't felt that sense of reward in a long, long time. It was also a hell of a feeling being part of a team again. Over the years, bureaucracy had often times made the police department and military more frustrating than satisfying, and it felt damn good to get my hands dirty once again.

"This is where we hose down," Gil said, pulling open a set of double doors that lead into a large locker room. I felt like I was in high school again as we moved through rows of lockers framing long wooden benches. There was a shelving unit filled with clean, white towels on the way into a shower room of ten or so single unit showers broken up by curtained walls. The smell of soap was marvelous.

"I like single showers," Gil said. "It's the only thing that isn't like high school. Those communal showers are friggin' nasty, man. And kinda prison-y. They give me the willies." He shivered. "No pun intended. Anyway, you're a big guy, so I'll guess you wear XL in most things, right?"

I shrugged sheepishly. "Sometimes 2X."

"Cool." He strode over to an adjacent locker and pulled it open. "I got some clean clothes in here for you. Jeans, a t-shirt, and a button down in your size I picked up at the Big 'n Tall," he said, pulling out a plaid shirt and faded jeans. "Gotcha some Avengers underoos, too. And some PJ's in case you wanna stay here tonight. It is gettin' late." He pulled out a set of folded pajamas that had cartoon drawings of cowboys on them. "I've got plenty of spare bedrooms and... well, I don't get a lot of visitors. Or I can call a cab to take you home, if you like. It's totally up to you." He smiled. "Oh and I can get those clothes cleaned for you, too, although you may just wanna toss 'em. They're prolly gonna smell a little funky come tomorrow. Anyway, I'll let you get cleaned up." He smiled, patting me on the back (his hand made a wet slapping sound in the goo). "Welcome to the team, Dylan."

After he was gone, I took a long shower and scrubbed the flecks of undead blood and monster goo out of every crevice imaginable. Thank the gods I had a shaved head or it could have been a real horror show.

By the time I was done, it was late. I dressed in the silly cowboy pajamas–which were at least two sizes too small, leaving inches of exposed ankle and bare stomach. The buttons felt about ready to burst. I sighed and returned to the apartment side of the penthouse. It was tough without a map.

At some point in my wandering, I passed Finch. He sat at the kitchen table, running a damp cloth across the edges of each soiled weapon, sopping up still damp blood and scraping off bits of hardened detritus. He took his time, patient, showing care and diligence I'd never before seen in someone his age. I'd guess him to be 23 at most, but that felt generous. I moved on before he noticed me.

I found Gil asleep in a leather recliner that faced a massive flat screen television mounted on the living room wall. The chair was one of those big vibrating massage jobs, and Gil was snoring, dead to the world. In his lap lay an open bag of sour cream and onion potato chips. His face and clothing were still mottled with brightly colored ooze, except for the two perfectly clear circles around his eyes where his welder's goggles had been. On the television there was some crazy sword and sorcerer program with awful special effects. I left him snoring in the vibrating chair and made my way to a random guest room down a hallway. A marvelous view of distant City Hall–its golden lit clock face shining like a beacon in the night–awaited me. I laid down, and it was not long before I slipped off into a deep and dreamless sleep.

***

I had no nightmares of monsters or terrible gruesome death, although waking to Gil's earsplitting metal music thrumming through the walls of the guest bedroom was a little jarring. A bedside clock told me it was nearly noon. I hadn't slept that well since I was about sixteen. I dressed in the clothes my host had provided and went looking for food.

Gil was not in the master bedroom enjoying the serenade of power metal. Even with Gil missing, his presence was unmistakable. The room was a mess of dirty clothes, soiled medieval weaponry, and a blizzard of multi-colored Lego pieces. Gil in a nutshell, really. I found myself wondering just how old my new boss was. It took me a minute to remember he had greying hair.

On a well-polished and expensive wooden dresser was a half finished Lego construct of the Starship Enterprise. My obsessive-compulsive urges kicked in at the hodgepodge of colors making up the model instead of a uniform grey. I ignored them and instead followed the sound of voices back towards the penthouse's main living room.

My teammates were in the kitchen. Gil stood before an open cupboard, talking to Finch, who sat in the same place at the kitchen table where I'd seen him the night before, although he'd showered and dressed in clean clothes–black shirt, black jeans. The same weapons lay before him in immaculate condition, in one hand he still clutched the oily cloth.

"No, Boss, I do not want chili."

"How 'bout some Dinty Moore? You want some Dinty Moore?"

"I thought Dinty Moore made chili?"

"Don't be ridiculous! It's beef stew."

"Oh. Well, I do not want beef stew."

"Beefaroni?"

"Absolutely not."

"What about Manwich? You want some Manwich?"

Finch took the can from Gil's hand and read the label. After a moment, he said, "This is just sauce. There is no meat in this."

"Is that a no?"

"Yes, that is a no."

"All right. Hey, I've got some taco kits here, but I don't think I have any ground beef."

"No. No tacos and no burritos. No more Mexican food, I beg."

"Oh, okay." He shuffled in the cupboard once more. "Here we go, I can get real fancy; How 'bout some Hamburger Helper? Although I still don't think we've got any hamburger."

"No. As I said, I want breakfast. *Breakfast.*"

"How 'bout macaroni and cheese? Or Shake 'n Bake?"

"No. And you said you didn't have any meat."

"Come on, you don't *really* need meat for Shake 'n Bake. That's just a silly technicality. Trust me, I've eaten it plenty of times without any chicken. It's great."

"No, breakfast. Must we do this every morning? I want eggs and sausage and coffee and toast."

"I don't even know if I have any bread," Gil muttered. "What have I got that you'll like? Hmm... I've got some sardines here. And... mayonnaise?"

Finch covered his face with his hands. "I need to get my own refrigerator," he said to himself.

I cleared my throat.

"I can cook, remember?"

Gil turned around with a huge smile on his face. "Ahhh, yes, yes! I remember! Brilliant! Cook on, master chef. Amaze us with feats of magical frying and baking and stuff!"

Any good vibes I'd brought with me into the kitchen went up in smoke when I got a look inside the fridge. There was an industrial sized jug of Kool-Aid, a spray can of Cheese Wiz, two half-filled jars of mayonnaise, four different kinds of mustard, and a loaf of bread that was completely green. The freezer had two boxes of frozen waffles and about sixty spicy beef burritos. I shut the door and looked at Gil.

"There's really not much I can do with moldy bread and fruit punch," I said.

He chewed his lip. "What about those beef tacos?"

I stared at him. "No," I said. I couldn't turn frozen beef tacos into eggs and sausage. Did he think I was an alchemist?

"Oh," he grumbled. "Oh, boy. Well... everybody get dressed! We are going out to eat. Someplace... *fancy*." Finch and I shared a glance. We were both dressed, while Gil wore only plaid boxer shorts and a Jimmy Buffett t-shirt. He caught the glance and understood. "Uh. Erm. I'll be right back."

***

The "fancy" restaurant was called Harold's Meat Shack (wrap your head around that). Tucked away in the suburbs between a gas station and a laser-tag gaming complex, the Meat Shack was a squat red building designed to look like a barn. Inside pictures of cowboys hung on the walls between kitschy props like saddles, mounted bull horns, and bandoliers. Gil fit in perfectly with his cut off jeans, Velcro sandals, and red Hawaiian shirt–this one had parrots and erupting volcanoes on it.

Finch sighed when I pulled the Tank into the parking lot and killed the engine. Gil, on the other hand, was beaming.

"You will love this place," he said to me. "*Love it.* It's great, trust me. They've got like eighty-six kinds of barbecue sauce. Plus, they give you buckets of peanuts and you can throw the shells *right on the floor*!"

"That sounds... fun," I said.

"And maybe if we've got time, we can hit up that place later." He pointed at the laser-tag joint next door and smiled.

Inside Harold's, half a dozen busty waitresses greeted Gil by name. A few even winked at him. He blushed and waved back, knowing every name. The host, a spunky brunette name Maureen, led us to a booth along the back wall. Above our table hung a mounted bison head big enough to break my sightline with Finch when he sat across from me.

"This is my favorite table. I love that thing," Gil said, reaching up and rubbing the stuffed animal's huge, furry cheek.

A blonde waitress sauntered over, looking just as giddy as Gil. "Hey there, Gil! Who's your new friend you got with you today?"

"Jeannie, this is my new colleague Dylan. And of course you know Finch."

"Hi, Dylan!" Shaking my hand enthusiastically, she struck me as the kind of girl who ended every sentence with an exclamation point. "Can I get y'all somethin' to drink?"

"I think we're all set, dear," Gil said. "Why don't you just do my

20

regular, okay? For the table. So three of 'em? And bring all the barbecue sauces, too."

"You got it, baby," Jeannie said with a wink to Gil. She pried the menu from my hand before I'd had a chance to open it. Finch leaned around the bison and shook his head apologetically.

"So I got us each a full rack of baby back ribs, mashed potatoes, gravy, corn on the cob, potato salad, and beans and bacon. How's that sound? And you heard that we'll have *all* the kinds of barbecue sauce, right? It comes in like this big barrel thing that opens and spins and has all these little cups..."

I nodded, although I could hear my large intestine groan in anticipation. "Yeah, that sounds, um..."

"All right, down to business," Gil said, cracking his knuckles. "I'm sure you've got questions, but let's start things off easy, okay? Monsters are real, yeah, yeah duh, I hope you figured that out by now. But it's more than that. Fairy tales aren't fantasy stories, they're more like... well, cautionary tales. Most of that stuff's real, too. Same goes for mythology. Mythology should just be lumped in with history, really. It'd be a hell of a lot more accurate."

"Wait, that's all real? All of it?"

Gil laughed. "Well, no, not all of it. I mean, the tooth fairy? Come on, who cares about baby teeth? Nobody's gonna pay some kid for his *teeth*. It's just gross. But most of of the other stuff is real, yeah."

A bucket of peanuts came and Gil attacked it, covering the floor around us with crushed shells.

"Okay," I said. "What about last night?"

Gil had a mouth full of peanuts. He chomped down and waved for Finch to continue.

Finch cleared his throat. "Well, as I said last night, a revenant is usually a dead body that's been reanimated into one of various states of being, never to be mistaken for living, remember?"

I nodded.

"That is true, but really only half of it." Finch leaned forward. "Necromancy is the most elementary form of dark magic, so the simple reanimated corpse is the lowest manifestation of a revenant."

"Why is necromancy the most elementary form again?"

"Because magic is about *will*," Gil said as he spit a peanut shell across the table onto the floor. "Your will to create a fire or your will to make something explode, stuff like that. Necromancy is easy because the dead don't have a will anymore, so there's even less resistance with the dead than with inanimate stuff like a rock. You see, a dead body can't resist *anything*. They're like an empty glove that can be filled by anybody's hand. Any dope can make the dead walk. Especially a zombie. That's just like the crassest magic ever."

"That's correct," Finch continued. "Revenants can be created by a host using a person living or dead. Although living revenants are very rare because of how much power they require," Finch said as he daintily picked one peanut from the already half-empty bucket.

"The host?"

"The guy in charge. The one who's doin' the magic and imposing the will," Gil said.

"The person in command of the magic, essentially," Finch added as he shelled his one peanut, leaving the remains in a tidy pile on the table before eating the nut. "The person with the dominating will is called the host because everything stems from his or her mind."

"I guess that makes sense," I said.

Finch continued. "Generally, when we go to the warehouses on the harbor, we are cleaning out zombies or revenants created by children just beginning to dabble in dark magic. As we said, necromancy is the most elementary magic, so that scenario is fairly routine, although anyone with formal training knows and understands how despicable an act it truly is."

"Reanimating the dead?"

Gil nodded. "Imposing your will upon another living being is a decidedly *uncool* thing to do. In the circle of magic, it's generally understood that it's *not* all right."

"Long ago, there were punishments for people who broke the elemental laws, but they're gone now," Finch said. "After the Alchemical Wars, magical government was destroyed. That's why more people knew and understood magic a hundred and fifty years ago than they do today."

Alchemical wars and magical government... huh. I decided to keep my questions to a minimum. "All right, what about that skull last night? What did you call it?"

"Yorick," Finch said, as Gil chomped a mouthful of peanuts. "That is the Boss' death channel. Essentially it acts like a... a *funnel* to return the spirits of the dead to where they belong. We use Yorick to free the dead from the hand of another's will and return them to their grave. Because channeling the dead requires a lot of power, it is fairly typical to rely on a channel like Yorick to supplement one's powers."

"Hey, I've got *plenty* of power, man," Gil said. "Age doesn't matter a bit. Just sayin'."

I nodded. "So what was the deal with last night?"

Gil spoke up as he signaled for a waitress. "Last night was a big revenant-raising spell, not especially strong on the surface. There wasn't enough power to control a living person, only the dead. The weird thing, though, is that last night, that bonkers djinn musta been pullin' the strings."

"Ah yes, so… the djinn?" I said.

"That was a surprise, huh?" Gil said as another waitress arrived. "Hey, Charlene, can we get some more peanuts?" She smiled and disappeared with the bucket. "Like I said last night, I wouldn't have brought you along if I knew we'd find a damn djinn there. They're nasty buggers."

"Djinn are spirits with a free will who are able to split their time between different worlds," Finch explained. "That green fire you saw was the djinn's way of moving between parallel worlds. When there is a flare of green fire, it means that the beast is either moving into our world, or out of our world and into another. Generally, djinn do not get involved in this world or our business, but when they do, they tend to be fairly unpleasant characters. If they're involved here, they must be tied up in something worrisome. Certain religious traditions say that the devil himself is a djinn, which will give you an idea of how bad these creatures can get. That is also why I was a little surprised to find the djinn involved in waterfront revenant raisings."

The peanut bucket appeared and Gil giggled with joy. He scooped a handful onto the table as he spoke. "Yeah, that whole thing was pretty abnormal. See, djinn are usually humanoid–and that guy wasn't–and I didn't think they did magic in that sense."

I had a peanut. "So the djinn was responsible for casting the revenant spell?"

"That'd be my guess, yeah," Gil said as he tossed a handful of peanuts into his mouth. "There weren't any other living people there to control them."

Finch nodded. "Logic does say the djinn controlled the revenants considering when he left, whatever bodies remained ceased to function. Although, this is all very out of the ordinary, as djinn do not generally have the capacity to animate the dead."

"But he's still out there somewhere."

Gil nodded. "Probably. Djinn are tricky. We may see him tomorrow; we may never see him again. I know one thing, though: if he don't wanna be found, we ain't gonna find him."

Jeannie the waitress reappeared with a tray stacked high with plates and lowered a massive partitioned barrel of barbecue sauces to the table, further cluttering the already packed space. Gil clapped his hands and leaned back. I was hungry, but the sight was a lot to handle.

"Ooooh darlin' baby girl," Gil said (to the barbecue sauce barrel?). "Am I glad to see you or what?"

Finch sighed again. I agreed.

CHAPTER 4. REALITY CHECK

When lunch was over, we piled into the Tank and puttered on back to the office. After the meat-stuffed-meat lunch, I felt about ready to explode all over the faux leather interior. I convinced the crew to let me take a detour back to my house to pack a bag. I live alone, so there was no one home to worry about me when I didn't make it back at the end of a late night, no pet to feed or plants to water. Finch explained the benefits of having things at the penthouse in the event of late hours. "Last night was not exactly unusual," he said. "We're generally out until two or three in the morning and often come home covered in something else's internals. Seriously."

The Zeros waited in the car while I filled my green and black Philadelphia Eagles carry-on with essentials like jeans, clean socks, a couple of mysteries (two about chefs and one about a librarian), and my toothbrush. There was a good feeling in my chest as I locked the front door. How quickly things can change. On top of my recent unemployment, the past few weeks had also heralded getting dumped by an on again/off again girlfriend and the officially maxing-out my *second* credit card. Each problem had faded into little more than an afterthought when Gil Abercrombie had sent his hearty check and note promising a change. As it was, the possibilities I now had at my fingertips seemed endless. Not to mention exciting as hell.

"This is gonna suck so bad," Gil said as I climbed back into the Tank and slammed the door behind me.

Holding my carry-on in my lap, I froze. "What is it? What's wrong?"

Gil stuck a thumb over his shoulder towards the back seat. "Mr. No Fun back there says that we gotta go to the office. I was plannin' a team bonding experience–something classy like go karts or dodge ball–but apparently his magical wireless phone thing says we've had a whole bunch of calls today. So we got work to do."

Finch leaned forward and into the gap between the front seats. He snapped an old flip phone closed as he spoke. "While you were inside, our office manager informed me that there have been numerous messages left by a young woman who seemed rather frantic to speak with us."

Gil froze. "Wait, a lady in trouble? Why didn't you say so? I figured it was just the mayor or something." He turned to me and nodded. "He's right, dodgeball can wait, big man." He pointed straight out the windshield. "To the office. Andiamo!"

Finch took the carry-on from me and tucked it into the back seat. After a few obligatory tries, I got the Tank started and we backed out, Gil going into some complicated rambling about his favorite Chinese buffet as we rumbled down the street.

Gil jabbered directions and led us back to the penthouse. I was tugging on the wheel to make a left turn into the alleyway that led to the garage when he jabbed me in the ribs and told me to turn right instead. A similar alley–okay, maybe a little more than just *similar*–led down into an underground garage not unlike the one in Gil's apartment building. As before, there was a reserved space marked with his name beside a private elevator.

"Is this the office?" I asked.

"You betcha."

"It's across the street from your apartment? Looks a little... familiar."

"Yep. Same architect, same design. Same everything."

I looked at him, raising my eyebrows.

He shrugged. "Hey, I like what I like."

We took an elevator up to the top floor and entered a large, sparsely decorated office. The spot-lit wall behind the main reception desk that usually bore the office name or corporate logo was blank. A stern, thick-necked woman with salt and pepper hair sat behind the desk typing. She wore a blue pants suit from about 1992. I think her biceps were as thick as my thighs.

"Hello, Dottie," Gil said as we pushed through the office's outer doors. She met him head on with a steely-eyed stare. "This is the new guy," Gil continued. "Mr. Dylan. Dylan, this is Ms. Dorothy Jane Caldwell, office manager. We would be absolutely lost without her."

She nodded stiffly and said, "How do you do, Mr. Dylan?" before turning her cool gaze back to Gil. "I've been trying to reach you all day, Mr. Abercrombie. Your cell phone seems to be turned off. Again."

"Oh I told you I can't work that thing."

She turned her icy stare at Finch. I may have heard him gulp. He raised his hands defensively. "Dorothy, I returned your call as soon as I learned you'd been trying to contact me. We were out, and I didn't have any signal."

She sighed. "You were in *that place* again, weren't you? Somehow your phone never seems to work in that *place*."

This time, it was Gil who blanched, the color draining from his face as he wilted. "Yes, m'am."

She took a deep breath and labored over each word, "*Harold's. Meat. Shack.* I can talk until I'm blue in the face, and still you don't listen. That place is bad for you, Mr. Abercrombie. Terrible, in fact. You heard what Dr. Hanas said about cholesterol and your duty to eat healthier."

"Yes, m'am."

"I expect better, Mr. Abercrombie."

"Yes, m'am."

"And from you, Alistair," she said, glaring at Finch. He nodded silently. After a long moment, she sighed again. "All right," she said. The flush of crimson that had crept up to her cheeks from below her high-buttoned collar began to fade. Slowly.

"Here are your messages," she said after a long moment. "Most are the usual fare: two possessions, a poltergeist scare, a mother who found a zombie in her teenager's closet, and one young man who swears he ran over a Wendigo in his pickup truck. The young lady in question is a Mrs. Willa Evelyn Bascombe. Here are her messages." She placed a stack of typed notes on top of the growing pile.

Finch took the pile and began flipping through it. "What exactly did she say, Dorothy?"

"Honestly, she said very little. Just enough to impress upon me that her life is in danger and the police are being... quite uncooperative."

Gil snatched Mrs. Bascombe's messages from the top of the pile and strode past the desk with a wave of his hand. "Keep up the good work,

Dottie my dear." Finch and I followed in his footsteps. She gave me a curt–but not unkind–nod as I passed.

The main office was large–covering the entire floor–and decorated by framed photographs of beaches printed with inspirational sayings. Finch noticed my confusion and explained, "Mrs. Caldwell decorated the office. She's been with us since the beginning."

"It's... peppy?" I said. The place felt like a giant high school career counselor's office.

The hallways were long and winding, lined by an impressive number of empty offices and conference rooms. At the end of the last hallway were three offices in a cul-de-sac. Each door included an opaque window with a name professionally stenciled on it, similar to what you'd find on Sam Spade's door. The left office door said "Finch;" the right, "Dylan;" and the center, "MR. BIG BOSS."

"That's your office, champ," Gil said, pointing.

I smiled. My first office. How many years did it take me? I opened the door and found an enormous room with huge floor to ceiling windows on the right-hand wall. The office itself was spartanly decorated with a few peace lilies and floor lamps. Against each un-windowed wall stood large bookshelves packed with hundreds of leather-bound books with titles I didn't recognize. An impressive antique sofa rounded out the rest of the room, along with a pair of guest chairs and a desk that appeared as big as a queen-sized bed.

"Wow."

"This is yours," Finch said. "So you can do with it what you will. Although, it would be wise to leave the books here, seeing as they are a wonderful reference. You certainly don't have to, of course." He shrugged.

"Whose are they?"

"The books? As I said, they're yours now. They did belong to the man who previously held your position."

"Oh? Who was that?" I felt silly being so cavalierly uninformed, but for some reason I hadn't imagined someone else holding the position before me.

"His name was Parker," Finch said. "He'd been with us for about nine years. He was killed just over three weeks ago." As he spoke, he didn't flinch. His voice was even and free of emotion, as I'd come to to expect from him.

I opened my mouth to speak but was interrupted by the ringing of a phone. "Excuse me," he said as he turned and exited the office. A moment later, the ringing ceased.

For the first time, I felt fear. Fear of what I didn't know and didn't understand; the deep-seated dread that comes from being in over your head and *knowing it*. Thus far I'd managed to keep my head down and go with it, enjoying the good times and trying not to get mauled during the bad, but I was getting too old not to know danger when it asked me to dance. And now this office thing. What had once been an exciting reward had morphed into a silent reminder of the worst-case scenario: an empty office and a wet-behind-the-ears recruit.

With well-insulated windows and a heavy carpet, the room was very quiet. I took a few steps towards the desk and could barely hear my own footsteps. I tried to imagine what I'd put on the desk to liven it up. I didn't have much of a family. What about my predecessor? I imagined portraits of a wife and children covering the huge desk, enough to spill over onto the cluttered blotter. I shook the image away and tried to be optimistic. Okay, no family photos; maybe I'd settle for one of those troll dolls dressed like a wizard and a *Doctor Who* mug.

I couldn't ignore the thoughts about Parker, the man who came before me. I took a seat behind the desk and leaned back in the chair. Having spent years in a city police department and the military, I'd seen my fair share of friends die in the line of duty, but the eeriness never passed. Superstitions lingered, including the feeling that death was contagious. Rather than fight against the fear, it would be easier to just swallow it and keep going. Didn't have any other choice, really.

Finch returned to the office, his hands in his pockets. "I'm sorry about that," he said. "That was a client. An eccentric one. Not exactly the best timing to take a phone call, I know, but she's quite high maintenance."

I waved him off. "No worries. Comes with the territory, I guess."

He paused. "What does?"

"Eccentric, high maintenance clients," I smiled. "And this. Empty offices. Some part of me always knew these were the stakes."

He nodded. "We... we had hoped to ease you into it. Last night could have gone very badly. For a minute there, I was worried for you and for Gil. The last few weeks were really hard on him. Rather than dwell on what happened with Parker, he instead chose to focus his attentions on finding Parker's replacement. Gil has friends in both the police and private securities. We were lucky to have your name land on our desks. But it's important you understand what you're accepting."

I smiled. "It's a little hard to claim ignorance when accepting a job that demands me to be armed and offers such ridiculously exorbitant pay."

"That's why he pays so well, you know."

"Because this job could easily kill us?"

"Because helping people and doing good sometimes isn't always enough to warrant running into a burning building or standing in front of an oncoming train. He understands he's asking a lot. More than a lot. But he has the money, and he wants to take care of those close to him. Honestly, it's the only way he knows how." Finch walked further into the office and took a seat across from me in one of the guest chairs. He lowered his voice and continued. "But believe me, when you're part of the crew he'd do anything for you. Anything."

I was silent. A little intense for the second day on the job.

"I'm not sure if he expects the same from his partners," Finch said with a shrug. "But he's got it from me."

I didn't know what to say, so I didn't say anything. Finch was quiet. The silence was heavy, but not altogether uncomfortable. From the hallway, a door opened.

"Whatcha doin' in here boys? Braidin' each others hair? Come on over to the *real* office." Gil stood in the doorway wearing a Sherlock Holmes deerstalker cap and puffing on his pipe. As usual, the smoke was rank. "We got a meeting set up with this Mrs. Willa Evelyn Bascombe in a couple minutes. Come on in so we can get up to speed."

Finch and I rose and walked through the reeking cloud. Gil pulled his door shut behind us. I wasn't entirely surprised to find an enormous model of the Millennium Falcon hanging suspended from the ceiling. It was impressive, at least four feet across. The rest of the office was a mix of the usual: sharp weapons and innocuous children's toys. On the wall behind his desk was a wide poster reading **HAN SHOT FIRST**.

Gil pointed to a pair of chairs before collapsing behind his desk. Scattered across the desktop in front of him was a jigsaw puzzle with puppies on it. The heavy book from night before sat open before him, a quill and ink pot beside its parchment pages. Yorick, the rune-carved skull from last night's escapades, sat nearby. Seated, Gil closed the old book, the leather cover creaking, betraying its age.

"She's in a state," he said, pushing the old book to the side and resting his pipe in a homemade ceramic ashtray. "This Mrs. Bascombe, that is."

"What did she tell you, Boss?"

"Very little. Anything Dottie couldn't get out of her, I sure as hell couldn't either. But I can tell you she's definitely spooked. Just talking to her was enough to put a bit of a fright into me, too. She sounds like a smart and balanced lady, not a loon or anything, but she didn't want to go into detail on the phone. Although… she did keep talking about her husband, so either he doesn't want her bringing in someone on the outside to deal with this problem, or he *is* the problem. Whatever's goin' on, we'll know shortly. She's on her way in now."

"How do we normally do this sort of thing?" I asked. "Do you meet with her first, Gil, or what?"

"No, no my good man!" he said as he returned the pipe to his mouth and took a few deep pulls from it and giving his best Holmes impersonation. "We'll all talk to her in the conference room together. I don't take notes. Good grief. That's what you two are for."

CHAPTER 5. MRS. WILLA EVELYN BASCOMBE

Dottie escorted her into the conference room less than twenty minutes later. Mrs. Bascombe was fairly tall, about 5'8", and lanky; dressed casually in jeans and a plain white t-shirt, she wore simple silver jewelry and thick-lensed red, cat's eye glasses that tended to slip below the bridge of her nose. Her brown hair was pulled back into a tight ponytail held high off her shoulders. There was no make-up on her face; nothing to mask the noticeable signs of recently shed tears. Other than the noticeable rings beneath her eyes, her dark skin was flawless. She had deep chestnut-colored eyes, the kind men are so apt to fall into. While her movements were stiff and wary, she carried herself with a quiet confidence and an intelligence that was unmistakable. She greeted each of us in a calm voice as Dottie stepped out and closed the door behind her.

"Thank you for seeing me on such short notice," she said, returning her glasses to the bridge of her nose with one finger.

Gil smiled. "What can we do for you, Mrs. Bascombe? Do you need something to drink? Are you hungry? We can get you pretty much anything you like."

She shook her head. "No, but thank you."

Gil smiled again, the glow of sympathy evident in his eyes. He was more formal than I'd seen him. Gone were the deerstalker hat and the pipe, as was his devil-may-care exuberance. Hell, his hair may even have been combed. It was a little disorienting.

"What can we do for you?" he asked. "Your messages had grown... a little frantic."

"I'm sorry. Your secretary must be sick of me by now. Or think I'm crazy." She forced a smile. "I called for the first time on Friday afternoon and probably left about a dozen voicemails over the weekend. I'm pretty glad you could meet with me today."

"It's all right," Gil said, making an effort to calm her. "Just start at the beginning. What exactly's goin' on?"

"Well, I... I believe my life is in danger. I, um..." She sighed. "I have reason to believe that my husband... that I'm going to be murdered by my husband."

Her voice dropped off, leaving the conference room in an awkward silence. Silence like this made me a little awkward, and I couldn't help but fidget. My partners had better poker faces. Finch stared straight at the woman, unblinking and stoic (as usual); Gil patiently held her gaze.

"What makes you think that, Mrs. Bascombe?" he asked.

She rested her hands on the table and began to pick nervously at the cuticles of her short, red-painted fingernails. "I have... *reason* to believe."

I understood why the police had been less than cooperative. Cops tend to need a bit more motivation than "because I think so" before a formal investigation can be opened. I was new to the Zeros, but unfortunately I was not new to this kind of interview. I'd conducted a fair share during my time as a Philly cop. These conversations left you feeling pretty damn helpless when you heard yourself saying, "Sorry, there's nothing I can do." I hoped this conversation would go differently.

"Mrs. Bascombe," Gil said gently. "I get the impression there's something you're a little cautious to reveal, and that's a-okay. But I'll tell you right now that bizarre occurrences ain't so bizarre here in this office." He shrugged, grinning a boyish grin. "We've each seen plenty of things that others would be... well, less inclined to accept. You followin' me?"

She nodded, but still said nothing.

Gil continued. "Okay, I'll be straight with you. I think something a little more concrete probably brought you to our door instead of some police precinct."

"I already spoke with the police," she said, shaking her head. "They laughed at me. Literally. But there was one who gave me your number. I think his name was Cobb."

Gil nodded, "Yeah, he's a friend. We... work with him from time to time. You must've said something to make your way to his desk."

"I..." She closed her eyes and took a deep breath. "I have dreams sometimes. Dreams of awful things."

We waited. She kept her eyes closed and continued.

"I've seen a floor soaked through with blood. I've seen walls stained in red as if they themselves were bleeding." She shook her head again. "I've dreamt of the bodies of women, all dead, impaled on hooks and hanging like slabs of beef in a meat locker."

I felt a cold sweat on my upper lip, and a nasty sick feeling started to fill my stomach. Over the countless witness interviews I'd given as a cop, I'd learned enough to know something in her voice rang true. I looked over at my partners. A pad of paper had appeared in Finch's lap, and he'd begun to take notes. Gil's brow was creased, but the kindness in his eyes was unwavering.

"Were you one of the women?"

Eyes still closed, she shook her head. "No, not at first. At first they were women I'd never seen before. There were a lot, but they were the same faces each time. At a certain point, it stopped being only a nightmare. I started seeing things while I was awake. And now... now it's always in my mind." She opened her eyes. They were glassy. She fought hard to hold back the tears and succeeded.

"Are you in the room now?" Gil asked. "When you see the bodies, are you one of the women?"

She nodded. "It happened last Monday. In the dream my husband grabbed me and dragged me into the room, and he closed the door. When the door slammed, I woke up. Now it happens every night. He grabs me and takes me in that room. And like I said, sometimes I see it when I'm awake, too." She took a deep breath.

"And you believe your husband is responsible?"

"Yes," she said, nodding again. She'd forced the word out, her voice shaking. "I know it, and that's what's terrible. It sounds ridiculous, I know. I mean, I love my husband. I *love* him and he's... he's a good man, but... recently he's been acting so strange." She shook her head. "I know it's true. Is that weird to say? This... this isn't the first time I've had something like this happen."

Finch perked up at these words. "What do you mean?" Gil asked.

"Dreams. I've had dreams before. I've seen things. Usually it's just insignificant stuff, sometimes it's not. Sometimes it's terrible. This isn't the first time..."

...But it could be the last, I thought. Yeah, it was dramatic, but that

didn't mean it wasn't true.

Gil sat back. "Thank you for trusting to us," he said. He took a deep breath and smiled warmly. "I am very happy to tell you, Mrs. Bascombe, you've come to the right place."

"I appreciate that, I really do," Willa said.

"You don't need to thank us, Mrs. Bascombe," Gil said.

"Please, stop that," she said, visibly shaken, her voice rising for the first time. Her breathing had quickened and her upper body had grown tense. "I'm sorry," she sighed. "I'm really sorry. It's just... Willa. Please, call me Willa. Since these... since these *dreams* started, I haven't been able to *bear* the sound of that name. *His* name. Alfred's name. I'm afraid and I'm angry because I'm never afraid. Can you just... Can you please call me Willa. Please."

Gil nodded, not batting an eye at her subdued outburst. His sly grin returned as if the stopper in the tub had been yanked and the heavy somberness had drained away. "Okie dokie," he said. "That's fine. Everyday here is casual Friday, anyway. I mean, check out my shirt." He smiled before he pushed his chair back and stood. "I'm Gil," he reiterated with a wink. "Gil Abercrombie. We're gonna take care of this for you, all right? I promise."

She nodded, her anxiety seeming to evaporate with a sigh. "Thank you," she said. "Thank you so, so much." She reached across the table and shook Gil's hand gratefully.

"Mr. Finch," she said, releasing Gil and shifting her gaze.

"Just Finch, thank you," he said, taking her hand.

"Abercrombie and Finch, huh?" she stifled a chuckle and shook her head. I cracked a smile as well. Finch and Gil looked baffled. "And...?" she turned to me.

"Dylan," I said as we shook hands.

I could feel relief in her touch. Looking into those deep chestnut eyes, I felt in danger of toppling in myself.

Gil touched a button on the phone in the center of the great table. Dottie's voice broke the quiet air with a bark. "Yes, Mr. Abercrombie?"

"Dot, my dear, I'm gonna send this beautiful little lady back your way. Get her something to eat and something to drink. Something from my usual lunch menu, like a meatloaf sandwich and a milkshake. Run through the usual paperwork yadda yadda and take good care of her, okay?"

"Yes, sir, Mr. Abercrombie." The line clicked off.

Gil lifted his gaze to Willa and smiled. "I'm gonna have my associate Dottie get you something to eat and help you relax for a bit. She's gonna ask you some boring questions and have you fill out some papers. All standard stuff, not to worry. I'll have a word with my partners here while you're with her and then we'll decide our next course of action. How does that sound, dear?"

Willa smiled and nodded. "That's wonderful. Again, thank you so much. Uh, about the money..."

"Ahh, forget about the money," Gil said with a wink. "We're not big on money 'round here." He smiled.

Before Willa could respond, the door opened and Dottie was there. Despite her sandpaper countenance, she smiled kindly as she led Willa through the doorway. The young woman cast a grateful glance over her shoulder at us just before Dottie closed the door behind her.

"You know, I did have a few other questions–" Finch began.

"Ahh stow it, old man. She put herself through the ringer to tell us what she did. I wasn't gonna have you hit her with a dozen more questions about blood and guts that woulda just made her break down. The poor girl needs a time out." Gil stood and walked to the window overlooking the congested Ben Franklin Parkway a dozen or so floors below.

Finally, he said, "What do you think?"

"I don't think she's lying," I said.

"Well, she doesn't think she's lying," Finch said. "Even so, she still may not be telling the truth."

"What do you mean?"

"He means that for all she knows, she *is* telling the truth. Whether or not it's actually true is the real question," Gil explained.

"Marriages are our most... sensitive cases," Finch said, leaning back and dropping his pad of notes onto the table. "The trust that's inherent in most marriages makes for a volatile environment in the wrong hands."

"One untrustworthy spouse can wreak havoc on the mind of the other," Gil said. "We've seen it more than you can even begin to imagine. If a private eye's meat and potatoes is stuff like 'is my husband cheating on me?' then ours is 'has my husband been messin' around in my head?' The client usually has no idea, but that's what we eventually uncover."

"This happens a lot? But why would he be forcing her to see these terrible visions?" I asked.

Gil shrugged. "Trying to scare her away? Or just scare her? This world's filled with some messed up people, man. It's sad but true."

"So it's the husband? How can he influence dreams like that?" I asked.

"That's the catch, D-man. Those aren't dreams," Gil said, taking a seat on the edge of the table. "It's a little hairier than that."

"They're visions," Finch said, closing his eyes. "Possibly precognitive in nature. That's why she's not asleep when they happen. Although, given the prior circumstances she described, I'm inclined to believe that the visions are true and accurate."

I looked at Finch. "Meaning?"

"Her husband is a murderer, and she is his next planned victim."

"So... that's it?" I asked. "The husband's gonna kill her? That was easy."

Finch smiled ruefully. "Not quite."

"It is more complicated than that," Gil said as he stood. "And we're really just playin' the odds when we say that Mr. Bascombe is the man behind the curtain, because there really are a jillion other possibilities. He's probably our man. But Finch is right, it's not quite that easy. What we really need to do is get to know this Willa Bascombe a little better. And her husband."

A half an hour later Dottie dropped a folder onto Gil's desk filled with "the usual paperwork." Half of it was routine information gathered directly from the client, in this case in a one-on-one interview Dottie carried out after Willa spoke with us. I learned that the second half of "the usual paperwork" was made up of police reports and documents from City Hall that had been faxed over by some of Gil's ferrets. He explained how easy it was to get pretty much any city bureaucrat to give up documents if you greased his palm with enough cash. But in the case of Mr. and Mrs. Alfred and Willa Bascombe, he was proven wrong.

"All I've got is a picture and a photocopy of the husband's driver's license," Gil said with a rare frown. "And if you look close, the photo is just a blow up of the tiny one on the driver's license. That's pretty lame, man."

"What about our client? Willa?" Finch asked, dropping the

photocopy of Alfred Bascombe's driver's license onto the table.

"Even worse," Gil said. "I got a copy of the last x-rays from her dentist and her driving record, which is totally blank. Not even a speeding ticket. This crap is useless."

I picked up the driver's license photocopy from where Finch had dropped it. "Wait a minute," I said, interrupting Gil mid-rant.

"What is it?" Finch asked.

"You guys don't recognize him?" I asked, holding up the photograph of Alfred Bascombe and pointing.

My partners shook their heads, bewildered.

"Hate to break it to you, but things just got a lot more complicated. I didn't even notice when she said... damnit." I took a deep breath and looked at my new partners. "Alfred Bascombe? As in City Councilman Bascombe? As in Member of the City Council in charge of the 11th District?"

Finch closed his eyes and groaned. Gil ran his fingers through his hair before stamping his foot and grunting, "What do you mean? What's the problem? I mean, this sounds like some Big Brother shit here, man."

"Forgive him," Finch said. "Politics aren't exactly Gil's strong suit. Are they, Boss?"

"Politics. Ugh. I can't stand that jibber jabber," he said with a dismissive wave of his hand.

"It was remarkable that I convinced him to register to vote before the last election. A few days prior to polls opening, he burned his voter registration card in protest." He shrugged. "Don't ask me."

"How does he not know about City Council with all his ferrets tucked into every bureaucratic office?" I asked.

"I handle most of that, not him. He can't even figure out a Rolodex," Finch explained with a shrug. "He gets confused when I hand him a click pen instead of one with a cap."

"How long have you lived in Pennsylvania, Gil?" I asked.

For some reason, he looked at his watch (maybe it had the year on it?). "Ooooh about... twenty-seven years and some change. I wasn't born here, but I'd say I've got some roots now."

"The City Council is the legislative branch of the city's municipal government. Didn't you take government in high school?"

Gil stared at me blankly.

"If Bascombe is on the City Council, then he's kind of a big deal," I said. "That's the bottom line. And we'll have a hard time asking questions around here without being pretty damn conspicuous."

"Conspicuous? Don't be absurd! I'm anything but conspicuous," Gil said, scowling.

I held my tongue, but images of Tiki shirts and battle-axes danced in my head.

"Actually," Finch said with a grimace, "I think I know someone who just might help us. Maybe."

CHAPTER 6. BLOODSUCKING POLITICIANS

Finch and I left Willa in Gil's care, seating her in his office and letting him wow her with promises that he'd show off his best magic tricks.

"We're going to run an errand," Finch said as he led me to the elevator, handing over the Tank's keys. "Just you and me."

It was a short trip, and the mid-afternoon traffic was light as we headed into the heart of Center City. The sidewalk crowd was limited to pale, heavy-set men and women in business suits taking a break from shuffling papers around on their desks. As a passenger, Finch was like GPS; he was silent save for short comments directing me to turn when necessary.

Finch led us past City Hall and down Market towards the river. At some point we turned north. Somewhere near Chinatown, he pointed out an entrance to a parking facility that spiraled endlessly underground, and I pulled in. It was crowded. We had to park near the bottom floor and walk up a few flights of stairs as the elevator was broken. We emerged on the sidewalk in front of a short and squat–perhaps five stories at most–municipal building, surrounded by glassy skyscrapers. The small complex was built entirely of faded bricks that had taken on a sour orange color. Beside the revolving door entrance were tarnished silver letters that spelled out "Department of Sanitation." The place had probably looked tired twenty years ago. Finch and I entered a wide lobby covered in putrid green tiles straight out of *Hawaii Five-O*. On our left, a heavy-set security guard behind a desk yawned and took a sip from a styrofoam cup. We passed him without a word and took one of the elevators to the top floor. I expected shag carpeting when the doors opened.

Instead of the 70's bachelor pad rugs and lava lamps I expected, the fourth floor hallway that welcomed us was constructed of black brick walls stacked above a dark-stained wood floor. Iron sconces capped by sandblasted glass domes decorated the walls at periodic intervals. Dim light angled upward and was lost in the peak of the high ceiling.

"Okay, I wasn't expecting this," I said as we stepped into the hall. Our footsteps echoed faintly down the corridor. Finch turned left and began walking. I followed.

"The top floor of the Department of Sanitation was leased out shortly after the building was completed," he explained as we walked. "Certain... independent contractors now call this home."

"What kind of 'independent contractors' are we talkin' about?"

We stopped before a black and white plastic placard screwed into the wall beside an open doorway. Finch pointed. It read:

We'd appreciate the temporary storage of all crucifixes, holy texts, genuine religious relics, children, and authentic Italian food below or in our waiting room.

Thank You!

Management

Below the sign was a compact metal shelving unit filled with an assortment of crosses on gold chains, a Bible or two, and a take-out container. A sign on the top shelf said "The Honor System, Please!" I leaned forward and peeked through the open doorway. A well-maintained waiting room sat inside, filled with sleek leather chairs and potted plastic plants. There was no window. In each corner was a table covered in magazines. From the doorway I could make out a few titles including *The Economist*, *Fortune*, *Business Week*, *Money*, *Entrepreneur*, *Forbes*, *Harvard Business Review*, and *Kiplinger*. A muted television set was mounted high in one corner with stock information scrolling across it in a bright array of colors. My gaze returned to the placard before meeting Finch's eye.

"Italian food?"

He cracked an uncharacteristic smile, but said nothing. After a moment it came to me and I nodded.

"Ahh, yes," I said. "Garlic."

He nodded before he continued walking down the long corridor with me beside him.

We came to a stop outside a heavy black door. The name on the door was "Arthur Greely." Finch knocked twice. There was a muffled sound from within, and the door creaked open.

The man standing before us was of average height and average build with average eyes and an average suit. His skin was deathly pale, the color eerily resembling congealed mayonnaise, and his black hair was slicked back and shiny. He wore thick-framed browline glasses and, with the exception of his pallor, would have been the perfect average Joe circa 1955.

When Mr. Greely laid his eyes on young Finch, his look of average Joe confidence sagged a little, as if he'd sprung a leak.

"Finch," he sighed. "I was under the impression that we had an understanding."

"I'm sorry, Arthur, I just need one more favor." Finch moved to step into the office, but Greely didn't budge.

"No, damnit, you said we were finished. Finished, remember? We talked about my *reputation*? Does that mean nothing to you?"

"I know, Arthur, believe me, I know. I wouldn't be coming to you if I had any other options."

"Your other option is to go to someone else, Finch. The details of it are your problem. You and your boss are poison around here. Talking to you is worse than getting my picture taken holding a giggling baby. I'm looking to move *down* in the world. If you've noticed, I'm still on the top floor, here. The *top*. Right where you left me, remember? The wife keeps getting on me about when I'll be getting the big promotions, the big raises, the spacious crypt-side office. I'm not getting any younger, Finch. There's a beautiful mausoleum waiting for me somewhere with my name all over it, I know it. If the big guys catch wind of you here..."

"You're right, Arthur. Really, you are. I just need one more favor. Please."

Greely stood firm, scowling with his hands on his hips.

Finch leaned forward and lowered his voice. "I'm sure that we can come to some sort of arrangement, Arthur. Gil has not been opposed to making certain... political contributions to campaigns that I advise him are worthwhile. And with the election not too far off... This is campaigning season, after all."

A hint of almost healthy light appeared in Greely's face. "Really?"

"Certainly, my friend."

Slipping his hands into his average suit's pockets, Greely licked his grey teeth and nodded his head. "All right, Finch. You got a deal." He stepped back to clear the doorway so Finch and I could enter and closed the door behind us.

"Make it fast, I've got houses to foreclose on." Greely rounded his spartan desk and took a seat.

The office was impeccably clean and designed as if for a monk. Any supplies were packed neatly into a cabinet beside us in drawers marked with labels handwritten in perfect cursive. Greely's desk was large and imposing, built from solid wood and stained black. Behind him was a window, covered with wooden blinds, slats drawn tightly. The only light came from small desk lamps scattered about the room, and even they had dark shades. To describe the office as gothic would be a gross understatement. The only decoration was a framed poster of the 1931 production of *Dracula*. Bela Lugosi grinned down at us, fangs bared.

"I'm a big fan of 30's film satires, and that one there's a real classic," Greely said, following my gaze to the poster. "Come on, Lugosi's great in that. Pure comic *genius* at work there. The Academy cheated him." He turned to Finch and pointed at me. "So who's your friend?"

"Oh, I apologize, Arthur. This is my new associate, Dylan. Dylan this is Arthur Greely, political maven and optimistic mayoral candidate for the upcoming election this fall."

Greely leaned forward and shook my hand. "Nice to meet you, Mr. Dylan. Though you have to understand that this relationship has to stay strictly between us. These are some sensitive political waters here."

I nodded. "Oh, of course."

Finch spoke up. "Arthur, I'll keep this brief; I need information on a member of City Council, and I'm hoping you'll be willing to provide it."

Greely's response was immediate. He shook his head, raising his hands as if being held-up at gunpoint. "Whoa, whoa, whoa, that is *not* a little favor, Finch."

"I understand it is sensitive information, Arthur, really I do. But this is very important."

"I don't care how important it is, Finch. I've been trying to curry favor with City Council to gain some political clout in this town for the past six years, and I'm not about to squash it by stepping on somebody's

43

toes. Now, of all times."

It struck me that Greely personified the worst of politicians. He saw nothing more than his own bottom line and felt immediately insulted by anyone else's agenda–professional or otherwise. The smallest flame of anger flickered to life in my gut.

Finch–ever true to his nature–remained patient. "I understand completely, Arthur; I'm not looking for you to sell anyone out. I'm only looking for some baseline information that will help me paint a more complete picture of a man."

"Baseline information to paint a more complete picture, my ass," Greely muttered. "If you or your loony boss are involved then you're not trying to figure out who to invite to your next fundraiser. You're probably two plot points away from carving his headstone."

Finch sighed. "Don't be dramatic, Arthur. At the moment, we're only involved in a preliminary investigation."

Greely was silent, groaning as he ran a hand through his hair. "This is insane and stupid, you know. But just out of curiosity, who is it?"

"Alfred Bascombe."

A caustic laugh sliced through the air. "Bascombe? In District 11? You must be joking! I've only just gotten to know the guy, and that in and of itself is a *feat*. He's private and well-insulated and doesn't associate with just anyone, you know."

I began cracking my knuckles and biting my lip. I was thinking about Willa and the other women in the bloody room. Not surprisingly, it wasn't helping to calm me.

Finch nodded. "That's why I came to you, Arthur; I knew you'd know him. As you said, not many people are close to him. But I knew you–"

"That's because he's smart and doesn't want to get screwed. You know how this business is–or maybe you don't–but if he lets someone like me in, it's because he *trusts* me. I'm not about to undermine all that! I've got big plans for myself, Finch. You know that. *Big plans*. Whatever pitiful scheme you've got running, I'm not going to–"

Well, I lasted as long as I could. Perhaps I need to take up some Tai Chi or calming breathing exercise. Regardless, a split-second later I was standing over Greely's arrogant bastard face with clenched fists. I had his collar in one hand and the cord to one of his blinds in the other. I gave the cord a sharp tug. The blinds rose a few inches from the sill and generous rays of golden sunshine spilled into the office.

"Listen, you ass," I said through clenched teeth. "I don't have the patience that my young associate Finch here has got, so I'll give you one more chance to answer his questions before I pull this shade up and turn you into a smoking pile of dearly departed. If I were you, I'd drop whatever political aspirations you're clinging to and give us the damn answers we need. An innocent woman's life is at stake here, and she means a damn sight more to me than you, you piece of shit."

There was silence in the office, a deafening silence. Greely stared up at me, looking wide-eyed and genuinely confused. Across the desk, Finch had leaned forward with a sigh and rested his face in his hands.

"Are you serious?" Greely asked with a snort. "Who the hell is this gorilla, Finch? Batman? And what planet is he from?" Greely removed my hand from his collar as if it were a slug, stood, and snatched the cord from my hand. He gave it a pull and raised the blinds all the way to the top. Sunlight poured inside, covering his body and filling the office with overwhelming light.

Nothing else happened.

"Yes, I'm a vampire, you ape. But vampires that don't feed on the flesh of humans aren't susceptible to the sun's rays. I'm not sure what cut-rate book *you* walked out of, but vampires in *this* century have gone legit. And what is all this valiant 'good and evil' crap? Even children know it's more complicated than that. Why don't you ask your boss–or, better yet, *young* Finch here–to tell you about the fuzzy little distinction between the two? So if you've nothing else to add, dolt, why don't you sit down before you look even dumber, because it would be pretty embarrassing if a *vampire* was forced to explain to a *human* the nuances of a moral gray area, wouldn't you say?"

With that, Greely resumed his seat and turned back to Finch, all the while shaking his head like an incensed elementary school teacher. Without a word, I sat, feeling as nearly foolish as I was angry.

Greely cleared his throat. "Listen, Finch, I appreciate the problem that you've got. And as I was saying before your toddler here had his tantrum, there is one thing I can offer you."

Finch leaned forward and rested his hands on his knees. "I appreciate that greatly, Arthur. What is it?"

"An anonymous tip. And after I give you this, we're through. The only thing that'll make me speak with you again is if you guys can get me in good standing with Management. So unless something magical happens, we're done. Do you understand?"

Finch nodded.

"And I do expected a damn hefty donation to my campaign fund."

Finch smiled. "Oh, of course."

"All right," Greely nodded. "Honestly, I can't *give* you anything on Bascombe, because I just don't have anything with real meat. But I can do you one better; I can let you get things on Bascombe yourself." He pulled a pad of paper from a drawer and scribbled something on it before tearing the sheet free and passing it to Finch. "I don't know how you always manage it, but as usual, Finch, your luck is gold." He pointed a long finger at the paper in Finch's hand. "Bascombe's having a charity ball at that location *tonight*. Yes, this evening. He's hoping to raise even more money for his own mayoral run and he's hoping to bank a lot tonight. Because of that, a ton of people are invited. At a certain point, his people stopped distributing formal invitations, instead saying that a check made out to Bascombe's campaign was enough to get you in the door. If you want to get to know the man, why not do it yourself?"

Finch folded the paper and slipped it into the pocket of his black jeans. "Thank you, Arthur."

Greely nodded. "And that's it. That is *all* you're getting from me. And if I see you there tonight, you don't know me, do you understand? Don't you even look at me."

Finch nodded. "Agreed."

The office grew silent. Greely frowned and waved a dismissive hand, casting a sharp glance at me in the process.

"Now get the hell out of my office."

CHAPTER 7. GETTING RIPPED A NEW ONE

Finch was silent as we returned to the elevator. I was too, having just demonstrated the breadth of my political knowhow. Finch chewed his lip as he pushed the button marked for the lobby. The doors closed.

I sighed. "All right, I'm sorry I–"

"Quiet, please," he interrupted.

"But I really just want to apo–"

"Quiet, please." he said again. "Wait until we are outside."

As always, Finch was beyond curt, but I noticed him clenching and unclenching a fist. I waited.

The doors opened and we crossed the sickly green lobby without a word. Outside on the sidewalk, the wind had picked up, and ominous clouds were gathering on the horizon.

"Can I speak now?" I asked when Finch came to a stop at the entrance to the parking facility. "Is that all right with you?"

"That place is wired for sound, Dylan. I'm sorry, but I don't want anyone hearing anything that I don't want them to hear." He met my angry eyes head on and didn't blink. "Half of what happened in there was my fault, but half was yours. I should have given you more information before we went inside, but I brought you in a solely observational capacity, and observers generally keep their hands to themselves–not to mention their mouths shut. I have no doubt that what you did up there was well-intentioned, but it was also rash, thoughtless, and foolish, to say nothing of dangerous. Don't ever give a vampire any information–about yourself or anyone else–unless you're positive that he *must* have it. Vampires aren't like what you've seen in movies. They're not going to jump you in a dark alley and bite your neck or seduce you in some dank Transylvanian castle. They've given up being forthright in exchange for insidious business dealings and multi-million dollar machinations; they don't have the muscle to stab you in the front anymore, nor do they need it. These days vampires are more likely to become the majority shareholder in your company and run your business into the ground just to rub it in your face. When that's done they'll seize your remaining assets and quite literally let you starve. Vampires thrive on slips of the tongue, gathering knowledge like single bricks until they've got enough to build a mansion. I'll say this just one time: what happened in there will not happen again, do you understand me?"

I nodded. Finch's rant took care of my anger. Now I just felt like an ass.

"There's a lot we still need to teach you, Dylan," he continued. "I'm glad you took the initiative in there, but if you don't have leverage then you don't have anything. And what you did in there wasn't about business, either."

"What do you mean?"

"You did it for the woman. For Willa Bascombe."

"No, I did it because he was pissing me off."

"No, Dylan. You did it for the woman. You wanted to help her, and he didn't; that's why you got angry. Trust me when I say that getting personally involved in something like this is very, very dangerous."

"I'm not personally involved," I groaned. "I just wanted to *do* something."

"Something for her." He nodded. "I understand, trust me. But you need to understand the risk here. Remember what we said? Trust is an incredibly dangerous thing."

I paused, looking into his dark eyes. "Are you saying that you don't trust her? After what she said to us? Her life is on the line here, Finch. She could die."

"Dylan, the only person I trust is Gil. Right now I don't even trust you. You don't seem to be listening. Trust can do much worse than simply get you killed, do you understand? Trusting someone completely is the best way to open yourself to a frontal attack on both your mind and your *soul*, so trust is something that must be given with extreme judiciousness. So no, right now I don't completely trust her, and neither should you. Remember what we said about the visions being planted? There is still a possibility that they are indeed false and she was sent to us as a trap."

The thought had never occurred to me. Again, I felt like an idiot. Awesome.

"I'm sorry," I said. "Again, I had no idea."

Finch took a deep breath and sighed. At that moment, he looked much older than his twenty-something years.

"I know, Dylan," he said. "I will not fault you for what you don't know or understand. I don't expect you to trust me yet, either, but I at least need you to listen to the advice I am giving you. Believe me when I say it is for your own good."

I nodded. "All right."

"Now let's go."

I pulled the keys from my pocket and led the way down into the parking garage, once again cursing the "Out of Order!" sign taped on the elevator. The sound of our footsteps and our breathing filled the stairwell as we climbed down to the bottom floor. I pushed open the stairwell door and felt Finch close his hand around my arm, stopping me in the doorway.

"Wait," he whispered. I turned and looked at him. His dark eyes moved across the scene before us.

The stairwell opened in the corner of the second-lowest level. The way the garage was designed we'd have to walk around the spiraling structure down to absolute bottom before we found the Tank–parked near the very end of the line. There was no sound at all. Fluorescent lights hung on swaying chains at uneven intervals, casting dim light across the pavement. Finch was silent, but continued to hold my arm.

"What is it?" I asked.

"Shut your eyes," he said, "and imagine the feeling in the air before a thunderstorm. The feel of charged and ungrounded electricity."

I did what Finch instructed, but felt nothing. After a moment I opened my eyes again.

"I got nothing."

"Try it again," he said. "It's there."

I shut my eyes a second time and waited. After a few moments I noticed the thin electrical impulses that seemed to pull at the hair on my arms, standing them on end.

"I think I got it." I turned to him. "What is that?"

"Trouble," Finch said.

A car a few hundred yards away from us began honking rhythmically, its headlights flashing. Similar car alarms roared to life around the level. Finch returned momentarily to the stairwell and pulled the metal lid off a small trashcan. Gripping the handle tightly, he returned to my side, pulling the door closed behind him.

"Are you really using a trashcan lid as a shield?" I asked.

He ignored me. "We're going to move quickly, all right?"

I swallowed. "Uh, what's going on?"

"I believe there's about to be a fissure, a parting of the barrier between worlds. Something's coming through. Remember the green fire back at the docks?"

"Barrier between what? Something's coming through? Here? Now?" I noted a touch of hysteria had crept into my voice.

"Yes. I believe this is a trap."

Overhead, the fluorescent lights began to flicker, casting deeper, blacker shadows over the already dim floor. Then, one by one, they began to die. In a moment, we stood in darkness broken only by the blinking headlights from the cars' triggered alarm systems.

"Shit," I said, breathing heavily. "*Shit.* We're going into that?"

"It will just wait for us if we don't. There's something Gil often says," Finch said softly. "An old Abercrombian saying: The only way out of a storm is through it." Leading me by the arm, Finch pulled me into the darkness.

As we moved through the rows of cars, the honking became overwhelmingly loud, filling the spacious silence and ringing echoes out through the huge structure. I raised my hands to cover my ears but Finch stopped me.

"Don't," he shouted. "I need your ears."

I nodded.

"And your nose," he said. "Trust your nose. If it's revenants, we will smell them, remember?"

Worst case scenarios had only begun to come to mind when I saw a flickering emerald light bloom beneath a line of cars and spread, roaring towards us in a wave. The light cast shadows across the walls as the cars touched by the light violently began to rock back and forth. As quickly as it appeared, the light vanished, returning us to semi-darkness.

"Green fire," I said. "That's...?"

"Yes, it's the–"

Finch was cut off as an incredible force tore between us, throwing him in one direction and me in the other. I heard the smashing of glass as I slammed into a luxury sedan's grill and collapsed onto the cold cement. I pulled myself into a cover of darkness, and I searched for Finch. I couldn't smell anything, but I saw the grim, hulking outline of the djinn as it trundled past me, silhouetted by the occasional pair of blinking headlights.

"Get to the Tank, Dylan!" Finch screamed from the darkness.

I heard the clanging of metal and the first howls of the djinn. My hands were shaking as I pulled the keys from my pocket. From where I was hunched, the car was down half a level and around a bend, still a few hundred yards, at least. A second heavy impact on metal jarred me into action.

I bent low and sprinted across the open space of the garage. I saw Finch standing in a wide-open space, facing the beast with nothing more than the trashcan lid. A trickle of blood ran down his cheek, his makeshift shield already bent and deformed. I saw the djinn wind up one of its massive arms and unleash a haymaker. Finch met the attack head on. The impact drove him a half-dozen paces backwards and sent the shield spiraling into the darkness like a frisbee. He caught my eye and screamed again.

"Get the damn car! Go!"

The beast rounded on him, slicing him across the chest with a claw and throwing his body backward. He crashed against a small coupe, caving in the passenger side door and exploding the window. Pieces of glass rained down on him, blood darkening the pavement around his body. The djinn growled and moved towards him.

Without thinking–you'll learn that I'm damn good at not thinking–I abandoned the Tank and sprinted towards the beast's exposed back. I'd left my pistol back at Gil's penthouse, so my only weapon was the ring of keys in my hand. I spread them so one key slipped out between each of my fingers, creating my own set of claws to match the djinn's. I lowered my body and swung my fist, ripping the keys through the exposed tendons that stretched taut at the back of the beast's right knee. I heard and felt the keys dig into its thick hide and chew through the fibrous tissue beneath. A rush of hot blood sprayed across my hand and arm.

The djinn bellowed and staggered, its roar reverberating over the storm of car alarms. It turned and faced me, jaw opening hungrily. With an almost dismissive wave of its huge hand, it swung and hit me flush in the chest, tossing me through the air like a skipping stone. I hit the ground with a grunt and skidded halfway across the level before coming to a halt.

Finch and the beast were a good fifty yards away from where I lay, disoriented and shaking my head to clear the stars. I still clutched the keys, now sticky and wet, so I pulled myself to my feet and began stumbling back towards where the Tank sat waiting.

Finch had begun moving, crawling on all fours. The beast hadn't forgotten him. With a howl, it swung a great claw at my young partner and missed, claw cutting a path through the pavement. It shrieked and swung again, this time catching the crumpled frame of a minivan Finch had put between himself and the beast. The driver's side door ripped clean off with a metallic groan. Hooking one claw beneath the front bumper, the beast effortlessly lifted the entire van and tossed it backwards onto another car. Alarms continued squealing as more and more vehicles were roused.

Finch, now uncovered, rose unsteadily to his feet and hobbled from the cover of cars and into the open space of the garage towards a smoking car wreck. From a mess of sedan ruins, he hefted a thick bar of steel like a baseball bat and turned back to the djinn. I heard Finch shouting as yellow light coursed up and down the length of the steel bar. Blood ran down his face, one arm clinging uselessly to his stomach and bathed in blood. The djinn roared in response, raising a clenched fist and stepping towards Finch's comparatively tiny form.

Finishing his incantation, Finch stepped forward and swung the bar with one hand, the metal rod leaving wisps of yellow light in the air as it cut toward the monster. The beast caught Finch's hand at the wrist and twisted. I turned to unlock the Tank and heard the crack of bone as Finch's wrist was crushed. His scream was lost in the howling of the djinn. I pulled the door open and turned back to see Finch on his hands and knees as the djinn swung upward, burying its claw in Finch's chest, lifting his body and throwing him through the air in a spray of blood.

I pulled the driver's side door open and jammed the gory key into the Tank's ignition. Miraculously, the engine started on the first turn. I pulled the car out and floored it, the Tank living up to its namesake as I slowly rumbled up the ramp of the parking structure towards the djinn.

The beast turned to me at the last moment as the Tank's dented nose met its midsection with a bloody *crunch*, sending the djinn flying into a row of parked cars. Glass exploded and metal twisted as the massive body ripped its way through a line of six-figure vehicles and slammed into the concrete wall behind them. I kicked the driver's side door open and got out as a spider web of green fire whipped across the floor in all directions. Blinded, I continued forward towards Finch's huddled body.

With a thunderous clap, it was over. The waves of emerald fire were gone, and with them the djinn. Once again the structure was drowned in darkness, the only light cast by flashing headlights. Finch's body was twisted into an unnatural shape against a pillar, a pool of blood spreading beneath him. I knelt at his side, my breath catching in my throat. A long, bent piece of metal protruded from the center of his chest. His right wrist was crushed, and it looked like one of his legs was broken. Between the spatters of blood on his face, his skin was deathly pale. The remains of his clothes were stained through with gore. His eyes were open, but unmoving. I leaned his head forward and spoke.

"Finch... Finch can you hear me? Come on, buddy, please..."

There was no sound. I shook his limp body gently but he did not stir.

I felt shock hit my system like ice water. Dead. Finch was dead. I leaned back and swore loudly. I'd hesitated, and now the kid was dead. He'd died fighting the djinn. He'd saved me. I turned and crawled a few paces away before emptying my stomach onto the pavement. My eyes were wet when I turned back to him. One by one, the lights above flickered back to life. The car alarms ceased, and it was quiet in the parking garage. In that quiet, I heard a strange, soft sound.

It was whistling. Or at least whistling of a sort. I opened my eyes and saw Finch's head move. He turned to face me, one eye blinking slowly. His lips parted slightly, but I couldn't hear him speak. I crawled closer.

The whistling I heard was air moving in and out of the hole in his chest. Tiny red bubbles appeared along the wound where the air seeped in and out. He was breathing. Again, Finch's lips moved as he struggled to speak. I leaned forward, bringing my ear to his mouth.

"What is it, Finch? What are you trying to say?"

The sound was less than a whisper, and seemed impossible. Almost no air was moving over his vocal cords, and given the wrecked state of his body, there was no way he could still be alive. *There was no way.*

And yet, he spoke.

"I need… I need…" he coughed and there was blood on his lips. "I need help… getting up. I think you may… need… to take… me… to… a doctor." He coughed again, and the corner of his mouth twisted upwards in a slight grin.

I felt his pulse on his wrist. It was strong. My mouth fell open as I leaned back, disbelieving.

"What the hell?" I whispered. "This is… impossible."

Sure it was. Didn't mean it wasn't happening, though.

CHAPTER 8. THIS IS EXPOSITION

Getting Finch loaded back into the Tank was a bit of a smash and grab job. There wasn't much room for nuance with a hunk of shredded steel jammed through his sternum. No matter where I grabbed him or how I moved him, blood spurted everywhere, and he had to grit his teeth to keep from screaming. Eventually I got him up and into the backseat where he passed out. We were able to make some semblance of a getaway before the cops showed up.

I called Gil and he gave me directions to a nondescript medical office a few blocks from the Ninth Street Market in South Philly, promising to meet me there ASAP. We got lucky, crossing Market without getting stuck in gridlock. A few short minutes later, I pulled the Tank around back and killed the engine. On the outside, the building looked like a bacterial infection waiting to happen, but soon I'd learn that inside it was the model of sterilization. A huge man in a smart-looking suit met me at the building's loading dock—I figured he was the Doc. He was flanked by a pair of orderlies cloaked in white, big monsters straight out of *One Flew Over the Cuckoo's Nest*. The Doc wore a slate gray three-piece suit, black shirt, and a purple paisley tie.

"How are you, my friend?" he asked, shaking my hand and smiling. His teeth were large and there was a sizable gap between the front two. He spoke with a heavy, unidentifiable accent, mangling each syllable. "You are Dylan, yes?"

"That's right."

He spoke softly and calmly as the pair of orderlies pulled open the Tank's back door and began extracting Finch, who looked like he was still out cold.

"My name is Hanas," he said. "Constantine Hanas, but you can just call me Hanas. Everyone else does. I am a doctor, and I have a longstanding working relationship with Mr. Abercrombie, your associate."

I nodded. "Do you know what you're dealing with here?" I said, gesturing to Finch's bloody body as the orderlies struggled to get him onto the stretcher. His twisted limbs were uncooperative. "Because I'm a little... lost."

"Certainly, Mr. Dylan. Mr. Finch and I are far from strangers." He patted my shoulder. "Far from it. Now do not worry, I will have him back on his feet in a matter of hours, okie dokie? I know exactly what I am working with here." He smiled.

I breathed a sigh of relief. "Good."

He laughed and guided me up the ramp into the clinic, following the stretcher. "Mr. Abercrombie instructed me to tell you that he is on his way now and that you should not worry."

"Okay," I said with a shrug. "Boss knows best." No one else was worried, so I tried to relax–with mixed results, if you were wondering. Inside, the men in white coats pushed Finch through a pair of swinging doors leading to what I assumed was the operating room. Hanas pointed to a small waiting area on our left.

"You can wait there, friend. Mr. Abercrombie should be arriving shortly. Understand?" He smiled again, patting a gigantic hand on my shoulder. "Relax, I will take good care. Do not worry." Without another word, he turned and disappeared through the swinging doors behind the orderlies. On the floor, a long trail of blood ran from the top of the ramp at the loading dock through the waiting room and into the back, matching Finch's path. He was bleeding like a stuck pig. And yet... alive?

I wandered around the clinic's ground floor for a moment before finding a small kitchenette. Inside, I stood over the sink and washed the blood off my hands. I couldn't stop myself from running through the attack over and over again in my head, searching for something I could have done differently. I wiped up the floor and was washing my hands when Abercrombie finally appeared, bursting through the back doors, huffing and puffing.

"Dylan, how are you? You okay, man?"

"Yeah, I'm fine," I said. "Finch got the... he got the worst of it, Boss."

He grabbed me tightly, surprising me with a big bear hug. His skinny arms pulled me close for a long moment before he released me. He took a deep breath and blew it out. "Good." He shrugged. "I was worried."

I opened my mouth to speak, but for a minute I was lost. Where to begin? Finally, I said, "What's the story here, Gil?"

He looked up at me and gave me a strained smile. "Yeah, there's always a downside to that 'just go with it' crap, right? And this is it. Confusion and fear, I'd say. Listen, I'm really sorry. I should have been there with you guys. I should have been more upfront about everything. I should have... I dunno. Done better. Things could have gone differently."

"No, it's all right," I said. "I'm just a little..." I couldn't even think of a word. "I don't know. Overwhelmed, I guess."

"It's all right, bud." He grabbed my arm and led me into the waiting room, gently depositing me in a high-backed leather chair. "Take a breath, big guy, take a break. I'm gonna get you some water. Hold on a sec."

He stood and walked from the small alcove, disappearing for a few moments before returning with a plastic cup in his hand. "Here you go."

The water was an ice cold boot in the ass. I was grateful. My head started to clear. I took a deep breath and felt a little better. "Thanks, Gil."

"No worries, my man." He took the cup and dropped it into a nearby trashcan before he sat down across from me. "Okay, first things first. Finch. He's... uh, different," Gil said. "He's not like us."

"Yeah, I think I saw that firsthand," I said. "I mean he had a steel bar in his chest and his pulse didn't drop below fifty-five."

Gil fidgeted. "It's weird, I know, but... Well, I don't want to tell you everything; I'll leave some of it up to Finch. But I'll tell you that he's... shit, I'm so bad at this." He shook his head. "This is totally his thing, not mine. I just like swords and stuff."

"It's all right, Gil. Just talk to me."

He nodded. "So, Finch is, uh... well, he's... immortal."

It was silent in the clinic. Gil stared at me like he'd just said *I love you* and I hadn't responded.

After a moment, I said, "Oh. Okay."

"Bonkers, right?" He smiled uneasily. "I mean, our boy Finch'll literally live *forever*. When stuff like this happens—and it's happened plenty, trust me–he feels pain and all that but it doesn't kill him. At the same time, he *is* alive. His heart beats and stuff, so he's not undead or anything; he's a living, breathing guy. He just… doesn't die. Or age, for that matter. Does that make sense? Finch is so much better at expository dialogue it's ridiculous."

"Yeah, it makes sense," I said. "Is this immortality thing normal? Or common?"

"No, not at all," Gil. "I mean, except for gods, of course. And some demons. And a couple witches I used to date." He stuck his tongue out like he'd just bitten a lemon. "Then there are people like the Weird sisters. And Aos Sí. Duh. Sorry, I'm on a tangent. Bottom line: it's not as common as it sounds. I mean Finch is a special case."

"Okay."

"But I'll leave it to him to tell you the details. It's not really my place."

I nodded. "Makes sense." After a moment I asked, "How old is Finch?"

Gil groaned and leaned back. "Ahh, the million dollar question. Damn it, I can never remember *that*. I mean, I'm always real vague around his birthday because I can't remember, I give him a cake that says something like 'You're So Old!' and try to leave it at that. He's… old. Way older than me. I've known Finch for as long as I can remember. Literally, I met him when I was like eight or nine."

"Has he always been like this? I mean, immortal?"

"Yep. He's been like this for as long as I've known him. Hasn't aged a day."

"That is crazy."

"I know, right? He's an expert on a lot of stuff and now you know why." He smiled. "He doesn't drive, though."

"He doesn't drive?"

"Nope. He never learned. I have *no* idea why. I mean I'm sure the old bastard predates the invention of the automobile, but no go."

I didn't respond, I was too busy trying to wrap my mind around the idea of immortality, the prospect that time was as inconsequential as weather on the other side of the world. No matter how I looked at it, a timeless existence struck me as a never-ending experiment in isolation.

"So anyway," Gil said, clearing his throat and leaning back. "What the hell happened?"

"It was the djinn. Hit us in a parking garage on our way back to the Tank."

"The djinn?" He looked baffled, biting his lip and staring off into space.

"Yeah, it didn't seem so interested in me, but it was mighty interested in Finch."

Gil's eyes slipped out of focus as he stared down at the floor, the cogs in his head turning.

I nudged his arm. "Boss?"

He snapped to attention. "Yeah, sorry. I was just thinking. This is weird. It's really weird, actually."

"What do you mean?" I asked.

"Djinn aren't generally malicious like that. They're more pragmatic. But they're not, um... as violently goal-oriented as this, if that makes sense. Like, a djinn would only attack you guys again for a specific reason. A djinn's not gonna attack you because you pissed it off. Djinn's are big picture monsters." He scratched his head and cleared his throat again. "Are you sure it was after you guys? I mean this couldn't have been some kind of accidental run-in?"

"Casual meeting in a parking garage? No, absolutely not. We were the only ones there. It popped up, attacked, and disappeared."

"Yeah," he shook his head. "That's bizarre-o, man." He sat back and ran his hand across a bristly five o'clock shadow that had begun to appear on his jaw. "Where exactly were you guys? What were you doing?"

"Finch didn't tell you...? We were leaving the Sanitation Department."

"Sanitation Department?" The confusion that clouded his face only lasted for a moment. When it evaporated, a dark cloud of anger took its place.

"Damnit, who did you see there?"

I swallowed. "His name was Greely."

He swore and stood, walking a few brisk paces back and forth in the waiting area. I heard him take a few deep breaths before he turned back to me. Most of the anger was gone. *Most.*

"He's not a man, Dylan."

"I know, Gil. Finch told me. He's a vampire, right?"

"Don't be so blasé about it, man. He's a vampire. A *vampire*. Finch might try to soften you up to them, but don't let him." He swore under his breath. "That explains why he told me to stay behind. Take care of the girl, he says. Keep her safe, he says. Show her a magic trick, he says. Jeez Louise."

"What's wrong, Boss? I mean he gave us good information. It seems pretty solid."

"Of course it's solid. 90% of the intel vamps give you is *pitch-friggin'-perfect*. They're goddamn masters of pulling you close enough to get those teeth into your jugular."

"But Greely sounds all right. He made it very clear this was the last time he'd be speaking to us. And he isn't feeding on people anymore," I said, remembering my little lesson about vamps and sunlight.

Gil sighed and fell back into a chair. He closed his eyes, looking very tired. When he spoke, his voice was low and weary.

"I'm sorry, Dylan. I don't want to give you the wrong impression. I trust Finch. I trust him more than I trust anyone." He sighed, resigned. "We'll follow his lead."

For the next few minutes I spoke with Gil, about Greely and the djinn. His smiles became easier as the stress of the day seemed to wane. It was not long before he was searching for his pipe while he extolled the virtues of hot sauce and the microwave while condemning mustard and what he called "the sacrilege that is shredded lettuce." When Doctor Hanas returned to the waiting room–dressed as impeccably as ever–I'd forgotten all the fear, confusion, and self-doubt I'd been so absorbed by.

"He is doing well," Hanas said with a big-toothed grin. "You can see him now."

He led us back through a maze of rooms. One last heavy door opened to reveal Finch lying in bed, wrapped in thick coils of gauze and Ace bandages and half-covered with a hospital blanket. His body looked as it had that morning, all limbs reasonably straight, no big metal bars jutting from his ribcage. He wasn't even wearing a cast. He smiled at us, seeming totally at ease.

"Finch," Gil said with a booming voice, grinning like a fool. "You had me worried, old man!"

"And as usual, I'm still here." Finch said, the ghost of a grin on his face. "I'm sorry if I scared you, Dylan," Finch said, shifting his gaze to me. "It would have been prudent to bring up the whole immortality bit prior to my getting mauled by a djinn. But as you know, these things do happen."

"No worries. I'm just glad you're all right."

He nodded his thanks.

Gil spoke up. "Dylan here hinted that you had a lead with your Greely buddy. Some political stuff? Whatchoo got, boy?"

"I had Hanas pull the paper from my pocket before he tossed the clothes," Finch said, pointing his finger. "It's there on the table."

Abercrombie lifted the paper and read while Finch explained. When he was done, Gil smiled and stamped his foot. "This is great! I *love* getting dressed up," he said, beaming. "It's like one of my favorite things. Really."

"It's a shame Finch can't come, too, eh?" I said, patting his blanketed leg. "Sorry, man."

"What are you on about, big man?" Gil asked, his eyebrows rising.

"He's all messed up," I said. "You don't think he's okay to..."

Finch shook his head at me. "I'm fine, Dylan. Trust me. Hanas has a magic touch. I'm going to be right there with you guys."

Gil was giddy. "Great!" he said. "I am so friggin' pumped! I'm gonna wear my dancin' shoes."

Finch rolled his eyes, but couldn't help grinning.

CHAPTER 9. HAVING A BALL

In the short hours before I was introduced to Gil's strange, sometimes inappropriate, and yet oddly personal sense of style, I believed Gil to be the type of eccentric billionaire who was never far from a tuxedo beneath break-in-case-of-emergency glass. Strangely enough, it turned out that I wasn't wrong. Gil was exactly that kind of eccentric billionaire; he literally had closets full of pressed tuxedos ready in case of emergency. What I *was* wrong about was that the tuxes weren't for him; they were for his guests. Or in this case, me.

While we Zeros dressed in the penthouse, a few of Gil's "service specialists"–as he bureaucratically called them–cleaned out the Tank downstairs in the parking garage. I tried not to think of the rivers of blood that would pour out of the old Mercedes the moment they opened the back door. I tried to voice my concerns, but Gil waved me off, saying, "This isn't the first or the last time my boys'll have to clean up something weird and keep quiet about it. As they know, mum's the word." Disconcerting, but rather handy in a pinch.

Despite Finch's brutal injuries, he seemed almost well. When he came down from his room, dressed to the nines, he was almost grinning. It seemed even he was not impervious to the delight taken in formal wear. Gil and I were standing at one of his emergency tuxedo closets arguing over sleeve length when Finch emerged. He was stiff and slow with his movements, leaning on a discrete black metal cane for support.

On our way back to the Penthouse from Hanas' clinic, Finch sat shotgun, and Gil spread out in the back while I drove. At some point Finch had dialed a number on his cell and passed the phone over his shoulder to Gil.

The conversation was a little awkward but inevitable. Yes, Willa

Bascombe knew about the fundraising ball. No, she had no intention of going. Yes, she knew her absence would be conspicuous. No, she didn't care. She had friends outside the city who were willing to give her shelter until the troubling matter involving her husband was resolved in one way or another.

On the phone, Gil had used every ounce of charm he possessed and somehow managed to convince her to attend the ball. Finch and I rode in silence as Gil explained the situation to her, taking his time to spell out how important it was that she was there to feed us information and put names to faces. Without someone present to open doors and make introductions, the only thing we were likely to accomplish that night was donate money to a bad cause and eat some rubbery catered chicken.

God knows how, but eventually she agreed, only on the condition that we were responsible for her safe exit. Just after disconnecting, Gil repeated her words gravely. "She said, 'I won't spend another night with that man. Every night I sleep in his bed is another night I'm inviting my own death.' Worse part is, there's a good chance she's right."

He recited the rest of the conversation back to us in usual Gil stylings (including lots of hand waving and shouting). I understood our need for her to be at the ball, but I couldn't help but feel the risk outweighed the reward. It was hard to forget the look on her face when she implored that we not even speak her husband's name in her presence, and here we were asking her to share dinner and a dance with him so we could have a measly introduction. Loyalty to Gil aside, I was having trouble swallowing my doubts. *How could this be worth the risk?* I needed to believe that Gil and Finch knew better. If I was going to work with them, I had to trust them.

With the sun setting, Finch and I sat ready and waiting. I rested on the sofa, watching a baseball game while Finch leaned back in a recliner and read a book with a long French title. Gil had disappeared into the huge master bedroom more than an hour earlier and had yet to return. He finally made his appearance a few minutes before the party was set to begin.

"We're going to be late, Boss," Finch said with a disapproving glance over his book.

"Late," Gil shrugged dismissively. "That's a good thing, bud. Only the *most* important people are late." He turned his back to us and straightened his coat–tails and all–in a full-length mirror. When he finished he walked into the living room, smiling. "You fellas look hot.

Hopin' to get lucky tonight? It may be your night. There's probably gonna be a buncha *foxy* ladies there. That's why I look *extra* spiffy. You guys better go in ahead of me, though. Because once the ladies see me, they ain't gonna have eyes for anybody else." He laughed. "That includes you, Mr. Tall, Dark, and Handsome," he said, pointing at Finch.

Gil's "extra spiffy" get-up was a long tuxedo coat and pants with a cobalt blue Hawaiian shirt tucked in as if it were completely normal. His shirt sported flower blossoms and huge Easter Island heads. His shirt collar was buttoned tight and and he wore a clip-on yellow bow tie. On his lapel, a button shone proudly, reading, "#1 Dancer Man!" Incredibly shiny patent leather shoes completed the questionable ensemble. He gave me a thumbs up before waving us to the elevator. "Time to go," he said.

Stepping off the elevator in the garage, I'd expected a stretch limo to be idling before us, complete with a chauffeur holding the rear door open. Instead, there was nothing but the Tank. It may have been cleaned, but I couldn't really tell except for the thick smell of bleach. Gil slipped into the back and Finch took shotgun, once again. I drove.

This was my first ball, and I had pretty high hopes of seeing a movie star, but when Finch read me the address from the back seat, I was surprised. The shindig was way down in Southwest Philly. Even from the backseat, Finch read my confusion and explained.

"About four years ago, not long after the old water treatment plant had been shut down, a handful of investors bought the property with plans of renovating it and turning it into a private horticultural facility. Untold millions of government historical restoration funds and private donations have been poured into the complex in hopes of attracting tourism, although I don't believe it's been opened to the public quite yet. I recognize this address from the stories in the Inquirer when it was announced, and I must admit I'm rather curious to see it. It's called the Waterworks."

"Finch likes gardens," Gil sniggered from the back seat. "He's a big flower nut."

A sigh from beside me. "I admit, I enjoy the craftsmanship of a good garden," Finch said, a touch defensive. "I have read a great deal about the Waterworks, and it is supposed to be very beautiful and tasteful."

"He's excited," Gil said, smiling in the rearview.

Finch was silent, frowning. I liked that a person who was probably a few hundred years old still pouted when teased.

As per Gil's wishes, we arrived late, pulling into a long gravel circle and coming to a stop beside an arch of ivy that rose over a majestic stained-glass doorway. Men in tuxedos stood on either side of the door. A young valet took the Tank's keys from my hand with a disapproving glance that disappeared when Gil slipped him a fifty-dollar bill with a wink.

"Give us a good spot, son. I don't want any dings or dents, you hear?"

Behind us in the center of the circular drive was a huge marble fountain. Jets of water sprayed into the air, raining water over ostentatious sculptures of mermaids. Beyond the gravel drive–where the valet struggled with the Tank–and the subsequent parking area, I saw dark silhouettes of refineries and smokestacks in the not-too-distant skyline. I knew that surrounding this grand structure were countless blocks of low-income housing, dilapidated factories, and neighborhoods ravaged by crime and poverty. As the tuxedoed butlers standing before me pulled open the stained-glass double doors, I felt a little uncomfortable.

"So this is what gentrification looks like..." I muttered, stepping inside.

Living up to its namesake, the Waterworks had all the pipes and concrete pillars of a high-volume water treatment plant, but the wide expanse of the buildings had been heavily gutted, the dirty factory machinery and factory workings of the compound having been removed in exchange for a lesson in architectural amalgamation. In the center of each room were tiered, glass cathedral ceilings that rose upwards in a step pattern. Colorful lanterns were strung from the pipes, casting soft light across the great gardens.

We followed the maze-like cobbled walk as it wound its way through room after room. On either side of the walkway were huge flowerbeds, bearing bright and flawless rows of flowers so perfectly uniform that they seemed factory-made, everything from long-necked daisies to massive florabundas. Shiny brass piping covered the walls of each room, maintaining the heavily industrial feel of the complex. Occasionally, an empty glass or cocktail napkin marred the landscape from a party that had moved on.

Numerous artificial streams ran through the main building, crisscrossing what I realized were some of the most impressive indoor gardens I'd ever seen. Interspersed throughout the endless oceans of color were blossoming dogwood trees, the pink petals moving gently in a breeze. I looked up to find big metal fans hanging from the ceiling, quietly circulating the air and giving each room a serene sense of motion.

Gil and I walked with a purpose, but Finch moved slowly, seeming to take in every blooming flower and tree. The only three on the path, we were apparently the last to arrive. Regardless, Finch was in no hurry.

Despite my misgivings about the evening, I was impressed. Unlike Finch, gardening was not my thing, but everything I'd seen was tasteful and organically worked with the water station's industrial aesthetic. The copper piping that ran up and down the walls offered a bright metallic juxtaposition to the vivid colors that filled each room.

After crossing through countless ornately decorated rooms, we came to a set of doors even larger than those at the entrance. They were tall and arched, like those of a medieval castle. The frame looked like brass, but the body of the door was a mosaic of stained glass arranged in the shape of a sunflower. Grand, as was everything else here. Part of me wondered if they had gilded toilets in the can. Another set of tuxedoed butlers opened the doors for us and we followed the cobblestone path outside into the cool spring air.

A huge slate patio, lit by rows of hanging Japanese paper lanterns and old-fashioned candelabras, spread out before us. Women in evening gowns danced with men in tuxedos to the music of a string quartet playing somewhere off to our right. A few of the guys wore top hats; most of the women had long white gloves unfurled up their slender arms. I felt like I'd just walked into some gothic Victorian wedding.

"This is some Anne Rice stuff right here, guys," Gil said.

"Should've worn a monocle, Boss," I said.

"Indeed," Finch added. "Although perhaps a cod piece would have been more apropos."

To our left was a small desk occupied by a balding tuxedoed man in wireframe glasses. Before him was a long wooden box sealed with a gilded antique lock. On top of the box ran a long, narrow slit in the center of the lid. The balding man looked up at us and smiled.

"Gentlemen, welcome to Councilman Bascombe's formal fundraising ball." He smiled again–obviously a bureaucrat. His smile faltered when he saw Gil's yellow bowtie and novelty lapel pin. "Gentlemen, do you have, uh… invitations?"

Gil cleared his throat and pulled an envelope from his inside tuxedo pocket. "We're special friends," he said with a grin of his own. "Councilman Bascombe will be grateful we came, trust me." He lowered the envelope and pressed it against the narrow slit where it got stuck, too thick to fit through. "Oh golly, what a faux pas," Gil said with a dramatic hand on his cheek. "I brought cash and look what's happened." He pushed ineffectually against the envelope with a frown.

The balding man's smile returned. "No problem, Mr...?"

"Abercrombie."

"...Mr. Abercrombie. Here." He unlocked the box and lifted the lid, showing off a large pile of checks intertwined like snakes in a nest. Gil dropped the envelope on top with a wink. The man giggled before returning the lock to the lid. "Thank you so much, Mr. Abercrombie. I hope you and your guests enjoy the evening."

Gil smiled. "I'm sure we will. As long as they play 'The Electric Slide' I'll be happy as a clam." The balding man nodded, his smile wilting slightly.

We passed through another vine-covered archway and made our way towards the grouping of tables along the edge of the dance floor. Finch and I gave the dance floor a wider berth than we would have an alligator pit. Gil, on the other hand, was like a child standing before a Christmas tree. He did his best to skank to what may or may not have been Edvard Grieg–hey, I said I *looked* like a meathead, not that I *was* a meathead; I know some classical music. A few awkward minutes later, Finch and I pulled Gil off the dance floor and towards a table near the patio's edge.

After taking our seat, we ordered drinks from a waiter in a white tux. The Grieg sonata ended and a smattering of weak applause filled the air. For the next few minutes we were silent as we studied the crowd.

The patio was large and quite full, though most of the guests occupied the dance floor, moving in perfect time to a slow waltz I didn't recognize. On the opposite side of the patio, a long wooden bar had been set up, and a handful of disinterested guests milled about it. Willa and Alfred Bascombe were nowhere in sight, and I felt a little anxiety creeping up. We three were Willa's protection, and we couldn't even get to the damn fundraiser on time. I fiddled with the silverware and watched the rich people dance. I'd given up on spotting anyone I recognized when Arthur Greely plodded past our table, waltzing with a rather frumpy looking pale woman. He looked exactly as he did earlier except he wore a top hat. When he passed, he met my eye and scowled.

When our drink order arrived, I leaned back and took a deep gulp of the only brew they had on draft, some shitty light beer. "This is not my kind of scene," I said after a moment.

"Nor mine, as a matter of fact," Finch added softly, sipping a dry martini. "I prefer real Victorian balls. Even they weren't this... *tight-assed.*"

"Under most circumstances, I'd be loving this," Gil said, taking a sip from his drink, a bright green concoction laden with slices of fruit and a paper umbrella. "But there's no friggin' way this place plays techno. I mean, what is this crap?" He gestured at the string quartet with unmasked disdain. "Ugh, boring old people music. Finch, how much of this guest list do you think is made up of unfavorables?"

"Quite a lot, honestly," Finch said, pensively. "Though I must admit, the mix is rather interesting."

"What are you guys talking about?" I asked.

Gil slipped off his jacket and draped it over the chair beside him, showing off more of the Easter Island heads on his shirt. "Let's just say that we don't have to worry about anybody wanting to sit at our table."

Finch took a sip and said, "We have been involved with nearly every guest at this ball in some fashion or other. In a business capacity, that is. And rarely are they *our* clients."

"Are you serious? These are all... bad guys?"

Finch nodded at me. "Essentially, yes. I was expecting it, to be frank, but I don't particularly enjoy it."

"Hey, look at that guy," Gil said, pointing his finger. "I think I killed that guy once. No, really. He better not see me here," he muttered. "He'll be pissed."

"We need not worry," Finch said, taking another sip from his martini.

"Why not?" I asked.

"I have a strong feeling nothing will happen while we're here. All these guests rarely get together for such an event. They won't allow it to be sullied by the likes of us."

"We're gonna have to leave eventually," I muttered as the string quartet finished the waltz and fell into silence. Another polite applause swam through the crowd before the sound rose. Above us, two figures had appeared on a balcony overlooking the dance floor. Willa Bascombe stood hand in hand with a barrel-chested man in a three-piece tuxedo and top hat. A silver watch fob ran across his sizable gut and I was disappointed to see him without a cigarette holder clamped between his teeth. Even from my vantage, I saw the fear radiating off Willa like heat waves. Her face was twisted in a false grin that looked like it took a lot of effort to maintain. I knew the man beside her was her husband, but it took me a minute to recognize him from his photograph. He had a thick beard that I'd never before seen. It was long and bushy, covering his mouth and rising high on his cheekbones before it twisted upward and met his curly hair at his sideburns. With the hat on, only his eyes and nose were visible.

Councilman Bascombe waved off the applause dramatically, but it continued. The three of us shared a dubious glance as the clapping grew to include catcalls and whistles. When he finally managed to silence his army of well-wishers, I heard Finch's voice across the table. He spoke softly, but his words rang with all the force of concussive blasts on a battlefield.

"I *know* you," he said, leaning forward. "It's been a long time, you son of a bitch, but how could I forget?"

CHAPTER 10. CHANGE OF PLANS

"What?" I asked, keeping my voice low as the applause died down. "What are you saying?"

Finch shook his head and shushed me. Above us, leaning heavily on an ornate balustrade and grinning, Alfred Bascombe was preparing to make a speech, and Finch had every intention of hearing it. I repeated the question, and he waved me off. I didn't really care to hear some political stump speech, I wanted to know what the hell was going on. I snapped my fingers to draw Finch's attention.

"Quiet," he said, his voice stern. "I do know the truth, and I will still know it in five minutes. So calm down." Finch turned away and focused on Bascombe as the big, bearded man cleared his throat and pulled a few folded pieces of paper from his jacket pocket.

"Thank you for coming, my constituents and dear friends. We have waited a long time for this evening. Far too long, really." He spoke slowly and deliberately with a voice that sounded like a rusted brass instrument. I didn't see a microphone, but from where I sat his voice rang loud and clear as though he were standing right beside me. "I am so glad to be here with you all tonight. It is truly an honor."

More applause broke out, and I rolled my eyes. Willa stood beside Bascombe, statuesque, her lips pursed. She looked stricken and maybe a little ill, and I couldn't help admire her poise. She wore a long red silk dress, her hair down from her characteristic ponytail. As Bascombe spoke, the lines of stress painted across her face eased as she got her feet under her. She was even stronger than I'd first thought.

Bascombe smiled as he made some ham-handed political joke and paused for the yuck-yuck-yuck response of his guests, some even clapping their hands. The chortling of pale-faced, undead cronies made me feel like someone was jamming splinters under my fingernails as I watched Willa fake a smile. I remembered Finch's warning about keeping my distance, but it was getting harder by the minute. I leaned back and looked longingly at my empty beer glass.

I turned to look for a waiter, raising a hand to signal a young man, when a *crack-crack-crack* of repeated gunfire snapped through the air, silencing the subdued laughter. Every muscle in my body tensed as the evening's forced cordiality was put to bed. Despite the fact that a good number of the guests had little to worry about in regards to gunfire–being undead, and all–screams broke out as the crowd of well-dressed bodies scattered. A second burst of shots rang out over the patio, then a third.

Instincts kicked in (thank you, years of training). I'd served overseas in official and unofficial capacities, and I'd heard my share of gunfire. Before Gil could lower his colorful drink, I'd tipped over the table, sending empty glasses and flatware to the ground with a crash. I yanked Finch and Gil from their seats, pulling them to the ground with me.

Gil looked surprise; Finch looked annoyed. For the first time, *I* was the one in his element. *Ahh, so this is what they pay me for*, I realized.

"What the hell's going on?" Gil barked. He crawled to peer around the overturned table before I grabbed him and yanked him back.

"Stop, damnit," I said. "Can't you hear someone shooting?" More shots. "That?"

"Hmm," he said. "Now that you mention it..."

Loud cracks echoed through the now mostly-empty concourse, followed by the sound of shattered stone and plaster raining to the ground. Somewhere, bullets chewed into the building facade. I liked the report of bullets hitting concrete; it meant they weren't hitting a person. From the sound of the discharges, I pegged the gun to be a Beretta 92 or 96. I sat back and counted off shots, waiting for the end of his clip. Around us, some guests had followed our lead, overturning tables and crawling behind them for cover. Others ran for the gardens. Somewhere, someone was crying.

"Guns are cruel instruments," Gil muttered, shaking his head as another shot ripped through the air. "Not really my bag."

Finch crawled on all fours towards the table's edge. As quickly as it came, the gunfire ceased, an eerie silence filling the concourse before panicked voices began rising. Finch was the first to stand before he gave me and Gil the all clear.

My eyes immediately went to the balcony, but it was empty. Not really surprising. The French doors hanging at the rear of the balcony swayed in a breeze, glass panes shattered. Ominous bullet holes speckled the pale stucco wall on either side of the doorway in a ragged pattern. I swore. "Either Willa or Bascombe was the target," I said. Running on automatic, I took off, crossing the patio at a run, looking for any stairwell that could take me up to the roof. Behind me, Finch shouted my name. I screeched to a halt and turned back. He stood pointing back at the roof across the patio from the balcony. I followed his finger and saw the silhouette of a thin man crossing the roof's edge at a sprint. As I noticed him, he changed course, leaping from the ledge down onto an adjoining building leading towards the center of the complex. In a moment, he'd disappeared from sight.

"Get him," Gil shouted. "We'll get her!" I nodded and took off.

They say a successful pursuit is half skill and half luck. Well it's more like nine-tenths luck and one-tenth skill because there always comes a time when whoever you're pursuing gets away from you. When that happens you don't *stop* chasing them, you just have to *guess* where they're going and hope to high hell you're right. Sooner or later, your luck runs out; it's inevitable. The hope is to end the chase before that happens.

I burst through a frightened group of women in ball gowns before crossing beneath the ivy archway that led back into the gardens. Many of the guests had run inside for cover, and the cobblestone paths were all jammed. I pushed a few dandies aside and leapt a low fence into a bed of tulips, stomping across a shallow stream with all the grace of a hungry grizzly bear chasing a camper. The voices inside the gardens were loud and shrill, filling the placid scene with rabid, wide-eyed fear.

I struggled to focus over the noise and commotion, my eyes moving across the ceiling, following the contours of the roof. Ocassionally I caught the blurred silhouette of the gunman pass an opaque window. Eventually, I knew the shooter would have to take a stairwell down–the roof was too high to jump, and I just had to be there when that happened. I'd gone through a few rooms, passing the small orchard of trees with pink blossoms and a fountain or two before I cursed it all and threw logic aside. At a certain point, you have to trust your gut. I picked the first maintenance door I saw and charged it, crashing through it as if it were nothing but paper.

I spilled onto the floor in a long straight hallway lit by a few bare bulbs hanging from the ceiling. Thick pipes and ridged conduits ran the length of the seemingly endless hall; in a few places steam vented into the path from seams in the old pipe fittings. My breath was coming in gasps, but I managed to hold it long enough to hear what I'd had my fingers and toes crossed for: the quick patter of shoes on tile. The sound rang back at me from somewhere down the tunnel ahead. Through the swirling clouds of steam, I saw a shadow flickering as it moved away from me. I peeled myself off the floor and took off after it.

My footsteps pounded against the wet tile of the hall as I fought a mounting cramp. I'd grown lazy in recent years, beginning the slow backslide out of shape, and I hadn't done any serious running in a while. Thankfully, whoever was ahead of me wasn't doing much better–the first good news of the evening. As I ran, the shadow grew larger.

Long flashlight beams were beginning to appear behind me. I heard muffled voices and men shouting. Either the cops or security, I realized. I only moved faster. The guy ahead of me was running out of gas, his breathing becoming more frantic while his outline became clearer through the steam. I was close enough to tell he was tall and as thin as a bone. A stumble had also crept into his step, the fatigue preventing him from running in a straight line.

Ahead, the endless straightaway finally bore a sharp left turn. The shooter skidded as he slowed on the wet ground. Squeaking shoes and groaning signaled his turn as he awkwardly puttered around the bend. I could catch him if I didn't lose too much speed, I realized.

My patent leather shoes hit on the wet tile like ice, but I made it around the corner without slowing too much. I rounded the curve and saw the shooter just ahead of me, staggering as he desperately tried to regain speed. Legs shaking, I gave one last push and closed the gap. Gritting my teeth, I reached out and grabbed the tail of a suit jacket. I locked it in my grasp just before my legs gave out. I fell, but I took him down with me.

The cloth of the man's coat didn't tear as I'd feared, instead it held strong, pulling him backwards. We fell in a tumbling heap. I heard him howl as his legs twisted beneath him. In the shuffle, his arms and legs flailed wildly. I raised my arms to protect me, but his left elbow connected perfectly with my nose.

And with a wet *splat*, my luck ran out.

There was a crunch and thunderous pain spread across my face set to the charging beat of my heart. Blood sprayed down my once immaculate shirtfront as my grasp on the man's coat released.

His chest rose and fell raggedly, a swatch of scarlet across his pale cheeks. Sweat poured off him and his whole body shook, racked with exhaustion. He turned, his eyes wide with desperation when they met mine. The need to escape was intense, but the shock playing across my face was enough to halt him, if only for a moment.

After a beat, he turned his back and ran. Dizzy and covered in my own blood, I felt the cold touch of shock run through me. The adrenaline faded and the pain began to worsen. I collapsed against the wall.

He was gaunt, sallow, and clean-shaven, but there was no doubt. It was the face we'd seen on the driver's license only hours earlier.

It was Alfred Bascombe, and he was gone.

CHAPTER 11. THE MAN IN QUESTION

"Please keep your head back, sir," the paramedic said as he pressed a rubber gloved-hand to my forehead and tilted my bloody face to the night sky for the umpteenth time. I grunted as he returned to pushing cotton balls up my nose. I tried to be tough, but it was excruciating, and he was enjoying it a *little* too much.

"Is that really necessary, Donald?"

"Don't tell me how to do my job, Finch," the paramedic said through gritted teeth as he pushed an index finger halfway to my brain. "Gil pays me well, but not well enough to take your shit, buddy."

I sat on the ambulance's open tailgate while Donald the paramedic stood facing me, apparently trying to Q-Tip my frontal lobe. Gil and Finch were behind the EMT, pacing and awaiting a chance to speak with me privately. Around us swarmed clouds of guests and a handful of trench coat detectives. Swirling police lights lit the scene. After the shooting, no one had been allowed to leave the Waterworks. So, here we were.

"What a waste of time," I groaned as Donald pushed what felt like his whole arm into my head. "This charade." I slapped a hand on my bloody tuxedo shirt to illustrate.

"This was far from a waste, Dylan," Finch said.

"Yeah, I mean Finch got to see those pretty flowers," Gil said.

Ignoring him, Finch continued. "As a matter of fact, we learned quite a bit."

"Yeah? Like what?" I grunted. "And where's Willa? With the cops?" I tried to catch my partner's eyes over Donald's shoulder. "You said you'd get her when I chased after what's-his-name."

"We need to talk to you about that, Dylan," Finch said, grimacing. Gil turned his back and faced the distant skyline, scratching his head uncomfortably.

"Gil? Gil, where's Willa?" I asked.

"Everything's fine, good buddy. I just got somethin' in my eye."

Donald tweaked my nose again, and I groaned. "Enough," I said, leaning away from him. "We're done." He frowned and reached towards my face again. I dodged him and slipped off the tailgate.

"Mr. Abercrombie, can you get your associate to sit down again? I'm not done packing his nose." He lifted a bag of cotton balls with a wounded frown on his face.

"I think he's had enough, Don," Gil said, stepping between us. "Thanks for your help."

I scowled at Donald the paramedic as he shuffled off. Gil took my arm and led me away from the larger crowds. He stood on my left, Finch on my right.

"All right, so we've got some new problems, big man," Gil began. "But we need to start with what happened with you in that hallway."

"Yeah, no shit," I said, yanking my arm free. "So are you going to–"

"What did you see?" Finch interrupted. "You were pretty disoriented when the officers dragged you out, do you still remember?"

"Oh, I remember."

"Apparently, the fuzz kept on chasing the shooter for a while, but they lost him somewhere in the sewers," Gil said, pulling his pipe from his coat.

"You know, you guys are probably going to have to tell me this again later," I said, rubbing my temples as a headache bloomed. "I feel a little... spacey. But I need to know what happened after I ran off. Where's Willa?"

"As Boss promised, we did make our way to the balcony, although not without some difficulty..." Finch began.

"...but the lady was missing," Gil said. "Sorry, man. I dunno if she was taken or... or what, but her husband–beardy Mr. Bascombe–was hit twice in the chest, so the odds that he ran off with her are kinda slim. Paramedics carried him out. It didn't look so good." He shook his head.

"What? What the hell does that mean? She's gone? Where could she have gone? This place is locked down!"

"I know, big man. I mean, we looked..." Gil began.

"We went through every room of the place that we could get into. All of them were empty," Finch said patiently. "Access to most major back rooms was restricted, but we got into more than a few of them. Again, they were all empty. Inquiries with security personnel as well as waitstaff led nowhere, either. We do have a source of ours waiting at the hospital to give us an update to see if she was brought in with her husband," Finch concluded. "Although I am not optimistic."

I groaned. "Why not? And where the hell could she have gotten to?"

Gil said something like "Uhhh errmmnn..."

"How can we find her?" I asked.

"Now calm down, Dylan," Finch said. "We've got eyes all over this town. Boss has got people with their fingers in every pie. I have a feeling that she slipped out when the shooting started. Right now, this place is locked down tight, so no one is getting out. Right now, we're just going to have to be patient."

"Well the damn shooter got out, no problem," I said.

"Yeah, but we don't know who or what that was," Gil said. "Maybe they could fly or walk through walls or turn into a goldfish. Finch is right, we just gotta be patient, okay? It could've been a specter or a demon or a magic school bus–"

"It wasn't," Finch and I both said at the same time. We froze and turned to face each other. "What?" we asked in chorus.

"You two been practicing this? It's kind of weird," Gil said.

Finch turned to me. "How do you know?"

"What do you mean, how do I know? I got a pretty good reason: I *saw* him. How do *you* know?"

"Because I know what's going on," he said.

"What does that mean, 'what's goin on'?" Gil asked, turning to face Finch.

"Bascombe is not Bascombe," Finch explained.

"That's right! That's right!" I said, pointing at Finch. "Bascombe was the shooter."

"What?" Now Finch and Gil were speaking in stereo.

"Yeah, Bascombe was the guy with the gun," I explained. *"That* was who I saw in the tunnel. The face on the driver's license," I said lowering my voice in the milling crowd. "See, I chased him and caught him, but there was a tussle and I got... well, you know." I waved a hand at the drying blood and all.

"Wait, Dylan," Finch said, casting a wary glance over his shoulder as we continued walking, slowly moving away from the biggest plume of guests. "Are you certain? Are you *certain* it was Alfred Bascombe you chased?"

"Absolutely," I said, nodding. "He looked a little different, though. Like the driver's license picture but really, really thin. Gaunt-thin. But I'm sure it was him."

Finch offered a rare grin. "I knew it," he said. "I *knew* it." He opened his mouth to speak when a thick southern accent exploded from behind us.

"My lord, Giles Abercrombie, is that you?!" Beside me, Gil and Finch froze, panic on their faces. A tiny grey haired woman tottered towards me in one of the most exotically gaudy ensembles I'd ever seen. Stripes of green and yellow and red and blue ran up and down her dress like Joseph's Amazing Technicolor Dreamcoat on crack. Wire frame half-moon glasses sat on the tip of her beakish nose. Peacock feathers shot madly from a wild beehive of curly hair. She couldn't have been more than five feet tall in high heels, no more than a hundred pounds soaking wet.

Gil turned around, the panic replaced by feigned joy. "Oh hey there, Mrs. Robbes-Grillet! You have turned this evening into a knock-out success despite all those awkward shoot-out missteps. And you look positively... *gorgeous*."

She blushed. "Now Giles Anthony Abercrombie you have positively made my evening." She stepped over to Gil, a shiny cane tapping across the pavement beside her, and turned a waiting cheek to him for a kiss. He obliged.

"It is certainly a treat to see you here, Mrs. Robbes-Grillet," Finch said. He was smiling so hard he looked in danger of pulling a muscle.

"Alistair Finch you always look so... I don't know, what's the word, Giles?"

"Tall?"

"No. Though you're taller than me, Alistair." She laughed hysterically and tapped her cane repeatedly against the pavement. The three of us stared at her.

"And who is this?" she asked after her spell of self-imposed hilarity had ceased. She turned to me and jabbed me with her cane. "*He* is tall, Giles. And he's got a big head. Why's he all bloody? Oh dear, that is *awful*."

"This is Mr. Dylan, Mrs. Robbes-Grillet; he's our new associate," Gil explained patiently.

"What happened to the other fellow? What was his name? Brian, wasn't it? Brian Parker?"

The smile on Gil's face faltered. He stood tall, surrendering his accommodating huddled stance. Confusion and distress tugged at his eyes like fatigue as he struggled for words.

"Mr. Dylan is our *new* associate, Mrs. Robbes-Grillet," Finch said, stepping in.

"How pleasant it is to meet you, Mr. Dylan," she said, turning away from Finch to face me for the first time. Over her half-moon glasses, she had smart and piercing eyes. I shook her small hand.

"It's a pleasure, ma'am," I said.

"Oh, such manners!"

Finch lowered his voice and leaned down to her. He lifted a hand to shield his mouth and whispered conspiratorially. "We're actually in the middle of some sensitive business, Mrs. Robbes-Grillet. Quite sensitive, if you follow." He winked for effect–pretty theatrical for the old timer.

"You talkin' about *monsters*?" she all but shouted. A few guests behind her threw their glances our way. Finch tried unsuccessfully to hush her. "What're you boys after this time? You came to the right place, either way. This place was a damn rat's nest, huh?"

Finch raised both hands and began hushing her full force as more eyes turned in our direction. Onlookers were increasingly angry. Beside me, Gil seemed to be surfacing from whatever dark waters he'd sunken into.

"What... uh, what were you doing here this evening, Eleanor?" Gil asked, his voice froggy. He cleared his throat.

"Oh you know me, Giles, I can't say no to a ball. And you know I've got the *money*, so I'm on all the lists of invites. Like you gentlemen, I'm here in a professional capacity, as well. I'm the face of the public library systems, you know. However ratty this nest, they still do make donations, you know."

"Oh, of course, of course," Gil said, nodding. Whatever had detoured him was gone. The easy smile returned to his face.

"And speaking of a professional capacity, you never got back to me, Alistair. Ignoring my calls now? Shame on you," she said, turning an accusing eye to Finch.

"Uhh... oh dear," he muttered. "I'm sorry, Mrs. Robbes-Grillet, we've been *terribly* busy, you see."

"I told you, Alistair, this is serious. Very, very serious. I'm missing the lead gargoyle from my Walnut Street branch. This isn't some suburban branch, this is *downtown*. He will be missed, I assure you."

Finch handed me his cane before pulling a notepad and pen free from his jacket pocket. He began to write as Gil took over questioning. "What information can you give us, Ellie?"

"Information? He was there on Sunday and he was gone on Monday. That's that. Now, I understand that he enjoys going out and having some fun at night, but the deal we signed when he was granted guardianship stated that he'd be on that facade when the branch opened at sun up." She punctuated each word with a wagging index finger.

"Okay. Do you know the name of the gargoyle that's missing?"

"Of course, I do, Giles. You know perfectly well that I am on speaking terms with all of my guardians." She rolled her eyes. "His name is Ron."

Gil paused. "Ron?"

"Yes, his name is Ron, and he is missing. I'm not sure whether I should be angry or worried, but I'm both, and I need you gentlemen to find him."

Finch scribbled a few more notes. Eventually, Gil convinced her that the cops were about to open the gates. Wide-eyed and eager to leave, she excused herself, sauntering away. That old bitty wore me out.

"Good gods," Gil said, sighing. "That woman is a gauntlet."

Finch nodded. "She's been calling me non-stop, trying to get us onto that gargoyle caper. I've been trying to convince her to be patient. Apparently it did not work."

Gil patted Finch's arm. "It's all right." He turned to me. "As she said, she's the main benefactor behind the city's public libraries. She also plays some sort administrative role, too. Like the head, head, librarian. Libraries are a big deal for us. Books are powerful, but you'll learn. Anyway, we helped her out once a few years ago with a ghost in the stacks, and she's been pretty regular customer since."

"Okay, good to know." I paused, trying to pick up the conversation where we'd lost it. "Where were we?" I finally asked. Gil looked baffled, but Finch hadn't missed a beat.

"I was about to explain who the man making a speech this evening actually was," Finch explained. "Who the man posing as Willa Bascombe's husband is."

"Wait, so that wasn't the real Bascombe?" Gil asked, finally bringing a lit match to his pipe.

"I don't believe so, no," Finch said. "I felt certain I was right the moment when I first laid eyes on him on that balcony. Dylan's story confirms my suspicion."

"And what is that?"

"That the true Alfred Bascombe is as much a victim in this as his wife Willa. That is, no villain at all. Rather, he is another victim."

There was a silence in our group as we exchanged glances.

"You better start at the beginning, bud," Gil said.

"You said you *knew* the man, is that right?" I asked. "I did hear you right, didn't I?"

"Yes, that's right. When I saw him on the balcony, I recognized him. He did look a bit like the photograph we saw of Bascombe, but something about him looked eerily similar to someone else, as well. I believe it was his eyes; they were unmistakable. You see, this being has no true face, but I met him in one form or another a long time ago. A long, *long* time ago. After you've met him once, he's hard to forget." Finch took his cane back from me and leaned heavily on it. "He was a mad killer then, and if I'm correct, nothing has changed."

"I'm sorry, did you you say 'mad killer'?" I asked.

"What is he, like a shapeshifter or something?" Gil asked, puffing on his pipe. Pungent clouds of smoke billowed around us.

"No, not quite," Finch explained, waving plumes of smoke away and stifling a cough. "It's more complicated than that. From the little I understand and remember, he uses the love between a husband and a wife to take the form of that which the wife loves. Sort of like a bond that he can latch onto and replicate. Only those who love each other truly and deeply are vulnerable to him. Without that love, he is rather toothless."

I felt a twinge of regret somewhere in my chest at Finch's words. I thought of Willa and Alfred Bascombe and grimaced. Was that jealousy? Oh man. I pushed the thoughts aside and focused on the matters at hand.

"So the man in the tunnel...?" I asked.

"I assume that was the real Alfred Bascombe," Finch said. "And now he's missing, as well. Somewhere he's confused and on the lam. He came here attempting to do the only thing he knew to do: try to kill the man who'd taken his place."

"But who is this guy, Finch? Who is it that wants to kill Willa?" Gil asked, taking his pipe from his mouth.

"I don't know his true name, but he calls himself *Bluebeard*," Finch said, shifting his weight on his cane. "He draws his power from the women he kills. It has something to do with using the love they carry. I haven't figured it all out, but it's definitely love-involved. Love and trust."

"I know that name," Gil said, slapping Finch's shoulder, almost knocking him over. "I know him! He's bad business."

"You knew him, you said?" I asked, turning to Finch. "Like, knew him knew him? Why didn't you take care of him the *last* time you met him? Huh?"

"Because at the time I didn't have the power, nor did I have the knowhow," Finch explained. "And that much hasn't changed in the last hundred and fifty years. Also, I didn't have a reason to care, quite frankly."

I opened my mouth to speak, but was interrupted by the ringing of a cell. Finch held up a finger before pulling a phone from his coat and answering it. He mumbled something curt before hanging up.

"That was our man at the hospital," he explained, "This Bluebeard/Faux Bascombe gentleman was never brought in. Nor was Mrs. Willa Bascombe. Wherever Bluebeard is, he's off our radar again, and I am assuming on the loose. Whatever plan he is working from has hit upon a snag."

"Yeah, the *real* Mr. Bascombe just stood up," Gil mumbled.

"We still need to find Willa," I said. "And we need to find her *now*."

CHAPTER 12. THE GREAT AND TERRIBLE SECRETS OF FINCH

By the time we'd spoken to our third or fourth detective and were finally cleared to leave, Finch had called half of Gil's contacts in the city. Apparently Gil had paid employees buried in most of the major businesses throughout Philadelphia. Major hotel's busboys, SEPTA bus drivers, cabbies, owners of shitty motels around the airport, garbagemen, hospital surgeons, power trippers from L&I, Amtrak conductors, some of those TSA jerks at the airport. You name it, he had 'em in his pocket. He assured me that patience would win out.

Back in the Tank, we finally pulled out of the quickly emptying parking lot. Finch pocketed his cell and sighed. "Dead battery," he said.

"Get anything, though?" Gil asked.

"Not a thing. I did speak with one of the detectives while you were filling out our contact information," Finch said, leaning back and squeezing the bridge of his nose between two fingers. "Mrs. Bascombe is most definitely missing. The entirety of the Waterworks has been searched, top to bottom, and it has now been officially confirmed that neither Willa nor the evening's assailant are on the premises."

"And the bearded Councilman Bascombe?" I asked, keeping my eyes on the road.

"I called Penn, Jefferson, Penn Presbyterian, Hanhemann, and Einstein, pretty much every hospital in the metropolitan area. Councilman Bascombe has not been admitted to any of them," Finch said. "Nor has Willa." His voice lowered, "I don't mean to be morbid, but I checked with the morgues as well. Nothing."

"I guess that's good news," I mumbled.

"We're just gonna have to wait and trust the lady," Gil said, puffing on his pipe. "She'll turn up, big man. I've got my boys out looking for her, my ferrets. We'll find her, all right?" In the backseat Finch rolled down a window and coughed. The Tank rumbled along as usual, but no one spoke. A terrible mixture of fear and anxiety swirled around inside of me, and I'm sure that Gil and Finch could feel it as much as they could feel the humid air pouring in through Finch's open window. The sad fact was that we didn't know each other well enough to have any idea how to handle it. Finch looked out the window, Gil smoked his pipe, and I drove. It was silent all the way back to the loft.

By the time we'd stepped from the elevator into the lush Penthouse, I'd manage to backseat the nasty cocktail of emotion in favor of good ol' understated seething. Angry at our powerlessness, angry at the circumstances, angry at this Bluebeard guy. Just angry. As my performance with Greely demonstrated, my temper is by far my worst trait. Half of me wanted to leave, carry my bag out the door and take a cab back to my house (the other half was divided between having an *Incredible Hulk*-like meltdown and eating a hot dog with Gil while watching a ballgame–essentially anything to calm down). I realized I hadn't slept in my bed in a few nights, but the thought of being alone sounded worse than anything else. I opted to stay. With that in mind, I wandered to the kitchen and took a seat in the semi-darkness, pondering a snack.

Gil followed me in and began clanging around in the cabinets. He emerged with a bottle of Lagavulin single malt Scotch and two cut crystal tumblers. Without sitting, he set a glass in front of me and gave a generous pour. The pipe still sat clamped between his teeth, tucked just beneath his scraggly mustache–incredibly incongruous when paired with the mix-and-match tuxedo he wore. To top it all off, he'd once more donned his deerstalker cap. Still silent, he poured a liberal dose of whiskey into his own glass before placing the bottle before me on the table. He put a hand on my back for a moment, then stepped out of the kitchen and left me to myself.

I tried the Scotch and relished the burn as it crept down my throat. Delicious gasoline. In the other room, Gil took a seat in his vibrating chair and leaned back. I could just make out his deerstalker hat as it peeked over the top of the headrest. The television snapped on and he commenced to flip channels aimlessly.

The Lagavulin was delicious. A friend had given me a bottle of it when I formally left the police force, and each sip took my hand and pulled me back through the years. Unfortunately, most of those memories were not welcomed. I stood and dug a few ice cubes from the freezer. Finch interrupted me just as I plinked them into the glass.

"Ice in your Scotch is a sacrilege," he said. He wasn't smiling.

"Sorry to disappoint," I said, a faint sneer creeping into my voice.

Finch pulled a highball glass from a cabinet and took a seat at the round kitchen table across from me, his back to the living room. He took the Lagavulin and filled the glass halfway with a heavy-handed pour. I watched him as he drank from the glass. He did not sip.

"This was not the most productive day," Finch said softly.

"It was plenty productive," I said. "Just nothing good happened."

Finch tossed back the glass, finishing it like a real champ. "We need to listen to Gil," he said as he poured himself another glass, the line of Scotch creeping even higher than it had been the first time around. "Boss is right. We need a little faith."

I took a deep sip of my own glass and had a hard time with it, marveling at Finch's stomach. The tumbler returned to the table with a slam. "Faith," I muttered, shaking my head.

"I'm sorry to say this, but you need to keep it together, Dylan. I know we don't know each other well enough to admit that, but it's true. We have to keep our heads clear here."

"Clear heads, that's grand," I laughed. "Look at the way you're downing that shit," I pointed at his glass.

He paused, slow to meet my eye. His glass was a little less that halfway filled. With evident hesitancy, he pushed the glass away.

"I'm sorry," he said, his voice low. "There is a reason I tend not to drink." He closed his eyes and took a deep breath. "You do know that Gil is right, though. We need to trust the woman. We need to trust Mrs. Bascombe."

"Willa," I said. From behind Finch, I heard a raucous laugh track from the television set. I ignored it. "She preferred to be called Willa."

Finch didn't respond, so we stared into our glasses for a little while. I hadn't had much to drink in a long time, and I could the Lagavulin getting to me. The glass had gone straight to my head. Whiskey will do that when you skip dinner. Still, it was an effort not to fill the glass again.

"Why aren't you in charge of this merry group?" I asked. "We Zeros. Is it because Gil is the rich one? Is it just the money?" Rude words, but it seemed my tongue had decided to do as it pleased.

Finch smiled. "It was inevitable that you'd ask such a question. The other men who have been in your position usually found more tactful ways of asking, but I admire your candor."

I raised my glass and pulled an ice cube into my mouth, crunching on it. "What's the answer?"

Despite what Finch had already said, his hand snaked toward the Lagavulin bottle once again. He poured himself two fingers before returning the cork. "I couldn't do this without Gil. I couldn't."

"Why?"

He took a sip. "Gil told you about me? Right?"

"You're immortal, right?"

"Yes, but it is more complicated than just that."

"More complicated than immortality, huh? If I had a dollar for every time I heard that one..." The dregs of my anger were mixing with the Scotch to form a nasty concoction. On any other day, I'd feel some kind of pity for the man across the table from me. At the moment, however, I was just angry enough and just tired enough not to care.

Finch took a drink from his glass and returned it to the table, his eyes studying what remained of the swirling amber liquid as a blush crept into his cheeks. Regardless of how many times he may have had this conversation, it didn't appear to get any easier.

"When I was twenty-two years old, my then fiancee and I made a deal for our immortality. But when you're twenty-two years old, you don't yet fully understand what it is you're making a deal with, or making a deal *for*."

"What kind of deal was it?"

A wan smile spread across his face. "A hasty deal," he said. "We decided to do it on a bit of a whim. There was a bottle we'd stolen from her father not unlike this," he said lifting the highball and swirling the Lagavulin around the glass. "This makes me think of her."

"What was her name?"

"Nora." The word escaped his lips like a sigh. Despite the intervening years, the name was still dear to him.

"What did you decide, Finch?"

A long moment passed where only badly scripted sitcom chatter and a laugh track broke the silence. Behind Finch, Gil watched without making a sound, something I'd learned was quite unusual. The look on Finch's face told me that he was somewhere far, far away.

"With the help of her sisters, Nora and I prayed to the Morrígan, the great queen, the crow of the battlefield. Do you know the Morrígan, Dylan?"

I shook my head.

"She is a war deity, a fierce and terrible goddess that men pray to for life and victory and finally death, in the end. That which you find on the battlefield is only found through her, given or taken from her hand. Do you follow me, Dylan?"

I was a soldier; I understood. Silently, I nodded.

"She promised us immortality, an endless life spent together in a world that loved us as much as we loved each other. In exchange, we need only give her one thing, one measly token of ourselves."

He paused and took another drink of the Lagavulin. He grimaced as he swallowed, his eyes sliding from focus as quickly as they became wet.

"We were children," he said softly. "It seemed so small, so...*unimportant*. We couldn't see it and couldn't understand how it meant anything to us at all; we could not fathom its worth. How hard it was for us to believe in something we couldn't see, couldn't feel. To us, it was nothing."

I didn't respond. His words were rough with honesty, and I realized he wasn't speaking to me anymore.

"A soul. That was what she asked of each of us. *Our* souls. And as children, we barely thought before nodding our heads and surrendering them. For... *this*."

His glass empty, Finch pushed it away. It clanged against the Lagavulin bottle that rested at the center of the table. He looked away, disgust clouding his face.

"This is all I can get angry about anymore; all I can regret. Because with each year that passes, it becomes harder and harder for me to *be* a human. I have fought for so many years to do what is right, and with each passing moment it becomes more difficult. They say that without a soul, a person is liable to collapse, as likely to fall into evil as despair. In the end, I chose despair; Nora chose evil. And because of that... I left her." The words came out as a grisly revelation, as difficult for him to tell as it was for him to experience. "Faced with that, I left. And now, what good is immortality when you are forced to live it out alone, as I was forced to do? As I *am* forced to do. As I ultimately chose to do."

Finch's words were a kidney punch. I had nothing to say because I could think of nothing worth saying. Nothing could offer comfort.

He looked at me. "Why am I not in charge of the Zeros, you ask? Because I cannot be. Despite my unending efforts, I care nothing for those we set out to help. Nothing. I try, the gods above know I try, but it still means nothing. The fact that I don't care does not even hurt me anymore. That is why Gil leads us. Sometimes his heart is bigger than his head, but I would have it no other way. I would rather follow a fool destined to do only what he believes is righteous than a pragmatic, empty-hearted son of a bitch." He pushed his chair back and stood, half-shrouded in shadow, looking down on me with fiery eyes. "And if you think for a goddamn moment that the missing woman is not *killing* him, then you're the biggest fool of all. He fears the death of an innocent more than his own death. He would gladly embrace the latter to save only *one*."

He turned away, stalking past Gil's huddled form and humorless sitcom to disappear into his bedroom. He closed the door behind him quietly with little ceremony.

CHAPTER 13. THE COLLECTION AGENCY

I nursed one more glass of Lagavulin (a little heavier on the ice) before going to bed. Whatever anger I'd been harboring towards Gil and Finch was gone, leaving me feeling bummed. It had never occurred to me that I wasn't the only person having trouble with the disappearance of Willa Bascombe—I said I'm pretty good at *not* thinking, didn't I?—or that I wasn't the only person cursing our powerlessness. As usual, I hadn't been able to see past the end of my own nose. As it often happens, we are blinded by our own troubles. So it goes.

About an hour after Finch went to bed, the flat screen TV snapped off. Gil dropped his deerstalker onto the chair with a quick wave in my direction and walked to the double doors leading into the huge master bedroom. His movements were slow and labored, betraying Gil's true age. Not the kind of fatigue that comes from getting up early after a late night, but rather the kind of exhaustion that comes after endlessly facing things that seem so much greater than yourself.

Left alone in the dark penthouse, I realized I'd been struggling to prove something to myself. Maybe prove that I was different than they were; better, perhaps. I wasn't. I was insecure. And afraid, living in a world that had become something far outside my comfort zone. In the past few days, I'd begun to understood Gil and Finch as well as I'd ever understood anyone (perhaps betraying how few friends I truly had). A true grasp of motive is a priceless commodity, and often overlooked, even among the dearest of friends. I'd overlooked such a gift before; I'd promised myself I would never do it again. A long story for another night perhaps.

When I finished that final glass, I put it in the sink and went to bed. Sleep came easy, but on that night it was laced with nightmares of an innocent woman's terrible fate, and the uneasy feeling that we were running out of time.

***

I woke first. The sun was bright in a clear blue sky marred only by thin traces of cotton-white clouds. I took Gil's key ring and drove the Tank out to a grocery store on Columbus Boulevard, stocking up on some old reliables that Gil either didn't have or had let spoil. Barbecue sauce and mayonnaise weren't key ingredients in any kind of breakfast I'd want to touch.

When I got back, I set to work putting together some worthy breakfast for a day I hoped would bear more fruit than the previous. Dropping strips of bacon into a frying pan managed to summon Gil and Finch almost instantly. Bacon has a magical way of rousting even the heaviest sleepers. Finch was already dressed in black; Gil had on plaid boxers and a *Star Trek* tee. Both had bed-mussed hair.

Gil pointed. "Is that *bacon*?"

"Yep."

"Wait, you can *make* bacon here?" Gil waved his hands around the kitchen skeptically. "You don't need a bacon-cooking machine or something?"

Finch shook his head and rubbed the sleep from his eyes.

I smiled. "Bacon's actually not that magical, Boss. You just need a skillet."

"Not that magical? HAH! I think it's a little more complicated than some frying pan."

"Sorry to disappoint," I said.

"Bacon never disappoints," he said. With a smile, he elbowed Finch. "I told you he was a helluva cook. I woulda bet the farm on that, you know what I'm sayin?"

Finch nodded. "What's the status on the coffee?" he asked.

"Coming soon," I said.

I poured a few glasses of orange juice before going to work on a couple of omelets. For a guy whose cooking experience extended only so far as deciphering microwave instructions or preheating an oven, Gil had a beautifully stocked kitchen. Stainless steel non-stick pans, copper

90

pots, and Japanese knife sets in matching knife blocks. Similar items filled about four different cabinets, cookware ready to compete in *Iron Chef*. Most of the stuff still had tags dangling from the handles. Sacrilege.

I dropped a thick omelet onto Gil's plate. Bright yellow egg chock full of mushrooms, peppers, red onions, and broccoli. His eyes opened wide as he ran to the refrigerator for one thing he actually stocked: ketchup.

"I can't believe this. I thought you had to be a scientist to make this. This is amazing."

"It looks delicious, Dylan. Thank you," Finch smiled as I poured the coffee. "Eggs for breakfast. How novel."

Gil pushed his coffee aside, making a sad face. "Ugh, can't drink that," he moaned. "The caffeine messes with me. But, oh, how I love coffee."

Finch grabbed his mug without pause and took a heavy drink. He smiled. "As do I," he said. "And how I've missed it. Living with this man is hard. No real food, no coffee. Just baby back ribs. And barbecue sauce." His face twisted at the thought.

It only took a few quiet minutes for the food to disappear. Gil leaned back in the kitchen chair and burped loud enough to make the pots hanging over the sink rattle. Finch scowled.

"So what's our plan for today?" I asked, sipping my coffee.

"I was on the horn already with one of my boys," Gil said, leaning forward and resting his elbows on the tabletop. "I may have a lead on Mrs. Bas–err, Willa. Maybe. I want to be optimistic, but I don't wanna... well, let's just wait. I'm gonna look into it."

"I've got something for you, Dylan," Finch said, taking a deep drink of coffee. "I think it's something you'll be able to handle on your own."

I wanted to be optimistic, too, I realized, but my patience was waning. I turned to Finch. "Okay, what's the gig?"

"I want you to meet with a man named Jonathan Keats."

"Brilliant!" Gil said, slamming a hand down onto the table. "I had totally lost track of that, old man!" He grinned.

"I know, Boss," Finch said with a clipped grin. "That's why I'm here."

"It's perfect for you," Gil said, turning to me. "I'm certain you can handle it alone." Finch nodded, smiling.

"Who is this Keats guy?" I asked.

"Man, we got a lot of balls up in the air," Gil said, ignoring my question, "and it seems like the only guy who can keep from dropping 'em is Finch, here," Gil said, wagging a crooked index finger in his partner's direction.

Finch shook his head and looked at me. "Jonathan Keats specializes in... collections, let's say. Backtracking for a moment, I'm hoping Mr. Keats will be able to assist with our little djinn problem. I'll put a phone call into his office in a few minutes and then you'll be on your way. How does that sound?"

"You'll have no problem with old Keats," Gil said reassuringly. "He's a paper pusher, but the paper he pushes is particularly valuable in this case."

"I had completely lost track of the djinn," I admitted. "But if it's important, I'm there. Are you guys going to tell me anything else here? Do I need to be... prepared for this?" I couldn't help but think of my stellar performance at Arthur Greely's office.

"No," Finch said. "He's just a man."

Gil smiled. "Pretty much."

The kitchen was silent for a moment as Gil and Finch shared a glance.

"Pretty much," Finch agreed, shrugging.

"Don't worry," they said in tandem.

***

The scrap of paper in my hand spotted by Gil's child-like handwriting had led me to a small bunch of offices located above a fortune-teller/laundromat/video rental joint. I climbed the stairs and rang a bell. After a moment, I was buzzed in.

The offices were larger than I expected, sprawling across the breadth of the building's top floor and broken into an ungodly maze by cubicles. The room smelled like five-year-old cigarette smoke and fried food. A gentle murmuring of indoor-phone-voices filled the room like the hum from a swarm of bumblebees.

"Can I help you, sir?" a blonde Amazon asked me from behind a cluttered desk. The nameplate on her desk read *PAM - RECEPTIONIST*.

Beneath it, a logline read *Kharon Debt Collection Agency.*

"Hi. I've got an appointment with a Mr. Keats." My eyes ran to Gil's handwriting for backup. "Jonathan Keats?"

She thumbed through a thick spiral-bound daily schedule before stopping and running a long red fingernail down a page cluttered with handwriting. "Yes, Mr. Dylan. One moment please." Without looking up, she lifted a phone and punched in a few numbers. After a moment, she spoke a few muttered words before returning the handset to the cradle. "He will see you now," she said, standing. "Follow the outer cubicles around the floor. Mr. Keats' office is located at the far end on the left-hand side. He's expecting you."

"Thank you."

I followed her directions as best I could, moving past row upon row of frumpy middle-aged men and women pounding coffee and droning into hands-free headsets. The carpet was beige, as were the cubicles, the coffee mugs, the motionless ceiling fans, and the desks. The walls were different, though. They were off-white.

As Pam the receptionist had said, I found the door to Mr. Keats' office at the far end of the main room along the left-hand wall, the same wall that faced the street. His door was closed but marked with his name on a gold plaque. Beneath his name were the words *Collections Specialist.* Apparently, I was moving on up; I'd skipped the cubicles and made it straight to the corner office. I knocked.

"Come in."

I pushed open the door and was met with an office that I'm fairly certain was, at one point, a janitor's closet. So much for the corner office. The floor was cracked tile and the walls were green cinderblocks. Piles of paper were everywhere, stacked precariously on the floor, on his paltry little desk, and crammed onto metal shelves hanging from the wall. Above his desk was a framed poster of a smiling business man pointing out from the frame with a bright cartoony word bubble that read *Go For It!.* I felt sorry for the man already. If I extended my arms straight out from my sides, I'd have no problem touching both walls simultaneously. I decided against testing it out for fear of his morale.

"Mr. Keats?"

A chubby balding man with incredibly thick glasses looked up at me and raised a finger, begging my patience. He wore a brown suit and a remarkably ugly yellow paisley tie. A phone was pressed to his ear and he spoke with a dry and nasally voice.

"Is this Mrs. Antonioni? Yes, m'am, my name is Jonathan Keats calling with the Kharon Death Collection Agency. Is this a good time to talk, ma'am?"

There was a pause and Keats waited with his mouth hanging slightly open, a dopey smile on his face. He nodded.

"Oh, I'm terribly sorry," he said, "this will only take a minute. The paperwork I've got here has you past due for your scheduled departure by approximately seventeen days. As you know, we granted you a temporary forbearance, but unfortunately it has... expired, yes, ma'am. I have down here for cause of deferment the attendance of a great great grandson's wedding, is that correct? Well, by my calendar the wedding has passed, so I'm calling to see if you would be available to set a new departure date."

He paused again, and I could hear subdued but inaudible vocal chatter from the other end of the phone.

"That's fine, Mrs. Antonioni, no problem at all. Let me just confirm my information here." He lifted a paper and squinted to read from it. "Is this still the best number to reach you? Okay, and is this still your current address?" He read it back and paused. "Great, great. And are you still anticipating a Catholic service following your departure, ma'am? Wonderful, wonderful. Thank you very much for your time, Mrs. Antonioni. We'll be seeing you on the seventeenth, then. Lovely. Have a great day!" He hung up, still smiling, and made a notation on the open file in his hands. When he was finished, he looked up at me, his eyes huge under the magnification of his glasses.

"Sorry about that. Time is money, you know, Mr...?"

"Dylan," I said, shaking his clammy hand. "Finch made an appointment for me, hoping you'd be able to help us out with something."

"Yes, yes, Mr. Dylan. Mr. Finch hinted at it a little when we spoke. I've always got time for one of Team Abercrombie. Good golly you're a tall drink of water, aren't you?" Keats spun in his chair– kicking over a few stacks of paper in the process–and opened a filing cabinet with a *squeak*. He pulled a manila folder from inside and handed it to me.

A date was scrawled on the folder's tab. A quick look at my watch confirmed that it was a few nights ago, the night of the raid on the warehouse at the docks. My night of formal induction into the Zeros.

"What is this, exactly?" I asked.

"Oh, of course." He smiled, leaning back and trying to put his feet on his desk, his chair wobbling unsteadily. Further stacks fell as he dropped his legs to the floor again with a dissatisfied grunt. He forced a smile. "Those are my records of incoming and outgoing souls for the night in question. Mr. Finch explained that you had a bit of an unlikely encounter on the evening, and you were hoping to get further information on the summoning. Circumstances surrounding it, and such." He tapped the folder and smiled. "That's what you've got there, my friend. Pretty fascinating stuff!"

With the door closed behind me, I leaned back against it and crossed my arms over my chest. "Fascinating, huh? And um... how's that?" Really, I had no idea what he was talking about, but I wasn't about to admit ignorance to my new middle-management comb-over buddy.

"Well, the souls in question were very recent burials, most within the last twenty-four to forty-eight hours. And you know what *that* means!" He laughed way too loud and leaned back, again trying to put his short legs onto his desk, again failing. This time, he knocked over his own coffee mug (beige) and a photograph of him standing beside an old blue-haired lady (probably his mom). He smiled again and checked his comb-over. I couldn't help but like the little guy.

Keats rolled his chair towards me and lowered his voice, leaning his sweaty, balding head close as he spoke. "Hey, you guys up to anything *exciting*? Eh? You planning on busting any ghouls or goblins or anything? Fighting mummies? Digging up treasure?" He blinked his eyes, thinking. "Do you guys do treasure? Because I got this here," he spun and pulled open a desk drawer. From inside he removed a wooden stake, but dropped it before he could face me. It clattered to the concrete floor.

"Vamps or anything? I fought a vamp once. A nasty one, too! Oh yeah, you better believe it. I was at the mall and a couple of teenagers with black fingernail polish were being mean in the line at the food court. Well, anyway, suffice to say I'm a big asset, let me tell you, Mr. Dylan. Big. I set those kids straight, right quick." He nodded. "I mean, the mall cop helped a little, but anyway. All I need is a good word from you to Mr. Gil and I think I'm in the gang. Seriously." He smiled so wide that I could see his uvula. All the while he fidgeted with the stake in his hands. Him + that weapon = me nervous.

"I'll talk to him," I said. "No promises, but–"

"Would you, really? I mean, I'd *love* to get in the field, you know. This office work is great, but a little tedious, you know. Just look at me. This bod was born to fight monsters, man." He shadowboxed for a moment, bouncing around on his office chair. His top lip quivered with exertion.

"It's true, Jonathan, I have to agree." I found myself smiling. "Listen, I gotta run." I tapped my hand against the file folder. "Thanks for this. We really appreciate it. Gil, especially."

"That's great, just *great*, Mr. Dylan. Can I call you Dylan?" He shook my hand with a fervor rarely seen in your common everyday bureaucrat. "I sure hope we'll be working together soon. Very, *very* soon!" he gave me another hugely good-natured smile.

"Yep, sure, bye Jonathan. Thanks again!" I pulled the door shut before he could ask for my autograph.

CHAPTER 14. ADDITIONS

Finch's eyes lit up when I dropped the folder onto the kitchen table.

"Bloody brilliant," he said.

"See? I told ya you could handle lil ol' Keats, big man," Gil said with a crooked smile.

"Anyone *could* handle the guy," I said, taking a seat. "You guys just didn't *want* to."

"I assumed that was perfectly evident," Finch said, opening the folder. "But I must say, I am glad you were so amenable. I believe this will prove quite illuminating."

"The new guy pulls the short straw," I mumbled.

On the table, Finch began laying out documents. Nearly every inch of the white sheets of paper was covered with tiny figures printed in black ink. If I squinted, I could make out letters and numbers–just barely, signaling that I probably needed glasses. Anyway, it looked like English that had been chopped into some kind of shorthand.

"What is this, exactly?" I asked.

"A tracking sheet," Gil said, taking a seat beside me and stuffing his pipe with knotted tobacco. "It's a way of following the soul traffic on the night we first met the djinn."

"Soul traffic?"

"Despite what you may believe," Finch said without looking up, "souls are tangible things. As real as this paper. When a person dies, their soul travels to another plane of existence, call it what you will. Likewise, when a soul moves in the other direction, in this case being pulled back onto this plane through some form of necromancy, there is a record of it. This."

"I thought you said that necromancy didn't have anything to do with a soul? It was about the will of one animating the corpse of another."

"Sort of, and sometimes, but not always, and not really," Gil said, scraping a match into light and holding it up. "Oversimplification and generalization." He smiled. "Confused yet?"

Finch ignored him. "A small percentage of a person's soul is bonded to their body for life. Effectively, it's what makes a person who they are; what makes them more than just an empty vessel filled. So when necromancy raises a dead body, some measure of a soul *is* torn back into this world."

"Jesus," I mumbled. "That sounds... awful."

Finch looked up. "It is."

When he'd laid out every sheet, Finch rose and left the kitchen, returning a moment later with a small magnifying glass in hand. He held it over the tabletop and began moving it slowly over the codified sheets.

I turned to Gil. "What is he looking for, exactly?"

"An idea of who's movin' back and forth. Necromancy's not the only thing that brings a soul back. Like anything else, this stuff's pretty involved. It's like tax law: there's a loophole for everything. Think of ghosts or hauntings, as just one example of a soul slipping through."

I nodded. "There was something else," I said, leaning forward and squinting at the gibberish. "Something else that Keats mentioned."

"What was it?" Finch asked, not breaking his concentration.

"He said something about recent burials? Yeah, that was it. He said souls here were buried in the last day or two. For some reason, he was impressed by that. Does that sound right?"

"Yes," Finch said, lowering the magnifying glass. "Exactly. Here," he pointed. "And here. And here. Gods above, they're everywhere."

Gil and I leaned forward, squinting. I stared long and hard, my eyes grappling for some pattern or meaning in the countless markings Finch scrutinized. Unfortunately the gibberish was still gibberish. I sat back with a sigh.

With his face nearly pressed to the table, Gil swore and leaned back, his eyes wide and pipe bobbing uncertainly in his mouth. "Good gravy," he said.

Finch nodded.

"And what exactly does that mean?" I asked, pointing. "Are these good dots or bad dots?"

Finch laid the magnifying glass on the table with a thud. He rubbed his eyes for a moment before speaking. "Souls become easier to free and bring back into this world the *longer* that they're on the other side, the longer they've been dead and buried. By that rationale, souls are very, very difficult to free in the time immediately following internment. Do you follow?"

I nodded. "But Keats said within twenty-four to forty-eight hours. That's not really 'immediately following' anymore, is it?"

Gil and Finch shared a glance. "Look at it with a little broader lens, Dylan," Gil said.

Finch cleared his throat. "'Immediately following' means at least twenty *years*. And that's a conservative estimate. Souls stirred before must be ripped free with an extraordinary force, a force so powerful we have no way of controlling it. Or fighting it."

"The stuff of legend," Gil said. "The kind of thing that gets turned into scary blockbuster movies," Gil said, resting his elbows onto the table. "Bad ones. With Nicolas Cage. Or that girl from *Mega Python vs. Gatoroid.*"

A silence descended on the kitchen. Gil and Finch returned to the coded sheets sprawled over the table while my mind paged through a few CGI-laden images of cities being laid to waste; your typical 4th of July Hollywood fluff that makes kids wanna buy tie-in action figures. So something–most likely the djinn–had raised revenants using "extraordinary force," a power greater than I could even begin to conceive. I didn't know what to say, so I settled for "uhh."

"What exactly does that mean?" A soft voice from behind us asked. My partners and I turned to face the mysterious newcomer.

My jaw fell open when my eyes met those of Willa Bascombe. She stood in the center of the living room, dressed comfortably in jeans and a tank top, hands buried in her pockets and hair up in its customary ponytail. A duffel bag sat beside her on the floor. Cool, calm, and collected, a complete reversal from our first meeting. Upon seeing our collected shock, she smiled. She looked good. Very good.

"Man, my boys are so fired," Gil mumbled.

***

She took a seat and dropped her duffel bag on the floor beside her chair. "So," she repeated, "What exactly does that mean?"

Gil picked his fallen pipe up off the table and wiped a smattering of ashes to the floor. "Um, well, Mrs. er, I mean, Willa. This stuff's a little... complicated."

"You've monitored soul traffic from a recent night where you seem to have encountered a beast of some sorts. You said djinn, right? That's interesting. Anyway, on the night in question, this document shows that souls were brought back to this world that required a great strength and power to do so. Is that correct?"

"How long were you standing there?" I asked.

"Long enough." Pushing her glasses up her nose, she smiled again. It was radiant. "So when I asked what it all means, I guess I really just want to know what your plan is from here."

"As a matter of fact, we're working that out now, ma'am," Finch said.

"Does it have anything to do with me and my husband?"

"Honestly no, I don't believe it does," Finch said, leaning back.

She didn't respond. I expected she was thinking exactly what I'd be thinking if I were her: *how was this relevant?*

Instead, she proved as level-headed as I was not. "Good. I was hoping this was simply another case. We've got enough problems."

Gil leaned forward. "Hey, where the heck have you been, little lady? We been worried sick!"

She fidgeted. "Sorry, guys. After the shooting at the Waterworks I took advantage of the craziness and slipped out. I was... really frightened, and I think I was in shock. Escaping wasn't so hard considering everyone on the upper level was worrying about my husband instead of me." She shrugged. "Needless to say, I wasn't missed."

Gil continued. "Well, all right, but what about after that? I had my boys lookin' all around for you. Those dopes are still lookin'." He paused, repacking his still smoking pipe with an unsteady hand. "How did you dodge them for so long? I mean... we were fearin' the worst."

"Again, I'm very sorry. Like I said when we first met, I've been so scared, and because of that so *angry*. The night of the shooting changed it all for a few reasons. First of all, I decided that I wasn't going to be afraid anymore. That's just not an option. So after the shooting I caught a cab and abandoned the city for the 'burbs. A person can only stand being a victim for so long before they've had enough of it, you know?" She adjusted her weight on the chair and continued. "The second thing– and the thing that really got me motivated–is the fact that the man who was speaking beside me the night of the shooting wasn't my husband."

We Zeros shared a knowing glance. Gil spoke carefully.

"Well, how... or what makes you say that, Willa?"

She took a deep breath and continued. "We've been married for thirteen years, and after that much time a wife gets to know her husband. I'm not talking about where he's from, I'm talking about how he sleeps or how he dresses, what he eats and how he does it. Last night in the hotel I had the chance to think about things with a strangely clear head. It was the first time I'd done that kind of thinking in a while. I pushed aside all the dreams and the fear, and I started thinking logically. And he's... well, that man? He's not my husband."

"We know," Finch said.

"What?"

Gil and Finch turned to me expectantly. I spoke, a slight tremor creeping into my voice. "After the shooting I chased the guy responsible. The one who pulled the trigger. I followed him through service corridors in the Waterworks, and I caught him."

"And?"

"The man I caught... *he* was Alfred Bascombe. He was your husband."

"What? And you let him go?" Anger seeped into her voice.

"No," I said defensively. "He escaped."

She sat back and sighed, relief creeping onto her face. "Oh man, I half expected I was crazy. I half *hoped* I was crazy. Like, maybe I was just... wrong. Maybe there were no dreams, maybe no one was going to kill me. Perhaps Alfred is still Alfred." She stopped, lowering her dry eyes to the nest of documents on the table. "I guess he still is. He's just... gone."

"He's not gone," Gil said, trying to comfort her. "He's just missing."

She turned to Gil. "Mr. Abercrombie–Gil–I love my husband. And this..." she trailed off, moving her gaze from Gil to Finch and finally to me. "I have to find him. I have to. He needs my help. He needs *me*. And I need him."

Her words rang with a love that made my chest hurt a little. Damn, if I didn't feel like I was in high school again. Beside me, I felt Gil rest a knowing hand on my shoulder. He cleared his throat.

"Alrighty," he said. "We're gonna find him. Now that we know he's alive and that the man in office is a big fat bearded phony, we've got real proof to start looking elsewhere for your husband. While we investigate that big fakey, too."

"I want to help," she said immediately.

"No, no, no," Gil said, raising his hands. "That is a crazy and terrible idea. Based on information we've got about the man impersonating your husband, your dreams *were* right, Willa. He wants you dead. The last thing I'm gonna do is bring you into this now."

"But I'm valuable, and I can help with this. First of all, I'm supposedly his wife. I've got access you don't. I can get into his office, I can get into our house, and as of right now, he *trusts* me, remember? Or at least, doesn't suspect me. I can open doors for you, remember? Plus, I'm a pretty good asset for this operation anyway. I've got... let's just say a useful skill-set. I mean I got in here, didn't I?"

Gil opened his mouth to speak and froze. "Wait, how *did* you...?"

She smiled and lifted her bag. Dropping it onto the center of the table, she unzipped it and pulled it open. A tangled mess of electronics winked back at us. I remember being proud I could hook up a VCR correctly. Great, my second chance in one scene to look confused.

"I figured you'd need some convincing before you agreed to bring me along. You read Dottie's file on me," she said smiling. "Right?"

Gil's mouth began moving wordlessly as he searched his memory. "That file was useless. There was like one line about your job, something about a tech specialist for a securities firm or something, right? But that was it. What the hell does that mean? Tech specialist for a—"

"I got in here," she interrupted. "Let's just leave it at that. My bosses prefer I keep a low profile. Suffice to say, I know my way around electronics and computers. And things."

"A valuable asset," Finch said, nodding, pragmatic as always. "I agree with her, Gil. I can't drive, and you can't even change batteries in a remote control."

"Now you wait a second," Gil began, raising a finger at Finch. "Those little pluses and minuses always—"

"And I came to you first," Willa interrupted. "Technically, this is *my* case. And I have a right to help save my husband. And myself."

Gil closed his mouth, scowling. He relit his pipe and began puffing on it stubbornly.

"Right?" she said, turning to me.

"I think she's right, too, Gil," I admitted.

After a minute, Gil yanked the pipe from his mouth. "All right, all right fine, damnit. I guess you're in. But only cause these two softies want you in. I want the record to reflect that I think this is a bad idea. A *really* bad idea. It's dangerous."

Willa smiled. "Duly noted." She waited a beat and put her hands on her hips. "So, I'll ask again: what's our next move?"

CHAPTER 15. BLUEBEARD HQ

We were riding the bus. I had assumed that when Gil the eccentric billionaire hired me, I'd kissed SEPTA public transportation goodbye. Apparently I was wrong.

After welcoming Willa as an honorary (albeit temporary) member of the Zeros, Gil had decided the group should split up. He pointed the stem of his pipe at Willa and me, saying, "Okay smarty pants, you get us access, then you get into his campaign offices. I wanna know who set up that fundraiser last night. And I want a list of the original guests from before the attendance ballooned. I want personnel lists, copies of staff IDs, and any other information you can get about this new big trouble. If Bluebeard's got some kind of corporate sponsor, I wanna know about it. For all we know, evil just incorporated. I'm a little disconcerted that Bluebeard picked Bascombe as his target. It doesn't really make a whole lot of sense unless he's got big, *big* plans. I wanna know why a loner psycho has all of a sudden turned to organized politics and started looking at the bigger picture."

"It is a disconcerting thought," Finch said as he stood. "And as you say, Boss, it doesn't make sense. It has been festering since I first saw our esteemed company at the ball. Bluebeard doesn't work this way."

Willa raised her eyebrows. "Bluebeard?"

"I'll explain later," I said. "You got it, Boss. Where are the campaign offices?"

"I know where they are," Willa said, picking up her duffel. "Let's go."

"Now?" I asked.

"Now," she said.

"Wait a second," I said. "Don't we need to plan this out a little better? I mean, where are you guys going?" I asked, pointing at Finch and Gil.

"We have a meeting," Finch said, standing. "A fairly unpleasant meeting that you will want no part of. Trust me."

I raised my eyebrows and looked at Gil. He forced a smile. "Yeah, really. Honestly, this is a meeting I'd just as soon avoid. You two go have fun. If the lady is right, and I imagine she is, you'll have no problem. Snoop around. Keep your ears and eyeballs open. Get as much dirt as you can. Willa, you should be able to handle most of it on your own, honestly. Just try and tread lightly, okay? Don't get too ballsy. Be smart. And be careful, yeah?"

She nodded.

"Dylan, I want you keeping her safe, you hear? You're the muscle, so... muscle. She's gonna be in a rough spot if this thing goes in the hopper. Hopefully, old Blue ain't even gonna be around. If he is, you get her ass out of there. I don't need her falling into the lion's mouth right now. Got me?"

"Just the lion's den, eh?"

He smiled. "Yeah. Trust the lady, okay?"

"I will."

"All right. Ya'll be good now," he said with a wave.

I grabbed the keys.

"Oh hey, wait a sec. What are you doin' there, champ?" Gil asked, stopping me.

"I figured you wouldn't need to be driving," I said. "I mean I'm the driver and all, right? I didn't really think you drove."

"Of course I drive, you boob. You saw me do it in chapter one. I just prefer not to," Gil said, taking the Tank's keys from my hand. "I'm a *very good* driver, as a matter of fact–fender benders aside." He pointed a finger at Finch. "*He* can't drive."

"Okay, how 'bout another set of keys then?"

Gil stared at me blankly. "What do you mean?" he asked.

"Another set of car keys. Car keys? As in another car? To get to the campaign offices."

Silence.

I groaned. "You're rich, Gil, you must have more than one car."

"More than one car? Don't be ridiculous. I'm just *one man*." He dug into his pocket, shuffling change about. After pulling out a handful, he sifted through the coins. "Here you go," he said, reaching out with a few coins in hand. "Public trans money. Have fun!"

And so, Willa and I rode the bus. She sat beside me on a bench seat in the center of the half-filled vehicle. Around us, people silently watched the city pass them by. The sun was rising high in the sky as afternoon wore on.

"Thanks for backing me with Gil," Willa said, breaking a silence that had been getting uncomfortable.

"I agreed with both you and Finch," I explained, which was mostly true. "You deserve the right to help out. It's fair. And if you're going to help, it may as well be in a substantive way." I paused and could feel a slight blush creep into my cheeks. "I mean he's your husband." A bit more emotion had crept into my voice than I would have liked, and my voice was just a *little* bitter-sounding. I cringed, hoping she hadn't noticed (but knowing she must have).

She paused. I stared straight ahead, but I could feel her look at me. "Yeah. Well, thanks."

Another few blocks passed in silence. I wasn't sure whether I should feel shame or embarrassment. I settled on a bit of both just to be safe.

"So what's your plan?" I said as the bus ground to a halt and the doors opened with a hiss.

"We split up and go in separately. I don't want to be seen with you. That won't help my inside-job cover story."

My cheeks burned brighter as I maintained my gaze straight ahead. "You go in first, I guess?"

"Yeah," she nodded. "The place is pretty big and the main offices are located on the twelfth floor. I'll go up and start digging around. There's security, too. I didn't go to the offices much, but I've never been hassled before. I shouldn't have any problem."

"And what am I supposed to do?"

"You're back-up. You're there in case I *do* have a problem."

"Okay. Am I supposed to just get all commando and kick the doors down if things go to hell? I don't really like the sound of that."

She shrugged. "I dunno, you're the army guy. But I should be able to walk in and walk out. Trust me."

I nodded. We lapsed into silence, and I didn't have the courage to break it again.

When Willa finally spoke, her voice was low and a hint of uneasiness had crept into it.

"The man impersonating my husband, Gil and Finch were careful not to say anything about him. Bluebeard?"

I didn't respond. The bus engines seemed to roar as we moved beneath an overpass, passing from darkness into light once again.

"Who is he? Do you know?"

I remembered Finch's advice and tried to haul my professionalism back to the surface. Sometimes around a beautiful woman, professionalism's a heavy weight to lift. "Well, his name is Bluebeard, and Finch said that he preys on women. He preys on their love and their trust for their husbands." I paused, letting the words sink in. "I guess you can take that as a compliment? A weird one."

"Compliment?" She said, an edge in her voice.

"Well, he wouldn't have targeted you if you didn't love and trust your husband deeply," I said softly.

"*I know* that I love and trust my husband, Mr. Dylan. I don't need any validation from a psychopath. Or anyone else."

Zing.

"Is that all you know?" she asked with a sigh.

"Finch didn't say much, really."

A few more minutes passed. Passengers came and went to the sound of squealing hydraulics.

"So, you saw him?" she finally asked. "You saw Alfred? I mean, the real Alfred?"

I nodded. "In a maintenance corridor in the Waterworks. I chased him." Subconsciously, my hand touched my black and blue nose–still sore, by the way. Compliments of the real Alfred Bascombe.

Her voice lowered further, little more than a whisper remained. "How… How did he look?" Concern creased her brow and her body tensed.

"He was…" I struggled to remember. I'd been a bit distracted with gushing blood and all. "Thin," I said. "He looked thin."

"Thin?"

I nodded, picturing him in my mind's eye. "The beard wasn't there.

He was pale and very thin. Otherwise he looked all right."

"Pale and thin," she mumbled. "So he was being held captive."

The thought had never occurred to me. I cursed my stupidity while admiring Willa's simple logic. There was a reason I'd never made detective. "I imagine he was," I conceded.

She blinked a few times and took a deep breath, letting it out slowly. In a moment, the fear evaporated as she steeled herself. "We'll need to talk to Gil and Finch about that," she said.

There was much that she left unsaid, much that even I could infer through my thick skull. If Alfred Bascombe had been held captive, then he must have escaped to make his appearance at the Waterworks. And if Alfred Bascombe escaped his imprisonment, then there were most certainly people chasing him.

***

The circuitous path of the bus finally dropped us off on the corner of 16th and Market. Huge skyscrapers rose above us, casting dark shadows over entire city blocks. Work had not yet let out, so the sidewalks weren't too crowded. Newsstands peddled lotto tickets and cigarettes. Street vendors sold umbrellas and maps. I followed Willa east towards City Hall and Dilworth Plaza.

We stopped. She pointed across the street. "There, that's the one."

The building was massive, rising at least thirty stories into an azure sky, dwarfing the huge *Clothespin* statue that guarded the stairs leading down to Suburban Station. While the surrounding skyscrapers were built from blue or even silvery white reflective glass, this building looked dull, a dirty, faded grey/brown.

"There? In the Prava?" I asked. "He must do okay for himself."

She nodded. "He just moved to that office. A local politician making that much money should have been my first hint something was amiss." She shook her head. "Wait here. I'm going in, all right?"

"I don't really like this..." I said.

"It'll be all right," she said. "Trust me. Didn't your boss say that?"

I nodded. Without another word, she left my side, crossing the street and disappearing through a gold-plated revolving door. Resigned, I took a seat on a bench and checked my watch. Fifteen or twenty minutes was as long as I was willing to wait. I felt sheepish at my recent behavior–maybe even a little ashamed. The years that had passed since my last serious girlfriend were proving fatal to my social skills. Was I really that attracted to her that I couldn't mind my damn manners? The trip on the bus alone was a lesson in the art of foot-in-mouth.

The pessimist in me expected police sirens or a private security patrol to appear, lights swirling as uniformed agents swarmed the building and locked it down. Just a matter of time, I figured. The minutes ticked by on my watch, but there was nothing. An uneventful twenty minutes later, I crossed the street and pushed through the rotating door into the building. Enough waiting.

A bronze plaque adorned a thick marble column that faced the main visitor's entrance. It read *Welcome to the Prava Center!* Beyond the column sat an imposing visitor's desk manned by two linebacker-sized men who sat behind it scowling. To their right, stanchions cordoned off a red-carpeted walkway that narrowed to a single-file line, funneling visitors through security before reaching the elevators. At the end of the stanchioned path was a pair of metal detectors managed by another pair of linebackers.

I patted down my pockets, pulling out a few metal objects as I walked towards the metal detectors. The line moved slowly, each person having to go through multiple times before the red lights stayed dark and they were cleared to enter. Beyond the metal detectors stood the golden doors of an elevator bank that ran the length of a marble hallway. Self-consciously, I straightened the plain black tie–borrowed from Finch, of course–I'd donned for the occasion and headed for security.

When my turn came, I dropped a handful of change, my wallet, and my cell phone into a tray and stepped through the detector. Against the wall, a taciturn woman sat behind a desk staring down at an obscured computer screen, bored. My turn. I stepped through. The red light above me blinked, and I heard a soft gameshow wrong-answer buzz. Fail.

I patted down my pockets again and dropped a pen into the metal tray. I stepped back through and the red light still flashed. I swore, kicking off my shoes, and walked through again. The red light continued flashing.

"I don't know what else I have on me," I said, frustrated. "Do you have one of those wands you can wave over me?"

The woman at the computer ignored me and began typing. A scowl had appeared on her face as her fingers danced over a keyboard. A guard appeared by the elevator banks with a walkie-talkie in hand. It was only then that I realized I should be nervous.

"Oh it's my belt," I said, soothingly. "Just my belt. I always forget *that*." I pulled my belt off and waved it apologetically at the guards before stepping through again. Still, the red light flashed. Sweat appeared on my brow as the line of visitors behind me stirred impatiently.

"I don't know what it could be," I said, my voice wavering.

I turned to try and go through the metal detector again only to be met by the two barrel-chested guards from the visitor's desk. They each had six inches and about fifty pounds on me. No small feat.

"Can you please come with us, sir?" one guard asked in a sub-baritone voice. His companion nodded slowly, cracking gorilla-sized knuckles.

I raised my hands. "Everything's cool," I said. "What seems to be the problem, officers? I forgot my belt, that's all. No worries." Without another word, the two goons lifted me by my arms and carried me from the lobby, my shoeless feet dangling the whole way.

***

The two apemen finally returned me to the ground after a short express elevator ride and a trip down a few winding corridors. They'd made certain to stand between me and any identifiable signs. I could have been on the third floor or the thirtieth.

The room I found myself in was a perfect square, about ten feet by ten feet. In the center of the room was a nondescript table with two chairs pushed under it. On one of the room's cinderblock walls was a wide one-way window.

"Your offices come with an interrogation room, huh?" I asked no one in particular. "That's little strange."

I took a seat at the table and stared at my frazzled reflection. Despite any brazen courage I tried to exude, I was pale and sweaty, moisture dotting my bald head. If I'd been busted so quickly, I could only imagine where Willa was. The thought did a number on my already knotted stomach. I took a deep breath and tried to look calm, but it's tough to look all together when you're awaiting your own interrogation.

The tie didn't look too bad, though. I straightened it for effect.

Sometime during my wait, my shoes reappeared. One of the linebackers pushed the door open and dropped them without a word. I was just tying my shoes when the door opened again and a tall, dour-faced man entered. He wore a suit that was formal but disheveled. Wrinkles ran up and down the otherwise bland outfit, and there was a popped seam on his right shoulder. From the tattered cuffs sprouted veiny wrists connected to hands that looked more like the djinn's claws. Despite his thick chest and strong arms, his hair was little more than grayish wisps that fluttered around over his skeletal face. His yellowed complexion made him look very sickly. A curly secret service-esque wire twisted around his ear and connected to an unseen earpiece.

He took a seat across from me and set his hands flat on the table in front of him. Balling one hand into a fist, then the other, I listened as each of his knuckles cracked. After a moment, he reached into his coat pocket and pulled out my wallet. He threw it onto the table in front of me. I picked it up and slipped it into my back pocket.

"We take security around here very seriously, Mr. Dylan," he said with a voice that sounded like sandpaper being dragged across stone.

I looked around the room. "I can see that. Although I didn't get my change back. Or my pen. Did your guys carry me to Guantanamo Bay?"

The man gave me a rather humorless closed-mouthed smile. It looked like it took a lot of effort. "My name is Altimerach," he said, straightening in his seat as if he expected applause. I felt my eyebrow rise dubiously. He looked more like a John to me.

"Councilman Bascombe appointed me head of his private security staff after the little… event at the Waterworks. I also happen to be head of security here at the Prava Center, so I care very much who walks through my doors and why, do you understand?"

"Yes."

"We have a policy here that is posted and enforced rather stringently." He licked his dry lips with a worm-like tongue and continued. "All sorcerers, witches, mages, soothsayers, warlocks, thaumaturges, diviners, necromancers, wizards, shapeshifters, shamans, as well as members of the Red Cross, United Way, or the Peace Corps must register in advance for an in-depth background check before gaining access to the Prava Center."

Did he say wizards? "Oh."

He leaned forward, staring down his long nose at me, perhaps expecting to hear a startling confession. He didn't.

"Can you tell me what you're doing here?" he asked.

"I have an appointment with a lawyer," I said. A thin lie, and getting thinner by the second. I tried not to blink. "A personal injury job."

He smiled and raised his eyebrows. "Personal injury?"

"Yeah, I slipped on a banana peel."

"I seriously doubt that, Mr. Dylan. In fact, I know you're lying. So, I'll give you one more chance. Is there anything you want to tell me?" he asked.

"It was from a really big banana."

I smiled, but remained otherwise quiet. I had no idea why he was holding me, but I knew that tight lips and patience would see me either released or handed over to the police. After all, I'd done nothing wrong. Right?

"You've done something terribly wrong here, Mr. Dylan," Altimerach said.

Well, shit.

"I don't mean to sound difficult, Mr. Altimerach, but I have no idea what you're talking about."

His voice rose and he leaned forward until I could feel his hot breath on my cheek. "I take the protection of my client, Councilman Alfred Bascombe, very seriously, Mr. Dylan. The rules that are imposed here at the Prava Center were brought into effect for a reason: safety. Fear of domestic or multiversal terrorism as well as retributions and reprisals are certainly not out of the question, and a disrespect for edicts that seek to curb such activities will be met with swift and terrible justice. Not to mention the fact that it pisses me off."

With that, he stood, towering over me as he slammed his knuckles down against the metal table. In the tiny room, the impact rang out like a gunshot. I grimaced. He saw me start and smiled.

"Don't lie to me, Mr. Dylan. I don't appreciate liars." Slowly, he returned to his seat.

"Then we have that in common, Mr. Whatever-Your-Name-Is."

"They make me *sick*."

"Lucky for you I'm not lying."

He didn't respond and silence filled the room. After a moment, the air conditioning kicked on, rattling ducts in the ceiling. Altimerach stared at me with beady animal eyes that sparkled in the harsh fluorescent light. His body moved slightly as he settled back into the chair, and I could hear occasional creaks of bones and joints like rusted hinges. After a few minutes of some awkward you-stare-at-me-as-I-stare-at-you, he stood, pushing his chair in and walking around the table to stand beside me. He leaned over and spoke softly into my ear. His breath smelled like rotten eggs.

"There is one person who wishes to speak with you, Mr. Dylan. You are fortunate that he has a curious mind. But after that, I'll enjoy dragging you from this room and throwing you off the roof. I won't even have to clean it up afterwards. There are many in this city who would gladly eat whatever's left." He straightened and left the room, pulling the door shut behind him.

I didn't much like the sound of a short plunge to pavement. *What the hell's going on here?* I wondered. *Thauamaturges? The Red Cross?* I felt adrenaline begin bubbling through my system. I heard muffled voices coming from the hallway and knew I must've done something to make a great many (dangerous?) people angry, even if I had no goddamn clue what it was. I bit my lip as my mind wandered to Willa, and I hoped she was faring better than I was, because I was in over my head. *Way* over my head. I tried to bury the thoughts of Willa in the same circumstances, alone and frightened in a cold interrogation room, waiting for her accuser to decide her fate. I had to trust her. I had to. And if I was going to be any help to her, I had to get out of that room alive.

That's when the door opened and Bluebeard walked in.

CHAPTER 16. THE STRANGE PROVIDENCE OF ROTTEN LUCK

He was a big man, the buttons on his white shirt pulling taut against his formidable gut. If anything, his beard seemed larger and fuller than I remembered, leaving a tiny slit for his mouth. When he smiled, grey teeth were barely visible.

"Mr. Dylan," he said.

"How you doin'?" No amount of flexing my muscles was gonna intimidate the guy, so I just smiled. If ever I'd needed to exhibit some restraint, it was now. A little bravery probably wouldn't hurt, either.

"You've made quite a stir today," Bluebeard said, taking a seat.

"You know, I was gonna visit a lawyer friend of mine in a law office on sixteen for some advice and then get a hot dog. Apparently stir up some shenanigans here at your office in the meantime. Oh, and who are you again?"

He laughed a deep, rich laugh. "Visit a friend, you say, sure, that's fine," he smiled. "I've good friends of my own working in Cabot & Shaw as well as Robinson, Robinson, & Moon, both located down on sixteen. You did say sixteen, didn't you? Unfortunately, no one in either firm has heard of you. We're searching for your... *friend* now." He smiled. More grey teeth. "I'm sorry to say, your afternoon snack will have to wait." I bit down on my lip and tried to look nonplussed. Searching for my friend. *Willa.*

Bluebeard smiled. He affected a warm Santa Clause affect, but it was tainted by an undercurrent of ferocious power and cunning. Each time he smiled, I had to stave off a chill as it threatened to run up my spine. It may have been a Santa Clause affect, but this was spooky John Wayne Gacy perv Santa.

He tapped the table with his hand. "Are you listening to me, Mr. Dylan?"

Actually, I hadn't been. "Why are you holding me here?" I asked.

"My security coordinator informs me that you came here with the intent to murder me, Mr. Dylan. And while such enthusiasm is generally promoted here at the Prava Center, my head of protection–the gentleman you just met–would rather I not be marked for death. What do you make of such allegations?"

"They're ridiculous." It was the first thing I said since entering Bluebeard's gulag that wasn't a lie.

He smiled. "Yes, they are. Ridiculous. You must understand, everyone here is a little on edge since the near miss last night at the fundraiser. My campaign managers are promising big things, and many loyal constituents are holding their breath in anticipation."

I didn't respond. Somewhere in his fat face, his beady eyes moved over me. He raised his bushy eyebrows; he must have found what he saw quite amusing. I was trying not to imagine Willa's strained face in similar questioning. Looking into the black circles of Bluebeard's eyes, I cursed our naiveté. What the hell made us think we could waltz in and pull off such a moronic errand in the first place?

"Mr. Dylan, I assure you that that there is literally nothing you can do against me. My dear Altimerach isn't quite... on the same page. I didn't hire him, you see. My... benefactors did. You must understand that there are certain events in motion, events which will change this city forever. Soon Altimerach and all the others will be standing by my side with full faith and knowledge that together we are working towards something grand. Truly grand."

Okay, so evil had *definitely* incorporated, and with Bluebeard behind the wheel. Evil Inc: Now consolidating power and taking over the world, one city at a time.

"Alas," he continued. "As it stands now, you–like most others–lack the spine to raise even a finger against me." He smiled again. "Much to my chagrin."

"Sounds like you wish I *had* come here to kill you."

"Well, it would be quite convenient if you were responsible for what happened at the Waterworks. It would save me the legwork of finding the real shooter."

"Any ideas who that may be?" I asked feigning ignorance.

His face may have shown a smile, but what I felt was white-hot fury. Bluebeard didn't seem to have any problem tipping his cards, but he sure wasn't prepared to lay out his whole hand. Apparently he assumed I knew who he was–probably because he figured we'd spoken to his wife–but he wasn't going to say anything outright. I was a bit disappointed that he wasn't going to get all James-Bond-villain and tell me the whole plan.

"I'll answer your question with one of my own." He lowered his voice to a menacing growl. "Where is the woman?"

At the mention of Willa, a current of tension ran though my body. He chuckled.

"Ahh, my *wife*. My dear, sweet Willa." He leaned forward and clasped his hands together, sarcasm dripping from each word like venom. "Wherever has she gone? I do pine for her so."

My heart was pumping. I could feel a vein do the macarena on my forehead.

He relished every moment. "Please tell me," he crooned. "Do you know where I can find my *love*?"

"Why am I here?" I demanded, slamming a hand down onto the bare table. "How long are you gonna ask me these stupid goddamn questions?"

"As long as I damn well please," he said, his voice rising like a shout from a bullhorn. "That's what you get for walking into *my* building, brazenly intending to snoop in *my* offices. *You* coming to *me*?" He laughed. "You will sit here and wait until I'm bloody well satisfied. And when I've gotten my answers, I'll feed you to the goddamn dogs."

Ah-ha. "So you want her," I said. "Willa. You want her dead."

"Dead?" he laughed. "Don't be silly, Mr. Dylan. I *love* my wife. I love Willa Bascombe. I want her back here at my side, back where she belongs. A good politician is nothing without a fine decoration draped over his arm."

"Asshole," I mumbled through gritted teeth.

"No need to be rude. After all, soon I will be Mayor of this town. It's a shame you and your partners won't be around to see such a glorious day. Give Finch my regards when you next see him, will you?"

With a wave of his hand, he rose to his feet, wiping his massive palms across his shirtfront as he turned to the door.

"What? You're letting me go? What about feeding me to your

goddamn dogs?"

He stopped and turned. "I'm sorry?"

"You said, 'next time I see Finch.' You're letting me go?"

He laughed again, another loud and full-throated roar that seemed to make even the screws in the wall shiver. "No, no, no, my dear man. Next time you see Finch," he took hold of the doorknob and smiled. "In Hell."

"You stupid son of a bitch, you can't kill him, he's–"

A muffled gunshot silenced me. Through the supposedly soundproof walls, I heard the faintest hints of a commotion. Voices rose and fell in tempered chaos as the sound rose. In one corner of the room, a tiny light bulb I'd failed to notice began flashing red. It froze Bluebeard mid-laugh. He released the doorknob and turned to face me, concern clouding his face for the first time. "What have you done?"

"What are you talking about, fat man?"

The lights above us flickered, dropping the room into momentary blackness before they returned to life. "Something has been summoned," he said. "And I imagine you are to blame."

"Summoned? What? *Imagine* is right."

He turned and pulled the door open, disappearing into the hall and slamming the heavy door behind him. Above me, the lights flickered again and died. This time, they didn't come back on.

I stumbled to the door and yanked on it. Locked. No amount of tugging or kicking budged the damn thing.

I picked up a chair and turned my attention to the one-way glass against the opposite wall. Through the walls, from all directions, I could hear muffled shouts break up occasional gunfire. I lifted the chair and swung, slamming the wooden legs across the pane. The glass reverberated with a heavy, unnatural clang that sent shivers down its length. It held. The roar of gunfire outside picked up.

I heaved the chair at the glass again. Something broke and it wasn't the glass. The wood cracked and splintered in my hands. The glass, on the other hand, held strong and as far as I could see in the dark, wasn't even scratched.

There was a loud crash as a heavy body hit the door behind me. Rounding on the table, I pushed a hip against it and shoved it against the door. It hit with the wood just below the knob, barricading it. The door shook again, rattling inside its frame and against the table, but it held.

Through the door, I could hear the sound of shuffling, dragging footsteps retreating. *Eerily familiar*, I thought. I lifted the remaining chair and carried it to the glass. With my shitty luck, even if I could break it the room behind would be another dead end. Even so, I couldn't stop. Willa was trapped somewhere in the building, trapped but hopefully alive. We were separated and stranded, and whatever was after me would probably be going after her next (if it hadn't already). With that thought as an energy boost, I swung the chair full force at the glass. The glass held and again I dropped little more than wood scrap to the floor. Outside the hallways had fallen into an ominous silence. Just those slow, heavy, shuffling steps.

My military training took over. Fear, anger, and helplessness disappeared in a blind visualization of schematics and tactics. My mind took me through the remaining scenarios of my escape. I decided on the keep-hitting-it-really-hard tactic. There weren't many other options. I had dropped to my knees, groping in the darkness for the heaviest, sharpest thing I could find when an emerald light shimmered through the darkened room, illuminating it enough for me to grab a chair leg with a brutally splintered end.

"Oh man," I said. "This is bad."

The window exploded, launching shards of glass over me like jagged teeth. Pain lanced through me as glass shavings sliced into my skin, bringing blood to the surface. I raised my hands to cover my face, but it made little difference.

The djinn stood on the other side of the busted window, staring me down with its bestial eyes. Its shoulders rose and fell with each breath the huge monster took. One hand lay across the windowsill, knives of glass crushed beneath the bloody talon-like fist. The second claw was reaching for my throat.

I stumbled back a few paces and lowered my hands. "Great timing!" I groaned. Green light was radiating from the djinn and throwing awful shadows across the tiny room. Behind the beast laid the ruins of an observation room, a crushed camera and smoking control panel filling the small space. Behind the beast, a door hung open, showing the hallway beyond. Two technicians were making their getaway. I liked their thinking.

The djinn stepped over the half-wall and stepped into the interrogation room. I pulled the table free from the doorway and dragged it between us. With a casual swing of its arm, the beast buckled the table, bowing it across the middle and collapsing it to the floor with a metallic moan.

I choked out a wimpy roar of my own and swung my table leg cudgel, cracking the djinn across its golf ball-sized knuckles with the flat of the wood. The djinn shrieked to the sound of bones breaking, it's knuckles cracking like walnut shells. The beast howled and withdrew, its short legs dragging sluggishly while it grasped at the bare walls for support. I jumped over the crushed table, swinging the sharp end of the table leg in a wide arc ahead of me. I raked the sharpened stake across the monster's chest before I fell and swung downwards, burying the spike in the beast's foot. The point passed through muscle and between bones, meeting the concrete floor with a *crunch*. Blood sprayed across my hands. I let go and recoiled, disgusted. Fierce screams filled the room as the djinn ripped the stake from its foot and launched it at me. I ducked in time to hear it punch through the door behind me. A pillar of white light shot into the room like a flashlight beam. I turned and lowered my shoulder into the door, but it still wouldn't budge. Above me, a claw ripped across the wood as the djinn swung for my skull. I rolled beneath its arm, getting behind it for the first time. With the monster's back turned, I jumped the half-wall, ran through the tiny observation room, and darted out the open doorway into the hall.

The office beyond was in ruins, blood staining the carpet in large pools around crushed desks and shredded bodies. Business men and women ran past me, stepping around huge misshapen footprints outlined in blood. A peril of working for the bad guys: possible devastation at the office via large otherworld creature.

I turned to follow the diminishing flow of traffic when Altimerach's stony gaze met mine through a crowd of secretaries. He stood sentinel at an emergency exit, funneling worried faces into a stairwell. On seeing me, he lifted a pistol with his bony hand and fired. Seriously? Couldn't I get one damn break?

I ducked and bolted in the opposite direction as bullets slammed into the plaster over my head. All around me, the sound of his gunfire rattled like out of control fireworks. Screams from errant office workers were thrown in for good measure.

Zigzagging my way through corridors, I begged the gods for an elevator or stairwell, but, no surprise, they were on a lunch break. Instead I found myself in empty halls surrounded by empty rooms. Deserted offices ran on forever. Behind me, I heard the djinn's bellows and Sasquatch footfalls approaching as it followed me through the maze of Bascombe's offices. Apparently it was not satisfied by the tasty office staff. I was on the menu. Dylan a l'Orange.

Turning one final corner, I skidded to a halt in a narrow cul-de-sac; conference rooms split off on either side and a huge floor to ceiling window faced me. Below, traffic pulsed slowly down Market Street. I pushed open the conference rooms, but they were useless. Filled with nothing but perfectly shined tables and desk chairs. Were we in Gil's office, I would've found a samurai sword and 30.06. In the hall were two potted plants, so I grabbed one and smashed it against the floor. A big jagged piece of ceramic caked with dirt was the best weapon I could muster. It didn't rate high in the *Zagat Guide* to intimidation.

When the djinn turned the final corner and stood before me, green blood dripping to the carpet and winding a twisted trail behind it, I couldn't help but question my recent employment decisions. The monster's huge mouth hung open, gore dripping from its fangs as it drew breaths in heavy gasps. If the beast could feel pain, I hoped it was feeling it now, because armed only with a dirty piece of ceramic, I'd need all the help I could get.

I dove beneath an errant swing and skidded along the carpet as I heard–and *felt*–the djinn's fist connect with the drywall. Vibrations pulsed through the carpeting beneath me. For a minute, I worried the floor was buckling. I stood and took off down the hall. I think I made it about four steps before I felt a hand close over my shirt at the nape of my neck and lift me into the air like a bad cat. With the cotton came a fistful of skin. I howled and kicked my legs against nothing as the djinn threw me against the windows. I felt hot blood on my skin as I spiderwebbed the window and collapsed to the floor. The djinn stood over me, its mouth opening wider and wider, quite committed to the idea of, well, eating me.

I felt the pull of the monster's breath as I raised my legs and kicked, the tip of my stained boot connecting with the heavy bone of the djinn's lower jaw. Its mouth snapped shut on a long reptilian tongue, its own razor sharp teeth severing it and dropping it onto my chest where it writhed like a worm. I yelped and rolled away, swinging the shard of ceramic as I did.

Somehow I connected with the djinn's face, the makeshift blade slicing through the leathery hide and spilling green blood across the carpet with a splash. The beast screamed in pain and frustration as it backpedaled. An undeserved smile met my lips for an instant before one of the djinn's errant blows connected with my chest, knocking the air out of my lungs and throwing me through the already spiderwebbed window. It shattered. Massive shards of glass exploded outward with the impact and fluttered around me as my body flew through the air. Above me, the djinn disappeared in a green explosion of flames as the Prava Center sped away from me.

It registered, however momentarily, that the people moving some thirty stories beneath me looking terribly small before I slipped from consciousness.

CHAPTER 17. EVIL INC.

Glass. Glass mixed with swirling currents of air. More glass. Glass everywhere.

I remember flashes of light and the tugging of multiple hands across my body. There was hot air and cold, and at some point the splashing of lukewarm water across my skin. By the time I opened my eyes, night had fallen. I was lying in a hospital bed, propped up by a stack of pillows. I felt the steady burning of fresh cuts exposed to air. The effort it took to raise an eyelid was far more than it was worth.

Gil stood over me, his pipe in hand, rank clouds of smoke rising over him.

"Holy Hannah! He's awake!" he shouted, waving a beckoning hand over his shoulder.

"One moment," I heard Finch calmly say from a distance.

Wide fuzzy blobs were floating across my field of vision, and it felt like half a dozen flat head screws had been twisted into my skull during the past few hours. My mouth was dry and when I pried my lips apart, I think the skin cracked. I coughed, half expecting a moth to fly out of my mouth.

"Where's the Doc? Call the Doc, Finch."

"It is my understanding that Dr. Hanas is on the phone with his wife, Boss."

"Go get him, will ya?"

I pushed myself upright in the bed with a gasp. Everything hurt. Absolutely everything. Dizziness hit me in a wave, making my head spin like a top and for a moment I was certain I'd throw up everywhere. I shut my blurry eyes until the feeling passed.

"Don't move, dummy, just take it easy, all right? Take it *easy*," Gil said, gently pushing me back down to the bed. I shook my head.

"…Wa… water," I choked out.

"Yeah, right-o." Gil turned and disappeared from the small room.

Wide windows to my left overlooked the city. Darkness covered everything, a heavy blackness dotted by street lamps and the slow passing of cars on the interstate. I heard the sound of plastic being punctured, then torn. The room was quiet for a moment before I heard what sounded like marbles or pebbles falling across hard tile floor. I rubbed my eyes, feeling a thick band of gauze around my skull just over my eyebrows. The strange sound ceased momentarily.

"Boss is right," Finch said softly. "You need to take it easy."

I opened my eyes and the cloudiness had dissipated somewhat. Finch stood just beyond the foot of the bed, a heavy sack of rock salt clutched in his arms. He met my gaze for a moment before recommencing his pouring. Streams of the crystals were spreading across the floor in an uneven line. As I watched, Finch took a few steps, emptying the bag across the floor until it met with another thick line near the base of the wall. With a final shake, he righted the bag and dropped what remained of it in the corner.

Finch followed my gaze. He stepped over the thick band of salt and stood at the bedside. Without speaking, he pointed down at the floor. I followed his finger as he began moving it along the path of the salt. It started just to my left near the headboard and continued around the bed in a shaky circle. I looked up at Finch and cocked my head questioningly.

"For protection," he said.

Gil busted back into the room before I could croak some semblance of a response. He carried a big plastic mug with a red bendy straw in it. He held it by a thick handle and passed it to me delicately.

"Nice and cold," he said with a grin.

I grasped it with an unsteady hand and took a long pull from the straw. The icy water hit my throat like a fistful of nails. It hurt, but it got the job done. With a labored swallow, I cleared my throat of its drug-induced clog. Gil took the mug back before I dropped it.

I coughed. It was dry and gravely. "What… what *happened*?"

Finch and Gil exchanged a glance. "We were hoping you could tell us that, man," Gil said.

I swallowed with a grimace. "Willa. Where's *Willa*?"

As I finished, I heard her. Her delicate but strong voice echoed from down the corridor.

"Come on, Doctor, *please*," she pleaded. In a moment, she appeared, pulling our ever-reliable, ever-mysterious Dr. Hanas by his arm. As she stepped into the room and my eyes met hers, I felt my runaway train heartbeat slow, calming, coming under control. The tremor left my hands. I took a deep breath and felt almost human again.

"All right, I am here," Hanas said, prying her hands from his thousand dollar suit before returning a cell phone to his pocket. "I told you, Ms. Willa, your associate needs rest." He straightened his sleeves before stepping up to me. "Mr. Dylan," he said smiling. "Pardon my tardiness, but I was speaking to my wife who is currently experiencing a rather difficult third trimester of pregnancy. How are you feeling?"

I snatched the mug back from Gil and took a few more drinks, the rust in my throat beginning to dissipate. "All right, I guess. What exactly happened?"

"Well, your friends brought you to me in a... uh, remarkably poor condition." He lifted a chart that hung from the foot of my bed. "Six broken ribs, a fractured femur, two broken humeri, cracked pelvis, two broken clavicles, a broken fibula, a cracked tibia, and a fractured skull, as well as numerous *internal* injuries." He returned the chart with a sly grin.

"Good God, man," I rasped.

He smiled his broad gap-toothed grin. "But you are fine, now," he said, raising his hands in an attempt to curb my fear. It didn't work.

"Fine? It sounds like I got stepped on by an elephant!"

"Actually, dude, you got tossed out a twenty-eighth story window," Gil said. "But the Doc's got a way, really. Don't worry!"

"Perhaps the most remarkable piece of information is that we found you in a twelfth story office. In a *different* building," Finch said slowly. "It looks as if you were thrown from the window on the twenty-eighth floor of the Prava Center, crossed over Market Street in mid-air as you fell, and landed in an empty office on the twelfth floor of an adjacent building. Needless to say, you were lucky. Incredibly lucky." He paused. I let it sink in, marveling at the fact that I was still alive. "What do you remember?" he asked.

My head felt like an egg that had been dropped on the kitchen floor, but a smokey memory was starting to take shape. I wasn't sure what I was seeing until I remembered the fire. The green fire.

"It was the djinn," I said, looking at Willa's worried face. Even worried, she was just as beautiful as I remembered.

"The djinn?" Finch asked. "Are you certain?"

I nodded. "Did it come for you?" I said to Willa. "Were you chased? Were you questioned?"

Her brow creased. "What? Dylan, I got in and out with no problem. I was outside waiting to meet you when I saw you get... come flying out the window." She swallowed, and I could see the remnants of terror surfacing on her face. "I called Finch and Gil. I was..." She shook her head. "I was sure you were dead."

I closed my eyes, the strange memories coalescing. "I thought I was dead, too. And I was certain *you* were dead."

"Why?"

"They stopped me as soon as I walked in the door. The security. I figured they'd already gotten you."

"What did they do when they stopped you?" Finch asked.

I looked up at him. "I set off some metal detector at the door. A couple of goons took me to some interrogation room. What floor did you say? The twenty-eighth?"

"That's our guess. We basically had to count the windows from the outside 'til we got to the busted one," Gil said. "Right now the place is totally shut down. No one in, no one out."

I smiled. "Except me, I guess."

Gil laughed and patted my leg. "Yeah, you got out, all right."

"Who did you speak with, and what did they want to know?" Finch asked, scowling at Gil's merriment.

"At first I spoke with someone named... Alt... um, Altimerach?"

Gil scowled and looked at Finch. "I told you that useless sack of crap would resurface somewhere."

Finch ignored him. "Exactly what did Altimerach want to know, Dylan?"

"Why I was there. He had the idea in his head that I was there to kill Bascombe."

"You mean Bluebeard?"

"I don't think Altimerach knows that Bascombe is Bluebeard."

"Why?"

"It was something that Bluebeard said later."

"Wait, you *spoke* with Bluebeard?" Gil said.

I nodded.

"What did he say to you, Dylan?" Finch asked, his voice lowering.

"Well, he wanted me to give you his regards," I said. "I think this is a lot bigger than we thought. And a lot worse."

***

As I recounted what had happened, Hanas worked over me, redressing my bandages and running his big hands up and down my arms and legs, squeezing and bending my limbs. For all the broken bones he'd described, I was inexplicably without a cast or brace. Instead of pain, I felt pins and needles jabbing at my muscles each time I moved or Hanas touched me, like my entire body had fallen asleep. As for my story, I took my time, recounting every detail I could remember. I watched the faces of my friends, looking for something I could use to elevate my lagging spirits. I didn't find much.

When I'd finished, the red-lettered digital clock above the doorway read almost nine o'clock. Hanas had finished and was seated contentedly by the doorway, hands folded patiently. He looked tired, but Finch, Gil, and Willa were still fully charged.

"This is bad," Finch finally said, "and terribly unusual. Bluebeard is notoriously independent. History attests that he's never collaborated with another. Instead he rather prides himself on his pigheaded self-sufficiency. If he is making a move like this, it's because he thinks it is worth it. Bluebeard... as Mayor." He shuddered. "This is very bad, indeed."

"But why would this Altimerach not know about it?" Willa asked. "Especially if he's part of some kind of inner circle?"

"It means that Bluebeard's backing isn't ready for his coming out party yet," Gil said, lighting a freshly packed pipe. "Which means that whoever's backing him is a lot smarter and a lot more subtle than Bluebeard."

Finch nodded. "I agree. Someone big is pulling the strings. Bluebeard is not the most popular man to put in a public office in any election–even in the otherworld community, so there is an argument that by keeping his identity secret you'll strengthen your chances for electoral victory. He's no one to trifle with, but apparently he is merely the beginning of our worries."

"So what are we saying?" I asked. "Evil just got a damn corporate sponsor? Great. That's just great news. There must be someone we can talk to about this. You said he's not that popular, so not every vamp or ghoul or whatever is gonna be united behind him, right? Is the... supernatural community a solid community? If they just think he's Bascombe, then not *everyone* will be on his side."

"The ball at the Waterworks may have even brought that into question," Gil mumbled, chewing on the stem of his pipe. "A lot of people will think he's more than just a man, now."

"Indeed. At the very least, it showed that this City Councilman Bascombe had some mighty otherworld support," Finch added. "The kind of signal that *will* help gain him votes in the otherworld community."

"I thought you said that Bluebeard was a pretty polarizing guy. He's got enemies like anyone else. What would make all these people fall in line and throw their support behind him?"

The answer was pretty clear, but when Gil said it, a shiver still ran down my spine. "Fear," he said. "If you see a shift in the tide that you can't change, it's best to go with it before you're washed away."

"This is new," Willa said, "all this popularity. Alfred barely got re-elected last time out. Do you guys remember? He almost lost the district. He's never had the kind of support that has turned out in the last few months."

"So someone's tossed a big endorsement his way," I said.

"It's not necessarily the same person who's pulling the strings behind it all, though," Finch said.

"We'd be dopes if we didn't assume that immediately," Gil said, leaning back against the wall and crossing his arms. "I mean, what makes us think that it's not the same person? Is that too convenient?"

"It *is* pretty convenient," I said shrugging.

"But it makes a lot of sense," Gil insisted. "The same person corralling support is the same person funding this new campaign."

"Actually, I agree with Finch," Willa said slowly. She met our eyes warily. "The kind of clout we're talking about here is *political*, right? But political clout is different from what you're talking about, Gil.

You're talking about supernatural stuff, not political stuff. Political clout is public. In order to give real political endorsement and have it be worth a damn, it's gotta be from a well-known and visible person in the community. It wouldn't be worth a damn if it came from someone who made his living based on the anonymity of underworld contracts."

"*Other*world, my dear," Finch said with a smile.

"Well, whatever. But in this case it's the same thing, right?"

We were silent for a moment. Finally, Finch nodded. "That is correct."

"So either it's the same person, in which case he's a fool and it'll be easy to expose him," Willa concluded, "or else we've got *two* big problems to worry about."

"The man behind the curtain and the political operative," I said.

"And Bluebeard makes three," Gil said sullenly.

We all shared a despondent look.

"Well, shit," I said.

CHAPTER 18. ALL IN

"Now that you're, you know, *alive* again, I don't wanna bring you down but we gotta go," Gil said, tapping out his pipe in a trashcan beside my bed. "Seems a bit rude, but sorry. This salt ring here'll keep out any beasties 'til we get back and figure out what's after you and why. And you little lady," Gil said to Willa. "You can stay the night at my apartment. But now it's time to go."

"Whoa, wait a second," I said. "You guys are leaving? Where are you going?"

"There is a... sensitive matter that needs attending," Finch said, slipping into a long black coat.

"Does it have to do with you meeting today?" I asked. "How did it go? You were both dreading it, but you look to be in one piece."

Finch moaned. "We met with a rat," he said.

"What like a traitor?"

"Yes, he was a traitor," Finch said. "That's how he became a rat."

I stared at him. "So, once again, you were being... literal?"

"I never joke about my work," Finch said.

"There's a dude named Roberto who pissed off a warlock a couple years back, apparently stabbed him in the back. Bad move, Roberto," Gi said, laughing. "Anyway, he got himself turned into a rat." He shrugged. "You know, it happens. He's about as big as a terrier, real nasty bastard, and he smells even worse than he looks. We had to meet him about three hundred yards underground in a sewer drainage pipe over in Cherry Hill."

"Ugh," I said. "New Jersey." Gil nodded.

"You would not believe how many pairs of shoes I have ruined in meetings with Roberto," Finch said.

"What did he tell you? Did he know anything about Bluebeard?"

"If he did he kept it to himself," Gil said. "He gave us some good dirt on Ron, though."

"Ron?" Willa asked.

It took me a minute to remember. "The gargoyle," I realized.

Her eyes widened. "Ah-ha. A gargoyle. Of course."

Finch looked at her. "You're taking all of this quite well."

She shrugged. "I've seen some things that have made me wonder. It's really not *that* surprising."

Gil nodded. "My kind of woman," he said. He looked at me. "Just roll with it, remember? She gets it."

"Yeah, yeah," I said as I threw back the hospital blanket. "Oh, and I'm going with you," I said.

"No, no, no," Gil said. "Absolutely not. There's already a chance this could be dangerous and you're in no condition to fight. You were almost dead six hours ago."

"Doc," I called to Hanas, "I'm clear, right? Clear to fight crimes and save the innocent?"

"Well, your bone structure is weaker than usual–" he began.

"Hah!" Gil shouted. "Told you."

"–but I don't see what danger you'd be in. Unless you get into a very bad fight. Your ribs, in particular, are rather tender. A direct shot in the wrong place will land you back here in my care, Mr. Dylan."

"See?" I said, pulling the blankets back and sliding from the bed. "Magic bone-mender here did whatever hoodoo he needed to put Humpty-Dumpty back together again. And you let Finch go to that fundraiser. I'll be ultra careful, I promise. Plus, with you guys by my side, I'm safer than if I stayed here alone, right?"

My feet touched the cold tile floor and I felt those pins and needles jab into my muscles and up and down my legs. My knees felt a little weak, but I could stand. Gil reached out for me, but I waved him off. I steadied myself on the bed until the weakness dissipated.

"I'm in, too," Willa said.

"What? This is getting to be ridiculous!"

She shrugged. "Like I said, if I'm on the team, then I'm on the team."

He groaned, but seemed more troubled by me out of bed.

"I can do this," I assured him. "Really. I can. Anyway, I'm not the hospital type. Please."

Gil sighed. A few minutes later, I was dressed in a pair of jeans, a Hawaiian shirt, and an extra pair of my sneakers he'd brought from his penthouse. My friends didn't look so sure, but that didn't stop me.

***

I slid into the Tank's back seat beside Finch and let Willa drive. She drove with one hand on the wheel and one hand on the radio dial. The first thing she did was turn off Gil's brain crushing heavy metal.

"Uh, excuse me," he said. "Why'd you do that?" She spun the dial with renewed fervor and static filled the car. "You are killin' the vibes, man."

"I'm driving, I need to concentrate," she said with a yawn. "That garbage is liable to get us in an accident."

Beside me, Finch smiled when she settled on a jazz station. Fast tenor sax lines of hard bop filled the car. Finch closed his eyes and leaned back, content.

"So where are we going?" Willa asked.

"Just an underground illicit gambling den run by the most well-connected otherworld crime boss," Gil said casually, reaching for the radio dial. Willa slapped his hand away and continued driving. "You're gonna wanna get on 95 South," he said. "Heading for Chester."

She nodded. "And who exactly is this Ron again?"

"Ron is the guardian of the downtown public library," Finch explained from beside me. His eyes were still closed as a pensive rendition of "Autumn Leaves" filled the cab. When he wasn't speaking, he was humming along.

"I meant to ask you about that," I said. "What's a guardian exactly?"

"Old buildings are different from new ones," Gil explained. "The accumulated past plays all kinds of tricks on the place's mojo. A lot of accumulated years sometimes carries bad mojo, which is why a lot of really old buildings have guardians that watch over what enters and what leaves. A lot of times, the guardian is a person. You know, some janitor who's worked at an old school for like a hundred and thirty years. Something like that. In the case of the public library, the guardian is Ron the gargoyle."

"That's all the Robbes-Grillet lady was talking about?" I asked. "A missing gargoyle?"

"Yes, indeedy," Gil said. "And we gotta get on it, right quick. A library without a guardian is bad news."

"Bad news is right," Finch said. "In truth, there is more at play than Boss' 'bad mojo' explanation, but in essence he's correct. It is incredibly dangerous for certain places to be without their guardian. The most notable examples being hospitals and libraries."

"Okay, I get hospitals," Willa said. "But why libraries?"

"Knowledge is sacred," Finch said. "There are many secrets that must be kept."

"And the downtown library's got plenty of secrets that our Evil Inc. would love to get their hands on," Gil muttered, making another play for the radio knob.

Willa slapped his hand away without taking her eyes from the road, a grin playing across her lips.

***

Gil gave her directions that took us deep into the heart of Chester. Ahh, Chester, a sad story of urban decay eerily similar to Detroit. It had been a thriving community until their hub of manufacturing–ships and cars, mostly–crumbled in the 60s. Since then, it had been a nest of crime, its population dropping steeply with each passing year. Now it stood as a shell of a city, most of the buildings in downtown either empty or sliding slowly into disrepair.

Gil's directions took us into one of the worst neighborhoods I could remember seeing. Storefronts were boarded up and pockmarked with graffiti, some buildings collapsing in various states of ruin, the worst of which was simply a gigantic pile of bricks marked by a plywood sign with the words **CLOSED FOREVER** spray-painted on it.

Lighting his pipe, Gil leaned over the seat and gave me a wary gaze before turning back to Willa. "Before we go in, I want to warn you two newbies that you're gonna see some weird stuff in this place, okay?

Like, *weird* weird. Just be cool. If you're with us, you'll be safe. Just don't freak out, all right?"

Willa and I nodded.

"All right," he said. "Pull over here."

We parked in front of a pizza parlor–the only business on the desolate block with an open sign–and spilled out of the car. A pigeon paced back and forth on the faded awning hanging over the pizza place. With each step, the little bird angrily cooed at us. A wave of nausea hit me on the sidewalk, and I had to steady myself against a parking meter. We began moving, and I struggled to keep pace with the group. I felt pretty bad.

Gil led us up a narrow alley between the restaurant and a burnt-out apartment building. More tunnel than alley, the walkway led deep into the center of the block, finally opening up in a small concrete yard that was ringed by the high stone walls of surrounding buildings. The tiny cube was empty but for a pair of metal doors built on an angle leading down into the ground. They were painted black and bare except for a slat you'd expect a pair of eyes to be glaring out from.

Gil knocked twice on the metal doorway, the impact echoed in the enclosed space. After a moment, the slat slid open and a lone, unnaturally large yellow eye peered out at us.

"Password?" an inhuman voice growled.

Gil hastily pulled a slip of paper from the pocket of his chartreuse Hawaiian shirt and read it by the light of the full moon above us. "Halifax," he said.

The huge yellow eye blinked once and the slat slid closed. Nothing else happened.

"Damnit," Gil groaned, "if that Roberto stiffed me on the password I'm gonna beat his little rat ass."

He kicked against the doors with a clang. I was ready to leave when the huge sound of groaning and grinding stone roused my attention. I turned to see the concrete wall behind us splitting and opening like a pair of monolithic French doors.

"Uh, guys?"

The group turned and took a collective step back. From inside, a dim golden light poured over us, illuminating a wide wooden staircase that descended into a large subterranean room. Gil took a step forward and was stopped by a hulking, dark shape.

For the first time since joining the Zeroes, I was truly speechless. The beast that stood before me was massive–probably just over seven feet tall–and overloaded with muscle. Despite its ungainly size, the creature moved with the agile grace of a dancer. Instead of skin rippling with thick veins, I saw fur, short thick fur similar to that of a black Labrador retriever. It covered every inch of the beast's otherwise humanoid body, the onyx pelt even winding between his long human-like fingers. It wore black pants, jackboots, and a leather vest, giving it the appearance of a biker dogmonster. As my eyes traveled up its body, I realized I was wrong with my black Lab analogy. Sprouting from between the beast's thick shoulders the head of a Rottweiler, huge and ferocious. Its mouth hung slightly open and long cords of drool dangled from a row of white fangs.

"Oh my," I said, agog.

"Enter," the beast said in a voice deep enough to shake dust from the doorjamb.

Gil waited while Finch passed the beast first. Willa skittered behind him. He grabbed my arm and pushed me through. He followed not far behind. As the doorway was pulled shut, I could feel the dog's wet breath on my neck with each careful step I took down the stairwell.

We descended silently, the only sound coming from the panting breaths of the sentinel behind us and the heavy footfalls of its boots on each wooden step. At the bottom of the stairs, we found ourselves in a large basement, clouded by smoke, the soft hum of conversation filling it. Countless green-shaded lamps hung over a sprawling field of round card tables, dimly lighting the room. Games of all kinds were in progress, and creatures I'd never dreamed of were everywhere, cards in hands, cigars in mouth. Later, Finch and Gil would tally off a list of creatures present, including vampires, werewolves, ghouls, nixies, sprites, elves, manticores, fairies, demons, ogres, trolls, brownies, witches, and a few other things I couldn't even pronounce. Added to the motley otherworld crew were a few overweight chain-smokers you'd expect to find in such an abysmal hole.

Gil turned a wary eye over his shoulder as the hulking guard strode past us and took a seat on a stool beneath the metal doors Gil had knocked on. Shaking his head, Gil turned back to us. "Dog soldiers," he said, "I never get used to the sight of 'em. And you can't trust 'em worth a damn."

He took the lead, slowly winding his way through the maze of tables. The constant buzz of chatter was low, so we spoke quietly.

"Dog soldiers?" I asked.

"They're mercenaries," he said. "Nasty sons a'bitches," he said, spitting disdainfully onto the concrete floor. "They're kinda famous for tearing guys limb from limb just for giggles, so you don't wanna know what they're willing to do for money. Trust me."

I tried not to stare as we slipped past groups of players huddled over ashtrays and packs of pristine playing cards. Dealers tossed cards over brightly colored chips piled high in the center of each table. Instinctively, my eye found the banker's cage cut into the far wall, a steel-barred enclosed vault with an attendant inside bundling stacks of cash. On the other side of the room a stubby wooden bar extended out from the wall. Half a dozen inhuman shapes huddled over drinks as they waited for seats to open.

"Where are we going?" I asked.

Gil pointed up ahead. "The private room," he said.

Past the playing tables, a thick red velvet curtain hung against the rear wall, obscuring a passage beyond. Flanking the doorway was a pair of dog soldiers as big and imposing as the doorman. Unlike their colleague, these two were Dobermans.

"We're going in there?" Willa asked, unsteadily raising a hand. "Past them?"

"You betcha, babe," Gil said with a grin. "The high roller's room. Get ready for some fun."

I met the smoldering eyes of the dog soldiers. Fun seemed... unlikely.

Gil dug into his pockets and pulled out a thick manila envelope. With a grin, he waved it before one of the Dobermans like a bone. Its beady eyes followed the yellow envelope greedily. It lifted a hand, but Gil took a step back.

"Ah, ah, ah, this isn't for you, Mr. Pooch," he said. "It's for your boss."

The beast clenched two ham-sized fists and growled.

"My friends and I want in on the high stakes," Gil continued. "You know, the high, high stakes." He opened the envelope and pulled a trio of hundred-dollar bills free. "Well, maybe you can have a taste," he said as he slipped the bills into the Doberman's vest pocket with a wink. "Use that later when you're playing poker with a cigar-smoking bulldog.

And don't say Uncle Gil never gave you nothin', ya hear?"

The Doberman growled something inaudible, but pulled the curtain back. Gil stepped through, and we followed him.

Other than the stone busts on old buildings, I'd never seen a gargoyle, but as I stepped through the curtain I got my first good look. Ron the gargoyle was huddled alongside a long roulette table. He was crouched on a red plush carpet while a few fat cats stood around him in tuxedos, smoking cigars and idly tossing thousand-dollar chips onto the green felt mat beside the spinning wheel. Ron's skin was a stony grey, a lot like the cut granite I'd already seen representing gargoyles in their daylight incarnations. His hands and feet were similar to a human's, but capped off by long talons similar to a hawk's. He wore what looked like a heavy denim kilt cinched by a leather belt with a novelty western buckle. Tight around his waist, above the belt, was a neon orange fanny pack.

"Mr. Abercrombie," a nasally voice said from the back of the room.

"Q, why do I never get invited back here unless I've got somebody to rescue?"

"A fair question," the voice responded. "From what I remember, Gil, you're usually carrying plenty of currency, making you the ideal guest."

A tall blonde-haired man circled the table and walked to Gil, a wan smile on his lips. His hair was combed straight back over his head, nice and sleazy, and pulled into a tight ponytail that stuck straight off the back of his head. He wore a white tuxedo–who wears a *white* tuxedo?–and sunglasses. He looked like a prom date from 1975.

"Quentin, these are my associates," Gil said, opening his arms towards us like a proud father.

Blondie tipped an invisible hat brim and smiled. I expected to see a gold tooth, but was sorely disappointed.

"Pleasure," he said. "I am Quentin Cally, and this is my establishment."

"My condolences," I said.

His host smile never faltered.

"And nice suit," I continued.

"And you are?" he asked.

"My name is Dylan. I'm the muscle in this operation."

136

He smiled. "That is good, as you're certainly not the brains." He pointed at me, then Gil. "Your matching Hawaiian shirts are *adorable*." Without giving me a chance to respond, he turned to Willa. "My dear, aren't you the belle of this ball? Please, come, have a seat." He took her hand and led her across the room to a seat at the roulette table. Ron the gargoyle remained huddled beside the table, ignored. I spared him a look, and he met my gaze, two large blue eyes pleading for help. As I watched, he shifted, revealing a heavy iron manacle anchoring one of his ankles to a steel plate, firmly bolted to the floor. He wasn't going anywhere. I gave him my best reassuring look before following Willa to the table.

"Dylan, wait..." Finch whispered as I passed him.

"Ah, the brawn decides to take a stand?" Cally said with a grin. "Good for you."

Gil took a place on my right and Finch on my left. They shared a glance before Gil poured out the envelope onto the table, spilling out thick bands of cash with a thud. The chuckling chorus of gamblers grew quiet, their eyes locked on the fat wads of money. Finch cleared his throat and spoke. "I believe we'd like to make a few wagers, Mr. Cally," he said. "What's on the table this evening?"

Cally grinned. "Since when is currency not enough?"

"Like you said, Q, I got plenty of that," Gil said, lighting his pipe. "I want me a pet."

The smile may have still been glued across Cally's face, but it seemed more out of habit than anything else. He slipped his hands into his pockets and sighed. "Who are you rescuing tonight, Gil?"

The room had grown silent. From behind the curtain, we heard a few muffled laughs or exchanges from the game room beyond, but inside the high stakes suite, the only sound was the spinning of the roulette wheel.

"Him," Gil said, pointing one finger at the grey-skinned creature that crouched beside the table. Ron raised his eyes and met Gil's for the first time, shame and fear playing across his face.

Cally ran a hand across the pile of hundred-dollar bills that lay on the green felt. He snapped through one of the banded stacks like a flipbook, the crisp bills flapping loudly against each other. He smiled and dropped the money before turning back to Gil. Slowly, he shook his head.

"Not nearly enough," he said.

"How much?" Gil asked. "You know I got more. I got plenty."

"No," Cally laughed. "You don't understand. *Money* is not enough. You know as well as I that some things are worth more than currency, Mr. Abercrombie. And your dear guardian friend is one of such things."

Gil didn't respond. Instead, he puffed on his pipe, chewing on the stem pensively while his eyes moved from the pale faces of Cally's yes-men to the plaintive eyes of Ron. The gargoyle shifted against his bond. When he moved, the soft *clink* of chains seemed quite loud against the spinning of the wheel.

"Tell me," Gil said. "What did you have to do to get him here?" He cracked his knuckles and scowled. "How did you trick him, huh? How did you get him trapped down here in this pit, chained like a dog?"

"Gil..." a voice whispered. It was deep and raspy like an old man's voice, and it took me a moment to realize it was Ron's. He peered at us over the edge of the table. "Gil, wait," he whispered.

"There's been a misunderstanding, Mr. Abercrombie," Cally began.

"Misunderstanding, my ass. You're rotten, Cally, do you know that? A two-timing piece of industrial slag, a sheisty operator of an illegal gaming establishment–a sub-par one, at that. I wouldn't trust you to spit-shine my shoes." For emphasis, Gil lifted his leg to show off one of his huge white orthopedic sneakers. "No, wait, even worse: I wouldn't trust you to scrub my toilet bowl with your face. This creature that you've chained here like a lawn ornament is a valiant, honorable creature. He is a guardian and a hero. You may *say* that you're fair, Mr. Cally, partial only to the cold currency you so proudly wave in everybody's face, but you are not. You, sir, are a liar and cheat."

"Gil," Ron whispered again, tapping a long talon on the tabletop. "Gil! Psst!"

"I won't stand here and let you treat him this way, do you get that? I won't stand for it. It's disgusting and it's a crime. I'm here to liberate my friend if it's the last thing I do. *You* are a monster, Mr. Cally. A truly despicable creature."

Gil finished with a nod of his head. Silence reigned. Even the wheel had stopped spinning, perhaps it was embarrassed. Cally glowered, his cheeks flushed a deep red. I could even make out a few veins popping from his forehead. The yes-men around him looked scandalized. At least one began inching slowly towards an exit somewhere at the back of the room.

In the terrible silence, Ron's blue eyes poked once again over the lip of the table. He stage-whispered again, sheepishly, each word long and clear. *"Gil,"* he said. *"I have... a bit... of a...* gambling... *problem..."*

Gil blanched, most of the blood draining from his face. He swallowed and his jaw fell open. After a long moment, he gave Cally an uneasy grin. "Eh... errrmmm...." he said.

Cally spoke. "Listen to me, Abercrombie, you moronic slime. This 'honorable creature' you are praising came to me of its own volition. He came to me with cold cash and ambition to *win*." He straightened his cuffs. "Being the *fair* man that I am, I offered him an equal opportunity, despite my own urgings to him not to do it. He knew the risk when he decided to make the ultimate bet and it proved foolhardy. I implored him more than once to walk away, Abercrombie, and I even fronted him a sizable advance in hopes that he would cut his rather significant losses and leave. Unfortunately, he declined my generous offers. As it stands, he made the ultimate wager and lost. And now he has *nothing*," Cally said. "The last bet he made was for his *soul*, and now even that is mine. So unless you want me to have my friends outside forcibly remove you and your innards, I suggest you leave, empty-handed and tail between your legs."

Gil's mouth fell open as if the hinge had broken. He responded to threats almost as badly as I did. Angrily, he slammed a fist down on the table and let loose an incredibly impressive caravan of profanity–unusual for him. He would have continued for quite a while before Finch stopped him with a hand on his arm.

"Mr. Cally," Finch said. "I have a rather unique perspective on this... problem. You, as a businessman, can appreciate the advantageous circumstances of the double or nothing bet?"

Cally was silent. Without speaking, he reached out and spun the roulette wheel. He dropped the small white ball onto the track and watched it circle the wheel before descending and ultimately falling onto a numbered slot. He watched silently from behind his dark sunglasses.

After a long moment, he turned his attention back to Finch and his offer. Slowly, Cally slipped the dark sunglasses from his nose and dropped them into his jacket pocket. His eyes were large, too large for his face, and unnatural in more ways than one. Where I'd expected irises and pupils, there was nothing. His eyes were *all* whites, where each pupil would be, there was nothing but a tangled array of veins, as if his eye had been turned around in its socket and now faced the wrong way. He smiled.

"Mr. Finch, there is no bluffing under my gaze, do you know that? I read your lies like letters on a page. You've nothing to offer in such a wager. The easiest bet to make is that which has already been lost. You have no soul to offer."

Finch remained quiet, his poker face as good as always. Gil looked down at the cash helplessly. On the other side of the table, Willa looked up at Cally, disgust plain on her face.

On the other hand, I couldn't keep my damn mouth shut. It was something about Cally, maybe his smugness, his superiority, or his house-always-wins mentality. And there was something about Ron and the chain on his ankle. Unlike my partners, I was neither smart enough, tricky enough, or frightened enough to remain quiet. I heard my voice before I even knew what I was doing.

"I do," I said.

"Dylan, wait!" Willa said. I waved her off.

"Dylan," Finch said softly. "This is a terrible mistake. Please, believe me."

"Quiet," I said through gritted teeth. "Well, Mr. Cally?"

His veiny white eyes moved over me. I didn't have any lies for him to read, but it didn't stop him from trying.

"Mr. Dylan," he said, "I don't know you. Not like I know Finch. I can read lies in a person's face and body language, but most importantly in their words. I don't see lies in you, but now I must *hear* the truth." He leaned forward, resting his palms on the green felt table. "Will you spin this wheel honestly, without otherworld intervention or the aid of divinations? Will you freely chance your soul without... cheating?"

I looked into his pale eyes, straight into where I believed his pupils should be, and spoke.

"I will spin the wheel honestly."

After a long beat, he smiled. "All right," he said. "Let's play."

CHAPTER 19. BUSTED

Finch closed his hand over my bicep, tugging me back from the table. His eyes looked grim with an understanding I could not fathom. "Dylan, no," he said. "This is wrong. Please, trust me. Do *not* do this."

"It's already done," I said as I shook him off and leaned forward against the game table. Cally's lackeys were slipping out a back exit with wide eyes, leaving the room empty except for my partners, Willa, Ron the gambling gargoyle, and Quentin Cally. Somewhere behind us, I could hear the low rumble of a growl issuing from the unnatural throat of a dog soldier.

Cally gave the roulette a dramatic spin as he looked up at me with his bottomless white eyes and grinned. "You understand the rules, Mr. Dylan?" I met his milky gaze but didn't respond. "We play on a single-zero wheel here, and we accept inside and outside bets." He leaned back and crossed his arms over his chest. "Only an inside bet will be enough to win back your precious gargoyle. And only straight up. That is, exact number, of course."

"But of course," I said, forcing a smile.

Roulette is a pretty simple game, and I understood enough to know that Cally was giving me a fairly decent screw. When it comes to roulette, like Cally said there are two types of bets: inside and outside. Outside bets are more general; you choose the color the ball will land on, or whether it'll be even or odd. Outside bets are preferable; you've got a much better chance of winning. Inside bets force you to choose either the exact number that will hit or a small window of numbers. Croupiers use the term "straight up" to mean a bet on an exact number, and Cally had already said as much. I felt my stomach lurch at my odds.

The roulette took another practice spin while Cally enjoyed watching my face lose its color. The numbers spun in a red and black blur. I felt a little faint, but my moronic single-minded determinedness didn't falter one bit. Hello stubbornness.

"Let's do it," I said, taking a deep breath. From his pocket, Cally pulled a fractured shard of black stone that looked like obsidian. He reached out and dropped it into my clammy palm.

"Make your bet, Mr. Dylan," he said.

The volcanic glass was surprisingly cold in my hand as I surveyed the tabletop. The numbers on the green felt table looked as blurry as the numbers on the spinning wheel. I blinked my eyes and reached deep for some sort of divine guidance. Maybe there were enough gods for at least one to take pity on a moron like me and give me some direction here. Without it, I feared I'd end up another hollow man like Finch. In my mind's eye, I imagined seeing a huge number magically appear in strobing neon, providence directing my unsteady hand. I imagined a miracle or a bolt of lightning or *something*. I squeezed my eyes shut and hoped, waiting for that huge blinking answer to appear.

But there was nothing. Zip, nada, a big fat goose egg. After a minute, Cally cleared his throat and tapped the table impatiently with well-manicured fingernails. I opened my eyes and looked at him. He was still grinning. I could taste desperation at the back of my throat, or maybe it was just an unpleasant preview of stomach acid and bile soon to come.

I cast a glance over my shoulder at Gil, Finch, and Willa, realizing how dumb I had been. Employed for a few days and already about to reduce the Zeros by one. Again. Finch looked disappointed and a little angry. Gil's face was white as a sheet, his eyes locked on the floor. Beside them, Willa looked stricken. Her hands were clasped tightly against her stomach and her eyes were glassy. I swore under my breath and turned back to the table, dropping the obsidian onto the wide marker at the head of the green felt tabletop.

It rolled over once and stopped in the center of the marker I'd chosen: 0. It seemed appropriate.

"As fine a bet as any, sir," Cally said, coyly tossing the small white ball from one hand to another. His white eyes moved over me, digging for that shred of dishonesty he was certain I maintained. I wasn't smart enough to cheat. Or lie, for that matter. I didn't even have the immortality thing going for me like Finch did. I had nothing, and right now nothing was *not* a real cool hand.

Cally grinned. "I'll be happy when this is done and you are *both* mine," he said, turning from me to Ron. He patted his breast pocket, as if he'd slip us both inside it right next to his sunglasses.

"Spin the fucking wheel," I said.

He spun it and launched the ball. It shot round the table with maddening speed, rattling against the wheel with each rotation. All eyes followed the tiny white ball as it continued, each of us holding our breaths. I looked up and saw that Cally was not watching the ball; he had fixed his lifeless gaze on me. I looked from him to the cowering form of Ron peeking over the edge of the table. In his eyes were a deep fear, sadness, and guilt. He looked up at me and blinked, raised his head slightly and mouthed the words "Thank you." I looked back at Cally. I may have been about to lose my soul, but it wasn't for nothing.

The ball began to slow, becoming less of a blur as the Zeros behind me all took a step forward. I felt Willa's body against my arm. Some part of me quietly enjoyed it. I took a deep breath and focused my attention back on the wheel, closing my eyes and praying for some shred of luck to appear and undo what my stupidity had so successfully accomplished. I bit down on my lip and exhaled, imagining the number 0 in my mind. I saw it and grabbed it, willing it to appear beside the stationary ball on the wheel before me. Resting my hands on the table, I bowed my head, crushing every ounce of my will into it.

I can't explain it, but something happened. Eyes closed, breath held, I felt something begin in my gut and flow through my body, something strange and unnatural that unquestionably came from *me*. It began as a tickle and radiated outward like a soft breath of cold air. In a second, it grew, taking on the subtle but persistent jab of electricity. If you ever touched a Van de Graaf generator in high school chemistry when learning about static electricity, it felt like that; the long unbreakable flow of static electricity lancing through your hand from a large conductor; the feeling that the current you had tapped into was inexorably connected to something much larger hidden from the eye. It felt like something between the jabbing pain of a knife point and the slight discomfort you feel when you press your hand against the bristles of a hairbrush. Rather than flowing from the table into my hand, it flowed out from my touch into the table. I can't explain it, but the moment I felt it, I knew I had done it. Before I knew what happened, it was over.

"Holy jumpin' gigolos, man!" Gil screamed, slapping my back.

I opened my eyes and saw the tiny white ball resting in the nook beside the black 0. My mouth fell open. I felt my friends' hands shaking me as I looked up at Cally, eyes wide.

His forehead was creased with anger, and his hands were shaking. I couldn't tell if he was looking at me or the table, but I didn't care. I burst out laughing and slapped the flat of my hands against the table in a raucous drum roll.

Finch patted my arm once and nodded, a look of palpable relief evident on his face. "Well done, Dylan," he said. "Although I believe you've put us in a spot of trouble."

Across the table, I watched Cally raise a hand, slip two fingers into his mouth, and whistle. The sound was piercing, effectively crushing our enthusiasm. Any joy that remained was squashed by the barking of the dog soldiers as they stormed into the room behind us.

Cally raised a hand and pointed straight at my face. "I don't know how it is that you've accomplished such a cheat, Mr. Dylan, but I can assure you, you have won *nothing*." He pulled a revolver from his white tuxedo pocket and aimed it at my heart. With a particular flair for drama, he cocked it, and his grin returned.

A huge hand closed around my neck, choking me before it lifted me off the ground. I kicked my legs against nothing.

Finch flicked his wrist beside me and I turned to see a straight razor fall from his sleeve into his waiting hand. He turned and swung the blade. The razor sliced through the dog soldier's snout, bloody pieces of flesh pattering to the floor. The Doberman holding me yelped before dropping me to the carpet. Finch spun and stepped in front of me in time to catch the bullet from Cally's gun. Droplets of blood spattered across the table as he leapt across the green felt and slammed into Cally, the pair of them falling to the floor in a writhing heap.

Weaponless, I grabbed Willa and pulled her behind me as I turned to face the two hulking dog soldiers blocking our exit. The Doberman had stepped back, blood streaming from his mangled face. His second stood tall, ready to rip us limb from limb. Gil put his arm across my chest, pushing me back as he stuffed a hand into his inside jacket pocket.

"Stop!" he shouted, raising a *hand grenade* and pulling the pin.

"Um. What the hell?" I muttered in shock.

The dog halted. Somewhere behind us, I could hear squabbling.

Over my shoulder I saw Finch rise with Cally, blood running from the blonde man's nose. Finch held the straight razor to Cally's neck and led him around the table to join the rest of the group. A second line of blood trickled down Cally's neck from where Finch already nicked him a good one.

"Abercrombie," Cally bellowed. "You are dead! *DEAD!* Do you hear me?"

"Shut up, Q," Gil grumbled. "We played you fair and square and you screwed us with our pants on. We had a deal, man."

"Fair and square? *Fair* and *square?* He's a cheat," he said, pointing at me. "That partner of yours fixed the spin. I couldn't tell at first, but I felt it through the table." He knocked on the green felt with a knuckle for effect. "Your *man* there is a goddamn liar, Abercrombie. He's dead, and you're dead with him. Your lives are worth *nothing.*"

"It seems you are in no position to make threats, sir," Finch said, moving the razor up and down against Cally's bouncing Adam's apple. "If I were you, I would be careful of your choice of words. I'm liable to lose control of this blade."

Cally trembled under the razor. "Now wait, Finch, you won't get five steps with me dead."

"None of us will if I let this cookie bust, you got me, Quentin?" Gil said, waving the grenade about.

"You wouldn't."

Gil smiled. "Old Abercrombian saying: Never trust a man with a hand grenade." He shrugged. "He could go off at any time."

"Where the hell did you get a goddamn grenade?" Willa asked in a stunned whisper.

"Never leave home without one, my dear."

"Get your mutts out of our way and free our friend," I said, pointing at Ron. "Or else we're gonna wallpaper your high roller's suite with guts."

"Yours as well as mine, Mr. Dylan," Cally said bitterly. "You cheat."

"I didn't cheat," I said, although I honestly wasn't so sure.

"You know damn well you did. You cheated," he grumbled. "More impressively, you lied. I don't know how you did it, but I will find out. I promise you. I do not *ever* forget."

I smiled. "No worries," I said. "Gil? What's next?"

He smiled, waving the hand grenade about like a child with a party favor. "It's your move, Quentin," he said.

From his pocket, he pulled a thick ring of old, toothed Victorian keys. He handed the ring to Finch, the set dangling by one old rusted key. "That's for the manacle," he said.

Finch took the ring and pushed Cally away from him. Stooping, Finch slipped the key into Ron's ankle cuff and unlocked it with one turn. The rusty binding fell to the floor. Ron stood and stretched, smiling a very human smile.

Cally raised a finger at me again. "You may walk out of here, Dylan, but don't ever think I've forgotten this. You are a dead man, do you understand that?"

I shrugged. "Mortal enemies. You gotta have 'em."

Gil seized Ron's arm with his free hand and pulled him towards the entrance. The dog soldiers begrudgingly separated, allowing a narrow passage between their huge bodies. I pushed Willa behind Gil and Ron. Finch followed them out, his bloodied razor still in hand. Gil held his grenade high like a prize.

We crossed the gaming floor as quickly as we could. A few pairs of curious eyes followed, but no one made a move to stop us. At the exit, the Rottweiler growled but opened the door anyway. As I slid past, its yellow eyes followed each of my tentative steps.

"Cheat…" it rumbled beneath its breath.

"Ugly."

With a lightning-fast ratchet of its huge arm, the Rottweiler hit me in the low chest with a gut-busting punch. It felt like something inside me broke. Air flooded out of me as I rocked back on my feet and nearly collapsed. Willa caught me with a groan, glaring at the dog. Beside her, Finch whipped his razor in the beast's direction, forcing it back a step. It growled, but didn't move.

"Foul play," Finch muttered, his free hand pressed to the bullet hole in his chest. "Do that again and I'll have your jowls over my mantle."

The soldier growled again, but didn't move. Finch elbowed us out. Without another word, we slipped up and into the cool night air.

CHAPTER 20. RON'S HOUSE

We left the alley and rushed out onto the sidewalk, happy to leave Cally's den behind. A few people had appeared outside the pizza place, smoking and laughing. A handful of baffled glances found us thanks to Ron, but otherwise we were ignored. Gil and Finch conferred about our next move while I leaned against the brick façade and tried to feel human again, fairly certain that everything from my neck down had been turned into corned beef hash by that dog soldier's punch. Sharp pain lanced through my chest with every breath. There was a good chance I'd be pissing blood for the next week, and gods only knew what else.

"Are you all right?" Willa asked me.

"That damn dog really gave me a good one," I said, hoping I looked tough. "I feel like I swallowed a gallon of milk and then ran the mile. Step back if you like those shoes you've got on."

She cringed. "Remember what Dr. Hanas said? About fighting?"

"Yeah, I'm... I'm fine," I waved her off. "Don't worry. I'm just out of shape. Haven't been hit like that in a long time. Anyway, it worked out all right." I glanced over at Ron.

She squeezed my hand as her worried expression melted away. In its place was something much sweeter. I smiled back. I may have eased her worries, but not my own. "What's our next move?" I asked after a long moment. "I think we'd better get going."

"Yeah, please get me far, far away from this place," Ron begged, looking uneasily over his shoulder. "I wanna go home."

"That does seem wise," Finch said, nodding. He looked well enough considering there was a bullet in his chest.

"Yeah, looks like in addition to your special djinn friend, you've got somebody else who wouldn't mind seein' your head on the end of a pointy stick," Gil said looking at me. "And Quentin isn't the best guy to have on your bad side. He's got some nasty clout, and I think you pissed him off mightily."

I shrugged. It hurt. "Whatever."

Gil grinned. "That pup's punch looked like it hurt. Here, have a drink." He lifted the grenade and gave the top a twist. The lug and fuse came off, revealing a hip flask's screw cap. His grin widened.

"That's a damn flask?" I asked. "You're kidding me. You bluffed him?"

"Oh, it's a flask, all right," he said. "Old Abercrombian saying: Never trust a man with a hand grenade, remember? In this case, 'trust' in a literal sense." He giggled. "Seems like Q's truth telling magic thing didn't work so well under pressure, huh?" he laughed merrily as he handed the flask to me. I took a sip. Bourbon.

"Speaking of truth, how did you do it?" Finch asked, raising an eyebrow.

"Do what?" I asked.

The group had quieted. Everyone was watching me.

"How did you manage the roulette?" Finch said.

I took a deep breath, wondering if my entire chest cavity was crushed. In the back of my mind, I thought about what happened, remembering the feeling of the power as it slipped from my palm into the table and carried me through the wager safely. I shrugged. "Luck, I guess."

No one said anything. I saw doubt in their eyes. And maybe a little fear. It was eerie.

"What?" I asked.

Gil shook his head and grinned. "Nothin'. Just glad you're still in one piece, big man."

Finch remained silent, his eyes locked on mine.

"Well," I said after an awkward moment, "shall we go?"

"Wait a goddamned bloody minute, you jokers," a voice shouted from behind us in a fractured British accent. "You ain't goin' nowhere without me." We froze at the commanding voice. It sounded like it was far away, but it was deep and aged, booming with all the resonance of a huge diesel rumbling to life. I turned to look over my shoulder.

The pack of smokers had vanished and the storefront was deserted. I peered down the alleyway, but it too was empty.

"Up here, you poncey twits," the voice said.

I raised my eyes–following the sound–to the pizza shop's withered awning to find a grey pigeon staring down at me with strangely human eyes. My mouth fell open and the pigeon mimicked my face with surprising accuracy.

"What are you lookin' at, you tit?" the pigeon said, its beak opening and closing in time. "I got spaghetti sauce on my face or something? Nuffin to see here."

"Archie!" Ron bellowed from behind me. He tromped forward, raising his huge muscled arms happily. "You waited for me!"

"For too damn long, buddy boy. Do you know how many pizza crusts and cigarette butts I've eaten since you were dragged in there? Plenty. Just sayin' the word pizza is making me constipated. All that cheese. Ugh."

Willa and I shared a look as the pigeon fluttered off the awning and landed on Ron's stony shoulder. He looked at us and cooed wordlessly before speaking again. "Where we headed?"

"Home, little buddy," Ron smiled.

I pointed at the bird. "What the *hell* is that?"

"Calm down, Dylan," Gil said. "Friends come in all shapes and sizes."

"I got a problem with birds, man," I confessed, taking a step back.

"That bloody Hitchcock movie really made things tough for a spell," the bird said, shaking its head. "You're the only dope who apparently still shits the bed over it."

"No," I said. "No, no. It wasn't that... it was," I tried to make up an excuse. "All right, maybe it is that movie. I don't really like that movie, okay?"

Gil laughed a thunderous laugh. "Hey, guy, no judgment." He lit his pipe and threw his match into the gutter. "Let's get going. We've got a lot to do and I don't feel like a tête-à-tête here on the sidewalk with one of Cally's goons."

Gentleman that he is, Gil conceded the front seat to Willa, choosing to cram into the back seat with Finch, Ron, and Archie the bird. *Gil should invest in tinted windows*, I thought as I steered the Tank onto 95 with our gargoyle and talking pigeon.

"To the library, brother!" the bird howled in his accent that I was beginning to suspect was fake.

"Lady and gentlemen, let me introduce a dear, dear friend of mine," Ron said from the cramped back seat. Beside me in the passenger seat, Willa turned, resting her hand on my shoulder, a smile on her face. I peeked into the rearview mirror at the grand introduction taking place.

"This honorable avian champion strutting proudly before you is Archimedes Jacob Von Albatrosser the third, son of one of the most lauded and respected carrier pigeons of his day and bearer of a most prestigious and prodigious family mantle," Ron said, grinning. "And he's loyal, to boot."

"Did you say Von *Albatross*er?" I asked, skeptically. "What is that? A stage name?"

"Certainly not," Archie scolded. He began pacing up and down Ron's muscled arms, his head bobbing with each step. It sounded like Archie had picked his accent up from watching Errol Flynn movies for about ten years straight. "Even the insinuation is dastardly, Yankee swine."

We pulled up outside the public library shortly before midnight. The adrenaline that had carried me so well was beginning to ebb. I fought through the fatigue and parked the Tank on the empty curb out front. The whole crew tumbled out of the car.

The library was closed, but Gil led us around to a side entrance. From his wallet he pulled out an ID badge and swiped it through a card reader. A red light turned green and he pulled the now unlocked door open. We filed into a long, plain corridor. Gil pulled the door shut behind us.

A few paces from the doorway was a turnstile similar to one you'd find at a baseball game. Beside it stood a common everyday rent-a-cop security guard with clipboard in hand. Holding the same card, Gil slid it through a second reader before passing through the entry. Finch followed behind him. Ron pulled a similar card from his neon fanny pack, granting him access, though he had quite a time squeezing through the turnstile wings and all. From the same fanny pack, he pulled a second card that Archie snatched from Ron's huge fingers with his beak. I watched the pigeon swipe the card deftly and glide over the turnstile on his delicate feathered wings.

"Um…" I began, raising my empty hands in question.

Beside me, Willa dug around in her purse before inexplicably pulling out a card, swiping it, and passing through. She turned back and smiled. "A library card. I guessed!" she laughed. I scowled. "It makes sense," she added defensively.

"Well, I don't... I don't have a library card," I admitted.

The whole crew stared at me.

"Does that big ape even *know* how to read?" Archie asked.

"Hey," I said, "Yes, I can read. I'm just a busy guy."

Gil shook his head. He turned to the security guard. "Well, Tommy?"

A few minutes and a pair of forms later, I was a proud library card carrier. I didn't feel any different. I swiped my new ID and passed into the library.

"Of course they've gotta have a way to keep track of people who enter and leave, you know? *And* what they read, of course. It's genius, really," Gil said as we cleared the entry corridor and entered the huge first room. "Plus, it means I can read a ton of comics and never have to buy *any* of them. It's win-win, my man."

His voice echoed up into the huge cathedral ceilings. I have to confess, I'd never been inside the downtown public library, choosing instead to get my dose of academia via the History Channel and the underside of Snapple caps. Huge columns supported a second floor balcony, rimmed by an ornate balustrade. The room was mostly dark, lit only by dim security lights over emergency exits and small green glass shaded desk lamps adorning reading tables that ran down the center of the room. Ten-foot tall stacks of books were everywhere, meticulously arranged and organized in cases that each included a built-in ladder on runners that followed the contours of the shelves. Despite the darkness, I could see the faint outlines of stained-glass windows on the second floor. An impressive building, I had to admit. When we left, I hoped to see some spires, crucifixes, belfries, turrets, and a shitload of flying buttresses. As good as visiting Rome.

"This way," Ron said, taking over. He walked quickly, his taloned feet clicking against the marble floor. Archie stood sentinel on his shoulder, big eyes peering around in the darkness.

The gargoyle led us through a maze of stacks I wouldn't have been able to navigate with a GPS and a team of PhD's. After what felt like forever, we stopped at a huge oak door. Ron knocked on it gingerly, his huge knuckles casting echoes throughout the stone building.

After a moment, he opened the door. If we'd been invited in, I didn't hear it. Inside was a wide study, carpeted with thick Oriental rugs and lined with bookcases that actually did stretch all the way to the ceiling. In the dim lighting, I couldn't make out how high that actually was. A fire roared in a broad stone fireplace against the wall. Beneath a great stained-glass window of library stacks was a wooden desk, behind which sat Mrs. Eleanor Robbes-Grillet herself. I'd expected her to have a huge leather-bound tome spread across her lap; she was instead reclined in a high-backed chair, her pink slippered feet propped on the desk, watching a Phillies game on a flat screen television that hung above the fireplace.

She smiled at us and gestured at the television. "I missed the game earlier. Season just started and I'm already missing games." She shook her head. "Glad I've got some... *interns* ready and willing to record it for me." Eleanor laughed before leaning forward and dropping her feet to the floor. "It'd be a lot better if this reliever of ours could keep it together," she said, waving an angry hand at the TV. "He's gonna give me another heart attack."

Unsteadily, she rose to her feet, resting her withered hands on the desktop. "Ron," she said, her voice soft. "Welcome home."

The gargoyle crossed the carpeted floor in a moment and folded the old woman gently in his arms. The embrace was short but genuine. When Ron stepped away, Archie chimed in. "What, no hug for me you old bat?"

"Oh shut up, Archimedes," she snapped. She looked over Ron's shoulder and her eyes met Gil's. She smiled. "Thank you, Giles. Thank you so very much."

"Anything for you, Eleanor," he said, smiling. "I think you need to have a sit down with your guardian, though. Go over the evils of organized gambling." He winked.

Mrs. Robbes-Grillet scowled. "I do not know what you're talking about, Giles." She turned a knowing eye on Ron and glared at him. He wilted and shuffled away, his wings wrapping protectively around himself. "Alistair," she said, looking down over her half-moon glasses at Finch. "Have you been shot?"

"Yes, madam," he said, bowing slightly. "But it's nothing. Do carry on."

"Very well," she said. "Let's get down to business." Pressing an intercom on her desk, she said, "Bring in the books, please."

The door behind us opened, and a weary young intern pushed in a cart stacked high with thick reference texts. The young man looked exhausted, his arms and legs moving as if strapped to heavy weights. His misery was evident. Leaving the cart parked beside a huge wooden table opposite Mrs. Robbes-Grillet's desk, the intern pulled a few chains dangling from reading lamps to cast light across the table before quietly stepping out. He pulled the door shut behind him.

"What're these?" Gil said, pulling out his pipe.

"All the reference materials I have at my disposal that relate, even tangentially, to Bluebeard," Mrs. Robbes-Grillet said smiling. "And I hope you don't plan on *lighting* that in my library, Giles."

Gil snapped a match to life and held it up to his pipe. "Don't be stodgy, Eleanor, pipes were made for libraries." He lit the pipe and took a few puffs. The old woman frowned. "Now what in tarnation makes you figure we need such materials?" Gil asked.

Mrs. Robbes-Grillet shook her head slowly. "I was at the same dinner you were, Giles. While I don't have quite the experience of young Alistair there, I have a fair share more than you." She surveyed the group. "And isn't that Mr. Bascombe's wife?" she asked, raising a crooked finger in Willa's direction.

"A pleasure to meet you, ma'am," Willa said politely.

"Welcome, dear, welcome," Eleanor said, bowing slightly. "I do hope you know you are in perfect hands with these gentlemen."

Willa smiled. "I do, indeed."

Gil smiled at Eleanor. "Okay, sweetie pie, ya got me. Bluebeard it is. And you saved me the time and trouble of having to track all these books down myself."

"Don't be silly, that's what Allan is for," Eleanor smiled. "Thank goodness for his late fees, I'd be so lost without him." She pushed the intercom again. "Allan!" she shouted. "Refreshments, please!"

The door behind us opened and the weary young man returned, pushing a tea trolley decorated with a coffee urn, a tea pot, and a plate of croissants. Faint wisps of steam rose from the spouts of the two kettles. He moved them to the table along with a collection of cups and saucers before wearily trudging back out.

Surveying the expanse of literature spread across the table before us,

Gil smiled.

"Well," he said. "Shall we?"

CHAPTER 21. ALL THE NEWS

I gave research the old college try, but it seems that while my spirit was willing, my body was not. Looking back, things got a little foggy around 1:30 before they faded out in a sleepy haze.

I awoke with my face pressed flat against the tabletop, a nice puddle of drool accumulating just outside my gaping mouth. Willa was beside me, leaning against my shoulder, her glasses open on the table and her hair falling over her closed eyes. I shifted her as best I could so I could stand up and shake off the cobwebs. The tall window behind Mrs. Robbes-Grillet's desk was lit with a fair amount of morning sunshine. My watch told me it was nearly 10 AM.

"It's good to see you're awake."

I turned to find Finch staring up at me. Unlike Willa and Gil, who were still pretty deeply conked out, Finch looked as if he'd never gone to sleep at all. A pile of books were spread out around him, open to various pages. A legal pad was on his lap, covered with magnificent handwriting that bordered on calligraphy.

"Morning," I said.

He nodded. "Well rested?"

"I guess." I stretched and heard a symphony of creaks and cracks as the bones in my back sang in protest. I felt a little better, but still far from ideal. I knew that if I lifted Gil's borrowed shirt and took a look, I'd find a generously sized welt on my stomach from last night's fierce blow. I decided to save that cringe for later.

"You didn't manage to stay awake for too long last night."

"I was pretty tired," I said. "Not used to 1 AM research sessions after almost selling my soul to an illicit underground demon gaming operation."

"Ah, to be young again," he said, smiling slightly. "How do you feel?"

I shrugged. "Well enough."

"What's going on?" Gil barked, sitting upright in a blur. A piece of paper was stuck to his face. He pulled it free and sat back, sputtering.

"Good morning, Boss," Finch said, turning his attention away from me. "Did you sleep well?"

"No. I miss my king-sized bed and sleeping mask." He shook his head again. "What time is it?"

"Almost 10 o'clock," Finch said.

"Good gravy. Too early," Gil mumbled.

Beside me, Willa lifted her head groggily, one hand rubbing sleep from her eyes. "Ugh," she moaned.

I patted her back, grateful for the momentary closeness our situation had allowed. "Good morning, sleepyhead."

"Good morning, my ass. Did Gil say 10 AM? I've been asleep for two hours."

"Man I really tossed it in early last night, didn't I?" I asked.

Everyone nodded in unison.

"*And* you snore," Willa said sourly.

Everyone nodded again.

"Oh. Um. Sorry. Productive night?"

"You bet your bootstraps, big man," Gil said shuffling through a squirrel's nest of papers. "Tons of stuff. About Bluebeard the man and Evil Inc."

Willa sighed and sat back. "I found the answer you were looking for, Gil."

"About 1862 or 1963?"

"1963," Willa answered, yawning.

"And?"

"Same thing. In each instance, the following year was a mayoral election. In 1963 it was for Governor, as well."

"Goddamn," Gil muttered, shaking his head.

"What?" I asked.

"This isn't the first time this has been attempted," Finch said.

"Nope," Willa said, "but it just might be the first time it works."

"Look at this here," Gil said, spinning a huge reference book in my direction. "This is the percentage breakdown for the 1963 mayoral election. The third party candidate in question was a guy named Edward A. Bathory. These books are great for tracking numbers over the last few weeks of the run, but they're only numbers. Somewhere in the last two weeks he took a huge dip in support, eventually only registering 13% of the final vote when tallied. Even his total fundraising numbers are here, and it looks like they hit a wall two weeks before E-Day."

"You sound pretty learned for a guy who didn't know what City Council was a few days ago," I said.

"Hey man," Gil said. "We worked hard last night."

Finch cleared his throat and continued. "As this candidate's support waned, so did his funding. Even when adjusted for inflation, the total fundraising figures are nearly nothing at the end," Finch added.

"Okay," I said, trying to follow.

"When fundraising is usually in a fever pitch of desperation, his fell off," Willa explained. "Those kind of numbers don't make sense, trust me."

"All right, so we're reading about mayoral elections. What makes this Bathory character raise any flags at all?" I asked. "Why aren't we reading about Ed Rendell or Frank Rizzo?"

"First of all, Bathory was a vampire," Gil said. "So there's that."

"Oh. Okay. Then what makes the election in 1963 have any bearing on the election this year?" I asked. "1963 was a little while ago."

"Not to vamps," Gil said, raising his eyebrows. "Remember, they've got a different idea of *time* than we do."

Willa leaned forward. "Take a look at this." She pointed a finger at a bit of smudged print in another book.

"I can't read that," I grumbled, rubbing my tired eyes. "What does it say?"

"Campaign manager," she read, "V. Altimerach."

A bell of recognition clanged in my head. "Altimerach," I said. "No way."

"You bet your ass, big guy," Gil said. "And here," he lifted a larger book that look even older. The ink was faded and smudged, but I leaned close enough to manage to read it. "V. Altimerach. Wow."

"In cases like this, common denominators don't bode well," Gil said. He turned to Finch. "Told you we should've smoked that P.O.S. when we had the chance."

"I don't think he's the mastermind," I said.

Gil and Finch froze mid-argument. Willa turned to me, crestfallen. "Why not?"

"He told me he was head of security, but he's got nothing to do with the campaign or political agenda. And remember what I told you guys? Bluebeard himself said that this Altimerach guy didn't even know that Bluebeard *was* Bluebeard."

"So that's a problem," Finch said. "But you do admit that this is more than a coincidence, correct?"

"Of course. But what does it all mean? Remember, I've been sleeping for a while."

"It means they have been waiting for the opportunity to do this for a very long time. Never before have they had the popular support, nor have they had the real likelihood of victory. They just might have the power to bring it all together this time," Finch said.

"Get him elected, you mean. But why? What makes this time any different?"

Gil pulled a newspaper from beneath a stack of books. It was folded back with a big black circle drawn around the headline and accompanying story. He held it out to me. "This is today's paper," he said. It read *MAYOR GARDNER WITHDRAWS RE-ELECTION BID*. Beneath the headline in smaller print, it continued: *Puts Full Endorsement Behind Dark Horse Candidate Alfred Bascombe.*

"Shit," I muttered.

"Yeah, it's just that, brother," Gil said, dropping the paper onto the table.

"What the hell are we going to do?" I asked.

"Dorothy landed us a few appointments today, scheduled for lunchtime," Finch said. "Gil is set to meet with Bascombe's head of policy and I'm set to meet with the Mayor's former campaign advisor. We need to figure out how far this thing reaches and *why*. 'Why?' is the big question right now. For all we know, the Mayor could even play a part."

"How'd you manage these appointments?" I asked.

Gil smiled. "The Bascombe rep is under the impression that I'm a possible campaign financier, so he's got no problem schmoozin' the hell outta me. As for the Mayor's former advisor, he's his *former* advisor, and right now that poor bastard's as good as unemployed. Easy pickin'."

I looked over at Willa. "What about us?"

"I've got somebody else for you two to meet," Finch said.

I didn't like the tone of Finch's voice, or the smug smile on his face. "Oh, great."

"Hold on a second, I've got some more things I wanna check out first," Willa said. "I was also hoping to find more extensive campaign documentation from the 1862 election." She stood up from the table and walked to the door. "I'm gonna dig around for a bit, all right? We've got time, haven't we?"

"You got it, lil lady," Gil said smiling. She stood and stretched. She smiled at me and walked out, a pair of books under her arm. The door shut behind her. "She's a catch," Gil said. "She knows this political mumbo jumbo like the back of her hand. Plus, she's got a great spirit," he grinned. "And other stuff, too, eh Dylan?"

"Come on, man, she's married."

"Yeah, I know, and we *are* tryin' to save her husband and stuff. Touché, I guess." He stood. "Anyway, I gotta hit the little boy's room before things get messy. I'll be back in a few. Give this a read, Dylan," he said as he strode out of the room, handing me a thin leather book. I turned the volume around in my hands to see a black and white engraving of a barrel-chested, bearded man eerily similar to Bluebeard standing before a large castle manor. Up above him a young woman looked down mournfully from a high window.

"That's his story," Finch said. "Literally."

I began to read, but being alone with Finch, the silence was awkward. Rather than read or entertain himself with something else, he sat watching me. It kind of gave me the heebie-jeebies. After a while, I dropped the book and looked at him, opening my mouth to speak when he beat me to the punch.

"What happened at Cally's last night?" he asked.

"What do you mean?"

"I sensed it just as Cally did," he said. "But like Cally, I have no idea what it was." He dropped his pad of paper on the table and stood. "The interesting thing is that Cally can't sense magic. That's not what he was doing when he asked you all those questions about honesty. He can only sense intent, and a true lie is a false statement made with intent. I believe the reason that he didn't think you were lying is that you weren't lying. You may have altered the outcome of the game by magic, but you didn't *intend* to, otherwise Cally would have been all over you."

"I don't know anything about magic, Finch."

"I know. But I also know that ignorance of magic does not preclude you from employing it."

"Um, okay," I said, frowning. "You're saying that just because I don't get it doesn't mean I can't do it?"

Silently, he nodded.

I sighed. "Outside of pulpy sci fi/fantasy books, I don't even know what magic is," I said. "I couldn't do it if I wanted to, and I *don't* want to. I like being the average joe in the group; the straight man, the boring non-magic guy."

He just stared at me, waiting.

I sighed and thought about it. After a long minute, I looked over the work the others had done while I'd slept. Like it or not, I was part of a team. And on a team, honesty is paramount.

"All right," I admitted. "I felt something. It was like..." I closed my eyes and visualized the situation. I saw Cally's porcelain eyes and the green felt tabletop; I saw Ron's unabashed fear and the red and black spinning roulette numbers. "...Electricity," I said. "It was like a jolt of electricity."

Finch smiled. "Come with me."

I followed him through the endless stacks, passing Gil and a few bored browsers on the way. "Be right back," Finch said without pausing. With a shrug, Gil continued back towards Mrs. Robbes-Grillet's study.

In the daylight, the library was a totally different place. Any ominous mystery I'd felt the night before was replaced by hushed tones and the pitter-patter of children's feet across the building's multiple levels. The library had a comfortable, welcoming air, and I couldn't help but be disappointed that it had taken me so long to cross the building's threshold.

Finch led me out the back entrance and around the building into an alleyway. Standing between a loading dock and a closed garage, Finch grabbed my arm and positioned me to face an overturned trashcan. He took a deep breath and stood behind me, pointing one arm over my shoulder at the pile of refuse.

"All right, I'm going to give you some simple directions, and I just want you to follow them, all right? Trust me when I say that you are completely safe right now. Nothing you are about to do is dangerous. Do you trust me?"

It took me longer to decide than I would have liked. "Yes," I said eventually.

"Good. Raise your hand–just one hand–and point it at that trashcan."

"Which hand?" I asked.

"Whichever is natural," he said.

"And point it there?"

"Yes, right there."

I raised my right arm, extending my hand out before me. I felt pretty stupid, but I could also feel the hairs on my arm stand on end.

"Now imagine fire, all right?"

"Fire?"

"Well," he paused. "Imagine that trashcan there *on* fire. That's better. And safer."

"Wait, what? Safer?"

"Nothing, nothing. Don't worry about it. Just imagine it. Think about the heat, the smell, the sound of the flames crackling."

I closed my eyes and tried to envision the overturned receptacle and its filthy contents awash in rippling waves of orange and red flames. Calling on all the imagination I'd once harnessed as a kid, I felt the warmth and smelled the burning fumes of the trash going up in smoke.

"All right," I said after a moment.

"Okay, now I want you to repeat after me, all right?" He stepped around to my side, lowering his hands and sliding them into his pockets as he walked. "And, remember, envision the trashcan on fire the whole time. All right?" I nodded. "Vatra," he said, his voice taking on an air of formality that was uncommon, even for Finch. "Vatra. Porast Vatra."

"Vatra. Porast Vatra." I spoke the words slowly, the uncommon sounds clumsy in my mouth.

"Again," he said. "Remember to visualize the fire. Visualize it. *Feel* it."

"Vatra," I said, my voice growing. *"Porast Vatra."*

I felt heat and a snap of static electricity crackle in the palm of my hand, as though a ruler had whipped against my skin.

I closed my eyes once more. *"Porast Vatra,"* I repeated.

From the tips of my outstretched fingers erupted a column of flame nearly a foot wide and traveling faster than my eye could follow. It crossed the alley in less than a heartbeat, exploding the garbage can and engulfing it in flames. I cringed, stepping back only to feel Finch brace me. The heat was harsh against my skin. Gasping, I closed my eyes and recoiled as I raised my hands to shield my face and turned away.

Finch grabbed at my hands, closing two of his over one of mine, curling my fingers into a ball.

When my hands closed, the fire ceased in a puff of smoke, leaving only the smoldering ruins of the refuse. My heart was racing, and I could feel sweat soaking through my clothing. I raised a shaking hand before disbelieving eyes, horrified.

"It's all right," Finch said, steadying me. "The fire is out. It's *all right*. You are in complete control, Dylan."

"What the hell are you talking about? Complete control? I just blew up that damn thing with my *hand*. My *hand*. Using what? Magic? I told you, I don't even *know* magic, Finch. Up until a few days ago, I didn't even know magic *existed*." All right, I was freaked, I admit it. The idea of having some power beyond my control—or even comprehension—really scared me.

"Yes, Dylan, I understand. I know you are frightened, but believe me, you can do this. You have control," he assured me. "Trust me, please. The only way you did that was with my instruction. *Please*, calm yourself."

I took a deep breath, focusing on my heartbeat, trying to push away the thought of everything around me exploding in flames. After a moment, Finch's concrete logic was enough to steady my wits.

"Tell me what's going on," I said.

He smiled. "That was a spell."

"You mean those words I said?"

"Well, no. Point of fact, that was Serbian. It was literally a call to raise fire. You can do it in any language, but I use Serbian. I know the language well enough and don't ever use it. It's not very likely I'll use it by accident one day."

"Hold on, any language? What?"

He sighed. "It is an incantation of words that you have imbued with a power, which was why I had you think of the fire while you said them. To you, they meant nothing; they served only as a way to focus your energies. When I had you think of the fire as you said them, you *gave* the words a power from inside yourself. The words acted as a conduit. Trust me, it's rather intelligent to use a language you don't speak in everyday conversation. It's a bit... safer."

"What stops me from imbuing normal everyday words with power?" I asked.

"Intent," Finch said simply. "Much of magic is channeled through good old fashioned intent."

"Shit man, I don't even believe this. I mean... why now? If you had done that whole thing with me last week would it have worked?"

"I'm not certain, but I don't think so," he said. "In truth, I was hoping nothing would happen, Dylan, nothing at all. But the spell you just unleashed on that unsuspecting trashcan over there could not have been accomplished by someone with no inherent power."

"What do you mean 'inherent power'?"

He took my arm and began leading me out of the alley. "I believe there is something inside of you that carries with it a heavy reserve of magic. That reserve is what gave the incantation the power to do that. Have you ever done anything strange or inexplicable before?"

"No, of course not. I've never exploded trashcans in an alley, or made panes of glass at the zoo disappear, or become invisible in the girl's locker room, or sawed my assistant in half at the circus. I've never done *anything*!"

"Hmm," he said rather matter-of-factly. "That's odd."

"*That's* odd? And why is that?"

"Because it means this power is new to you."

"New," I repeated. "How new are we talkin'?"

He chewed his lip as we paused at the library's busy entrance. Men and women walked past us, unaware. "Honestly I don't know," he said. "But I know someone who can tell us."

CHAPTER 22. MR. DOLAN'S TALE BEGINS

"That is *so* awesome," Willa said, grinning like a madwoman and taking a sip from her coffee cup.

"It is not awesome," I said seriously. "It scared the shit out of me."

"It just exploded? Like, fire everywhere?"

"Not really, it was more like a ray of fire thing," I explained, taking a bite of a breakfast burrito that felt like it weighed about seven pounds. She laughed, leaning back and running a hand through her hair.

We were sitting in a booth in the Midtown Diner III on 18th Street, a few blocks from the downtown library. After parting ways with Gil and Finch, Willa and I decided to share a bite to eat before our lunch meeting.

At the moment, I was catching her up, entertaining her with the story of how I was apparently a new magical wunderkind over breakfast. Eating eggs and bacon, she seemed to be taking the whole thing better than I was.

"I've always wanted to have some kind of power, ever since I was a little girl," she said. "I was a big fan of *X-Men* growing up."

"Me too, but like flying or something. Now that I've got it, I'm a little freaked out."

"I get that," she said, shaking Frank's Hot Sauce over her eggs. My kind of woman. "You have to admit, it is exciting, though."

"Yeah, I guess. I'm trying really hard to be cool, something I've gotten good at since becoming one of Gil's merry men."

She nodded, her face turning serious. "I know all about that, trust me." She fidgeted in her seat, stirring up her hash browns. "I had another dream last night."

"About Alfr–uh... I mean, about your husband? And Bluebeard?"

She nodded. "I'm looking forward to getting past this." She took a bite, still not meeting my eye.

I realized she was doing a good job of keeping it all together, and it made me admire her even more. Even after all this was done, she would still carry the burden of her prescient dreams. There was nothing we could do about that. She would live with the dreams forever, whether she liked it or not. Suddenly, she and I seemed to have much more in common.

I caught my eyes wandering to her ring finger where a hefty diamond sat. How easily it was to forget that this was a married woman; how easy it was to forget that this woman's life was in mortal danger, just as her husband's life was.

"I'm sorry," I said. "I don't want you to think you've been pushed a little to the back burner through all this," I admitted. "There's a lot going on, but we haven't lost sight of what's important. We are all working towards finding... *Alfred*. But how are you holding up?"

"I'm all right," she shrugged. "I trust my Alfred. He's a very capable man. You know, he set his mind on becoming a City Councilman, and he did it. He can do anything he sets his mind to." She shook her head. "I wish he was here with me now, but I trust him more than I trust anyone, honestly. I get we're a very unlikely pair," she smiled and it was radiant, "but that's what makes me so happy. Something about us just... *works*." She trailed off, her eyes losing focus as she stared off into space.

"We'll find him, Willa. I promise."

She blinked, returning to reality. "I know. I...." She nodded. "I know."

Our conversation had run out of gas, and we found ourselves eating our food in silence. I'd forgotten how bad I was at being comforting. I finished up my burrito, and I dug into my pocket for the crumpled piece of paper Gil had given me at the library. Scribbled across it in Gil's child-like script were a pair of addresses. At the bottom was a third address in Finch's impeccable cursive and a time for later tonight. His "magic man."

"Do you know where any of these places are?" I asked, handing Willa the paper.

Chewing, I watched as she read. "The first two," she admitted, "but not the last one."

"And that's the one I'm most curious about."

"That's Finch's weird Doctor, right?"

"Yes, it is."

"You two going together?"

I nodded. "I'd rather Finch be there to do the talking. Otherwise I'm not even gonna know what to even say. Hello, sir, I immolated a trashcan this morning. Please prescribe me."

"The first address here is somewhere in the Mainline," she said.

"From what Finch said, it's some kind of a retirement community. I think we're supposed to be meeting one of the pollsters who helped out in the mayoral elections back in '63."

"*1963*, I'm guessing?"

"Um, yes?"

"Hey, just checking," she said. "At this point, very little surprises me."

"That's a good way to be." I checked my watch. "Let's get going," I said, standing up. "I don't know what time this old timer's gonna need a nap."

***

We took a cab. It was just faster than however many transfers we'd need to get to this place. I offered to pay and we were there in twenty minutes.

As per my request, the cabbie dropped us off at the gated entrance to a well-manicured over-sixty community. The gate was black wrought-iron bolted into a beautiful brick wall, surrounding a nest of ranch houses. A similarly designed iron door was set into the wall by the sidewalk to allow for pedestrian entrance. I rang a buzzer set into the stone and waited.

"Green Lawn Estates," a rosy voice said. "How can I be of service to you?"

"Hi," I said, leaning to speak into the box, "My name is Dylan. My associate and I have a one o'clock appointment to meet with a Mr. Timothy Dolan."

166

There was a long pause before the crackling voice returned. "Yes, Mr. Dylan. Welcome to Green Lawn Estates. Mr. Dolan resides in bungalow twelve. Please don't hesitate to contact us with any questions or concerns, and have a nice day!" The radio clicked off and an electronic *buzz* unlocked the gate. I pulled the door open and held it for Willa.

As it turned out, Green Lawn Estates was no misnomer. Each bungalow was framed by picturesque lawns so green I'd venture calling them emerald. Flowerbeds were planted before each ranch house, huge pastiches of color bright enough to make me squint in the midday sun. Willa ooh'd and ahh'd at each home we passed as we followed the curving sidewalk deeper into the geriatric paradise. Golf carts buzzed slowly past us, complete with elderly couples happy to smile and wave. I had to admit, the place was pretty idyllic.

"There's number twelve there," I said as we came around a gently sloping curve. Smaller than many of the other homes, the number twelve bungalow was just as nice. It sat on a tiny hill facing a quaint man-made lake. From the center of the lake gushed a tiny fountain of water that sent soothing ripples across the water's surface. The front lawn was immaculately maintained, as each of the homes' were, but number twelve stood out thanks to the endless patches of daisies that filled each flowerbed. Beside the quaint front porch, a Philadelphia Phillies pennant fluttered in the gentle breeze.

"What an adorable little house," Willa said, smiling.

"It is pretty cute," I admitted, though "cute" was not a word that passed my lips regularly.

She took a step up the walkway when I stopped her.

"Hold on," I said. "I have to tell you, I'm not great with children or old people…" I trailed off sheepishly.

She laughed. "Relax, Dylan. Just let me handle it, okay?"

I nodded gratefully and took the rear, following her up the brick path to the small cottage's front door. She knocked twice and waited.

The door opened to a hunched old man with a shock of white hair sprouting from his head. He wore khakis and a white button down with red suspenders, thick glasses gave him a rather mole-like look. A thin oxygen tube ran over each of his big ears down to his nose. He smiled when he saw Willa, a big white denture grin.

"Hello, my dear. Hello! Welcome," he padded back a step in a pair of Philadelphia Eagles slippers, a scarred wooden cane in one knotted fist.

"Mr. Dolan?" Willa asked.

"Yes, that's me, I'm Tim." He smiled again. "Come in, please. It's so rare I get such a lovely visitor!"

Willa stepped inside and extended her hand. "Mr. Dolan my name is Willa Bascombe."

He switched his cane between hands and gave Willa a hearty shake, his grin widening. "Pleasure, it's a pleasure, young lady."

I stepped inside behind her, extending my hand for another one of Mr. Dolan's big shakes. His hand was a little shaky, but his grip was firm. "My name is Dylan, sir," I said. "Thank you for seeing us on such short notice."

"Not at all, not at all," he said, closing the door behind us. He checked on a thermostat before slipping into a sweater and drawing it closed around his small body. It felt warmer inside than out.

"Perhaps I would've had to think twice if the Phils were playing this afternoon, dear, but they're off today. Lucky you!" he smiled again. "Come in, come in, have a seat." He gestured us into the living room with ecstatic waves of his hands.

Willa and I took seats on opposite ends of a couch facing a pair of high-backed recliners. On one seat sat a withered paperback mystery with a brutally cracked spine. The other was empty. Across the walls were photographs of children and grandchildren, most yellowed with age. In many of them, an adorable white-haired woman stood beside Mr. Dolan. The pictures seemed to cover nearly every square inch of the small room's walls. As I followed the pictures around the room chronologically, I couldn't help but notice the abrupt disappearance of the kind-eyed Mrs. Dolan. I looked at the two recliners facing me and realized how quiet the cottage must be without visitors.

"Can I get you two lovebirds something to drink?"

"Uh, erm, eh..." I blushed, my eyes widening at his assumption. *This is awkward*, I thought.

Willa laughed, not missing a beat. "Oh, no thank you, Mr. Dolan. And actually, we're only associates."

"Oh dear, oh dear," he said, crossing the carpeted floor at a shuffle and taking a seat in one of the recliners after pushing the paperback aside. "I always assume," he said, grinning devilishly. He leaned back, struggling into the recliner, joints cracking and arms shaking, struggling to support his weight. I half rose to help him before Willa shook me off. Mr. Dolan didn't even notice. "I *love* this chair," he said, "but I have a dickens of a time getting in and out of it these days. But it's so comfy." Finally settled, he pulled a lever, raising the footrest. With a deep sigh, he relaxed. "Now, what can I do for you two youngens?"

"We're doing a retrospective study of mayoral campaigns in the city, Mr. Dolan," Willa began. "And your name came up more than once as a premier authority on the 1963 mayoral election. You worked in that campaign, didn't you?"

He squinted, arching his eyebrows. "1963. Hmm..." He tapped his wrinkled finger on his closed mouth, thinking back. "Ah, yes, 1963. It was Hardy the incumbent running against Dorosso, right?"

"Yes, sir. That's right," Willa said, looking over to me and making a writing gesture. I pulled the crumpled paper from my pocket and borrowed a pen from a cluttered coffee table. "Was there a third party candidate that year?"

"Um... '63..." he scrunched his face up, his tongue poking from his mouth like a small child as he thought. Finally, he remembered, his face falling slightly. "Oh. Oh dear, yes there was. A man named Bathory. Edward Bathory." He sighed, lines of worry creasing his forehead.

"That's the information I have, as well," Willa said. "And he's the man we're so interested in." She smiled, "The man that history seemed to forget."

He examined her carefully, a certain wariness creeping into his face. "Yes, the man that history seemed to forget..." he trailed off, his eyes narrowing behind their huge lenses. "What makes you ask about him, dear? I haven't..." he sighed again. "I have tried not to think about Edward Bathory for a very long time." One of his palsied hands crept across the chair to the curved head of his cane.

Willa sensed his apprehension even before I did. "I'm sorry, Mr. Dolan, I don't mean to make you uneasy, and the strangest thing is that this is exactly the response we're getting from everyone we meet with about this Mr. Bathory. We're only trying to get a fair and balanced glimpse of what the election was really like." She smiled innocently. "That's all."

His hugely magnified eyes moved over her face slowly before turning to me. He took a few wheezy breaths before exhaling and releasing his cane. "I'm terribly sorry, my dear, it seems that even after all these years, I'm still just an overly cautious old man."

"No, not at all. Don't be silly, Mr. Dolan," Willa flashed him another one of her grand smiles.

He sighed and shook his head, but the sense of unease hadn't totally evaporated. "I'd all but forgotten," he said softly. "Even when you asked about him, I didn't quite remember. Not everything, not at first."

"Remember what, sir?" I asked, leaning forward.

Straightening up in his chair, Mr. Dolan smiled, the wide grin betraying his true age as it spread wrinkles across his wizened face. "It seems like so long ago," he said. "I was hired into Mayor Hardy's campaign early, before Christmas, in 1962. I was so excited to land a mayoral campaign. It was the biggest campaign I'd been associated with. At the time I'd only been out of school for a few years. Peggy was so proud. The man I reported to was the head of political affairs, a man named Lionel, um... Abernathy, I believe? Now, Lionel had been working city politics for a number of years at that point; he was nearly the same age then as I am now. Lionel hired me as a private pollster to do some demographic work with specific age groups they were particularly worried about. This kind of thing wasn't done very much at that time, but Mayor Hardy certainly had the money. When I was brought on, I learned that it was for a very specific reason. I remember Lionel sat me down on my first day and explained that reason in just two words: Edward Bathory."

"He had already announced his intention to run?" I asked.

"Well, not exactly," Dolan said. "But he'd made enough ripples working on City Council to turn heads. From what I remember, Lionel was particular worried about the upper middle class vote."

"From what I read, Mayor Hardy was a fairly liberal mayor. What made Mr. Abernathy worry about the upper class vote at all? Didn't he expect to lose it?"

"Well, Lionel was more worried about the middle class vote, not the upper class vote, and from some preliminary numbers he showed me, this Mr. Bathory was extremely popular in his district–a heavily middle class district. And to make things even more worrisome, Lionel had reports that Mr. Bathory was seeing heavy support *across* income lines. In his district, he seemed to be universally admired."

"That's remarkable," Willa muttered.

"Why politically speaking, it was, dear," Dolan smiled. "Now you see why he worried and brought me aboard the campaign. It was my job to find out why Mr. Bathory seemed so universally popular within his district, and how that would translate across a larger field of play."

"What district was that, sir?" I asked.

"I'm sorry?" he leaned towards me, cocking an ear in my direction.

"I said, what district did Mr. Bathory represent?"

"Oh. Um..." he tapped a finger on his closed mouth again. "I know, I know, of course," he said smiling. "It was District 11, how could I forget?" He smiled innocently. "Peggy's lucky number."

"District 11," I muttered, red flags rising in the back of my head for some reason. I dug through my recent memory. After a moment, I turned a baffled eye to Willa. Her eyes were wide with recognition. That's when it dawned on me. District 11. Her husband's district. Another coincidence.

Fantastic.

CHAPTER 23. MR. DOLAN'S TALE CONCLUDES

"Everything all right, son?"

I looked up. Mr. Dolan's myopic eyes squinted at me through his thick glasses.

"Yes, sir. Fine. I was just... thinking."

He smiled. "It's all right. You looked a bit spooked, is all."

I shifted on the couch, glancing at Willa uneasily before Mr. Dolan continued.

"You two have to remember," he began, "1963 heading into '64 was a hell of a time. Politics meant something else back then. It wasn't just unemployment and foreclosure and the economy and all that bunkum, it was war and civil rights. Soon enough JFK would be killed and anger would spread like fire. It was the beginning of something... darker. Vietnam was young, but people didn't like where it was headed. It wasn't until '64 and the Gulf of Tonkin that Vietnam really exploded, of course, but you better believe we knew what was coming. It was... a different time.

"So when Lionel brought me onto Mayor Hardy's campaign, I felt like I was really doing something, you understand? I believed in Mayor Hardy, like so many others did, and it was a good feeling. Peggy was so proud of me. 'You're doing good, Tim, you know that?' She used to tell me that all the time. What's strange is that I believed I was doing a good thing." He paused, staring off into space, smiling. "Like I said, things were different back then." I looked at Willa, hoping she'd urge him on, but she was silent. After a long pause he continued.

"Lionel, my boss, he was a tricky bastard. A lotta the stuff he wanted to run in the campaign wasn't strictly legal. Kind of a precursor to Nixon and CREEP and all. But I knew what I was getting into. Lionel was pretty upfront with me, or as upfront as he was with anyone, quite frankly.

"'Bathory,' Lionel had said to me, 'Bathory is what you're hired to handle, Dolan. I want to know the ins and outs, and I want to know why his numbers are so damn *good*.' See, the Mayor got his start on City Council, too, coming out of the 5th District. Hardy was counting on that vote to help him carry the election. Bathory, on the other hand, was coming out of the 11th, which at the time was a mixed bag. Quite a bizarre district, let me tell you.

"Originally, the 11th was the closest to a red light district as you could find in the city. After the war ended in '45, it was mostly made up of gentlemen's clubs, streetwalkers, drug dens, tenements, and the like, the kind of thing you'd expect to find in the worst neighborhoods. But in the late 50's and early 60's, things started to change. All the uh..." Mr. Dolan paused and coughed, a noticeable blush creeping into his pale face. He lowered his voice, "Well, the *sex* stuff started drying up. Sorry, darlin'," he apologized to Willa with a tip of an invisible cap.

She smiled and waved him off. "Not at all. Please, continue."

"Well, it started changing into what it is today: a corporate hub. A lot of office complexes and corporate headquarters started appearing. Property values had hit rock bottom, and they say that's the best time to start turning a neighborhood over. So '62 and '63 were watershed years for the 11th, years that changed it forever. If you go down and walk the streets of the 11th now, you'll not find the slightest trace of what it once was. Most people wouldn't even believe what it used to be like."

He was right. I'd lived in the city for pretty much my whole life, and I couldn't even imagine the 11th district being considered a red light district, let alone remember it. I thought of the area, a ten or fifteen square block nugget located just north of Market Street around 3rd or 4th Street. In the past few years, it had become even more gentrified, with waves of upper class families squeezing into brick row homes adjacent to business high rises and office complexes.

"So when I came onto the campaign, the 11th was already a real wildcard. Every politician in the city was battling for its vote, but Bathory looked to have it locked. Not one to be elbowed out by a newcomer, Lionel brought me in to work on Hardy's campaign. He said I was just as young and fresh as the 11th's vote, so I was the perfect choice."

173

"You were responsible for capturing the 11th?" Willa asked.

"Not only that, but Lionel wanted me to dig into Bathory's campaign. He wanted to know who Bathory was and where'd he had come from. And he wanted to know about the strange support he'd marshaled.

"The first thing I did was visit Bathory's campaign HQ. Nobody knew who I was, so I didn't even bother with any undercover stuff like you see guys doing these days. I walked in the front door and said I wanted to volunteer. And how 'bout this: I got turned away on spec. I couldn't believe it until I got a look around. They had interns climbing the walls. Well-dressed, college-educated upper class kids with the palest skin and most expensive suits you can imagine. Not the kind of crowd that was known in the 11th at that time. Businessmen were just beginning to dig in, but at the time it was pretty unusual. Little did I know, it was *the future*.

"Naïve kid that I was, I started investigating as much as a political science graduate would know how. I started asking questions around the neighborhood, interviewing voters, talking to volunteers on their off time, making out timetables of the campaign staff, and even going through their trash. I read so many shredded campaign documents it was ridiculous. I got pretty good at taping things back together." He chuckled.

"Their campaign releases were weird and cryptic, but what I brought back to Lionel he accepted gladly. 'Don't ask questions, Dolan,' he used to say. 'Just get the dirt. Get me *all* the dirt.' So I didn't ask, I just worked, nose to the ground.

"One of the few interns who turned out to be cooperative was a woman named Eliza Adams, a sweet red-haired young woman with freckles. The first time we met, she caught me snooping through a dumpster behind Bathory HQ. I don't know if she was horrified or what, but I'll never forget the first time I saw her. Thank goodness I'd already married Peggy, that's what I always say, or else I'd a-gotten involved in that whole mess myself." He shook his head, his eyes clouded with nostalgia and fear.

"Whole mess...?" I asked.

Mr. Dolan looked up at me, his gaze sobering in the afternoon light. He adjusted his grip on his cane, his palsied hand shaking. "You've heard plenty of stories about politicians, right? That president a few years back and that lady intern secretary he worked with? Things weren't that different forty some years ago, let me tell you, especially with a woman like Eliza. Good golly, Miss Molly," he shook his head. "The more I looked into it and watched them, the more I began to suspect something was a little... unsavory."

I was ready to open my mouth and ask what when Willa shook me off. *Let him tell it*, she mouthed to me.

"Bathory himself was a bachelor, never married. There was a lotta hubbub about what that meant and all, but he was young enough for it not to be unusual. If anything, it *helped* his youth support. Eliza, on the other hand, she *was* married. No one came right out and told me, but it wasn't too hard to figure," he said. "That ring on her finger?" He shrugged, uncomfortable. "No one said anything, you know. But I watched them. It was my job.

"I watched Bathory and his troop of volunteers; I watched his policy advisor, a guy named Byron something; I watched his speechwriter, who I think was named Everett; and I watched his campaign manager, someone named Alter...something? Vincent was it? Altimer...?" He shrugged as Willa and I exchanged glances. "I don't remember," he finally admitted. "But even if Bathory may have... well, *been with* another man's wife, he was on the up and up. His staff was like an army, strong and dedicated. At first, I followed him to rallies around the 11th district, mostly taking place on the steps of office buildings or in corporate parking lots. After a spell, I began following him to meetings in conference rooms, churches, factories, and community centers all over the city. Something about Bathory was working. People liked what they were hearing. Where I'd originally waved Lionel off, telling him how silly it was to fear a third party candidate from the 11th, I started to understand. He was a real threat.

"Anyway, Eliza and I got to be friends. Soon, we were meeting once a week or so. She'd talk about the campaign, trying to convince me I was on the wrong side, trying to talk up Bathory and all the great things he was going to accomplish.

"'The 11th District is going to bring about change,' she used to say, 'this is where the city is heading; it's the future. The 11th is going to lead the way for the next twenty years; it's going to raise this city out of its depression to something *greater*.' I didn't understand all of what she was going on about, but what Eliza was selling, I was starting to buy. I brought back what she said to Lionel, giving him paper-thin strategies about counter-movements in neighborhoods adjacent to the 11th, about corporate interventions on our behalf. But whatever hackneyed plans we put together to counter Bathory didn't pan out. Nothing could touch him. For a few dark months that spring, I had nearly given up the hope of a Hardy re-election victory.

"The worst of it started in early that summer. If you remember, in May the first major student protests against the war started popping up. Not long after that, in July, the Civil Rights Act became law. Other riots started because of that. Riots that were… less well-intentioned. People were angry and politics were getting more volatile by the week. Lionel had fired three of Mayor Hardy's policy advisors in the two previous months and was looking to sack another. Our staff, it seemed, was like a revolving door. Fresh bodies came onboard only to quit a few weeks later, angry and disillusioned. It was the way the whole country felt.

"The really weird thing, though, is that Bathory's campaign *didn't* waiver. They didn't have any last minute policy shifts or firings because of public pressure or political missteps. Byron and Everett and that Alt guy–the men who had been there since conception–were *still* there, as was their army of volunteers. Loyalty in their camp was incredibly impressive. Us, on the other hand? We seemed to be coming apart at the seams. And our campaign wasn't the only one struggling, either. Franklin Dorosso, the main challenger for the office–the guy we figured would be our main competition–was doing even worse. He'd replaced his campaign manager so many times that fresh meat was being flown in from California because the local pickings had all been used up."

"Why were Bathory's numbers so strong?" Willa asked.

"That's what I couldn't figure out," Mr. Dolan said. "I did so many polls and questionnaires and Q&A's that told me nothing. Bathory had near unanimous support in the 11th, and it was spreading. The 6th, 7th, and 8th were all starting to topple like dominos. I couldn't tell if it was word of mouth or what, but his numbers were miraculous, and every day they got better." He paused, taking a sip from a glass of water on a nearby coffee table.

"I continued to meet with Eliza on a weekly basis. She pressured me, hoping to turn me onto Bathory's side. 'Join now,' she said. 'It's not too late to be a part of the victory. Be a part of the change.' I kept turning her down. I liked Mayor Hardy. I'd voted for him. I had party loyalty and he'd been good to me. Despite Eliza's preachings, I still felt like *I* was doing something I believed in, but it was just getting us nowhere.

"At the summer's end came the race riots. It was hot and people were unhappy. The riots busting out were the nail in the city's coffin. 700 people arrested and 300 people injured. I'll never forget it. It looked like half the north side was on fire.

"Dorosso didn't even touch it. He pulled back on all race issues and his numbers plummeted. People didn't want a mayor who stuck his head in the sand. Bathory and Mayor Hardy went at it head on, pushing for civilian boards to analyze police brutality and civil rights. Over those few weeks in September, things were at their worst. We were losing staffers to Bathory everyday, and for the first time his numbers passed ours. Time wore on, and I continued to meet with Eliza.

"As September wound down, things were bleak. There just seemed to be no hope left. Still, our campaign pushed on, but we were all beginning to feel disillusioned. Lionel called me everyday, asking for some kind of silver bullet. But I maintained that there was nothing.

"In the beginning of October, after endless pressure from Lionel, I caved and began a report that I would *forever* regret. See, Lionel had gotten to me, saying that if Hardy lost the election, the city would fall apart. Somehow he convinced me that the race riots were just the beginning, and the only man to hold the town together was Hardy. For some reason, I believed him. I was... frightened. The report I wrote outlined an illicit relationship that Edward Bathory was having with a married campaign volunteer named Eliza Adams. I knew it was enough to ruin him, I'd known all along it was the silver bullet Lionel had prayed for, but I'd done everything in my power to avoid it. With the the report written, I set out to find evidence."

Mr. Dolan grew quiet. For the first time, I didn't want to ask him any questions; I didn't even want him to continue. I knew what was coming. Dolan's eyes were closed, his arthritic hands clasped on his lap.

"In my own defense," he said softly, "I believed that I didn't have any choice. 1964 was not a banner year for the successes of politics, and to complicate things, Lionel had promised me a job in the Mayor's new term if I could help secure victory. On top of it all, that October I learned that Peggy was pregnant with our first child. I worried so much about our future," he conceded, lowering his eyes. "I worried for her and for our baby," he looked up at his picture wall. "For Carolyn. What would happen if the Hardy campaign lost and my job disappeared along with it?" He closed his eyes and took a deep breath. "I couldn't bear to think of it. So I followed her. I followed Eliza.

"We usually met for lunch at a diner not far from Bathory HQ. One week after lunch, I followed her. It was easy because she wasn't expecting it. She returned to the office and got back to work. At five, I watched as the volunteers began filtering out, heading home for the day. Soon, only Bathory and Eliza remained. They left together, and I watched them from my car parked across the street. They got into the same car and drove to a hotel outside the city.

"I took pictures of them leaving the hotel a few hours later, hand in hand. I knew that the images along with my report would be enough. I called home and told Peggy not to wait up. Then I went back to the office to type it. I finished late, sometime after midnight. The office was empty by then, and I could have easily left it on Lionel's desk. I almost did. That would have been it, done. I just... I couldn't. I was raised believing politics to be above that, to be *more* than gossip and scandal. Do you understand? Politics are supposed to bring people together; to give people hope of something better. The thought of ruining Eliza's reputation was bad enough, but to think of destroying both of them was... just too much." Mr. Dolan paused, his face twisted in remembered pain. "I *couldn't*. I'm not a bad man," he said, looking up at us, "and I *knew* that. I wrote that report, but that was all I was capable of doing. I packed it up in my briefcase and took it home with me, planning on burning it in my fireplace. Except, I never got it home.

"I learned the next day that someone hit me with a brick halfway to my car on a sidewalk in Center City. I wasn't found until almost five o'clock the next morning." Absentmindedly, he raised a hand and felt the back of his head, his unfocused eyes staring into nothing. "All I remember is when I awoke, my briefcase was gone, and the report with it. I've never doubted that it was the reason I was attacked." He trailed off.

"Mr. Dolan," Willa said softly. "What happened then?"

He shook his head. "I kept watching them. Lionel was angry with me because I told him documents had been lost, but he didn't do anything about it seeing as I'd gotten my skull split in the process. So I watched Eliza and Bathory, hoping against hope that I was wrong. It happened on the afternoon of October 1, 1964, the same day the riots broke out at Berkeley. I was there to see Bathory get forced into a car by his own campaign manager. Through my binoculars, I saw the manila envelope in his hand, and I saw the back of the photographs as they pressed them into Bathory's face. I saw the fear on the man's face, the *terror*. I knew they were my photographs; I knew it then and I know it now. They pushed him inside the car and drove off. I never saw him again. No one did.

"He was still on the ticket, of course, but it went nowhere. The funding dried up, the miraculous support all but vanished. There never was a scandal, or even a police investigation into his disappearance. I contacted my local precinct after a few days of terrible guilt, but they wouldn't listen. I quit my job with Hardy the following day. For the remaining weeks leading up to Election Day, I searched for Eliza. But it was all in vain. I did not find her. I didn't find *anything*. The election office that had once been such a hub of energy and change was now nothing, all but empty and manned by one young volunteer answering the phone." His voice had taken on a hollow distant sound and his gaze had lowered to the floor. "I got a job working in a library a few weeks later. I... I didn't look back," he admitted. "You can understand why."

With an unsteady hand he removed his glasses and wiped them off on his shirt. His hands shook badly, a shake that had to do with more than just age. The energy I'd seen upon arriving was gone, replaced by a slow, haggard weariness.

"It wasn't your fault, Mr. Dolan," Willa said.

The old man smiled. "It may not have been, dear, but it will take more than your assurances to convince me otherwise. The only person that can convince me of that probably died with Mr. Edward Bathory more than forty years ago." He was silent for a moment. I listened to the slow ticking of a clock as Mr. Dolan wiped a swollen knuckle against his wet eyes. "I've tried so hard to forget it all. And just like that, it all came back."

"I'm so sorry," Willa said, under her breath.

The old man sniffled and shook his head slowly, warding off the terrible thoughts that had plagued him so. He took a few labored breaths before forcing a smile, looking almost as he had when we'd first arrived, but not quite. He had forgotten about everything, pushed it deep into the recesses of his memory and moved on with his life. That is until we dug it back up. The guilt that weighed upon the old man had drifted across the room like a contagion. It settled around my shoulders and stayed with me until well after we were done comforting the old man and left his small cottage. I felt a terrible sadness at all that had happened and all we had learned.

Willa's eyes told me I was not alone.

CHAPTER 24. CHANGES

We were silent as we walked out of Green Lawn Estates, Mr. Dolan's words still weighing heavily on both our minds. It had occurred to me that if Willa and I had not appeared, the old man might have lived the rest of his days without dwelling on what had happened all those years ago. We'd done a bang-up job dredging it up. Thus, guilt.

I'd called a cab, and it was waiting for us at the front gate. As we rode in silence, I pulled the crumpled piece of paper from my pocket. I studied the addresses, déjà vu tapping me on the shoulder. After a moment it hit me. The second address was for the oft avoided Death Collector, Jonathan Keats. I groaned.

"What is it?"

"This address," I said, pointing. "It's... it's a joke." I thought back to the last time Gil and Finch had sent me into his office. "They're just busting my balls. It's no a big deal."

"Are you sure?"

"Yeah. We already got what we needed from him. They like getting under my skin, that's all."

"All right."

We lapsed into silence again, and I watched the 'burbs out the window, green lawns and minivans.

"We have to find her," Willa said finally.

"Who?"

"The woman, Eliza Adams."

"Dolan said she was gone. Disappeared. By now she's probably dead. If the..." I glanced at the driver and lowered my voice. "If the *vamps* haven't gotten to her in the last forty years, then she probably died of old age."

"I can find her," Willa insisted.

"What makes you think you can find her today if Dolan–her own friend–couldn't find her the day after she disappeared?"

"Because it's my job," she said. "It's what I'm good at: digging up info. I can do it."

She talked, and I listened. When we pulled up outside Gil's office building, I slipped a handful of bills to the driver before stepping out onto the curb and holding the door for Willa.

"Are you sure this is a good idea?" I asked for the fifth or sixth time.

"Positive." She scribbled a number on a piece of paper and handed it to me.

"What's this?" I asked.

"My cell. Call me if there's a problem."

"Wait, you're leaving *now*? I thought we were all gonna ponder it over some tater tots and you'd do it next week or something."

"Nope, now. I have to do this, Dylan. I have to know. This is important. I know it is. And I can get it done quickly on my own."

"No, Willa, this is a mistake. Let me come with you. Me or Finch. You shouldn't be alone. Bluebeard wants you, and he's got people out looking for you right now. You have to stay with us. We have to stick together."

"I can take care of myself, remember? The night of the charity ball? How long was I away from you guys? All night." She grinned. "I'm better at this than you give me credit."

"Well…" Point taken. "*Gil* isn't going to like this," I said, struggling for any reason to keep her from leaving.

She smiled again. "I know. That's why I'm leaving now, before we go upstairs and he can talk me out of it. It's just easier this way." She gave me a quick hug and my heart skipped a beat Middle School style. "Be careful," she said. "And good luck tonight with your mojo doctor. Sorry I won't be there."

Without another word, she turned and disappeared into the busy sidewalk crowd. I swore but let her go. She had that determined look in her eye. I knew there was nothing I could do to stop her, nothing short of physical restraint. I watched her bobbing ponytail recede into the distance and realized that the trying events of the past few days had somehow created a bond between us. It made me smile. When she was out of sight, I turned and headed back up to Zero HQ.

***

"You let her do *what*?" Gil shouted when I relayed the news. He was seated behind his desk, feet propped over his eponymous leather-bound tome, a mismatched LEGO construct in his hands. At my declaration his mouth fell open, spilling his pipe onto the desktop and scattering ashes across a pile of papers.

"I couldn't stop her, boss," I explained sheepishly. "I'm sorry."

"Damnit, big man." He stood, abandoning the LEGO thing beside his pipe. "Dot!" he shouted. There was a pattering of quick footsteps on carpet before Gil's ever-loyal secretary appeared.

"Yes, sir?" She peeked her head in the office door wearing a polka-dotted turtleneck sweater, her hair pulled up in a tight bun on top of her head.

"Get the tentacles going again. Willa Bascombe's on the lam again."

"Tentacles, sir?"

"You know," he said, waving his arms about. "The tentacles. The search things. The guys we pay to find people, remember?"

She nodded. "I think you call them the ferrets, Mr. Abercrombie."

"Yeah," he grunted. "The ferrets! Set 'em free."

She nodded once more and disappeared.

"Boss, this didn't work last time; what makes you think they'll find her this time?" I asked.

"What exactly is the problem?" Finch said, stepping into the office in Dottie's wake. "I heard your shouting halfway down the–"

"Gigantor here let Willa go off on her own," Gil said, pointing a condemning finger at me.

"I didn't *let* her," I explained again. "I couldn't stop her!"

"Blah, blah, blah, blah," Gil said, angrily sweeping a handful of loose LEGO pieces onto the floor. "We need her, Dylan. We need her *safe*. We need her *alive*. Capice?"

182

"Don't you think I know that? Do you think I wanted to let her go? I'm pretty sure I know exactly how important it is that we keep her safe, all right? I get it. It wasn't my idea, nor did she have my blessing. Get the hell off it, Gil. She's a grown woman, I couldn't stop her."

Gil straightened, the anger evaporating from his face. Surprise took its place. A long moment passed as he fixed a level stare at me. He may have been surprised, but just beneath the surface I could see the anger; it was unmistakable. A moment passed before Gil rounded the desk and began to pick up the LEGOS he'd scattered a few moments before. He didn't look at me again. I turned and walked out of his office.

I paced the office with my name on the door, although it couldn't have felt more *unlike* my office. I'd done nothing to make it my own—not even brought in my Flyers mug–and I hadn't been back home in days. The Zero summer-camp-immersion treatment was beginning to take its toll. At the moment I wanted nothing more than to go home and be alone. I swore under my breath and stood before the great floor to ceiling windows, looking down on the activity of the city streets below. Behind me, the door closed.

I turned to see Finch take a seat in one of the visitor's chairs. "What do you want?" I asked.

"Are you all right?" he asked.

"Just *dandy*."

His face was impassive. I knew that Finch wasn't Mr. Sensitive, as his hollow shark eyes reminded me. I stared him down. I blinked first.

"What?" I finally asked.

"What happened?"

"What do you mean?"

"What made Mrs. Bascombe leave in such a hurry?"

I sighed, taking a seat across from Finch in the other visitor's chair. "We met with Mr. Dolan, that pollster hired by the Hardy campaign in '63."

"Yes, I set up the meeting."

"Okay, well it turns out that this Edward Bathory, the third party vamp candidate, was probably killed by his own people."

Finch straightened up. "His own people?"

"Yeah. Dolan remembers our boy Altimerach being involved. Stuff went south. Next thing you know, Alt's hustling Bathory into some car, never to be seen again."

"And how does this involve Mrs. Bascombe?"

"It turns out that Bathory was having an affair with a woman named Eliza Adams. A married woman."

"And Mr. Dolan believes that is why Bathory was removed from the election?"

"Yes. To Dolan, a man caught having an affair with a married woman is plenty reason to undo his political campaign."

"Did Mr. Dolan pause on the fact that murder was a rather severe punishment?"

I shrugged. "He didn't seem to make the connection. But he blames himself. He was the one that outed them."

"And where is Mrs. Bascombe now?" Finch asked.

"Trying to locate Eliza Adams."

"She is most certainly dead now," Finch said, his voice level and cold. "If the vampires killed Mr. Bathory, then they certainly killed this Mrs. Adams."

"I know, that's what I told Willa. She was... stubborn."

Finch smiled. "All in all a quite productive afternoon meeting, I'd say."

I shrugged again, feeling more disheartened and annoyed than anything else. "What'd you guys learn?"

"Well, Gil's meeting was a waste of time. Bascombe's campaign head of policy cancelled, leaving Boss to talk with a finance intern instead. Nothing there. My meeting was a bit more fruitful. I met with our current Mayor's former re-election campaign advisor, and it was quite illuminating. His name is Allen Calder and he was incensed. Until the last few days he'd had no idea that Mayor Gardner had even considered not running. They'd made plans of policy and strategy, going so far as to outline things he'd hoped to achieve in the first fiscal quarter."

"So why did the Mayor withdraw?"

Finch smiled and raised his hands cryptically. "Mr. Calder had no idea. As I said, he was quite angry."

"We need to speak with the Mayor," I said.

Finch laughed. "Gil's connections are good, and as they say, 'money talks,' but a meeting with the Mayor will be hard to come by."

He was right, of course, but it was the only way to know anything for sure. I sighed and collapsed into my desk chair. I looked at Finch, and he stared back at me with unsympathetic eyes.

"What's going on with you?" he asked after a moment.

"I don't know. I'm a little freaked out. The djinn, Cally's goons wanting to crush my head, and now this whole magic thing I've got going. And Willa."

"You know she's married, Dylan."

"Yes, I know that, thank you. It's not that. I just worry about her. I know I have to keep my distance. Yes, you were right about that. It's just... hard, that's all."

"I imagine it is, Dylan." He smiled. His words felt well-rehearsed, but its intentions were true enough, so I didn't mind. I knew at that point that Finch didn't feel the same way the rest of us did, but I knew he tried to be there for us anyway. For that I was grateful.

"Thanks, Finch."

He nodded and stood. "Given the concerns on your mind, why don't we keep your mind a bit distracted? Come with me."

Finch led me from my office down the winding corridor back towards Dottie's desk and the main entrance. A few twists and turns of the hall later we were walking into one of the offices I was certain was deserted. Finch closed the door behind us.

The office was far from deserted. Weapons lined the walls and stood on archaic wooden racks, filling much of the room. Swords, shields, axes, maces, spears, chains, and a scattered assortment of firearms covered most of the room. Finch walked over to a wall mounted rack and grabbed a short sword that looked very familiar.

"This is yours," he said, handing it to me. "It's the same weapon you used that first night on the dock against the djinn. I like to believe that a person has a special relationship with a weapon they've used in defense of their own life. So, without getting too caught up in ceremony, I give this sword to you." He handed it to me. It was a solid weight in my hand, not too heavy, but just heavy enough to remind me that it was a dangerous weapon.

"This one is mine," he said, pointing at a long sword that hung nearby. "Sometimes I use an ax or a mace, but I always come back to this sword. She has saved me–if not my life, then my skin–many times. I think it's equally important to find a suitable name for your blade as well," he said, his voice becoming oddly nostalgic. He ran a hand up and down the flat of the long sword's blade. "So, I named her Aenesthethema de La Roche de la Mort." He smiled. "It's a family name."

I looked down at the short sword in my hand, a rather quaint–albeit wholly respectable–weapon next to Finch's Aenesthethema. "I dub thee... Carlyle," I said. Finch gave me a crooked stare. "What?" I asked. "It's a family name. Mother's maiden."

"All right, we have a little time before we have to meet the good Doctor, so I thought I'd show you one or two things." He lifted his sword from the wall. In the enclosed space I took a step back. Finch smiled.

"Fire is the most volatile of elemental summonings, so in a way it's actually the easiest to conjure, but at the same time, it is also the most dangerous. You have to be focused when you conjure fire, or else it will dissipate. For example..." Finch turned his focus from me to the blade of his long sword, his dark eyes locking on the slightly wavering blade as his lips began to move. His incantations were low, just under his breath, so the words were lost to me, but soon after he began speaking, a flickering light began to run up and down the length of the blade.

At first it was clear and colorless, a translucent shimmering light that cast ripples over the dull grey steel. Finch continued his incantation, his voice rising to a nearly audible level as the colorless waves began to take on a pale yellow light, casting a glow over his face. The yellow light began to grow in intensity, becoming denser and more tangible before the shimmering was transformed into a controlled burning flame that sheathed the length of his sword. I stepped back, feeling the heat from the blade. Finch looked impassive, but I felt some sense of awe at the near biblical image before me.

His eyes locked on the wavering blade, Finch concentrated fiercely as the fire grew in tangibility until the metal of the blade was completely lost, totally covered in the consuming flame.

He ceased his incantation, finally raising his eyes to mine. The flames burned and burned. "How's that?" he asked.

I laughed, my mouth falling open. The flames flickered as Finch moved the blade side to side. "I'm going to teach you to do this," he said.

"I can't do that," I mumbled.

"I know you can do it," he said. "It is easy." Yet even as he spoke, the fire burning on the sword flickered, like a light bulb at the end of a faulty wire, and dimmed. He turned his eyes back to the blade and began the incantation anew, but it was too late. The flame flickered again and dimmed once more, this time severely. The steel blade showed itself through the fire. He continued the incantation, but after a few seconds the fire was completely gone. "Damn," he said, shaking his head. "It seems I am rusty."

I reached one hand out warily, holding it close to the blade. I could feel no heat. After a moment, I tentatively touched the metal with my bare skin. It was cool.

"Fairly impressive, right?" he said, smiling.

"Uh yeah?"

"I will let you use my incantations again. Remember, it's *Porast Vatra*. But you'll have to visualize it; guide the flame. Channel it into your sword this time. Hold the blade with two hands," he lifted my second hand to the grip. "It will take much more power to channel the flames, but if you focus you may be able to begin the conjuration. Ready?"

I gripped the sword between my two shaking hands and stared up and down the length of the short blade. Taking a deep breath, I closed my eyes and envisioned the fire growing from the hilt upward, fierce yellow flames flickering in the enclosed room, casting strange shadows across the walls. I imagined the heat against my skin from the unnatural flames, and I imagined the cold metal I'd touch when they'd ceased to exist at my command. In my mind's eye, the flames were real enough to exist, palpable enough to touch with the tips of my fingers. I opened my mouth to speak when Finch stopped me.

"Dylan," he said, his voice just above a whisper. "Open your eyes."

I opened them, struggling not to lose my concentration and the hard image I'd formed in my mind. But as I opened my eyes, I *saw* exactly what I'd been envisioning in my head: a fierce sheath of fire. The flames writhed over the surface of the blade, not wavering or flickering like Finch's, but burning an intensely bright blue, hot enough to make beads of sweat form on the surface of my skin. Now it was Finch's turn to take a step back, a look of shock painted across his face.

"Bloody hell," he said. "You're a little more powerful than I had expected, my friend."

I swallowed. "Okay, great. But how do I make this *not* on fire anymore?"

CHAPTER 25. DOCTOR ELROY PONDEROSA

We left the office with a brief "We're going out" before adjourning to the Tank for a scary ride into the ghetto. Finch assured me that Gil wouldn't mind some space.

We drove due west into the wastelands, our destination Haverford and fifty-something. Finch talked the whole way; I'm fairly certain he was trying to calm my frayed nerves.

"I didn't know if I'd be able to come," Finch said, "but I am glad I could. I imagine this will make you... uncomfortable. But it shouldn't. The best analogy is a visit to the doctor's office. Although not like Dr. Hanas. A little different. Dr. Ponderosa will administer one or more of a few simple tests, all quite painless, in an effort to find the source of the... the *power* you seem to have acquired in recent times."

"You're certain this is new, right?"

"Reasonably certain, yes. It would be nearly impossible for you to have carried such power with you for your entire life and not have unleashed it at some point."

"Just out of curiosity, how powerful are we talking? Because you're beginning to make me nervous."

"Relax, Dylan, I assure you that everything is fine." He took to staring out the window as he gave me directions, not the most comforting response. "And it won't hurt at all," he repeated. "I don't think."

We left Penn behind and the campuses of University City. Slowly, the buildings began to slide downhill. Graffiti became more and more prevalent on the battered facades of faded brick or stuccoed townhouses. It wasn't long before vacant lots, abandoned storefronts, and burnt out, boarded-up homes became more and more common. The only greenery in the neighborhood was a handful of dead trees or patches of grass in empty lots. Tumbleweeds of garbage blew past us on the barren roadways.

I looked at Finch. "Are we almost there?"

"I assure you, Dylan, Dr. Ponderosa's office is perfectly safe," Finch said, reading my mind.

"At this point I'm just worried about getting there alive."

"You're being dramatic," he said.

"Says the guy who can't die," I muttered.

When Finch tapped the window and announced that we'd arrived, I figured he was kidding. His narrow finger was pressed to the glass in the direction of a large brick warehouse that could have doubled for a public school circa 1955. Most of the windows had been long since broken. The main entrance was chained closed and there were colorful pastiches of spray paint pockmarking the entire front of the structure.

I pulled the Tank up to the curb in front of the huge building and killed the engine. Finch opened the passenger side door and stepped out. I followed and locked up nervously.

"It's perfectly all right," he assured me.

"Better safe than sorry."

"Trust me," he said. "We could leave a handful of one hundred dollar bills on the front seat and they'd all be here when we came outside."

"I haven't cashed my first check," I said. "We can use hundreds from your wallet."

"Dr. Ponderosa owns this entire neighborhood. It looks the way it does because he chooses to keep a low profile. Nearly every building around is a research facility. He works very hard to keep up appearances, as you can see. Or so I have heard."

"Uh huh."

"Follow me," Finch said, turning and heading around the huge building towards the back.

One long walk down a trash-filled alleyway later, we emerged in a fenced-in lot surrounding a weary looking auto repair shop. The sound of hydraulic drills was loud in the enclosed space. Through the open garage door I could see a beat-up Volkswagen lifted from the ground with a worker standing beneath its chassis. A hanging light lit the mangled undercarriage, casting shadows across the ground. Above the gaping garage door was a sign that said **ZACK'S CAR SHOP**, but someone had spray painted a huge pink "Y" over the Z, effectively making the sign read **YACK'S CAR SHOP**. Beneath it, a neon open sign buzzed lazily.

"Is this the part where we clap and the wall opens again?" I asked, pointing at a blank brick wall.

"Don't be ridiculous," he said. I followed him into the open garage. The stink of oil and grease met me in a wave. Somewhere I could hear the muted sound of a radio playing classical music.

"Hello?" Finch asked. The tech standing beneath the Volkswagen turned to face us. He wore a filthy jumpsuit and a confused look.

"Yeah, can I help you fellas?"

"Hello, Mr..." Finch leaned forward to read the greasy name patch on the man's uniform. "...Jackson. My name is Finch, is the King available?"

Jack the automan smirked and shook his head. "Yeah, sure. One sec, buddy." He turned and disappeared into the depths of the garage.

Finch turned back to me. "It is just for show, you see," he said, waving his arms about. "All this."

I nodded. "Yeah, sure."

"I nearly forgot, Dylan, you must call Dr. Ponderosa 'the King,' all right? It is of dire importance. Do you understand?"

"Ponderosa?"

"Yes, Elroy Ponderosa. But that's the King to you and me, agreed?"

"Sure, okay." I shrugged. The situation was getting weirder and weirder.

After a few minutes, Jackson the automan emerged with a younger technician following behind him. "Here he is," Mr. Jackson said, waving at us before turning his attention back to the Volkswagen.

The man who emerged from behind Jack wasn't much of a man, he was a kid, sixteen at most. He had acne and was overweight. Like Jackson the automan, he wore a grease-stained jumpsuit with the garage's logo on it. The name patch said **EL JEFE**.

"Ahh," Finch sighed, smiling. "The King."

The kid nodded. "Yeah, that's right," he answered in a squeaky voice.

I stared at the kid and blinked a half-dozen times or so. Would you want to go to a twelve-year old doctor? It had to be a ruse. The garage, the kid, the ghetto, the grease? Finch was right, it was all just a clever disguise. No, a *great* disguise. Ingenious. I closed my eyes and waited for the pavement to open and a platform to lower me into the ground, depositing me in a beautiful study with Oriental carpeting, endless bookcases, beakers, and Bunsen burners. There was some mad scientist doctor somewhere down there just waiting to diagnose me, I was sure of it. I opened my eyes and I was still in the garage. With the kid. And the grease. And Jackson the automan.

Beside me, Finch introduced himself. "I called you this morning," he said. "This is the man I wanted you to take a look at."

"I was expecting you later," the kid said, running a chubby hand through an Elvis coiffe, pomade and all. "I'm still on the clock right now, know what I'm sayin', pardner?"

"I do apologize, it has become a rather pressing issue that we get my friend diagnosed immediately. We are more than willing to compensate you generously for your time."

The kid looked at each of us. "I know you," he said to Finch. "And I know your boss. You do good things 'round town." He nodded and tipped an invisible 10 gallon hat. "I appreciate that. So I'll help you out, pardner. What do you need?"

"An analysis here regarding my friend would be infinitely illuminating. He has recently shown some abilities that were... unexpected."

The kid turned and tipped an invisible cowboy hat to Jackson the automan. He turned back to us. "Why don't y'all come back into my lab?" he said.

He turned and led us into the garage's office. Stacks of paper were piled on a cluttered desk beside an open book and a statue of a hula girl in a grass skirt. On the wall was a periodic table of elements between a pair of Elvis posters. The kid crammed a handful of Bazooka Joe into his mouth and pointed at a pair of folding chairs. He took his place behind the desk.

"All right, out with it, pardner. What is your friend? A clone? A ghost? An automaton? A homunculus? A revenant? No, not revenant. I'm gonna go with zombie. He does look kind of... dumb."

I opened my mouth to speak when Finch stopped me.

"Er, no," he said. "This is my friend, his name is Dylan. He's just a man, a real live living human man. Recently he seems to have been imbued with some sort of power."

"All righty," the kid said, blowing a bubble with his wad of gum. "What sort of power?"

"Therein lies the problem," Finch said. "I don't know. I can tell you that it is powerful," Finch said, choosing his words carefully. "Very powerful. Dylan has never before been a magical practitioner. Not until just recently, that is."

"How recently?"

"Approximately two or three days."

"Conscious or subconscious?"

"I believe the summoning was subconscious," Finch said. "Though the outcome was quite consciously desired. However, my friend did not know he was capable of such a feat."

I watched the exchange with anxious fascination. They went back and forth as if I was, in fact, nothing but a zombie.

"Wait a second," I finally interrupted, "Just wait one damn second. What's going on here? And where's this Doctor Ponderosa? Is he your Dad or something, kid?"

Beside me, Finch grew rigid.

The kid had straightened up in his chair as much as he was able, though his eyes hit me about mid-chest. Puffing himself up, he looked up at me and scowled. "You can get outta here, you old fart, you got me? I don't need this kinda hassle. I'm a professional at work here. You got better things to do, you can go." He pointed a chubby finger at the door and chewed his cud of gum. "So buzz off."

"King," Finch said with a boyish grin. "I'm sure we can come to some kind of arrangement that would allow us to retain your services. Some kind of... incentive?"

"Yeah, and I'll give you a Twinkie if you're good," I mumbled.

The kid glared at me before turning his eyes back to Finch. "Double my fee," he said. "No, wait." He shifted the gum from one side of his mouth to the other like chewing tobacco. "Triple."

"Done."

"And I'm the King, remember? Nobody in this town's capable of doing what I can do." He pointed a finger at me. "You better remember that when I've saved your life, old timer, got me?"

"Uh, yeah, all right, champ."

He nodded smugly, a wide grin spreading across his face to reveal horribly crooked teeth. I grimaced.

"Dylan, was it?" he asked me.

"Yeah, that's right."

"This way, pardner." He stood and walked a narrow path between boxes filled with car parts and piles of old carbon forms. I followed with Finch a few steps behind. The path led out the office's back door into another condemned lot. The three of us huddled beneath a makeshift tent–the big plastic kind you're likely to see at family reunions–surrounded by stacks of tires. A Rottweiler chained to a nearby stake commenced going berzerk at the sight of us.

"Shut up, Burt!" the kid shouted (to no avail).

Standing against the rear outer wall of the office was a huge wooden chair outfitted with electrodes, dials, tiny engines, chains, and enough convoluted wiring to make a proud electrician cringe. On the armrests and the front legs were straps, similar to the kind you'd expect to find on the electric chair. My breath caught in my throat at the sight of the terrible contraption.

"Old sparky?" I said.

The King grinned. "Hop in, pardner," he said.

I looked at Finch, my eyes pleading. It looks like the kid was gonna get the last laugh this time. Finch looked at the chair and nodded. "It is important, Dylan. I swear," he admitted.

I took a deep breath, gathered my courage, and stepped up and into the chair. The kid took great pleasure in securing the leather straps to my wrists and ankles before closing a metallic claw-like covering over my right hand. The claw was outfitted with sprockets and cogs connected to long spindly fingers. The fingers ended with long needles that touched my skin when the contraption was closed. He turned a key on the claw's surface, winding the contraption like a music box from hell.

When the key was wound, he knelt and poured gasoline into a generator sitting beside me. Having filled the tank, he gave the pull-chord a tug, forcing a weary engine to turn over unsuccessfully. After a second and third pull, the engine caught, roaring to life. I looked up at Finch.

"Come on, man," I pleaded. "This thing has gasoline in it? And how about some alcohol swabs?"

The kid stood and smiled at me again, adjusting gears and calibrating knobs around the chair. "Don't you worry, chief! I'm a professional, 'member?" From a pocket on his jumpsuit, he pulled a stack of punch cards. He flipped through the stack, arranging and re-arranging before he knelt and slid the cards into what looked like a thousand-year old computer on the ground, one card at a time. Finally, with a flick of a few switches, electricity poured into the chair.

I sucked in a deep breath and held it as a cathode ray tube beside my face exploded to life, sending bright blue lines of power vibrating up and down the length of the tube. All at once, I felt the electricity, like the touch of a creeping caterpillar against every inch of my skin. Cogs on the chair began to turn, twisting against springs and winding cables, a long chain of events that seemed to bring the entire chair to life.

Against my hand, I felt the claw's needles jab painlessly into my skin. Drops of blood began to fall to the ground. The cathode tube turned from blue to pink to red, casting a wild shadow across my face. Against my back, I could feel smaller needles injecting themselves into my body against my backbone, touching nerves and sending waves of numbness up and down my body. Over the roaring of the generator, I could still hear the Rottweiler bark from across the tiny lot. Beside me, Finch looked on stoically.

When the cathode sputtered and fell into darkness, I was certain the test was nearing its end. I was about to exhale when a pair of thick electromagnets extended out from the chair on a mechanical arm and was pressed against my temple. A piercing bolt of lightning ripped through my brain as the magnet heated almost instantaneously from ice cold to fiery hot. I ground my teeth in pain and groaned, but the sound was lost in surges of electricity and dog barking.

I opened my mouth to holler when the pain abruptly ceased. The metal claw raised itself from my hand and wrist before retracting itself back into the chair. The electromagnets followed a minute later, steaming as they slid away from me and disappeared from my field of vision.

I was covered in sweat, and despite the warm April evening, I was shivering. With a kick, the King killed the generator, leaving the tiny lot in silence but for Burt the barking dog. My head was ringing, and I had a hard time seeing one of anything.

"Success!" the King said. "Perfect as pie. Probably." He motioned for Finch to release me from my constraints. He did so quickly and with an apologetic shrug.

"Are you all right?" he asked.

"No. And it's a good thing. If I was I'd kick that kid's ass," I said. "Yours too." Okay, so I tried to say that, but it probably sounded more like, "Hurrh. Erda udd ming, trick da mid's gasss. Errggs moo."

He pulled me from the chair and rested me on a low stack of tires. I hadn't eaten in hours, but I felt ready to vomit profusely. Like *Exorcist* vomit. Finch propped me up and turned his attention back to the kid.

"Did we learn anything, King?" he asked.

"You betcha, pardner." The kid turned his attention to a small vial he held in his hand. "Had to get the difference engine up to a certain speed. It separates neurological waves from hyperneurological waves. Does that make sense? In layman's terms it's like brainwaves versus magicwaves. I designed this machine to measure them. Also, when the blood gets polarized, it separates the physiological cells from the magical. So then what I'm able to draw out is a sample of non-physiological hypermatter." He raised the vial. "Got me, friends? The chair does all that. And I use the chair because magic can't be read by modern technology. As soon as we can find a way to make thaumaturgy and nanotechnology coexist, this process'll be a lot easier." He smiled. "Soon enough, I'll be pilotin' that program, too, pardner. But for now, we've gotta lean on the good old fashioned stuff." He patted the chair. "What can I say, friends? It gets the job done."

"Ah," Finch said, grinning. "Brilliant."

From my perch on the tires, I bent over and vomited on the pavement. Finch and the kid ignored me.

"What are the results?" Finch said, leaning closer to the vial, which had begun to glow.

"I'm about to find out, and I need to hurry. Hypermatter, or this stuff here," he said, raising the vial again, "is only able to exist on this plane for a few moments once separated from its host."

As he finished speaking, an old dot matrix printer snapped to life and began churning out a long report on perforated paper. The kid bent down, squinting at the faded ink numbers. I could see him move his lips while he read. I groaned.

"Holy Hannah," he said, standing back up. "Looks like you've been matched, pardner."

"He's been matched, King?" Finch said, taking a step back and tossing a glance at me. "Are you certain?"

The kid lifted the long document as the old dot matrix printer continued to spew out endless readings. "Uh, yeah." He ran a stained finger along the lines, reading. "Recently. The body is still changing to adapt to the vael."

"Vael?" I murmured.

"That's right, Dylan. A vael," Finch nodded excitedly, clapping his hands like a child. "Bloody hell. I've only read about it," he said. "I've never actually met someone who was *matched*."

The King nodded and blew a bubble with his Bazooka Joe. "Looks like it. His body is still changing on a chemical level to accommodate the vael. Though it looks like the changes are nearly complete." He read another few lines. "Yeah, definitely."

The printer finally ceased and the King tore the last page free. He turned from the printer and rifled a cardboard box from a pile of tires. Opening it, he pulled a tiny glass eye-dropper from a mess of instruments and a long rectangular paper filled with small colored squares. The colors changed in intensity from blue at the left to red at the right.

"Now we can do a strength test," the kid said. "Before this baby putters out and we gotta do it again. You don't wanna do that again, do you pardner?"

I looked at him. A moment later, I bent over a tower of tires and emptied whatever was left of my lunch. When I straightened, I saw the King drop a tiny circle of glowing fluid onto the sheet. He'd chosen the middle, the center square, which looked like it was a lush green.

When the fluid touched the magical litmus test, the paper erupted in blue flames. The King yelped and dropped the tester to the ground. With the heel of one battered sneaker, he stomped the small flame, extinguishing the fire in a puff of smoke.

Finch took a step back and eyed the smoking remains. "Um, King? What does that mean?"

"Hold on, hold on," he said, pulling a fresh test from the box. Drawing another glowing orb from the vial, he dropped a second dot of the material onto the litmus test, this time at the crimson red square at the far right of the test.

For a moment, the crimson square turned a neon yellow before the paper began smoking madly. This time, the young doctor was able to grind the paper into the ground *before* the fire started. He looked at Finch and took a deep breath.

"Well, King?" Finch asked. "You've had your second test. What can you tell us?"

The King raised the small vial of my magic goo to his eye. It glowed brightly for another moment before turning black and hardening into stone. He raised his eyebrows and turned back to us, his mouth hanging slightly agape.

"Well," he said slowly. "That little paper there's the power test, pardner. Simple but effective. And, your old friend here, Finch? He's, um... well he's off the damn charts."

My head spun with a new fear. I cursed not eating a heartier lunch. At that moment, I really could've gone for another good puke.

CHAPTER 26. THE SCIENCE OF IT ALL

"It's mostly physics," Finch explained. "And physics on a quantum level. When I first learned about magic as a younger man, we didn't know much about quantum physics, but years go by and they learn the real science of it all."

"I don't know what you're talking about," I said. I was driving the Tank back towards Gil's Center City office. After being dropped on the equivalent of the thaumaturgic rack, my "driving" was more like controlled swerving. I felt sick and not in the mood for cryptic explanations.

"My understanding is a bit arcane, I admit," Finch said. "Physics, especially physics on the quantum level, wasn't really discovered until I was, well, old. As you can imagine, I've had a hard time coming to terms with this new science of yours." We hit a pothole and I gagged, fighting back a dry heave. Finch didn't notice.

"You said vael," I said. "What the hell is a vael?".

"That is a difficult question to answer," Finch said.

"Well, try."

He took his time, looking out the window and formulating his thoughts. After a few minutes he began. "Magic is not the 'mystical art' you've come to believe that it is," he said. "As I said, it all comes back to what we now know as physics. Rather than believing that you are able to harness fire because of some strange and unnatural control of the elements, you have to understand that you are able to harness fire because you have been able to tap into natural powers present on another dimensional plane, although I've been told that 'dimensional plane' is a sort of a misnomer." He laughed offhandedly and shook his head.

"Lost," I said.

He sighed. "All right, have you ever heard of the cosmological theories of the multiverse?"

I shook my head as we came to a stop light.

"Popular culture may have adapted the term as 'parallel universes' or 'alternate realities.'"

"Yeah sure, I've heard of them."

"Essentially, each is referencing the theory of the multiverse; the theory that there are many different universes that together make up everything that *is*."

"Okay."

"The important thing to remember is that we live in *one* of these universes, one of many. Do you follow?"

I nodded.

He continued. "So while we have a set of physical laws and physical constants here, other universes in the multiverse will have a different sets of physical laws and constants *there*. For example, something normal and household that we take for granted here–something like a magnetic field–may be extremely volatile or even impossible to generate on a different level of the multiverse. Are you still with me? In essence, a person on another level of the multiverse that is able to tap into *our* physical laws to create a magnetic field would appear to have harnessed some sort of extraordinary and unnatural force, correct?" I nodded again. "Something quite analogous to a mystical or spiritual force, but it is in fact neither. What we call 'magic' is little more than a different matrix of physical constants. So when we use 'magic' here, we're simply tapping into the great pool of the multiverse and temporarily realigning our own set of physical laws."

It made a little sense. I put the Tank in gear and got us going as the light turned green. A light rain began to fall, pattering softly on the windshield. "I think I get it," I said.

"Unfortunately, you don't. Not yet," Finch said grinning sardonically. "Because I don't understand it yet and people who have been studying magic for their entire lives do not either. But that is the most basic framework. Most magics on this plane are an almost natural physical or psychological process that your body and mind are able to catalyze subconsciously. That's why a great many people who are born with the power to tap the multiverse do it unknowingly before they are even educated as to what magic *is*. Does that make sense?"

"You mean our minds and bodies naturally have a preconceived understanding of this 'multiverse' before we even do?"

"Yes," Finch said. "For some of us there is an ingrained notion that has left ... something like a watermark on our psyche. That is why magic is natural to some people. Some people are born with a powerful ability hardwired into them that makes them able to dip into the multiverse and to understand it *naturally*. To some people, dabbling in the laws of the multiverse comes almost second-nature. And then there are others–a great many others, at that–who are never able. Which brings us to the vael."

"The thing the King said I have?"

"You do have it, indeed, Dylan. We saw the proof firsthand already."

"You mean the test?"

"No, I mean when you altered the outcome of the roulette game, when you immolated that trash can, and when you were able to conjure flames on your sword without even using an incantation to focus your energy. That kind of power is not easy to come by. "

I swallowed. My throat was dry and I could taste the lingering burn of bile at the back of my mouth. Outside, the rain was picking up slowly. The windshield wipers scraped across the glass with a *grrrrrrrp*. "Go on."

"There has been a search going on since the beginning of time to harness something that will allow normal people to have complete mastery of what we now call the multiverse, to make use of the limitless powers there. The search has been going on for a very, very long time. Talismans and charms, potions and remedies, people have been struggling not only to understand magic, but to make it accessible. And accessible for *everyone*. But for literally hundreds of years, this Holy Grail of magical conjuration and control went undiscovered. Around the turn of the century, however, there were rumors around the otherworld community that someone had found something. Or, more to the point, some*thing* had found some*one*."

"I'm lost again."

"After searching, a group of investigators discovered a nun named Sister Margaret Clarendon had awoke one morning to find herself in control of a remarkable and apparently bottomless well of power. A power she had never before been in possession of and could not begin to fathom."

"And it was this… vael?"

"Yes. At the time, the magical community found her because of the disturbances she had been creating on this dimensional plain. These disturbances were leaving the equivalent of magical footprints all across our world–to say nothing of the so-called 'miracles' that had been attributed to her. After an exhaustive search, the investigative team found her in her own abbey, locked behind a brick wall she insisted was built around her. The poor woman was terrified, afraid of even lifting a finger or opening her mouth for fear of what she may do. You have to understand that this woman was a humble nun, a woman who spent her days in silent prayer and teaching children. One night she'd gone to bed only to wake the next morning with the ability to bend time and space at her will. It was an awesome force that she could not even begin to comprehend."

"How did she get it? This power."

"They did not know. And Sister Margaret was… unwilling to help contribute to the investigation. Shortly after she was found, she left and went on to live in isolation until her death a few years later."

"This thing killed her?" I asked, my heart rate launching into triple time.

"No, Dylan, not at all. Sister Margaret was frightened and unwilling to receive the help and training that she needed. If anything killed her it was fear, fear or misunderstanding." Finch shrugged. "It was a terribly unsympathetic time for the supernatural."

"And no one knows how she acquired this vael thing?"

"Investigations continued into this phenomenon for the next few decades, but no breakthroughs were made until just after the second great war. A powerful man named Avery Greenwalt was actually able to enter the multiverse, effectively shifting *between* universes for a short period before returning to ours. He was gone for seven and a half minutes, but to him he was gone for twelve years."

"But where did he go?"

"The answer to that question is impossible to give. He was… different when he came back. He spoke of worlds beyond your darkest nightmares, but somehow Greenwalt had survived. He told a tale of meeting a shaman on the other side, some sort of mage or sorcerer who taught him of this creature called a vael. What he learned under this sorcerer's tutelage is now all that we know of the vael. When he returned, Greenwalt was unstable and paranoid, and he disappeared not long after his return. But he did bring back the information we had been searching for."

"What was it? And did you say *creature*?"

"Yes, I did. The vael is a *sentient* being that is able to live on every level of the multiverse at once. It inhabits a host of its choosing and in doing so imbues them with the power to touch upon each level of the multiverse at their will."

"It's like a parasite?"

"No, it's not, it doesn't *take* anything. It exists only on a subatomic level, but without a host–or a *match*, as Greenwalt called it–vaels cease to exist. By living on every level of the multiverse at once, vaels are forced to surrender their concrete form. Without a match to inhabit, a match that lives on *one* level of the multiverse, a vael cannot exist at all."

"Wait a minute, go back a few steps. You said *sentient*?"

"Yes," Finch said. "Sentient. Vaels *choose* their match."

"Well why the shit did it choose *me*?" I shouted.

Finch raised his hands. "That I do not know, Dylan. Calm down. I've never had a sit-down conversation with a vael, considering I am not an electron, so do not ask me."

I shook my head. Whatever was left of my brain was spinning like a top. A few days ago, I was just a regular guy. A few minutes ago, I was just magical. Then I learned that I've got some sub-atomic not parasitic parasite living inside me and giving me all the powers of the parallel multi-leveled universe. I missed being the regular guy.

As Finch continued speaking beside me, he grew more excited by the minute. "There have only been a handful of cases of vael matches on this dimensional plane in the last fifty years, maybe two or three, but it has happened. This is a *phenomenal* gift, Dylan, a gift that a great many people would kill for."

"I wouldn't kill for it," I said, my voice shaking. "And Sister Margaret wouldn't kill for it either. I don't even want the damn thing."

"Maybe that's why it chose *you*. It did not choose Adolf Hitler or Pol Pot," Finch said. "Power is the greatest test of character. If you have been chosen by the vael, it is because the vael has found you *worthy*."

"Chose me," I grumbled. "Cursed me is more like it."

"It is not a curse, Dylan. Don't be dramatic."

"How would you know, Finch? You've probably wanted one of these... *things* since you and your girlfriend pulled a coup on the magic world all those years ago. Probably couldn't imagine having unlimited power at your grasp, right?"

Despite my outburst, Finch said nothing. His silence didn't stop me though.

"Well, just the thought scares the shit out of me. Right now I feel like my head's about to explode with all this weird stuff spinning around in it, and at this moment I'm actually turning to *you* for a sympathetic ear, which shows how crazy I must be feeling. You know, I kind of enjoyed being normal old Dylan, the guy who liked to cook and watch baseball in his split-level house and drive an ugly car. Big meathead Dylan, not expected to do anything but hit monsters with sharp heavy objects and not get in the way when the real important stuff is going on. I've been that guy my whole life and it's a little scary now that he's gone. And now I'm... different. Strange."

I stopped talking and Finch did not fill the silence. He threw me the occasional look, but I ignored him, instead staring straight out the Tank's cracked windshield as we left the King and his startling diagnosis far behind. I tried to gather my thoughts, but my head was a whole bag of crazy, and despite my ranting, Finch's subdued excitement was still kicking off him like embers from a campfire. Even if he was being quiet, I knew his mind was racing through all the possibilities I now held at my fingertips. The more excitement I felt radiating off of him, the more I wanted to be alone. For the first time, I cursed my new life as a Zero, instead wishing I could go back to being unemployed. *The Price is Right* and *Days of Our Lives* was starting to look mighty good. I was broke, but it was a whole lot simpler. Life as a Zero was anything but *simple*. Yeah, I may have been being overdramatic, but it was hard not to feel like everything in my life had changed in the last week. It had.

"I'm gonna go home," I said. Darkness had fallen and the workday was over. We had things to do, but I needed to grab my remaining sanity with both hands and hold on tight. It would be easier to do that at my crappy old split-level house. "I have to go home."

"Well, all right," Finch said reluctantly. "We still have some things we should discuss. And with Alfred Bascombe on the lam and the little problem of Bluebeard and..." He trailed off when he met my eye. "You know, I believe you do need some rest and a bit of time to sort all this out. That is good thinking, my friend."

I parked the Tank in Gil's space, handed Finch the keys, and left without a word. On the sidewalk, the April evening was warm and damp from the rain. A strong wind was blowing down the empty streets. More rain was coming. I hailed a cab and slipped inside. When the car started moving, I leaned back and shut my eyes, not looking back as we drove off.

CHAPTER 27. CHOSEN

My house looked almost unfamiliar to me when I got out of the cab. It pulled away and I stood on the curb for a minute in the dreary rain that had begun again. My yard was overgrown, the grass pocked with crabgrass, the flowerbeds spotty with dandelions and nests of weeds, and even from the street I could see that the gutters were clogged. Old leaves and twigs sprouted from the bent and soiled drainpipes, forcing streams of rainwater to run off the roof in rivers. It was a far cry from old man Dolan's house Willa and I had visited earlier, and an even farther cry from the house it once was when my parents were still alive.

I unlocked the door and pushed it open, ignoring the peeling paint that had once been so perfect. I tossed my keys onto a nearby table and locked the door behind me. It was dark inside. I hadn't left any lights on after I'd gone a few days ago, and no one had been there in the meantime. Come to think of it, I hadn't had a visitor in a while.

I circled the cluttered living room, turning on a smattering of lights. It was hot and damp inside, an early hint of the summer's coming humidity giving the air a heavy, stale quality. I cracked a few windows, allowing a sluggish breeze to blow through the house before I trudged upstairs. The dirty city rain had given my skin a slick, oily feel, and I needed a shower and a shave.

Going through the motions, I tried to keep my mind blank. Thinking about Finch's and the King's breaking news just freaked the shit out of me. Was I afraid? Hell, I'd be a fool not to be, right? Magic wasn't just a derivative crutch used by bad genre fiction writers. Well, not really.

I emerged from the shower feeling mostly human again. Clean and clean-shaven, but the hot water and steam had left me feeling sleepy. If I hadn't been so hungry, I would have just gone to bed. I put on a Cannonball Adderley and Miles Davis record and went into the kitchen to make some dinner: baked chicken with garlic, asparagus, red potatoes. Nice and easy.

I was standing in the kitchen barefoot, wearing faded jeans and a Hill Valley *Save the Clock Tower!* t-shirt when I heard the knock at the door. I felt my Hulk temper roll over. It was either Gil or Finch, two guys I'd have a hard time talking to at the moment. I was tired, hungry, and burnt out. The quiet swirls of Hank Jones' piano and Miles' muted trumpet were just getting going. I swore aloud and stomped over to the door, pulling it open angrily.

Willa stood on the stoop, a red and white polka-dot umbrella opened above her and a bottle of wine in her hand.

"Hi," she said, smiling. She had cleaned up and changed, herself. In addition to a smile, she wore jeans and a plain black t-shirt. Over her shoulder was a leather messenger bag. Her hair was wet and pulled up into a ponytail. Behind her glasses, her eyes looked fresh and lively, far from what I figured mine looked like.

She lifted the wine bottle and shook it temptingly. "I talked to Finch," she said. "And I figured you could use a drink. When it comes to drinking, however, it's about the only thing I'm girly about," she smiled and laughed. "Ergo, wine and not beer."

I was a little taken aback, but I realized I was smiling. Generally when I get surprised by unexpected visitors at home, my first instinct is to scowl. I guess Willa had a different effect on me than most other people.

"I'm sorry," I said after a long moment. "I'm a little spacey. Come in, please." I backed up and she stepped inside, shaking out her umbrella on the stoop before closing the door behind her. She handed the bottle to me.

"Gil said you're a great cook. I hope you can work with red."

"Thank you very much. Did you already eat? I was just gonna put something together."

"Oh, I'm sorry," she blushed. "I didn't mean to crash, I just wanted to check on–"

"Don't be silly," I said, waving her into my living room. "Have a seat, I'd love the company. Although it's a little... ehh... messy in here." I swooped a mountain of mail from one of the chairs and motioned for her to sit.

"No, not at all," she said. "And thank you for the offer, I've been feeling a little lost recently, not being able to go home and all." She took a seat and looked around the room. Now I was blushing. The place was a wreck; laundry, mail, books, and knick-knacks, all comfortable under a blanket of dust. Charming.

"So how are you doing?" she asked as she met my eye.

"Um... all right, I guess. I don't know." I put the wine bottle down on a coffee table and took to clearing off a second chair across from the first, feeling every bit as awkward as I probably looked.

When I finally sat down, I'd lost my train of thought. "Uh... how are you again?"

She smiled. "I'm all right. I met with Finch and Gil and we're making progress. I'm... I'm keeping up hope." She shrugged. "But hey, you had a pretty weird afternoon. Finch told me a little about what happened, but he was fairly mysterious about it all."

I took a deep breath and recounted as much of what had happened as I could. I skipped over bits I didn't understand, but did my best to flush out most of what I'd learned. She listened with sharp attention, holding my eye and digesting every word. When I was done, she leaned forward and commenced with the inevitable questions.

"So the origin of magic isn't technically supernatural? It's like some sort of byproduct of an intentional fissure between dimensions?"

"Um...? I think? I had Finch spend a half hour explaining it and you seem to have a better grasp already."

"Wow." She leaned back, blinking. "And this new sentient subatomic companion you've got is called a vael?"

"Apparently. This new parasite friend of mine."

"Well, to be fair, it's not technically parasitic," she said. "It seems more symbiotic than anything else."

"I guess that sounds a little better."

"And this doctor described you as being 'off the chart?'"

"That's what Doogie Howser said."

"Did Finch talk about physical side effects of this vael thing? You said the doctor mentioned physiological changes associated with the vael."

"Finch didn't mention anything about side effects," I conceded.

"What about permanence?" she asked. "Is this thing going to be around forever?"

"No clue. But if it chose me and came into my body, I'm guessing it can choose to leave just as easily."

"What about control?" she asked. "Did Finch talk to you about how to control any of this overwhelming power?"

"Nope."

"Damn, Dylan, you've gotta ask these questions," she grumbled. "This is why you take someone to the doctor's office with you."

"Well, technically I had Finch with me," I said.

"Oh, you know what I mean. Someone who *listens*. Finch stopped listening the minute that kid said you had the vael. He's not sensitive to how freaked you must've been feeling. You needed someone there to ask the questions. I would've gone with you."

"*You left*," I said, my Hulk temper getting one good shot in. "You went to go look for some lady. It was just me alone and I was feeling a little under the weather at the time. Remember?"

She opened her mouth to speak again but stopped. Shaking her head, Willa took a deep breath and let it out slowly. "I'm sorry," she said. "I'll..." she trailed off, her eyes falling to her hands in her lap. She shifted uncomfortably in her seat before looking back up at me. "I'll be there for you next time. I promise."

"No," I said. "It's..." I shook my head and forced a smile. She smiled back. It was encouraging. "I'm sorry. I'm feeling pretty stressed," I admitted.

"It's all right. I am too."

It was quiet for a minute before I said, "Come into the kitchen and talk to me while I cook."

She followed me in, Cannonball Adderley's alto sax solo filling the air as the record played on, filling the silence. Willa took a seat at the kitchen table as I got to work.

"Speaking of today," I said. "How did your search go for Miss Lady?"

Willa leaned forward. "I found her."

"You found her? Eliza Adams? Seriously?"

"Yes. I found her. I told you, it's my job."

"What exactly do you do for a living, again?" I asked, grabbing my bottle opener. "Because I'm wondering if you're actually employed by the CIA or something."

She laughed. "I only work as a technician for a private security firm. The CIA? Please, they can't afford me."

"Oh okay. But you have to admit, you've got weird connections. And you managed to elude Gil's searches for you twice now," I said uncorking the wine. "You're not exactly a computer programmer."

"I know some programming," she said. "A little bit."

"Still mysterious," I said, pouring two glasses of wine and handing her one. "I'll let it go this time, Secret Agent Bascombe." She smiled and accepted the glass. "All right, what did you find out today from the mother computer?"

"Mrs. Eliza Adams was declared legally dead in 1973, ten years after she was last seen. However, the paper trails that would have been invisible forty years ago are a little less than invisible now. Too easy." She smiled and took a sip after swirling the dark liquid around her glass. "It's good," she said.

I took a sip and agreed. "Yes, it is. Thanks again for bringing it. And thanks for coming over. It's nice to have you here." She smiled. "Now, what do you mean 'paper trail'?"

She took another sip. "Things like social security checks passed on to next of kin, health insurance, driver's licenses, birth certificates. When a person needs to create a new identity, there are a lot of ingredients that are getting harder to forge in the digital age. So I started out assuming that she was still alive and that she'd created her new identity in 1963. I had her old identity, including driver's license, birth certificate, and photograph, so from there, I just had to connect A to B."

"I'd wager it's a bit more complicated than that," I said, digging through the fridge. "You make it sound ridiculously easy."

"It's not as hard as you think. I imagine you'd have a hell of a time, but like I said," she smiled coyly, "it's my job."

I cooked while Willa talked. Most of it was technical jargon as she outlined the couple dozens of steps she went through in order to find Eliza Adams. Honestly, very little of it meant anything to me, but I liked seeing her sitting at my kitchen table as if it were her own, and I liked hearing the sound of her voice.

When I laid her plate in front of her, her face lit up. "Gil wasn't kidding, was he?" she said, smiling.

"I can cook," I said shrugging. "In addition to being able to handle myself with a gun and driving a car, it's one of the few things I'm good at."

She cut into her chicken and skewered a piece, bringing it up to her mouth eagerly. After a moment, she nodded, a grin spreading across her face. "Yes, you can cook. Thanks again, this is really fantastic. Any other hobbies?" she asked as she cut into the chicken again.

"Well, I like listening to jazz, I like reading, and I've always wanted to be a good gardener, but I can't keep a cactus alive."

"What makes you want to garden? That doesn't seem to fit the profile."

I shrugged. "My Dad loved it, and he was great at it." Even saying the words out loud made me think back to being a boy and helping my parents in the yard. Losing your parents makes you realize how lonesome being an only child can be. "Mom and Dad were so proud of this yard."

Willa smiled. "This is their house?"

"It was," I said simply. She nodded, inferring the rest.

"You've kept it up... pretty well," she said.

I laughed, feeling my face flush. "I really haven't, but thanks for saying that." I looked around the small kitchen and could only see the accumulated grease and dirty dishes. Living alone has a way of infecting your life with complacency.

"Anyway," I said, struggling to change the subject, "back to business. Now that we've found Mrs. Adams, what's our next move?"

"Gil has his private jet lined up for us tomorrow."

"Are you serious? A private jet? Where exactly is this Mrs. Adams? Hong Kong?"

"Actually, it's Ms. Burton now, and she lives in a town called Houghton in Michigan."

"Where exactly is that?"

"It's on the Upper Peninsula, not too far from Wisconsin. It's a small city up against Portage Lake, near Lake Superior."

I must've looked confused.

"It's a stone's throw away from Canada," she said.

"Ah, yes. Got it. And how did she end up there?"

"Well, from what I read in public records, Nancy Burton moved to the city of Houghton in 1965 when it was little more than a dot on a map. Eliza Adams' maiden name is Ellington, but I couldn't find any other related Ellington family members in the area. As far as I can figure, she moved there simply to get as far away from the whole Bathory scandal as possible. In the past forty years or so, little Houghton has done all right for itself. It's still a small place, but a lot bigger than it was when Ms. Nancy Burton first arrived."

"And we're flying into this burg?"

"There's a town across the river called Hancock that apparently has a small airport. Just a short drive from downtown Houghton."

I let her talk; watching her wave her hands animatedly and devour the dinner I'd made. She had a youthful vitality that I felt like I'd lost a long time ago. Whether it was the military, the years of living alone, or just the toils of each day, I always felt so tired, so worn down. Compared to her, I felt like a slug. And here before me sat a bravely smiling woman, even though her husband was missing, probably on the run for his life, a woman who was wanted dead herself. But still, looking into her eyes, it was hard to see it. I smiled as I listened to her. It had been too long since I'd shared a meal like this with someone in my own home. I had really missed it.

After dinner we carried a second bottle of wine back into my mess of a living room. I let Willa talk herself out, going over her plan of locating and questioning Eliza Adams, outlining our travel plans down to the last detail. When she was finished, it was late, but her bright eyes were still full of energy.

"So, cut the crap," she said, pausing to take a sip of wine. "How did you really feel about what happened today at the doctor?"

I emptied my glass and returned it to the table. As I gathered my thoughts, Willa filled my glass again. "Honestly?" I asked. She nodded. "It really... Well, it scared the shit out of me."

She nodded, her cheeks red from the wine. "Why, though?"

"A few days ago I was basically a chauffeur. Gil and Finch hired me to drive their ugly car around and swing swords at monsters. That's it, right? Sure, I can do that. Somehow in the last couple of days I got in over my head. I was in the military and I was a cop, but that was a long time ago. After that, I was a security consultant, meaning I walked around in navy blue blazers and pointed to corners where cameras needed to be installed. I made bad money, but it was a job. Now all this..."

"But why were you afraid?" she asked again.

I opened my mouth to speak, prepared to lay out a messy handful of details that added up to nothing, the usual smoke and mirror crap. But when I paused, I gave the wine a chance to act, loosening my tongue. Perhaps it was just the wine, or perhaps it was the fact that I was talking to Willa.

"I did badly in school," I said. "Really badly. Which is why I ended up joining the military when I got out of high school. My parents knew I worked pretty hard, but I just... couldn't do it. I told you a little about my parents. My Dad was a gardener, my Mom was a filing clerk in a law firm, not even a secretary. They worked hard, but neither went to college. They supported me, but they didn't really expect much from me. They were proud of whatever I did." I shook my head. "All my life I've had such low expectations, from others and from myself. And now this..." I raised my hands and held them before me, half expecting lobsters to burst from my palms. "Now I have this power, a power that Finch said some would be willing to kill for. Kill for? And I have it. *Me*. How do I deserve this? It's... it's insane. I don't usually find myself in this kind of position. What am I supposed to do? What if I totally screw it all up?" I looked down at my hands again. It felt like a pit had opened at the bottom of my stomach, a pit that would only get bigger and bigger in the days to come.

Across from me, Willa set down her wine glass and leaned forward. Silently, she took my hands in hers. Compared to mine, hers were so small, free of the calluses and scars mine had. She looked up at me. Her eyes were beautiful and understanding.

"You're wrong," she said simply. "You deserve this. It's not a mistake, Dylan. You are a good man, and this *chose you*, remember? Finch said that a vael matches itself with a host of its own choosing. You were the person it wanted. You've lived your life believing that you were incapable of being something greater, not because anyone told you that you couldn't, but because no one told you otherwise. You are amazing and capable of doing great things, do you know that?" She held my hands tightly. "You have to believe that you deserve it," she said. "Because you do. You've earned this."

My breath was stuck in my throat, and I couldn't take my eyes off of hers. In that moment, she was the most beautiful thing I'd ever seen. I wanted so badly to grab her and kiss her, to feel her against me, but I couldn't. Her hands entwined with mine, I could feel the wedding band wrapped around her finger. I thought of Alfred Bascombe, alone, desperately trying to stay alive and reclaim his stolen life. I knew I'd pledged to help restore her husband to her. Despite what I wanted, I knew it was something I could never have. I took a deep breath and blinked my eyes, breaking the gaze that had connected us for those few long moments. Then I leaned back and released her hands.

It's better this way, I told myself. *It's better this way.*

CHAPTER 28. WELCOME TO MICHIGAN

I woke up with a crick in my neck. My head hung back at an awkward angle against the chair, and as I straightened I heard a drum roll of joints popping and cracking. Morning sunshine was pouring in through the partially curtained windows that overlooked my unkempt front yard. Willa was sleeping stretched out over piles of my laundry–both clean and dirty–on the sofa at the other end of the room. She was fully dressed except for one flat that had fallen off in her sleep. Her bare foot hung off the end of the couch. From where I sat, I could see red painted toenails.

We'd talked late into the night. Sometime shortly after midnight, we'd finished the wine, and I could feel it. My brain felt like it was floating from one side of my skull to the other, my own personal wave tank. I closed my eyes and tried to rub the sleep from them. It didn't work. Unsteadily, I rose and stumbled into the kitchen for a glass of cold water.

It was the electrical shock I was looking for. I stood in the doorway, looking out into the living room at Willa's sleeping form on the couch.

It had nearly gotten awkward the night before. Sitting there, drunk, staring into each other's eyes, when she'd taken my hand. Good grief. She was a married woman, pushed and pulled not only by the bottle of red wine split between us, but by her missing husband, the threats, the danger, the fear. I was just as drunk as she'd been, and I could have led her down a dark road. I thanked my lucky stars for whatever had managed to slap some sense into me before I'd ruined a lot of things. "No more booze with beautiful married women," I said aloud.

"What?" Willa's voice murmured from the sofa. It was thick and full of sleep. Her eyes cracked open and she rolled over onto her back, groaning.

"Uh, nothing. How long have you been awake?" I asked, agape. "I said, um, no more... er, wine. It does things to my head."

She nodded as she stretched. "Ugh, me too. I don't really drink anymore. And this is why." She sat up and rubbed her face. "God, Dylan, what do you have in this sofa? Bricks?"

"It's not too soft, is it? You would've been better off on the floor, I think."

She stretched again and cracked her back. "You're not kidding." She turned and dropped her feet to the floor. "What time is it?"

I looked at the digital clock on the stove. "Wow. Almost eleven."

"Oh, man. Yeah, no more wine." She stumbled to her feet. Her ponytail had come free and her hair was a wild nest around her face. One hand reached out and felt around blindly on the coffee table for her glasses. After a minute I walked over and put the red cat's eye glasses into her open hand. She thanked me as she pulled her missing shoe back onto her foot.

"We gotta go," she said, shaking her head.

"Now?"

"We should've been up and out the damn door at about eight." She swore under her breath as she searched for her purse. "Are you ready to go?" she asked, turning to face me.

"Let me get changed," I said as I stumbled up the stairs to my bedroom. I found a clean pair of unslept-in jeans, a t-shirt, and a button down. After a minute I was back in the living room, pulling on a pair of boots. Willa had taken a minute in the bathroom to clean up. She'd washed her face and gotten her hair under control and back into its ponytail. Eager vitality had returned to her eyes.

"All right," she said. "You ready to go?"

I sighed, my hangover promising a long day. "Yeah."

"Let me call Gil." She pulled a cell phone from her pocket and dialed a number. "Hey, it's Willa, we're on our way to the airport now. Yes, I know we are very late. Okay, see you there." She hung up and returned the phone.

"Wait," I said, standing. "Gil's coming too? And Finch?"

"No, but they're gonna meet us there to see us off. Gil wants to get all our plans in a row."

"All right, whatever."

From my place we took a cab to the Northeast Philly Airport, a tiny little two runway place where Gil apparently kept one (he's a billionaire, remember?) of his planes. A Learjet was waiting on the tiny runway, engines roaring in a heavy crosswind. Beside the jet was the ever-loyal Tank, pulled right up on the tarmac. Gil and Finch leaned against it with their arms crossed.

"Took you two long enough," he said over the engines, a wide dumb grin on his face.

"Slept late," I shrugged.

Finch and Gil shared a brief glance. Beside me, I could see Willa blush. "What's the plan?" she asked.

"You got the info you need, right?" Gil said. "You're gonna meet the lady, this Ms. Burton, at her house?"

Willa nodded. "I have all the information I need. Did you make the arrangements for the car?"

"You betcha," he said. "There is a car waiting for you there now. I made sure the guy stuck a map in there for you, too. Just outta the goodness of my heart."

"Thanks," I said.

"No problemo. I didn't even know they had maps of towns that size," he laughed. "Anyway, get your asses back here ASAP. We got stuff to do. And I don't like either of you being out of my sight for too long. There are too many balls up in the air right now. I'd go with you, but like I said, we got stuff to do here. We may have a lead on your husband," Gil said, turning to Willa.

Her eyes widened. "You do? That's great! What is it? Where is he?"

"Whoa, relax there, girl. It's just a lead. That doesn't mean it's concrete. And until I see him and get him back into friendlier territory, I'm not gonna put a flying banana's worth of faith in any tip, you got me?"

She nodded, her face growing somber, but I could see a flicker of hope in her eye. "All right," she said. "We'll get back soon. We gotta go."

Gil saluted. "Safe travel, my friends." Behind him, Finch nodded.

We climbed the few steps up into the jet as the engine velocity increased. Behind us, the stairs folded up, rising as they retracted into the body of the plane. The plane was compact and the cabin tiny, only about eight seats squeezed inside. For a minute I felt a nagging tug of claustrophobia as I fell into a seat across from Willa. Between us was a small table. She rested her messenger bag on the floor beside her and began laying papers across the table.

"Going over the plans one more time?" I asked.

"Can't be too prepared," she said. "The last thing I want to do is screw up by getting lost or something." She spread out a map and pointed. "Here's where she is," she said, tapping a dot on the map circled in thick black marker. One long road led from the center of the small town out to the secluded location Willa was indicating. Surrounding it was nothing but wilderness.

I leaned back. "Well, navigator, you point the way, and I'll get us there. I'm the driver, remember?" Outside, the engines were roaring as the small Learjet began its taxi into position.

Willa looked up at me, eyes growing serious as she chewed on her lip. I'd seen that look on a woman's face before, and I knew exactly what was on her mind: last night. She opened to speak but I interrupted her.

"I hope you won't mind if I try to get some sleep," I said as I repositioned myself in the seat, avoiding eye contact. "I don't wanna be falling asleep behind the wheel up there in the middle of nowhere. I'm liable to run over a groundhog."

She closed her mouth and swallowed whatever conversation she was hoping to open. I felt a twinge of regret, but pushed it aside. The best thing to do now was move on. As the small Lear began to pick up speed, I cracked one eye and looked out the window in time to see the ground fall away. Sleep found me soon after.

**

"I can't believe we're lost," she said. "We have the map. And we planned this."

"We're not lost, we just don't know where to go next."

"You said you knew where we were going."

"I did. I was following your directions, Tonto. You spoke very declaratively. I can't help it you can't read a map."

"I can read a map just fine, Dylan. We left Hancock, we crossed the

Portage Lake Lift Bridge, we drove south through town, we got on 26 heading southwest. We almost missed Erickson and we would have if I hadn't shouted to turn. Remember where that Oldsmobile honked at you? Yeah, there. Then we took Erickson drive to County Road 65. We took 65 to Larson and from Larson to Rova. Now we're supposed to take Mullen Road straight to her house."

"I got that," I said. "I got *all* that. But where the hell is Mullen Road?"

"It should be around here," she shouted, waving her arms around in frustration.

"Ah, yes. Therein lies the problem. Nothing is around here."

Except trees. We were standing on the side of a narrow road in a heavy copse of trees. Beyond that copse was another copse. On the other side of the road were more copses. It was basically a forest. Most of the trees had wide flat leaves twisting in the wind. The rest were stately pines that leaned in the breeze blowing in from the distant Portage Lake. We had our map spread across Ye Olde '85 sedan, the stately car that Gil had arranged for us at the Houghton County Airport. It was purple and it looked like a fossilized grape. Willa was hunched over it, running her finger up and down the thin black line that demarcated County Road 65, a long line that connected major thoroughfares, and she continued tracing her finger along the other roads, the lines getting smaller and smaller as we moved southwest into the wilderness of Michigan's Upper Peninsula.

"We went wrong here," she said, tapping one spot.

I leaned over and squinted. "Yeah, I remember. We followed Larson until the road dead ended. Trust me, I remember."

She scowled. "Backtracked to Rova," she mumbled, sighing. "Now we're just looking for Mullen."

"Yup."

We'd passed a few homesteads on the way to our current spot, but they were empty. It was a weekday and everyone was at work. Mullen Road was on the map, a tiny little dotted line that ran off into a wide spread of forest to another dead end where I supposed Ms. Nancy Burton now lived.

Willa straightened and cursed as she shaded her eyes from the sun and turned her gaze up and down the narrow road for the umpteenth time. As we each stared off into the woods, the electronic chirping of a cell phone split the quiet. Willa pulled the tiny device from her pocket.

"Yeah," she said. "Hi Gil. Oh things are going swimmingly."

I walked over to her. She grumbled something and handed the phone to me.

"Hello?" I said.

"Howdy, boy!" Gil said merrily. "How you doin'?"

"We're lost in Michigan, Gil. Guess how we're doing."

"Be cool, brother bear, it could be worse," he said. "It could be January."

"Truth."

"Anyway, we got some weird stuff happening here. A guy from the Mayor's office called and wants to meet with us. What time you think you'll be back in the real world? Stuff here's getting interesting."

"I don't know, eight? Nine? It depends on when we find this lady," I muttered. Across from me, Willa walked up and down the street, hands on her hips, eyeing the woods. "Did you say a guy from the mayor's office?"

"Yeah, man. We got things to talk about. We're gonna have a team sit down dinner thing at nine. Try not to be late."

"Where?" I asked.

"Do you really need me to tell you where?"

I thought of barbecue ribs and clutched my stomach subconsciously.

"Oh, man," I groaned.

"Get in the car," Willa said as she began folding the map.

"I think I gotta go, Gil," I said.

"Where you goin'?" he asked.

"I dunno. Where are we going?" I asked Willa.

"We're gonna go up and down this road one more time."

"Looks like we're gonna drive around the woods some more," I muttered. "Gotta go."

"Right-o, bud," Gil said. "Good luck."

"You too." I hung up and tossed Willa the phone.

I slipped back into the driver's seat. We'd gone up and down the road half a dozen times to no avail. But we'd come a couple hundred miles already, so a few more passes seemed reasonable.

We coasted the length of Rova Road a few times before turning up

Larson. The area was nice and lush, with heavy foliage growing on either side of the road occasionally broken up by large fields that surrounded a home here and there. There was a slight chill in the air despite the sun overhead. Gil was right, it could be worse, it could be January. I shuddered to think of what it would be like during the winter out here on the Upper Peninsula, sandwiched by Lake Superior and beset by lakes. I'd turned back down Rova when Willa spoke up.

"Stop," she said.

My mind had been wandering as I looked out the window, thinking about the area's weather and respectable collection of big trees when she'd spoken up. I dropped my foot onto the brake, skidding the ugly grape to a rough stop.

"Back up," she said.

I put the old girl in reverse and drifted back a few yards.

"There." She pointed out the driver's side window.

On my left was a narrow opening in the thick canopy of green. We'd passed it five or six times and never paused on it. The covering of leaves and branches was only slightly thinner there than it was anywhere else on the roadside, but bracketing the slight opening was a pair of thick stumps from razed oaks. From the surface of the road, the ground sloped downward to a gulch before it rose again and led into the darkness of the woods.

"That's it," Willa said.

"That's what? A good place to dump a body?"

"That's Mullen."

"How do you know?"

She leaned over me and stared. Momentarily distracted by her face so close to mine, I eventually looked over when she said, "In the gully." She pointed. "Right there."

After a moment I located it. A hand-painted wooden sign that read **MULLEN** was lying on the ground, partially covered by a blanket of pine needles.

"You gotta be shittin' me," I mumbled as I looked up in the tangle of forest beyond.

"Looks like we're walking."

"I thought I signed up for *urban* fantasy," I said.

After struggling through the thicket barring our path, Willa and I trudged along Mullen "Road" for a few hundred yards before the foliage managed to thicken once again. Above us, the canopy of trees tangled together and the amount of light that seeped through diminished with every step. In the looming darkness, we followed the trail around stone abutments bursting from the ground and thickening clumps of thorny bushes before we heard the gentle trickle of a stream ahead.

Rounding one more twist in the path, we came upon a small cottage standing beside a creek, brown and turbulent from a recent heavy rain. The squat cottage was a mishmash of colors, as if cobbled together from parts salvaged from a refuse heap, and it looked like it had survived its fair share of hard winters. Its roof was bowed, and shaded from the sun as it was, streaks of mildew grew on the siding. One glance was enough to make me feel better about the current state of my house. Each window was shuttered and dark, and a sign stood a few paces from the front door, hand-painted in the same script as the fallen road sign. This one read **NO TRESPASSING**.

"I think we're here," Willa said, taking a deep breath.

"A real Shangri-La," I admitted.

Willa was silent as she walked the few remaining paces to the door. She passed the no trespassing sign without pause and climbed the few crooked steps to the door. She took a deep breath and knocked.

I followed and stood a few feet behind her. My instincts said that I should be a few miles behind her given my people skills, but a few feet would have to suffice. After a long moment, she knocked again. Nothing.

"Maybe she's... not home?"

Willa turned a skeptical eye to me. "Does it look like she gets out much?"

"Well, not really."

"And remember, she's about 75 years old."

"Oh, yeah."

Willa knocked again. "Ms. Burton?" She called. "My name is Willa Bascombe. I've come a long way to talk to you, ma'am." She knocked again.

"Maybe it's naptime," I said.

Willa scowled at me and knocked again. "Ms. Burton," she said. "Hello?"

As she knocked, I walked around the house. Other than the building itself, there were no other signs of life. No birdhouses or wind chimes, no pets or footprints. At the backdoor was a trashcan with bungee cords and locking clasps to protect against raccoons and bears. I pulled the bands free, opened the plastic locks, and lifted the lid. Inside was trash. A deep breath convinced me it was fairly fresh, so the house, thankfully, wasn't abandoned. I replaced the lid. Behind me, the stream was a beautiful sight, churning along past me in the bright sunlight, free of the oppressive canopy of trees. I turned back to the house and noticed the flutter of a curtain in the the only unshuttered window.

"She's here," I said after I'd trudged back around to the front of the house.

"How do you know?"

"The trash seems pretty recent," I said. "And there's a window open that overlooks the stream out back."

"So it's not all sealed up."

"Nope. It's the only human thing I can see in this whole place."

Willa turned a hopeful eye back to the door and knocked again. "Ms. Burton, please. I just want to speak with you." She sighed.

I walked up the few steps and pulled Willa back, taking her place. I knocked, louder than Willa had as I spoke, "Mrs. Adams, we have to speak to you. We're friends. We spoke with Mr. Dolan. Do you remember him? Timothy Dolan?"

I held my breath and stepped back. A strong gust of wind blew through the forest, rustling the trees and stirring up dried leaves from the ground. The canopy above us swayed in the wind, disturbing the thick covering of leaves enough to allow brief glimpses of light to shine through. I heard the door unlock.

Willa pulled me aside and took my place. "Mrs. Adams? Mrs. Eliza Adams?"

The door opened. From the darkness of the cottage emerged an old woman, stooped and fragile, holding a cane in a shaking hand. Her hair was long and fell around her withered face in white strands. Her eyes were milky and yellowed. She looked up at us warily.

"Who are you?" she asked, her voice low but firm. "My name is Nancy Elizabeth Burton. The woman... that woman you're searching for? Eliza Adams? She is dead. Long, long dead."

CHAPTER 29. THE MISSING WOMAN

"Who are you two?" the old woman asked. She squinted down at us warily.

"Mrs. Ad–um... I mean, Ms. Burton?" Willa asked.

"*I'm* Nancy Burton, young lady. Who are you?"

"My name is Willa Bascombe, and this is my associate, Dylan. We've come a long way to find you, Ms. Burton. May we come in?"

"What do you want?"

"To speak with you, m'am."

"About what? The weather?"

"No, m'am. We're looking for a woman named Eliza Adams."

"I told you, she's dead."

"You knew her, m'am?"

"A long time ago," she said. "She's gone now."

"Can we come in?" Willa asked again.

The old woman set her jaw, and her top lip quivered slightly. "For a moment." She stepped back to clear the doorway and Willa and I stepped inside.

The house was dark and cool. I had expected to find the cottage cluttered and dusty, the kind of house well-lived in and loved for years stacked upon years. Instead, it was nearly empty and spotless, as if a moving crew had just left after having wiped the place down with wet rags. Each window was curtained on the inside, preventing any light from entering, and the only furniture I could see was a kitchen table and four chairs. The foyer was empty, as was the living room, and the front bedroom.

"What do you want?" the woman asked again as she closed the door behind us, cutting off the one main source of light.

"Can we go somewhere to talk, Ms. Burton?" Willa asked.

"Back that way," the old woman gestured. "Into the kitchen."

I followed Willa as best I could, moving toward the small table and the gentle glow of sunlight shining in the window I'd seen at the rear of the house. The old woman moved behind me, her cane tapping on the floor with each step. In the darkness of the cottage, the threat of danger crossed my mind for the first time. If the woman behind me was who we believed her to be, then she was the one-time lover of Edward Bathory, a well-known vampire. I didn't know anything about vampires aside from Hollywood crap and the little I'd learned during my first and only encounter with Arthur Greely, but I had to assume there was a chance she was a vampire herself. An actively feeding vampire. And now Willa and I stood in the darkness of her home, alone and unarmed.

If the thought occurred to Willa, she showed nothing. In the soft light of the kitchen, she took a seat at the table. I sat beside her. The old woman poured steaming water from a kettle into a mug and added a tea bag. *No furniture, but she's got teabags*, I thought. Hmm. The old woman took a seat across from us and glowered.

"Talk," she said.

Willa cleared her throat and began to speak. "In 1963 there was a man named Edward Bathory who ran for Mayor in Philadelphia, Pennsylvania. Despite the odds against him and his small campaign, he garnered strong support across the city. Shortly before the election, he... disappeared." Willa paused and glanced at me. "We have reason to believe that you volunteered in his offices, m'am; that you were involved in his campaign."

A long moment passed. The woman betrayed nothing, staring Willa and me down with eyes of cold steel. She sipped her tea. After a moment, she said, "You're wrong."

Willa extended her hands across the table towards Ms. Burton and raised them reassuringly. "Please, m'am, you have to understand that we mean you no harm. If you are Eliza Adams, then you're safe. We understand that you've gone to great pains to disappear and we aren't here to expose you."

The woman laughed. It was a sharp sound, filled with bitterness. It fit her face well, a face shaped by decades of frowning.

"That woman is dead," she said again. "I killed her. I want no part of her here; I want no mention of her spoken in this house. You think I came here to escape that life? To get away from the dangers? To live?" She shook her head. "I came here to *die*."

Willa's brow creased. I couldn't tell if she was angry or confused. She leaned back, eyes locked on the old woman's. "To die?" she asked. "Why?"

"You stupid child," the woman muttered. "You know nothing. You believe you know the election, the men involved, the politics, *Edward*." She shook her head. "You know nothing. No, you know less than nothing. To ask you to understand would be like asking a dog to speak."

At each of the old woman's jabs, my temper started to wake up. Willa rested a preemptively restraining hand on my arm and spoke. "We know about the election, m'am," Willa said. "We know that Mr. Bathory was representing the... outside vote. We know that at the last minute his... his *own kind* turned on him and he was taken away. We know that–"

"Taken? You believe he was taken?" her voice grew loud and skeptical. "You foolish girl. He was killed. They *killed* him. Do you understand?"

"Yes, I do understand, we need –"

"You need to *leave*," the old woman said. She rapped her cane repeatedly against the floor. "Foolish *children*. Leave! Now!"

"Listen, lady," I said, standing as my temper popped a seam. "You need to relax. This has gotten a lot bigger than you and your crazy baggage, all right? This is about my friend and her husband and an entire city that may be in jeopardy. Do you understand *that*? Give up your self-pity for a second to understand that this is bigger than yourself."

"Moron," the woman said as she swung her cane at my head. I raised my arm in time and batted it away.

"Dylan," Willa said, standing and pulling me back from the table. "Go outside, please," she said. "Right now."

"What? And leave you with this old bat? Absolutely not."

"Please, Dylan," Willa urged. "Please, go outside."

I looked down at the old woman and bit my tongue. She looked smug, staring up at me as she clutched her cane.

"Please, Dylan," Willa said again. I looked down into her eyes and realized she was right; it wasn't about me. It was about the city and

Willa and her husband. She needed this.

"All right," I mumbled. "I'll go." I stepped around the old woman and walked outside, pulling the front door shut behind me.

***

The breeze had ceased, but it was still pleasant in the shade. I walked around to the back of the house and sat on a stump that overlooked the stream, waiting for my temper to ease. It didn't.

So I sat fuming, watching the water pass gently by. Inside I had exhibited my trademarked hot-headedness with aplomb. Nice job, Dylan. I looked over my shoulder at the house where Willa was doing her best to get anything useful out of the condescending old woman. I cursed, and threw a rock into the stream with a *plunk*. As time wore on, I watched the sun move slowly across the sky and waited for her to emerge.

I wasn't sure if I should feel sheepish or guilty or angry, but after a spell I settled on all three. I knew I'd done it because I wanted to help, but being the subtle man that I was, I'd probably done more damage than good. It didn't help that I'd been following Willa around and working in close quarters with her for days, and it was starting to get to me. My feelings for her were wearing me down. Add manchild Gil and heartless Finch to the mix and I was hurting for a vacation in my first week. Working for the Zeros was turning out to be tougher than I'd expected.

When Willa emerged from the house, I didn't even notice. My mind was busy putting together apologies for outbursts and confessions of unrequited love. I was totally zoned out when she tapped me on my shoulder. I turned and she beckoned me back to the road. I followed without speaking as we struggled through the thickets back to the grape colored sedan.

Inside the car, I waited before turning the ignition. Beside me, Willa buckled up.

"What happened in there?" I asked.

She shrugged. "We got what we needed."

"What'd she tell you?"

"It's complicated, Dylan."

"What do you mean, it's complicated? What did she tell you? And

227

why the hell did it take so damn long?"

"It would've been a lot easier if you'd kept it together."

"I kept it together just fine; she was being self-pitying," I said, my temper flaring again.

"Well, she sort of was," Willa conceded. "But sometimes you have all the tact of a six-year old child, Dylan. Like I said, it's just complicated."

"What are you talking about?"

"This whole thing is different than we thought," she said.

"How?"

"It's not about political scandal or even an election," she said. "We've been playing this whole thing in our world, which is wrong."

"What do you mean 'our world'? How else is there to play it?"

"Their way. This isn't about an affair, Dylan," Willa explained. "It's about an affair with a *human*."

"What?"

She took a deep breath. "Bathory was a vampire, right?"

"Yeah."

"And he was in love with a human, right?"

"Was he?"

"In love?" she sighed. "*Yes*. They were in love. She was planning on leaving her husband for him, but Bathory begged her not to."

"Why?"

"Because it would cost him his life."

"I don't understand."

"I didn't either at first," Willa said. "But she explained it to me. When I think of vampires, the stereotype that forms in my mind is the alluring romantic, right?"

"Yeah, Anne Rice and those *Twilight* books. I'm more of a Bram Stoker guy, but whatever floats your boat."

"She explained it to me," Willa said. "So vampires are all about *power*, right?"

"Yeah, I think Gil said something about that."

"And they're willing to seize this power in whatever way they can. Like any good organization, they've got tactics and trends, and like any good organization, they have changed over time. In this case, *centuries*.

Vampires originally began as crypt-dwelling monsters, snatching children in the night and feeding on the blood of humans to change people covertly into vampires in hopes of raising an undead army."

"Old school," I said.

She nodded. "Exactly. But after hundreds of years of hiding in shadows, they changed, abandoning fear and embracing something different. They hoped to grow their numbers with something new, something they called *seductive assimilation*. They took on roles of incubi and succubi, using love and sex to prey on the innocent. Still with me?"

"Now it's Anne Rice."

"Okay, it's a little weird you know this much about vampire fiction."

"Hey, reading is cool."

"All right. Anyway, this romantic non-hostile takeover approach failed around the turn of the century and was abandoned soon after the last great war. Apparently, history says that in the war, vampires were nearly wiped out. They were weakened and drastically reduced in numbers, so their tactics changed again within the remaining vampire communities. As I understand it, they came together and formed something called the Battery. It is the first and only ruling body that oversees all living vampires. Does this make sense?"

I nodded. "I think so. Man, once I was out of the room she must have gotten pretty talkative."

Willa rolled her eyes. " Anyway, the first thing the Battery did was create laws to ensure the future of vampires. In addition to changing tactics from seductive assimilation to incorporated power, the Battery formed the laws that now outline contemporary vampire culture, including one explicitly stating that mating with humans was *forbidden*."

"Hold on," I said. "Incorporated power... how literal is that? Does that mean like corporations?"

"Yes. Vampires were now on the level and wearing suits. She said they've got offices and letterheads. Apparently that's the new way."

"That makes sense with what I've learned recently. And this whole love thing?"

"A vampire and a human cannot be romantically involved in any capacity. It's more than just a faux pas, it's considered a slap in the face of vampire life, of the culture, of the law, and of the Battery. They

229

believe that crossbreeding weakens them. She said the Battery dismissed it as a show of weakness and faithlessness in the cause."

"That's why Bathory begged Eliza Adams not to leave her husband?"

"Yes. He couldn't be with her; he couldn't marry her. Do you understand? Their love is the reason that the support for Bathory dried up. Their love was the reason he was *killed*."

"But why?"

"By getting involved with Eliza Adams, Bathory proved he'd turned his back on the Battery. Their rulings and laws were no good to him. And here's the crux of it all: vampires thrive on solidarity, even more so than power. After the last great war that left them in such tattered ranks, they knew that the only way to survive was to stay together, which is why they formed the Battery in the first place and why eugenics became such an integral part of vampire culture. Now they follow the same laws, they listen to the same ruling body, they believe in the same ultimate goal. Because they realize without that solidarity they are lost. That being said, it is really disturbing that they are now apparently in bed with Bluebeard. The dynamics are shifting, and I don't think for the better. "

I paused to think about it. Then I stopped, because I didn't really want to think about it.

"How did the old lady know all this?" I asked.

"Bathory told her," Willa said. "They were together for a long time, Dylan, and this was why they couldn't *stay* together."

"What ended up happening?"

"Dolan's photographs," Willa said. "Remember? They were the proof the Battery needed. He was disregarding their law. Once there is any hint of dissent, it's considered a division of power. And once there's a division of power, everything goes to hell. When Bathory was fingered as a dissenter, a judgment had to be passed. The Battery decides if the dissenter has any grounds."

"In the case of Edward Bathory and Eliza Adams...?"

"They decided that Bathory was the problem," Willa said. "Bathory had to go."

"And they killed him?"

She nodded. "They killed him."

"Even though he was their best chance at political office?"

She nodded. "The laws must be followed, and like I said, the only thing greater than power is solidarity. There can be no insubordination, no independence, no schism."

"And Eliza Adams has been on the run since?"

"No, Dylan. She came here because this is Edward's home. This is where *he* was born. It's been knocked down and rebuilt countless times over the years, but he was born *here* over a hundred and fifty years ago. He arranged for her to be taken away, and he begged her to stay here, to live out her remaining years safely in this house. The Battery ruled against him more than forty years ago, and she's been alone since. At this point, she wants nothing more than for them to find her. Death and fear aren't really motivating factors anymore. Her own death doesn't scare her."

"Good grief," I said, leaning back. Cue guilt.

"I'm not even sure if anyone is still after her," Willa admitted. "But for years they were."

"Why did she tell you this?"

"When you said that my husband's life was in danger. It... it made her understand why I was there. So your efforts weren't totally wasted."

"That was all it took?"

"*All?*" Her face flushed with anger. "That's *all?*"

"No, wait, I mean–"

"Dylan, sometimes you need to give people a chance to explain themselves, and other times..." she looked away from me, across the creek, "you need to think about how other people feel. "

I was quiet. Her words stung, that's how I knew they were true. She wasn't just talking about my attitude towards the old woman, either. She was talking about her husband, as well. I'd been thinking of him only insomuch as a means to an end, a way of pleasing Willa. Alfred Bascombe wasn't even a real person to me. And Willa had realized it before I had.

"We've got a job to do, all right?" she said. "And we can't be doing... this."

I nodded. "You're right. I'm... I'm sorry."

"I'm sorry too. For everything," she said, her voice softening. "I just need you to know. I need you to know where I stand. All right? I love my husband, Dylan."

Where she stood. Ahh, yes. That answered any question that may have been lingering in the back of my mind. Quelled that fire with a big bucket of water. I nodded.

"All right," I said.

I turned over the ignition and the sedan's engine grumbled to life. I was embarrassed and a little sad. I focused on the road as we drove back, trying to busy my mind going over the information Willa had gotten out of the old woman.

We'd nearly reached the airport when it occurred to me.

"Solidarity," I said aloud, my mind beginning to put together a rough outline of a plan.

Willa looked at me. "What?"

"Solidarity," I repeated. "They're all about solidarity."

She nodded.

"That's it. That's the key. That's how we win."

She nodded again. "Yes, it is."

CHAPTER 30. THE ROUND-UP, PARDNER

"You ordered me what?" Willa asked for the third time.

"Baby back ribs, mashed potatoes, steak fries, corn on the cob with extra salt and extra butter, onion rings, potato salad, broccoli salad, macaroni salad, corn bread, cole slaw, macaroni and cheese, and a side of barbecue sauce."

"Starch and starch with a side of fat. And mayonnaise."

Gil nodded. "Yeah. I mean, the good stuff. What did you want? *A salad*? Good gravy Marie, woman. Old Abercrombian saying: Eat meats, not beets. Or is it eat meat, not peat." He shrugged. "It's a tough rhyme, but the sentiment is perfectly sound."

She sighed. She was fitting in quite well with me and Finch.

"I knew you two'd be hungry," he explained to us, smiling. "It's been a hell of a day, hasn't it?"

I would have nodded if I'd had any energy left. Jet lag would make the food taste better, but each bite would bring me closer and closer to the inevitable sleep. A few hours ago, Willa and I had been staring at a cottage in the woods of northern Michigan; now we were sitting across from Gil and Finch at Harold's Meat Shack, overlooking a spread of ribs that would make most competitive eaters fear for their lives.

"Okay, so now that the food's here, go back a few steps," Gil said, taking a huge bite from a rib. Barbecue sauce spread obscenely across his face. "You said this old lady confirmed the Battery?"

I nodded. Beside me, Willa remained speechless, her eyes locked on her plate, glazed over.

"Seriously?" he said. "I mean... the *Battery*? She said they're real?"

"Uh huh. Yeah. Why?"

"That is a breakthrough," Finch said as he tucked a large white napkin into the neck of his black shirt. "A rather remarkable one, in fact. The existence of the Battery has long been a rumor, but little more than that. Getting someone to go on the record about it is harder than getting someone to go on record about the multiverse or the future of social security. The term 'rumor' is a grand understatement; *myth* or *legend* is more like it."

"Legend is about right," Gil sputtered, launching kernels of buttered corn across the table. "Nobody I ever spoke to would say boo about it. Seriously. So either this old bat's nuts, or she's got balls the size of–"

"Yes," Finch interrupted, scowling. "Quite. As we've said, this is a rather surprising revelation."

"How can they be so powerful if no one can even confirm their existence?" I asked.

"It ain't the only powerful group you never heard of," Gil said. He dropped a gnawed rib to his plate and wiped his hands up and down the paper bib covering his pink Hawaiian shirtfront.

"Like many covert organizations, they stay below the radar," Finch said. "And they deal only with others of their kind."

"You mean other vamps?" Willa said, breaking her silence as she took a tentative bite from a brick of cornbread.

"Essentially, yeah," Gil nodded, dropping a bone onto a plate that was already frighteningly empty. A pile of pale bones lay in the center of the dish, picked clean.

Finch cleared his throat. "Myth holds that the Battery has agents that deal with various otherworld species and sects–for example, an agent who deals with covens, an agent who deals with demons, and so forth. But the Battery itself will work directly with no one beyond their own circle. In addition to agents, they have contractors, outsiders they hire to do their hands-on work for them. This withdrawn and detached management style helps keep them insulated. Half of it's for their own protection, and half to streamline everything they do."

"What exactly does all that mean, Finch? In non-supernatural scientist lingo."

"They are the managers, the overseers, the coordinators. But they remain in shadow. By making sure that everything comes through the Battery, it ensures that they're always in control but always safely concealed. If this is true, they have countless agents who are completely in the dark, forcing them to be loyal because they do not know who else is in the Battery's employ. It's how they keep the power consolidated and how they keep all their people loyal. Remember, the worst thing that could happen is some kind of faction. This policy ensures that power is kept in one place all the time. Trust me, if your congress implemented practices even half as stringent, they would accomplish a great deal more."

"Well it sounds like vamps work together a little better than we do," I said.

"If they didn't," Gil muttered, "they'd be extinct by now."

"That's correct," Finch said.

"What does that all mean for us?" I asked.

"End of the day, I think it means she's legit," Gil said, dropping the final bone to his plate and burping. A waitress in a pair of shorts that looked more like underwear appeared at his elbow to clear his plate in time for him to receive a fresh one. "Nobody mouths off about the Battery willy-nilly," he said. "They'd just get whacked."

"Yes," Finch said, nodding. "I agree. Given the limited knowledge I have about the Battery, what she says seems to fit with them perfectly. I'd wager that she's telling the truth."

"We were talking," I said, gesturing to Willa. "And we think this is the best way to go about splitting this whole thing up and landing on our feet."

Gil's eyes narrowed as he lowered a piece of meat from his mouth. "What do you mean?" he asked.

"This factioning," she said. "We need to find a way to undermine their main source of power, in this case, Bluebeard. It worked once with Bathory, so it should work again, right? If we can somehow split up their base of power, we can let them self-destruct just like last time."

I nodded. "Exactly. We find another candidate to drop into the mix. All we need is a little support, just enough to make the right people take notice, and it will crack this whole thing right down the middle. I mean, we already know how tenuous these otherworld power truces are, anyway. Bathroy's case was a prime example of it, and Eliza Adams proves it."

In Finch's eyes, I could see him turning the matter over in his head. Before he could speak, Gil chimed in. "Absolutely not," he said. "Out of the question."

"What?" I asked. "Why?"

"Because what you're proposing is actually *more* dangerous than a frontal assault. These 'otherworld power truces' you mention so cavalierly are really just gigantic consolidations of power. When you stick your finger in there and start meddling around, good things don't happen, believe me. And it's not tenuous, this shit's like nitroglycerine; it's volatile, man. It probably won't work and it's just gonna piss off a lot of different groups of people. Besides, we already have a solution: the mayor."

"Well this third party guy doesn't have to *win*," I said. "He just has to bust up what's going on. We basically just don't want Bluebeard to win, right? We need our own Ross Perot."

"I think you have chosen an inappropriate metaphor, Dylan, but I am following you," Finch said.

"No, goddamnit. We need to take Bluebeard out of this," Gil said, lowering his voice. "With Bluebeard still in the game in any fashion, the mayor is *out*."

"Wait, what do you mean?" Willa asked. "I thought the mayor had already withdrawn from the race."

"Not willingly," Gil said.

"What?" she asked.

"That's just one of the things Finch and I figured out today while you two were on your friggin' nature hike," Gil said, taking a bite of cornbread. "You'd be surprised what his campaign manager was willing to tell us after a few glasses of scotch."

Willa leaned forward, her eyes widening. "Hold on, you got him *drunk?*"

"Well, he wasn't feelin' particularly chatty," Gil said defensively. "Not at first, anyway."

"But we learned that Bluebeard's people have been putting the pinch on the mayor as well," Finch said, taking a sip from a glass of water. "It sounds like the same pressure is being applied on all sides."

"What do you mean?" I asked.

"There is pressure from Bluebeard for the Mayor to exit the race, but there's apparent pressure *on* Bluebeard as well," Finch explained.

Willa and I exchanged a glance.

"I got one of my bank guys to dig around," Gil continued, "and he found something... interesting, especially considering none of this matches Bluebeard's MO."

"His MO?" I asked.

"Modus operandi?" Gil said, his eyes opening wide. "Duuhhh."

"No, I mean *what* is Bluebeard's MO?"

"He works alone, remember?" Finch said. "This is not only incredibly out of character, but it simply doesn't make sense. There are recorded incidences and crimes attributed to Bluebeard literally going back centuries, and I told you that I've met the man. This isn't like him."

"He ain't pullin' the strings," Gil said. "That's what we figured out."

"What did you end up finding that supported this?" I asked Gil.

"Huh?"

"What evidence did your bank employee get his hands on?"

"Oh, yeah. So my bank snoop looked into the campaign committee's funds for me, the funds for your husband, Willa."

She grimaced. "Not so impressive, really. Explains why we weren't so popular, really."

"That's just it," Gil said. "It *was* impressive. I thought it was weird, too, so I had him dig deeper. We found two separate accounts. One was paltry, but the other was *crazy*. Tons of money. *Tons*. The larger, more impressive account is also the more active of the two, while the other hasn't seen any kind of deposits in weeks."

"Again, what does all this mean?" I asked.

"The big account, the one we figure to be Bluebeard's account, that one was only opened about five weeks ago."

"Seems pretty convenient," I said.

Gil nodded. "Yeah, and it's not linked to the name Bascombe in any way," he said. "It was opened by a third party."

"Well that's not all that uncommon when it comes to re-election funds, is it?" I asked.

Finch shook his head. "Of course not, funds for re-election are almost always run through third party companies or LLC's established for the sole purpose of electing a public official."

I shrugged. "Then what's weird about it?"

"This is a private account. A private *individual's* account."

"One person's account? Not a whole front company for the Battery? Just one guy?" I asked.

Gil and Finch nodded.

"This one mystery man is the guy driving the boat," I said.

"Another truly terrible metaphor, Dylan," Finch said. "But you are correct. The mayor's campaign manager alluded to specific private funding, as well. So there is a private individual with a large surplus of money acting as the catalyzing force here. Someone is literally writing the checks. Based on the information we acquired today, there's enough money behind Bluebeard to make all the recent fundraisers unnecessary."

"Then what is it for? Public opinion?"

"Support," Willa said, her voice low. Her eyes were out of focus as her mind wandered away at the repercussions of what Finch and Gil were saying. It was making more sense to her than it was me. "Junkets and dinners and ballroom dances, all this is for the sake of public popularity. There are more ways to support a candidate than simply donating money. And people who can't be bought with money can be bought in other ways."

"Precisely," Finch said.

A waitress came by and delivered another few plates of ribs to Gil's delight. I cringed. Somewhere by the bar a jukebox came to life, filling the room with raucous country music. Gil swooned with delight.

"Great tune, Delilah!" he said to the departing waitress.

"I put it on for you, baby," she cooed.

"What is this?" I asked. "Toby Keith?"

"You betcha, big boy," Gil laughed. "What do you listen to?"

"Jazz, folk, acoustic–"

"Snob," he growled as he lifted a forkful of macaroni and cheese.

Despite myself, I laughed. Beside me, Willa laughed too. She leaned back and took a sip from a beer on the table. Across from me, Finch almost cracked a smile (but not quite). "*Anyway*," I said, "this is bad, right? A big money player?"

"Yeah," Gil nodded as he took a sip from a stein of lemonade. "In politics, money's gold. Add a shitload of otherworld muscle behind it from the Battery and you've got a recipe for disaster."

"Then who's the money?" I asked.

Gil shook his head as he ripped into a thick slice of meat. "There's the problem. No clue."

There was a lull. Gil continued eating at a pace that couldn't be matched even by a teenage boy while the rest of us picked at our plates like lethargic birds. I mustered the courage to eat a few ribs.

"How do you eat this?" I moaned. "I can feel a heart attack brewing right now."

"You gotta be young, brother bear," Gil said, grinning.

"I'm younger than you are."

"Not at heart," he smiled.

"I think I'm with Dylan on this one," Willa said, turning to me. "Do they have salads in this place that don't come with mayonnaise?"

"No," Gil said, "And thank goodness for that." Finch opened his mouth to chime in and Gil turned to him, a greasy finger raised. "Don't you even say a word! I know exactly where you stand when it comes to quality eating establishments."

"I believe this is in reference to a past comment I made regarding a chain of restaurants called... Waffle House, I believe?"

"I'll never forgive you," Gil grumbled.

Willa and I laughed. In response, Gil waved over another waitress and ordered another rack of ribs. By the time Gil had cleaned his last plate, Willa cleared her throat and broke the silence. "So what are we going to do? We have to *do* something."

"You bet your sweet cheeks we're gonna do somethin'," Gil said, wiping his mouth. "We're gonna take out Bluebeard. We certainly aren't gonna stand by and watch."

"How?" I asked. "We don't have the muscle."

Gil flexed a bicep and looked offended. "We've got *plenty* of muscle, I'll have you know. And we've got surprise on our side, as well. That's the kicker."

I leaned back and sighed. "I hope your plan is better than us kicking his front door down and arresting him."

Gil scoffed. "First of all, wherever we go, we're gonna sneak in the back, not kick in the front, okay? Obviously. Second? We're not about to arrest this guy. He's been killin' innocent ladies for long enough. So we're gonna take him out and make the switcheroo with his better half–if we can *find* the good Mr. Bascombe, that is–so everybody's happy."

Willa spoke up. "This isn't the most..." she trailed off. "...the most well-formulated plan." Her face had blanched at the very thought of a frontal assault on Bluebeard inc., and I'm pretty sure my own complexion was following suit.

"Whaddya mean?" Gil asked. "We'll have my gargoyle champion Ron, as well as his formidable partner in destruction, Archimedes the pigeon. Not to mention the unkillable Finch, me with my awe-inspiring wit, you with your weird hacker whatever thing, and our big bad ace in the hole: Dylan the Magic Man. Didn't modest Dylan here tell you he can explode trash cans and stuff?" his face had lit up like a kid's on Christmas. "Can't touch this," he said, waving his hand around the table.

"Dylan mentioned it, yeah," Willa murmured. "I just don't know how realistic this is," she said.

"I have to agree here, Boss," I said. "We're absolutely not capable of any kind of assault on him. Are you hoping to hit him in his offices? At the Prava Center? I don't think having me and a pigeon is going to make a huge difference."

"No, no, good grief," he said. "Attempting an attack at the Prava would be like trying to storm Fort Knox."

"So where are we planning on hitting him?" I asked.

"I don't know that yet, but we've got time, don't you worry. The absolute details haven't been ironed out." He grinned. "Yet. I said *yet*, haven't been ironed out *yet*. You'll both be a lot more comfortable when we've got a plan, trust me. For now just relax, okay? Enjoy the musical stylings of Garth Brooks and indulge in the best pie south of Bob Evans."

"Pie?" I gasped.

"It just doesn't feel right," Willa said. "This feels like a bad idea. Any kind of frontal assault on Bluebeard is a mistake, pure and simple. We may *just* have the power to kick-start a coup, but we don't have the muscle to burn the damn house down. Which is why I really think we need to take a few steps back to our original plan," she said, glancing at me. "The third party candidate to split support. Snap this truce like a twig."

"I agree," I said. "It makes sense and it's safer."

"What did I say the first time?" Gil said, his voice rising. "This is *not* an option. You're not even talking about making a deal with a vampire, you're talking about trying to make a deal that might involve the damn *Battery*. You wanna use politics to fight the politicos. We can take on Bluebeard on his turf; we can't touch the Battery on theirs. It

would be like trying to get Hitler to mow your lawn. It's ridiculous. "
He turned briefly to Finch. "Put that metaphor in your pipe and smoke it.
And how do you two think you'll get the help of a group of vampires that
doesn't even want you knowing they exist, anyway? They killed
Bathory because he was with a human woman, that's all. So what are
you gonna do? Walk up to their front door and knock? Offer to trade
'em your favorite matchbox cars for their help? You'll be dead in two
seconds. No, less than two seconds. And has it occurred to you that
we're *assuming* the Battery is supporting Bluebeard? It adds up, but we
don't know for sure. The mystery financier could be completely
unrelated. We don't know what's goin' on in their evil peanut brains. No
clue. But bottom line: vampires are not to be trusted. Get that? Never.
Never ever. Never trust them." He turned to Willa. "Am I clear, young
lady? To them, we are insects to be squashed. They ain't gonna do our
dirty work for us."

"But isn't it worth a–" Willa began.

"No, it's not," Gil interrupted, slapping a hand down onto the table.
Dishes rattled at the impact. "This is for your own good, *both* of you;
please trust me. I'm protecting you, okay? It's out of the question. Out
of the question. Do you understand?"

Willa and I were silent.

"Do you *understand*?" he repeated.

I mumbled something inaudible but nodded nonetheless. Willa
looked up at Gil stubbornly. "Yes, Dad."

"Okay," he said after pause, finally cracking a smile. "Good. Now,
to the *really* important business; what kind of pie do y'all want?"

"No more," we all mumbled in unison, hands unconsciously moving
to our bulging stomachs.

Gil looked up to an approaching buxom waitress and grinned.
"Four slices of pecan pie, my love," he said.

CHAPTER 31. HELLO TROUBLE

I was driving. The traffic around us was light as we rumbled down 76 towards Center City. Willa was beside me in the passenger's seat while Finch and Gil shared the bench seat in back. When the first slug hit the Tank's body, it sounded like a stone thrown by a child. We had been laughing at something silly Gil had said. But when my window exploded, we'd figured out we were in a bit of trouble.

Willa kept her cool, surprising me, gasping for a moment before sliding down in her seat, tucking her knees beneath the dash as bullets smashed through the windshield. Gil was hollering wordlessly, any meaning lost in the hammering of gunshots. Finch leaned forward and grabbed the steering wheel as I ducked in time to feel the cold breeze of a bullet passing within inches of my skull.

"Gun," Finch shouted into my ear. "Gun!"

I looked up at him. "Not carrying," I screamed as the rear windshield erupted, showering glass debris across the backseat. I hadn't carried since the first night at the dock, a mistake I swore I would not make again. Beside me, Willa's eyes were pinched closed, her hands clasped over her ears. Blood spattered across my cheek as a bullet caught Finch just below the collarbone. He swore and bucked, releasing the wheel as the car began to swerve across the highway.

When the chasing car hit us, it nearly put us into the concrete wall in the center of the road, but the terrible shriek of metal on metal cued me to get my hand on the wheel. We were surrounded by civilians going about sixty-five miles an hour; at this speed they're not called "car accidents," they're called "car wrecks." Whatever the other car was, it was big. I swerved out of the left lane in time to feel a second impact push us into the right shoulder and within whispering distance of the guardrail. I sat up in my seat, just enough to see over the dashboard, and caught a glimpse of a hulking pick-up truck in the side view mirror just before a shotgun slug tore it off the car.

"GUN!" Finch shouted again, his face pale as blood ran freely down his chest.

"I don't have a gun, goddamnit," I yelled in response. "Don't you have some magic you could *throw* at him?"

A thunderous crunch of metal on metal sounded against the car's body, loud and hard enough for me to feel the impact through the steering wheel, and I saw wide circular holes opening on the Tank's hood. A half-dozen shots followed one after another. I didn't know shit about cars, but I figured that couldn't be good; shotgun shells and engine blocks probably don't get along well. A thin wisp of smoke began to flow from the hood that was beginning to resemble Swiss Cheese.

Finch disappeared from view for a moment, and I could hear hurried words between him and Gil. I dropped my foot on the pedal, gassing the Tank as much as its prehistoric engine would allow. Slowly, we began to speed up, the engine groaning under the stress. Ignoring petty restrictions like lanes and traffic laws, I swerved in between well-polished sedans and minivans as a rain began to fall from the dark night sky. In a moment, it was torrential. Big drops pattered across the smashed glass of the windshield as headlights flashed in my rearview mirror.

"Any ideas?" I shouted over the roar of wind as the bright lights behind us approached. I didn't have time to brace for impact before the huge truck hit us again, throwing us forward into a luxury sedan in front of us. The impact pushed the unfortunate sedan off the road and into the guardrail with a *crash*. I couldn't watch as it T-boned the rail and flipped over. Waves of water from the flooding roadway mixed with debris from the twisted undercarriage and flew up into our windshield. I spun the wheel to pull the Tank away from the crash as the truck hit us again.

Gil's head appeared in my rearview, his scraggly hair blowing in the gales of wind pouring in through the shattered back windshield. He hefted a compact revolver and extended it unsteadily towards our pursuer. He squeezed off a shot, the sound paltry compared to the pick-up truck's monstrous shotgun blasts. If the shot made any difference, I couldn't tell.

Finch appeared again at my side. "Get off at the next exit," he said. "Whatever it is, we need off this road."

A green highway sign flashed past on my right. Next stop, 30th Street Station. A hub of transit in the city. Septa, Amtrak, bus lines. That meant lots of civilians and lots of cops. I tried to decide how bad of an idea it was. My careful decision-making process was interrupted when I realized I had to get to the other side of the three lane highway with about a dozen cars in my way. I pulled my foot off the gas and twisted the wheel, the Tank slamming into a taxicab as the pick-up loomed in my rearview.

I couldn't outrun him, and I wasn't a good enough driver to out maneuver him, so I hit the breaks. All around us, I could hear car horns come alive from anyone who hadn't gotten the bright idea to pull over and let us go. A rusted hatchback swerved to go around us as the Tank's speed went from 75 to 30 in about three seconds. Before I was completely aware of what was happening, the pick-up had rocketed past, its red brake lights illuminating as it shot past. Before the truck stopped, I dropped my foot back onto the gas and turned sharply towards the exit, the monstrosity of the Tank creeping across the highway and up the steep ramp to 30th Street with all the speed of a sloth.

The pursuing truck was newer and in better shape than the Tank, but it was still a damn big vehicle, so it struggled, its diesel engine roaring behind us.

At the top of the exit ramp, the trickle of smoke seeping from the hood had become a heavy stream. It was loud in the car, everyone was shouting and the wind and rain were blowing through the busted windows. My hands were shaking, and I couldn't catch my breath.

"Is everyone all right?" Gil shouted over the din.

We each muttered, but nothing coherent. Somewhere outside I could hear approaching sirens and the distant sound of car horns from the highway. I tested the gas, and the engine was slow to respond.

"I said is everyone all right?"

"Yes," Willa said, pulling herself upright as she wiped water from her face. She looked at me. "Are you okay?"

I nodded. "Finch caught one, though," I said looking into the rearview mirror. I could see Finch collapsed back into the seat with Gil hovering over him. The color in Finch's face was a little better, but not much. "What about you, Boss?"

"I'm all right," he said. "We got lucky."

"I wouldn't call that luck," I said as a pair of high beams caught the rearview mirror. "Shit, here we go."

I dropped my foot heavily onto the gas, but the engine was dying. I could feel it turning over slower and slower, the wheels struggling to make every rotation. We curved around the station, masses of pedestrians running for shelter in the worsening rain. Behind us, I heard an engine rev.

"Hold on," I shouted.

The lights grew bright just before the hit. When the truck hit us, we were barely making 30 mph. My head hit the steering wheel, and I saw stars. I heard the squeal of tires as the driver behind us pushed the disabled Tank through a red light and into the heavy traffic of Market Street. Headlights poured through the rain-soaked windshield and I could hear the sound of car horns. My vision faded into darkness, and I felt myself slouch towards unconsciousness.

When I opened my eyes I was flat on my back in the gutter. I could hear shouting and the sound of gunfire. That's always a good sign.

"Get up, goddamnit!"

Willa was hunched over me, her hair soaked and hanging in her face. I sat up and almost vomited, nausea rising in me like a wave. Her hands were clutching fistfuls of my shirtfront and she was shaking me violently. I blinked a few times to clear my eyes and took stock of my surroundings.

The Tank was shielding me from the gunfire. Gil and Finch were huddled against the huge car's side paneling as pistol and shotgun fire tore through the already ravaged vehicle. Willa tugged at me again, struggling to get me upright. I closed my eyes, held my breath, and sat up, managing somehow to keep down the barbecue from dinner.

The rain had increased. Deep puddles were spreading across the road surface. Everything looked a little foggier than usual, and I didn't know if it was because of the weather or the state of my head.

"We gotta get outta here," Gil said, turning to me. He lifted his pistol and shook his head. *Empty.*

We were close enough to the heart of the city to be able to disappear, the only feat would be getting out of our pursuer's sight lines. From what I could hear, there were at least two shooters, and our current position held little defensible cover, especially considering we were unarmed. Pinned down. I shook the stars out of my head. Well, not totally unarmed, I realized.

"Step back," I said.

Willa looked up at me and pushed the hair from her face, her eyes wide. "What are you going to do?" she asked. Before I could respond, Gil took her arm and pulled her close to him, into the cover of the Tank. "Give the man space," he said softly.

I inched to the front of the car and peered around towards the truck as bullets took bites from the asphalt in front of me. The truck was about twenty or thirty paces away and lined up parallel to us. I couldn't see anything or anyone but the occasional muzzle flash. I had no idea who the bastards were, but their intentions were pretty clear.

"What are you going to do?" I heard Willa ask from behind me. "Dylan," she said when I didn't respond. "What are you going to do?"

"I'm going to try and get our asses out of here," I said, squinting against the rain. In the distance I could hear sirens, but whoever was taking potshots at us didn't seem to care. The last thing I needed was to bring more innocent people into this. I poked my head further out to try and see someone–*anyone*–that I could get a bead on. When it happened, I didn't see them, I *heard* them. It was a growl, a deep mongrel growl.

"Dog soldiers," I said. That answered a few questions. I looked back over my shoulder at my friends, huddled together in a mass. "Get ready to run," I said. They nodded.

I focused on the truck as the sirens grew louder, imagining not only the dog soldiers huddled behind it, guns trained on our ruined Tank, but also imagining the truck itself and the little bit of machinery I actually understood. In my mind's eye, I started at the ignition on the steering column and moved down to where I imagined the starter to be. Somewhere inside was the actual ignition, the point inside the engine where the starter ignited the gasoline. *All the makings are already there*, I thought to myself. *It just needs a little–*

Spark. But before I'd even connected the dots in my head as I'd learned to do, the truck exploded in a swirling miasma of red and orange as a storm of flames engulfed it. I felt the heat even before my eyes had fully opened. Before I had a moment's chance to dwell on the fact that at least two creatures were being burned alive, I felt hands on my back, pulling to get me on my feet.

"Come on," Willa was saying. "Come on."

"I think it's okay, Wil–"

Gunfire interrupted me, a frantic rattling of shots that lacked the patience taken to aim. I heard bullets ricochet from the Tank and the road. Willa tugged at me, pulling me to my feet and leading me down the street in a huddled run. Behind us, Gil was struggling with Finch's weakened form. In the distance, I could see two smoking shapes emerge from the flames, singed and angry dog soldiers looking for payback.

I pulled Willa to a stop and looked back at Gil, but he waved me off. "Go!" he shouted. "I'll get him. Split up, meet us back at the office." He slipped Finch's arm around his shoulders and hauled him across the street into an alley by the old Post Office, sparing a last glance in our direction to shout "Go!" once more. Willa didn't need another hint. She hooked her arm in mine and dragged me away from the burning wreck.

I was dazed, but I managed with her guiding me. She pulled me over the flooding Market Street Bridge as a fleet of police cars flew past us. On the other side, she led me north down a narrow street. We paused momentarily under an overpass before continuing. A few minutes later and I was lost in alleyways of garbage and flooded gutters. Dead on my feet, I was ready to lay down in a dumpster, and I probably would have if Willa hadn't been there. With each corner and alleyway, we lost speed, but we kept going. The buildings around us were getting taller and I knew we were creeping slowly into Center City. Gil's office couldn't be far off.

Willa stopped to get her bearings in the shadows at an intersection and left me leaning against a cool, wet, brick wall. I closed my eyes, trying to shake the cobwebs from my head, but I felt so tired. I covered my face with my hands and listened to the sound of the city around me, feeling the rain soaking through my clothes.

That was when I heard it: the soft tap of a claw on pavement. I didn't wait for a good look. Acting on instinct only, I grabbed Willa and pulled her into an alleyway and on to the ground. With a grunt, I pulled a particularly pungent bag of trash onto us. I clamped my hand over her mouth before she had a chance to say a word as I did my best to pull our legs beneath the covering of garbage.

Sliding as low as I could, I kept an eye on the alleyway and intersection while still covering my face. The intersection was empty of traffic, but the street was a slow river of water flowing freely over the sidewalks. Willa's body was pressed against me and she was still and silent. I could feel the cold water filling my shoes. The longer we were huddled in the trash, the more I began to believe the sound had been my imagination. Then I heard it again: a soft tap, like the sound a dog makes when it walks across a tile floor.

A huge dog's foot stepped from behind a dumpster. The fur was brown, although large patches of it had been scorched black. Chunks of fur were missing in other places, leaving raw red patches instead. My eye followed the inhuman body upward to the hulking head of the Rottweiler. The lighter fur around its jaw was bloody. The beast's eyes were sharp as they moved up and down the alley, but it wasn't the dog soldier's eyes I was worried about. At the end of the monster's great snout, its gleaming black nose twitched with each breath. I pulled Willa tighter to me and closed my eyes. From where we were lying, the garbage seemed pretty rancid. I hoped it was rancid enough.

The beast stood over us, moving its massive head from side to side for what seemed like a lifetime. A thick, strong hand slowly extended towards the pile of trash. From a broken bag to my left, a long-tailed city rat skittered free and ran across the dog's foot. The creature stepped back and snarled. Finally, after a long moment, it turned and ran back into the alley as a police car cruised through the intersection, lights flashing slowly.

Neither of us moved for a long while. Eventually, we pushed the trash off and rose from beneath the reeking protection in the alley. After a long, exhausted silence, Willa looked over at me and smiled a weary smile. Even in the terrible dank alley, in the midst of a torrential rain and perhaps flash flood, and covered with the remains of a bag of summer-ripened garbage, she looked beautiful. She reached out and took my hand for just a moment.

"Are you okay?" she asked.

"Yeah," I said. "I'm great."

She smiled again and nodded. After a moment she released my hand. "All right," she said, taking a deep breath and clearing her sopping hair from her face. "Let's get out of here."

CHAPTER 32. LET'S NOT MAKE A DEAL

There was a man waiting outside of Gil's building when Willa and I finally emerged from the tangled half-flooded labyrinth of side streets. We were both soaked to the skin, clothes clinging to our bodies, hair dangling in wet strands down Willa's face. I saw the guy from half a block away, and I stopped Willa with a hand on her arm.

"Who is it?" she asked.

I shook my head. "I don't know." The rain was still pounding down, keeping the streets empty of the usual foot traffic. The figure standing in the shadows was the only other person in sight.

"What do you think we should do?" she continued.

"Wait here." I pulled her out of the murky halo of a streetlight and into darkness. "Wait and see what happens, all right?" She nodded.

As I approached, the man took a step forward, cocking his head slightly to the side. He held a bright red umbrella, spotted with strange shapes, and he wore a long pale trench coat over what looked like a light-colored suit. In his free hand, he held a battered leather briefcase. A bit thick in the midsection but decidedly human, the mystery man didn't look to be one of Cally's dog soldier heavies.

I slowed down about a dozen paces from the stranger. "Who are you?"

The man stepped forward into the light and tipped his umbrella back, exposing his face to the light of the pale moon. Big drops of rainwater pattered against his unnaturally thick glasses. Despite the rain, he smiled. "Mr. Dylan," he said.

"Keats?"

"At your service, sir," he nodded to me as he stepped back into the cover of the building and lowered his umbrella. I noticed that the strange shapes were cartoon dragons. Appropriate.

He shook the umbrella off and handed it to me, grimacing in the foul weather. "Wanna go retrieve your partner?" he nodded back in Willa's direction.

I accepted the umbrella gratefully. "Thanks. What are you doing here?"

"I had a meeting scheduled with you for yesterday," he said. "But I guess you guys were all pretty busy fightin' monsters and whatnot." He lifted his briefcase. "I've got some things you need to see."

I swore under my breath. So the Keats meeting wasn't a fool's errand. I was lazy and impatient when I blew it off. "Sorry. We've been... eh, a bit bogged down," I said. "Knee-deep in a pretty ugly mess. Again, I'm sorry; it's been a weird twenty-four hours."

He smiled and wiped his thinning hair off his wide forehead. "Hey, no problem, Mr. Dylan, no problem at all. Why don't you go get your friend and we'll head inside. I don't much like the rain."

I could see that. Even under the partial overhang, Keats seemed to be wilting. His suit was rumpled and wet beneath his stained trench, and his thin hair looked even thinner when it was drenched. I pulled a recently acquired key ring from my pocket and tried a few shiny keys before locating the correct one. With a quick turn, I unlocked the front door to the office building. "Step inside," I said.

"Much obliged!" he said, smiling up at me.

I let the door close behind him and crossed the stretch of street back to Willa's vantage across the way, dragon umbrella in tow. As I approached, she stepped out into the light, her arms crossed over her chest, looking nearly as withered as poor Keats.

"Who's that?"

"A death collector named Keats who probably wishes he was born a Viking," I said.

"Huh?"

I shook my head. "Nothing, nevermind. He's a good guy. He's one of Gil's contacts. I've met with him already; a little eccentric, but just in a sad way. He says he's got some information for us."

"He's that guy you blew off yesterday?"

I nodded sheepishly and Willa shook her head.

"Let's see what he's got to say," she said.

***

We took the elevator up to Gil's offices and stepped out, all three of us shivering in the building's air conditioning. Dottie's dour face greeted us from behind her huge desk as we limped through the main entrance into the Zero's office.

"Where have you been?" she asked. "And where is Mr. Abercrombie?"

"I'm sure he'll be along shortly, Dottie," I said, shaking my head and sending water flying. "Don't worry, he's with Finch." I hoped it was true.

As we passed her desk, she stood, resting her palms flat on the tabletop. "Wait. There's someone here waiting for you."

The three of us stopped en masse and turned. "Me?" I asked.

"Well, Mr. Abercrombie, to be more specific," she said. "But he's waiting to speak with someone. Perhaps you could lend him your ear in the meantime, Mr. Dylan. He made an appointment with me this morning."

I nodded. "Yeah, okay. In the meantime. He's in the conference room?"

She nodded.

"Right-o."

I led the way with Willa a few steps behind me and Keats following at the rear. His eyes widened with each open door we passed. We almost lost him at the weapons office. I'm sure he was more than ready to grab one of those double-sided battle axes and go all Hercules on the first potted palm that came his way.

I knocked on the conference room door once before pushing the door open and stepping inside.

Across the table from the doorway sat an impossibly tall man with exaggerated features not unlike a Cro-Magnon man. A heavy brow sat over wide, sad eyes, and an enormous razor-sharp jaw hung at the base of his skull. His arms were thick and long, leading down to hands large enough to palm a pumpkin. To make the scene even weirder, he wore a gaudy black silk suit, a yellow shirt, and a pink tie.

Frozen in the doorway, I turned to Willa. "You see that, right?" I said softly.

She nodded.

"And you?" I asked Keats.

Slowly, he nodded, but unlike Willa and I, he was not so entertained. His dripping brow had creased, and his eyes, magnified by his glasses, scrutinized the huge man across from us with a ferocity I'd not seen before in the death collector.

"I see him," he said, his voice low.

"What's wrong?" I asked.

He nodded forward, his eyes lowering slightly to the tabletop. "Look."

I turned to face the silent giant and lowered my eyes to the well-polished wooden table separating us. In the reflection on the tabletop, I didn't see the giant. Instead, I saw the pale green skin of the djinn knotted by the twisted black tattoos scorched into its withered flesh. Its crushed beastly face broke into a horrid grin as I realized what it was that sat before me.

I stepped back a few steps, spreading my arms on either side of me, corralling both Willa and Keats backwards with me. "Get out of here," I said. "Now."

"Wait," the beast said, raising one of its monstrous hands. The giant's mouth did not move when the deep voice sent a tremor through the room, but I could hear it nonetheless. "I came to talk," it rumbled. "To negotiate."

"Negotiate? Are you serious?" I asked. "I'm pretty sure the last time I saw you, you tried to negotiate squashing my head. Remember that? Because I do. And you threw me out the window of that damn building." I felt the electric tingle of magic flow through my body like jets of ice water. At some point, my temper had begun to tap into that well of magic. Worrisome.

The giant eyes widened, and it raised both hands peaceably. "But it spared you."

I opened my mouth to speak but stopped, letting the monster's words sink in. *It*, he'd said. *It spared you.*

"What do you mean?" I asked, softly.

"The source of the magic, the *power*. It spared you. You understand that now, do you not?"

"Stop," Keats said, taking a step forward. "Don't listen to it, these creatures deal only in death."

"No, wait," I said, stopping Keats. "I want to hear what he has to say."

"He's right," said a voice from the hall. I glanced over my shoulder to see the sodden shapes of Gil and Finch enter the room. Finch was still leaning heavily on Gil and he looked pretty busted, even for him. "That creature wants nothing but your life, Dylan," Finch continued.

"What do you mean?" I asked.

Gil pulled off his soaked Deerstalker hat and tossed it onto the conference room table where it landed with a *splat*. "He wants it back."

"It?" I asked.

Finch met my eye. "The vael." He turned his gaze to the djinn for the first time. "Am I correct?"

For a moment, the beast was silent, turning the giant's huge eyes over each of us. It clasped its hands on the table before it and began to speak, the earthquake of a voice rising from nothing.

"I traveled through many lands and untold levels of the multiverse to find it, and it is mine. Choice is not a luxury for the vael to indulge, as it has. It was a mistake and I want it back," the voice said. "The power. It belongs to me."

"It's not his to give any more than it was yours to take," Finch said, stepping forward. "*It* chooses, that is the point. And when you touched him, it made its choice. There isn't even a way to get it back."

"Oh, but there is," the monster rumbled. "When a vael's host is destroyed, the vael is forced to revert to the closest entity, in this case: the destroyer."

"That means what I think it means, right?" I asked.

"It must kill you to get the vael back," Finch said.

"What could you possibly be here to negotiate?" Gil asked, his voice rising. "The slaughter of one of our own?"

"It is justice," the djinn said. "It does belong to me."

"You're a fool if you think we're going to hand him over to you," Gil said. "I'm not gonna lose another, do you hear me?"

"Gil, wait a minute," I said. My stomach was quickly tying itself in knots, but I understood the deal before the djinn even laid it out. My life or my friend's lives. I knew the beast wouldn't stop hunting us until it got the vael back.

"Wait nothing, Dylan, you're not gonna listen to this thing's deal," he said. "It ain't justice when it's returning something that was stolen, anyway," Gil grumbled. He looked at the djinn. "I'm sure you murdered for it in the first place."

A placid smile spread over the lips of the giant. "Would you believe that there are worlds where even a monster such as I could be considered benevolent? Such is the multiverse. There are many levels, and many great evils."

My breath caught in my throat. "I can't believe that," I said.

The smile spread further across the giant's face, widening to his oversized ears and opening to expose huge yellow teeth. "Believe it," it said. It's wide walnut-colored eyes met mine. "You know the deal already. I have your lives to negotiate with," the djinn said. "And that is plenty. I got to you once," the giant smiled. "Him," he said pointing at Finch. I turned and remembered laboring over Finch as I watched him expel what I thought to be his last breath. I believed the djinn; it could do it again, and it would. "Give me your life," it said to me, "or I will kill them all."

"There has to be another way," I said as I turned to my friends behind me, all people I'd come to care about greatly. My eyes lingered on Willa's for a moment before I turned around. "I wouldn't let them all die, not for me. There has to be some other deal we can–"

Gil stopped me with a hand on my shoulder and took a step in front of me. He leveled his fists on his hips in his best superman pose and smiled. He opened his mouth to spout his best quip when a sweaty arm elbowed him out of the way.

"Never, monster!" Keats shouted, raising his red dragon umbrella before him like a rapier. "We'll never turn him over to you! Never! Now en guard!"

The giant rose to his feet and bellowed an inhuman roar that was eerily familiar. From the plush carpeting below our feet, the emerald green flames flickered to life, firing across the floor into the body of the giant and engulfing his body. The giant's suit tore away and fell, turning to ash as it hit the floor. With the suit came the skin of the giant and the guise itself. What remained was the broad-chested tattooed monster in all its glory.

Keats leapt onto the conference room table and swung the umbrella over his head, bringing the plastic blade into the side of the djinn's head where it impacted solidly to little effect. As the djinn raised one huge claw to remove poor Keats' head, the heavy ratcheting sound of a pump-action shotgun filled the room.

"Get down!" Dottie shouted from behind us. Gil, Finch, Willa, and I hit the deck in time to hear the *boom* of the gun shake the room. Dottie's shot was perfect, going over Keats' shoulder and slamming into the djinn's chest, sending the monster tumbling backwards with a screech.

Keats began gibbering incoherently as he jumped from the table and tumbled to the ground, dragon umbrella in hand. Dottie racked the shotgun again, dropping a smoking shell to the carpet as she fired again. From our spots on the floor, we could hear the djinn stumble about, roaring angrily.

"Don't just lay there," Dottie said after a moment. *"Do* something!"

Gil and Finch were the first up, dashing from the office and pulling Willa with them. I stumbled to my feet and held my hands in front of me, reaching for some spell or incantation that could do something. What was that fire thing Finch had taught me? Serbian...?

Before I knew what was happening, jets of fire sliced through the air towards the djinn. I felt power running up and down my arms, and I staggered at the vael's single-minded fury as it sent flames roaring towards the beast.

The djinn batted the column of fire away like an insect, tumbling the conflagration into the floor to ceiling windows behind it. In the intense heat, the windows began to warp, losing their shape and consistency before exploding, firing shards of glass around the room.

With a miraculous concentrated effort, I managed to extinguish the fire that spewed uncontrollably from my hands as I staggered backwards. The djinn followed me, taking a step forward and slamming one hand down across the table, cracking the wood into splinters before flipping the two sections in opposite directions against the walls. I backpedaled away from the beast as it crossed the open space between us. It's mouth began to widen, clicking open on unnatural and inhuman hinges, the great maw slowly growing until it was large enough to accommodate a full grown man, namely *me*. I'd seen this trick before.

I pushed myself out into the hallway in time to see Gil and Finch emerge from the weapons room. Gil was swinging a long sword, the blade taking chunks out of the walls. Beside him Finch carried a compact mace and my short sword. Bringing up the rear was Keats, who had donned a heavy iron helmet and was dragging the biggest axe I'd ever seen in my life.

The sight of the motley trio re-inflated my flagging confidence and I focused my thoughts to clear my mind's eye. I raised a hand, visualizing the electrical cables that ran through the drop ceiling. I imagined them pulling themselves free and wrapping around the form of the djinn. I visualized it, and they obeyed. The lights snapped out as feet upon feet of colored wiring ripped free from the ceiling like angry vines and began wrapping themselves around the djinn. The beast slowed and stumbled as all the electricity I could muster pulsed through its body in terrible waves. In the darkness of the room, bright white claws of electricity lanced into the djinn's body. Outside, the lights in the hall flickered before sputtering out and dying, leaving us in pitch blackness. I forced more electricity into the monster, everything I could.

The djinn was screaming as the power jolted through its body. With a twist, the beast pulled one hand free and opened its claws wide. In the darkness, a burst of flame came to life momentarily over its hand. When the fire disappeared, the djinn held a long yellow chain in its hand, the links dripping sparks that burned into the carpeting like molten metal. The beast whipped the coiled chain, slicing through the wiring and freeing itself.

Gil leapt over me and charged the monster, sword in his hand. The djinn met him head on, the yellow chain clashing against Gil's sword and sending shreds of flame fluttering to the carpet. Gil swung for the djinn's head and neck, but the beast met each slash with its chain, its strength pushing Gil back one step at a time. Finch tossed me my sword as I rose to my feet, taking a few steps towards Gil. When my hand closed around the hilt of the blade, pale blue flames spread up and down the length of the blade from tip to pommel and began inching up my arm. The flames were cool, filling me with an endless well of strength unlike anything I'd ever felt before.

I stepped towards the djinn and raised the sword. Swinging its free arm, the monster pushed Gil backwards as it leveled a swing of its chain at my face. I met the chain with the short sword and pushed back, nearly upending the beast with one thrust as the power of the vael overwhelmed me. I felt invincible; the strength flowing up from inside me felt endless. I swung the sword again and the djinn met it with the chain, but only just. Sparks jumped from each impact and drifted to the floor. I swung again, forcing the beast backwards towards the ledge. With each impact the monster roared, but could do nothing to stop me. I pushed harder, leading the beast towards the edge and swinging with every ounce of strength I could muster.

Finally standing on the precipice of the window, I raised the sword to make one final swing, hoping it would be enough. But as I planted my foot, I felt the ground shift. In the face of the beast, my sneaker slid on a mess of shattered glass and my legs gave way, dropping me to my knees. I looked up to see the djinn raise his glowing yellow chain and prepare to bring it down through my skull.

Behind me I heard a shout. By the light of the emergency lamps hanging in the conference room, I saw Finch's mace spiral through the air and hit the djinn dead center in its chest. The beast gave a horrible scream and pitched over the ledge, tumbling out the shattered window.

I crawled forward and looked down over the edge to see the spinning mass of green fire fall through the endless rainstorm towards the street. The fire flickered and died before it hit the ground.

Once again, the djinn was gone.

CHAPTER 33. KEATS' BUSINESS

"Where'd he go? What's next?" Keats asked breathlessly. "Wait. Is that it?"

I slipped back from the threshold and looked back at the rest of the gang as the lights flickered back on. Keats stood at the center of the room, struggling to get the huge battle-ax off the ground. His knees were wobbling and the blade was shaking in his meaty fists. Gil appeared at his side and relieved him of the weapon before he hurt himself. After a moment, Keats collapsed gratefully in a desk chair with a huff.

"That's it," Finch said softly.

"Oh, man," Keats said. "That was incredible."

My own legs were feeling pretty unsteady under me. Willa was at my side in a minute, her arm on mine, guiding me.

"Let's sit down, shall we?" she said.

"In a moment," Finch said, as he blocked our way. "Can I have a word, Dylan?"

I took a deep breath and nodded, releasing my arm from Willa's grasp. "One second," I said to her.

Finch led me out of the ruined conference room and into his adjacent office. He shut the door behind me.

"I believe I should speak with you before Boss did," he said.

I took a seat in one of the visitor's chairs and closed my eyes, trying to steady my heart. "Talk with me about what?" I asked.

"About what happened back there."

"What exactly did happen back there?"

"You were willing to offer yourself up to the beast," he said as he took a seat behind his desk. "And that was a terrible mistake."

"I didn't nearly do anything."

"Yes, you did. For someone with my considerable age, I get underestimated far too frequently. I have learned to read people much better than I get credit for," he said. "And you were ready to give yourself up."

I shrugged. "What's your point?"

"My point is, do not do that again."

"Why? Wise man that you are, you must understand why I was about to do it."

"I understand it on a practical level, Dylan, but that doesn't mean I believe it wise. You have to think of yourself as part of a team now, and in this team, you're as important as Gil or myself. We are equal partners. Sacrificing yourself for any reason whatsoever would seriously damage us as a whole and our ability to help others."

I was confused. As far as I knew, the thought of self-sacrifice had only crossed my mind during a situation I considered most dire. Now Finch was asking me to think about the others and not just myself. I was under the impression that was exactly what I had been doing.

"Where's this coming from?" I asked, an edge more prominent in my voice than I'd intended.

"Where is it coming from? It is coming from the idea that we have a duty here to fulfill. And we cannot do it if we're dead. Understand? We need you alive if we're going to get Bascombe back, if we are to stop Bluebeard, if we're going to do *anything* to change this world. Self-sacrifice is a fine thing, but don't give away the farm for a glass of milk, do you follow me?"

I guess I did, so I shrugged. "I was under the impression that I was doing good," I said. "Or trying to."

"You were doing good for the moment. But as I said, you are on a team now, a team with no expiration date. It is better if you start thinking of it that way." He took a deep breath and sat back, checking his watch. "I believe that's all the time we have," he said. A moment later there was pounding on the door. It was Gil.

He pushed it open in a moment. His face was flushed and he seemed pretty angry. "What was that, huh? Give yourself up?"

I nodded and raised my hands. "It was a mistake," I said.

"You're goddamn right it was, buddy," Gil said, wagging a finger at me. "We're a team here! We've got good things to do! We've–"

"I know, I know that now, I'm sorry."

"That collector back there knew it before you did, and that's something you gotta figure out, got me buster? I'm not gonna have one of my boys be valiant or martyred or whatever you thought. Nobody's gonna be layin' down on the tracks around here, got me?" He took a deep breath, pulled a pipe from his pocket, and shook the stem at me. "I'm not gonna..." he trailed off. After a moment, lit the pipe. He took a deep drag and closed his eyes. A long moment passed as he puffed on the pipe, sending foul clouds up around his head.

Finally, he said, "I'm not going to be hiring anybody else 'round here anytime soon. Got me?"

I nodded.

"Okay. I just wanted that to be clear."

I nodded again.

Gil took a deep breath and nodded. "All right, boys. Enough therapy. Let's get back to work."

***

Keats had set up shop in one of the empty offices. Across a broad table was a spread of paperwork. It looked like Latin to me. Endless streams of characters, some recognizable and some far from it, covered every page. The papers reminded me of the last batch of documents I'd gotten from Keats. The death collector was bent over the desk with Willa at his side. Their eyes followed his chubby index finger up and down the pages.

I leaned over the table, my eyes roving across the smattering of code. The text meant little to me, but Willa was eating it up, nodding along with Keats' mutterings as she followed his chubby finger up and down the page.

"What is this?" I asked after a moment.

Keats looked up, annoyed. "It's the tickertape, of course."

I looked over at Finch to shrug, but he was also looking down at the mapping of characters.

"What's the tickertape again?" I asked.

"It's a record," Gil said from behind me. "Sort of like a play-by-

260

play itinerary of those who have been crossing back and forth, remember? Didn't we go over this? This particular ticker is exclusively from the Kharon collection agency."

"Exclusively?"

Keats looked up. "Of course, I can only get my own agency's ticker, man." He grinned at Willa and continued.

"Okay, what does it say?"

"The activity has shown a drastic increase," Willa said, "although even that seems like an understatement."

"Tickertape isn't exactly a misnomer," Keats said. "It's kinda like the stock market, you should be able to account for increased traffic in one way or the other. Like, a plane crash will cause a large number of people to go *out*. Following?"

I nodded.

"There's been a spike." He rolled up one wide sheet and pulled it aside to make room. From the floor he pulled a second roll, creased from storage in his briefcase. He opened it across the tabletop. "Look here. See the strings of numbers punctuated by time code?"

I saw it, but only barely. Long streaks of numbers running in a mass jumble across the page. Seemingly endless lines of digits that concluded with a few pairs of two digit numbers separated by colons. It meant nothing to me.

"These are people," Keats said. Running his hand over the paper.

"People?"

"They represent people," Willa corrected. "People... crossing over." She looked to Keats. "Do I have that right?"

"Crossing over is a bit flowery. I'm just a civil servant, remember?" he smiled. "They are going *out*. That's our preferred terminology." He tapped his finger against a block of time code at the end of a particularly long line. "Here is when this person went out."

I shook my head. Bureaucrats were bureaucrats, it didn't matter how macabre or supernatural. We were all numbers at the end of the day.

"So what's the big news?" I asked, a little disgusted with the whole thing.

"Okay, well this is a snapshot," Keats said. "It covers roughly a week. It looks like such a mess because there's really no way to chart this any better. It's a bit like trying to track the embers as they explode out of a firecracker. If you take a picture at just the right time, you'll be able to see enough, but it wouldn't be trackable, get me?"

I nodded.

"And when is this snapshot from?" Finch asked.

"About five weeks ago," Keats said. "It's absolutely average. Most tickertape snapshots look just like this one, follow?"

We all nodded.

"This one is from four weeks ago," he said, pulling another roll from his bag and rolling the crinkled paper out over the desk. The paper was blurrier, criss-crossed with more lines running in wilder and more scattershot directions. "A little busier, right?" Again, we nodded. He bent and pulled another from his bag. "This one is three weeks ago." Same result, the lines were longer and seemed to tangle further, curving and crossing each other at wild intervals. I had to blink a few times to focus on anything.

"Now this is from last week," he said. "I just saw it for the first time yesterday." He opened the last paper slowly, unrolling the snapshot over the others, his hand shaking slightly. The paper looked grey at first, but when my eyes adjusted I could see that the ink stained through the paper; there was just so much ink. Legibility had been sacrificed in favor of printing more numbers and more times, one on top of another on top of another. There wasn't a number in sight that wasn't stamped with the outline of another directly on top of it.

"So that's a lot," Keats said. "This snapshot tells us *two* things." He rubbed his hands together like a chef about to get to work. "First of all, the quantity. Many, *many* more people have gone from one side to the other here, which is obvious. What's not so obvious is what the numbers themselves tell us." From his briefcase, Keats pulled a magnifying glass, a wide lens mounted on an ivory handle.

"Here," he said, pointing to one of the least cluttered areas. "Look at the tail end of this account." I bent over with Willa, Finch, and Gil, all of us eager to get a better look (and not pause on Keats' use of the word "account").

It was an **X**, capital and stained with black ink. It stood at the end of a block of time code, marking the very end of this particular person's journey.

"What does it mean?" Finch asked.

"The **X** is a sign of a returned delinquent," Keats said, his voice wavering slightly.

"A returned *delinquent*?" I asked.

"Yes," Keats nodded, his face uneasy. "When you first met me, Mr. Dylan, I was on the phone, doing my job." He shuffled through his coat pocket and pulled out a business card. "Collections," he said, pointing at the title below his name. "*Death* collections. Kharon Collection Agency gives people a second chance. A few more days here past their time, to tie up loose ends or see the ocean or visit their sons or daughters. That's what we *do*. Most people are granted a temporary stay if they follow proper procedure and make a formal request. Now, my job is to make sure they come back. Most people understand that returning is what's *supposed* to happen, but some people don't. Some people resist. That's where the collections comes in."

"And so a 'delinquent'...?" I asked.

"Someone who does not come back," Finch said.

"Exactly," Keats nodded.

"Then what are these?" I said, pointing at one of the ominous **X**s. "A returned delinquent?"

"They mark when someone is brought back," he said.

"Brought back?" I said. "I'll need a little more."

He nodded. "We're a business, so we offer cash exchanges on people who are here past their registered stay. Exchanges for people who are unwilling to play ball, so to speak."

"You mean rewards," I said, spitting the word out. "You hire *bounty hunters*."

"We don't use any of those words," Keats said, clearly uncomfortable. "But they're essentially correct." He paled under my scowl.

Finch put his hand on my arm to calm me. He could feel my temper rising even before I could. "This is a second chance," Finch said, "nothing more. Neither Mr. Keats nor his employer is responsible for their deaths. This is the natural way. He only allows them the time to accomplish what they otherwise could not. The extra time is a gift, a gift they would otherwise not be afforded."

Sometimes Finch's inhumanity really pissed me off, but in this case, I knew he was right. It took a cold hand to guide me through the logic of this one. I took a deep breath and nodded for Keats to continue. "All right," I said. "All right. So tell me what all this means. Extrapolate for me."

He looked relieved. Keats didn't have the kind of job that made him a popular guy at dinner parties. Hell, he probably made IRS auditors look popular. "Well," he said, "these accounts have all been settled by outside parties. That's what the bold typeface implies. Following?"

Another collective nod from the group.

"All right, well let me tell you that this is incredibly abnormal. This returning of delinquents is a nasty job, and most people can't stand doing it. We rarely get these accounts settled. At a certain point, it's like a hospital bill, we just drop it, understand?"

We nodded again.

"So when I tell you that we've had a tenfold increase in delinquent party returns, you'll begin to understand how unusual this truly is." He wiped sweat from his brow and pulled a fresh stack of documents from his bag.

"Now these are payment forms, typical bank issued invoices, essentially. When we have a delinquent party returned, the returning agent fills one of these out in our accounting department and we process payment to them. The... uh, reward. Still with me?"

"Keep talkin', hoss," Gil said with a nod. "We're with ya."

"This is what I found when I began investigating paperwork in the accounting department." One by one, Keats laid the sheets down on the desk. The same handwriting and the same name, the same signature and the same bank account information marked each invoice. "They've all been settled by the same person."

I picked up an invoice. "Who's Talus Fox?" I asked.

Gil looked at me, his face paler and colder than I'd ever before seen it. "Talus Fox killed my wife."

CHAPTER 34. THE PLANS...

Gil left the office a few minutes later, leaving Willa, Finch, Keats, and me to figure things out.

"What else do you have for us, Mr. Keats?" Finch asked, eternally nonplussed.

Keats was shaken again. He'd taken off his Viking helmet and collapsed into the desk chair. His thinning hair was matted with sweat. Pushing his glasses up his nose, he looked at Finch. "Well," he said, "I have the name, but that's not all." He shuffled through a few more documents before finding one and handing it to Finch. "Here's the bank account. Mr. Fox has requested that all payments be made as direct deposits into this numbered account." He blanched and leaned towards Finch, lowering his voice as he spoke. "Is Mr. Abercrombie all right? I... this always happens to me." The small man frowned and I felt genuinely bad for him. "I'm so very sorry if I–"

"Don't worry about it, Mr. Keats," Finch interrupted. "Mr. Abercrombie is a professional." My soulless partner's cold heart had no time to comfort our bureaucratic friend. Instead, Finch looked down at the paper, business as usual, his eyes moving over the digits as if they were prey. After a moment he handed the paper to Willa. "Does this look familiar?" he asked.

"No," she said after a moment.

"It's the new election account," he said. "The one to which I was previously referring. The new account that has been running Bluebeard's Bascombe campaign."

Keats remained silent. Willa looked up at Finch. "Are you sure?" she asked.

Finch nodded. "Certain." He turned back to Keats. "Please continue."

The weary collector took a deep breath. "That's not all," he said. "Account verification in this case was accomplished through personal information. I imagine this is what you've been waiting for." He handed a second document to Finch, a document marked with thick lines of ink from a heavy black marker. "I removed some of the especially sensitive information," he said. "I could... well, I could get in a lot of trouble for giving you that."

"Your secrets are safe with us, Mr. Keats," Finch said softly. "You are certainly now a firm part of this investigative team."

After a moment, Finch looked up from reading the paper and handed it over to me with a nod. I took the sheet. It was what we'd been waiting for.

"An address," I said. I looked up at Finch. "What do you think?"

He shrugged. Willa took the paper from me and began reading.

"Hold on," she said, standing.

Without another word, Willa moved from Keats' makeshift office across the hall to an empty computer terminal and set to work. Finch, Keats, and I held camp, not speaking. A general pall had fallen over the entire group. After the djinn's attack and Gil's disheartening revelation, most of the goodwill we'd accumulated during our earlier feast at Harold's had evaporated.

When Willa returned, she held a thick stack of papers in her hand. Jaw firmly set, I could tell she'd made up her mind.

"That's the place," she said. She handed a paper to Finch. I looked over his shoulder at the document. It was a poor photocopy of a deed. The signature at the bottom of the document was illegible, but there were unmistakable initials smattering important clauses up and down the form. **BB**, they said. I couldn't speak for the others, but it left little doubt with me.

"How do you feel about it?" Finch asked Willa.

She looked back up and him, her eyes cold. "That's the place," she said again.

Finch nodded. "I'll take it to the boss."

***

We watched Keats pack up the mess of documents before leaving the office all together. The rain outside had slowed, but not abated. On the stoop, Keats snapped open his dragon umbrella and scuttled off to find his car. Willa, Finch, and I walked across the street, ignoring the rain, too tired to care.

Gil was in his room when we got back, the door closed. Finch told us to wait while he went inside with the documents in hand. Willa and I took seats on opposite ends of one of Gil's massive sofas. She leaned her head back and closed her eyes, exhaling a long slow breath.

"Are you all right?" I asked after a long moment.

"Yeah. You?"

I nodded.

"I know that's the place, Dylan."

"I believe you, Willa. How did you find that deed?"

"It's my job, I told you."

"*What* exactly is your job?"

She offered a weary smile. "I deal in information services. And computers. Not completely unlike Mr. Keats."

I nodded. "I used to be in the military," I said. "So I guess I used to kill people."

"Now you just kill monsters," she said.

"Yeah, and drive the car. It's a little better."

We fell into silence. Through Gil's closed door, I could hear muffled voices, but the words were lost. The huge windows that overlooked the city were awash in raindrops. The city outside looked dismal in the night. Beside me, her smile gone, Willa looked miserable.

"I'm gonna get your husband back for you," I said finally.

She looked down at her hands. They were shaking as she absently picked the cuticles of her fingernails. Without speaking, she nodded.

"I promise."

She nodded again. Behind us, the door to Gil's bedroom opened. Finch walked out, crinkled papers in hand. He dropped them onto the coffee table before us.

"We're hitting it tomorrow night. Get some sleep."

***

It was that easy. Willa adjourned shortly thereafter to one of Gil's countless bedrooms without a word. Finch disappeared as well. I turned off the lights and made my way to the bedroom I'd been calling home.

Sleep was hard to come by. A lot was on my mind. Somehow, Gil had turned Willa onto his frontal assault plan, leaving me the odd one out. I turned over our original plan in my head, trying to find a way to unseat Bluebeard without getting anyone killed. Nothing came to mind. Nothing would work. I needed a whole lot of support and leverage that I just didn't have. At a certain point, I fell asleep. The pattering of rain on the murky glass helped.

When I woke up, the light outside was pretty pale. It was early. I got dressed and walked out into the apartment. Finch was the only one awake. Sitting at the kitchen table, he'd spread out numerous schematics across the round table and was laboring over them.

"Good morning," I said.

He nodded.

"Hungry?"

He looked up at me and wiped the sleep from his eyes. "Yes," he said. "And I did not sleep well."

"Me neither."

"Why not?"

"This whole A-Team thing is making me a little nervous. It's not really our strong suit. Recently we've been more like the Keystone Kops."

He looked back down. "We've done all right."

"Why didn't you sleep well?"

He frowned. "For the same reason," he finally admitted.

"Oh dear," I said as I lined up what remained in Gil's refrigerator on the counter. It was enough to put together a halfway decent meal.

"What's the plan?" I asked.

"I am formulating our plan now. In this incarnation," he said, pointing at the papers on the table, "you will be up front with me. We'll keep Willa and Boss on the second line."

"I'm up front?"

"As the Boss says, you are the ace in the hole."

"Why does everyone keep saying that?" I asked. "It makes me a little uncomfortable."

Finch shrugged. "It's because you are, Dylan."

"Just because I can set a sword on fire and stuff doesn't mean I'm Batman."

Finch looked up at me as I cracked a pair of eggs into a skillet. "You do understand that bending the elements to your will is merely the tip of the iceberg, don't you? Your power is incredible, Dylan. You don't have mastery over it, but don't be mistaken, you are immensely powerful."

"People keep saying that," I mumbled. "Just because the Yankees have the biggest payroll doesn't mean they're the best team."

He squinted at me. "I do not completely follow, but I think I grasp the essence of your metaphor."

"Don't you watch sports?" I asked.

"Only cricket."

"What I'm saying is, if I don't have complete control over the power, I may as well not have it. So, yeah, I'm a little nervous."

"We have bigger things to worry about, Dylan," Finch said.

I let that hang out there for a moment as I dropped a handful of diced onions into the frying pan. "Like what?"

"It is very likely this is a trap," he said.

Again, I let it stew. I mixed the eggs, watching as they firmed up and yellowed. Behind me, I heard Finch rearrange his papers. When the omelets were ready, I dropped them onto a pair of plates with some toast and took a seat across from Finch.

"Why would you say that?"

He cleared his throat. "When you are dealing with a host of politicians jockeying for muscle, never for a moment believe that you are not being manipulated." He pulled a pile of papers from the empty seat beside him and laid them on the table between us. They were Keats' documents. "These fall into our hands with all the information we need after a particularly long dry spell? Why?" He leaned back and took a bite of his eggs. "These are good," he said. "Thank you."

"But why?" I asked. "If we are being manipulated, then to what ends?"

"Bluebeard is old and lazy, Dylan. He's used to getting exactly what he wants. He makes me look like a kid, so you'll begin to understand that he's been around for a long time. People like that don't change. I don't believe that he would let this information get out from under him; he may be lazy, but he's not that sloppy. It begs the question, is Bluebeard himself responsible for the leak because he wanted us to find him, or did someone else leak the information because they want us to find Bluebeard?"

"Either way, a trap doesn't bode well for us," I mumbled, suddenly losing my appetite. "There's no way this is just good fortune?"

"No," Finch said, shaking his head. "It is possible, but not probable. I've simply lived long enough to doubt things like this, do you understand?"

I nodded.

"Also, Gil's luck has never been this good."

"What do you mean luck?"

"Talus Fox?" Finch shook his head. "That is an incredibly large carrot to dangle in front of Gil. And in this case, it may just work."

"You're talking about revenge."

"Yes, of course. If you believe that Gil has always been the white knight in these parts, you're sadly mistaken, friend. There was a time when he was a reclusive billionaire who spent his days traveling the world with his wife, struggling to help me fulfill a lifelong quest. It was fine, until one year we stepped on the wrong foot. We stepped on the wrong foot, and Evelyn was killed. Fox was responsible. And since then, Gil's not been on any even half-way passable terms with vampires, and he's been more than willing to help those in need, free of charge."

"And you?"

Finch smiled. "I've stayed with him because he promised long ago never to stop until he helped me. And I promised Evelyn I'd never leave Gil's side." He looked up at me and ventured a smile. "I imagine you've wanted to ask that question for a long time. Why am I here with Gil?"

I nodded.

"Of course, it is a much longer story than that, but it must wait for another day. Today, we try to stay alive. All right?"

"Right-o."

He nodded once and that was that. Finch was back to the paperwork, back to the logical and the pragmatic. I was frightened of the imminent siege, if I could even call it that. Frightened for myself and frightened for my friends. I looked down at the schematics, ate my eggs, and tried to help formulate the plan.

When Gil and Willa rose, they set off together. "Shopping and recon," Gil said as they pulled the door shut behind them. Finch continued building on the plans he and I had laid out over eggs while I adjourned to the small gym Gil had on the second level of the penthouse. Dottie had brought a select few of our weapons back from the office after the clean up and left them in the sparring room adjacent to the gym. My short sword was there. I practiced for a few hours, calling up the magic, feeling it rocket up my arm like a jet blast of ice cold air, making the hairs on my arm stand on end. I practiced conjuring fire and extinguishing it. I took Finch's mace and Gil's axe, injecting them with the unnatural blue flame and swinging them about the room, feeling the effects. I swung the heavy iron blades around the sparring room until a sharp pain began jabbing me in the side from where Cally's dog soldier had very nearly ruptured my stomach. The pain lingered for a moment before it left. I decided that was enough.

I left my sword in the sparring room and took a long shower. Under the water, I concentrated, slowly moving the beads of water around the tile, controlling the direction and flow of the water with little more than a flick of my wrist as Finch's words played through my head: *bending the elements to your will is merely the tip of the iceberg.* I closed my eyes and I tried to imagine more, tried to imagine something greater, something *larger*. As I stood beneath the water, I felt a heat begin to build in my chest, like an open flame was being pressed against the inside of my ribcage. The heat grew, and I tried to control it, tried to shape it like an invisible ball of clay in my hands. I imagined the vael's power matching my will, granting me power greater than I'd ever imagined. Before I'd begun to bring an image to mind to steer the vael in the direction I'd chosen, I felt the burning begin to subside and I rested my hand on the tile wall to steady myself. I opened my eyes when I felt the substance of the wall begin to change beneath the palm of my hand, the tile turning from rock solid to gelatinously soft. I sucked in a deep breath and imagined the fire in my chest extinguished. The wall hardened beneath my hand once again, and I could all but see the molecules realigning themselves.

"Oh," I said. "Wow." I dragged my aching body out of the shower and didn't look back. Changing the physical properties of matter was a bit over my head at the moment, and I didn't have time to wrap my brain around that one. Not today. I dried off and put on a clean outfit from Gil's closet, another flamboyant Hawaiian shirt. This one had erupting volcanoes on it. Awesome.

Waiting for me in Gil's great room, playing video games, was Ron the gargoyle, seated on the sofa with his wings spread out behind him. Archie the pigeon perched on his shoulder, mumbling game strategy and dropping empty sunflower seeds onto the leather upholstery.

"Gentlemen," I said as I passed.

Gil stood over the kitchen table with Finch at his side. Willa was behind them, drinking coffee from a cup at the kitchen counter, listening. They were going over our plan again. Gil looked up when I stepped into the kitchen.

"About ready to go?" he asked me.

"Already?"

He pointed to the window. Darkness was beginning to fall. The day had gotten away from me.

"No time to waste," he said.

A cold pit had opened at the base of my stomach, and fear had set in, the worst fear I'd felt since my first mission overseas. I wanted the cold feel of a weapon in my hand.

"You all know the plan?" Gil asked.

We nodded.

"Ron!" he called. After a moment, the chubby gargoyle appeared in the door, pulling a pack of gum from his fanny pack.

"I been listenin'," he said. "I been listenin'."

"What he means is that *I've* been listening, Gil," Archie grumbled from his shoulder. "We're on it, don't worry."

"This is a big move for us, and I know we're gonna do all right, I just want you guys to remember two things," Gil said, pulling his pipe from the breast pocket of his Tiki shirt and lighting it. "One, if things start to go south, we're aborting. Got that? Like I said, this is big, but I'm not letting it all go to hell. Okay? Two? Talus Fox... If we find him here? He's *mine*. Got it?" He turned to meet us each in the eye, his face pale and stony. "I've been waiting years to find this bastard."

I listened to Gil's words and felt a chill run up my spine. Over Finch's shoulder, I met Willa's eyes. In them I saw much of what I felt chewing away in my chest. A nasty dose of fear.

I couldn't forget what Finch had said: *It is very likely this is a trap.*

CHAPTER 35. ...GO STRAIGHT TO HELL, BOY

Of course the shit inevitably hit the fan.

You know, in the military I learned about how to plan a mission and how *not* to plan a mission. Missions are put together by one person, but coordinated and hammered out by everyone working together. You need to have the plans imbedded so deeply in your head that no matter how terribly it goes, no matter how blown to hell things get, your brain will still move from the preconceived point A to point B to point C with almost no cogent thought necessary. At the end of the day it all comes down to preparation and training. It has to be automatic.

On this occasion, none of that happened.

The address we got from Keats was outside the city. It wasn't a house, it was a damn estate. The driveway ran straight up through a magnificent front yard with greener grass than I was likely to see at the Phillies Stadium. I didn't see any Venus de Milo knock-offs, but I wouldn't be surprised to find the real thing next to a koi pond or rosebush. Thick hedges stood behind the wrought iron fences that surrounded the property. In the center of the compound stood a red brick mansion dotted by enough French doors, balconies, and windows to rival the White House. Maybe Venus was inside.

"Split up," Gil said. "Follow the plan."

We'd been crushed inside the freshly repaired Tank. Once again, it was good as "new." Gil sat in the passenger's seat, reading off the directions as we drove, leaving Finch and Willa to fight for space with Ron in the backseat. I parked it in a small copse of trees about a quarter mile from the estate, leaving us to walk the remaining distance. Gil broke up the group at the first sign of the black iron fence. Light from the distant mansion poured through the gate that blocked the driveway, casting long shadows across the street.

"Y'all remember the plan, right?" His voice was tense, something I was unaccustomed to. Like the rest of us, he wore a black coat–his slipped over his yellow Hawaiian shirt–and black pants. Over his shoulder, he carried a batter's bag. Instead of a baseball bats and a glove, I knew it carried his swords of choice and a few other goodies, just like the bags Finch and I carried.

"We remember," I said in a hushed voice. I turned to Willa. "It's time."

Behind us, Ron gave a nod and lifted himself from the ground with a few hearty flaps of his leathery wings, kicking dust into the air from the empty street as he and Archimedes disappeared a moment later into the dark night sky.

Gil patted Finch once on the arm and they turned to leave, this version of the plan partnering Willa and me. "Wait," Finch said.

Willa and I turned back. Finch's eyes were wide in the dim light.

"Make sure to neutralize any and everyone you see, even if they don't see you. The last thing we need are heavies moving around behind our backs." He nodded at Gil. "We'll do the same."

I nodded. "You got it."

Still, Finch hesitated. After a moment, Gil rested his hand on Finch's shoulder. "Good luck," Gil said. "Let's go."

Finch gave a nod before slowly turning away.

We'd all done our best to memorize the schematics for Bluebeard's mansion and the surrounding grounds. It came second nature to me, although I imagine Willa would have been lost if I turned her loose. We were moving through the woods that ran parallel to the western fences of the compound, following the hedges and black iron as we made our way farther from the road and towards the mansion. Despite the full moon above us, the woods were nearly pitch black. I followed my old instincts as much as I did my crappy night vision, my feet crunching through the foliage with Willa two paces behind me.

I knew the spot in the fence the moment I saw it. Finch had given me a general location to choose our entry point while we'd planned, leaving the final decision up to me. Well, we'd found it. The hedges were thinning around the ground while still quite dense up around chest level, allowing Willa and I enough coverage to bust through the iron fencing without drawing too much attention. I slowed and pulled her close to the fence. "This is it," I whispered.

Her eyes were wide, and I could feel her breath on my face. She nodded once. I dropped to my hands and knees and began to clear the space in front of the fence of leaves. After a moment, she joined me. The last thing we needed was for the iron to kick a spark and set a damn fire in the middle of the woods.

"Are you going to cut through?" she asked, stage-whispering over the growing buzz of woodland insects in the late summer night.

"I think so," I said. Honestly, I had no damn clue what I was going to do. Finch and Gil had taken a host of spell fixings, enough to basically turn Finch's little finger into a welder's torch. With a wink Gil had told me I wouldn't need it. "You've got all the juice you need already, brother," he had said. Great. Thanks, Boss.

With the dry leaves and sticks cleared away, I took hold of the iron for the first time. Despite the mild spring air, the iron was cold in my hands, surprisingly so. I closed my fingers around the metal, thick bands that would have been tough to cut through with a welder's torch.

"Can you do it?" Willa asked, knowing full well that if I couldn't, this raid would be over pretty quickly.

"Um. I think so," I said again. I waved her back a few steps and extended an index finger towards the iron, taking a deep breath and closing my eyes.

I felt the heat before I saw anything. A rush of burning hot power flowed up my arm, totally unlike the cold power I'd grown accustomed to feeling when I ignited my sword. This was more intense, more focused. When the bolt of energy left my finger, I had to struggle to control it. It felt like I was trying to spray a fire hose through a hole the size of a pinhead. Even through my eyelids, I could see the white-hot light, burning with the intensity of a hundred acetylene torches. Behind me, I heard Willa took a sharp breath and back away. In my mind, I focused on the stream of power on the iron fence rail and pushed as much power through it as I could. After I minute, I relented, releasing the breath I'd been holding and cutting off the bottomless well of power I was slowly pouring into the iron.

"Good God," Willa muttered from behind me. "That was bright."

"Yeah," I said, taking a few quick breaths. "It was that, all right."

"Did it work?"

Tentatively, I put the back of my hand up against the fence, waiting for heat. There was none. I rested one fingertip against the iron, then two, then my whole hand.

"A little," I breathed, feeling the slight divots I'd managed to chip out of the iron. "It'll take a lot more to get even one of these spokes out." I looked up and down the fence. No other point would be any easier than this one here.

"Okay," she said. "What does that mean?"

I checked my watch. The numbers on the dark face were illuminated just enough to be read. "We've still got a few minutes until Gil's man in the power company pulls his strings."

"How few?"

I grabbed the metal again and tugged on it ineffectually. "Too few," I said after a moment.

I heard Willa swear under her breath. "Now what?"

"Hold on," I said. Pushing the thought of cutting from my mind, I closed both hands over one iron rail. I didn't close my eyes; instead I focused on the iron, feeling the material against my skin. I remembered everyone's words and assurances. I had the power to do nearly anything. Anything. I remembered what happened in the shower only a few short hours ago when the wall had begun to change under my hand. I had to believe I could do it, and for the moment, I did.

I felt the inflexible material yield against my skin, like I'd closed my hand over a lump of dough. What had once been cold, firmly rigid iron was quickly softening and becoming malleable in my fist. I pulled on the metal, feeling tendons of the melted fence stretch like bubble gum before giving way with a snap. With my two hands, I'd pulled a length of iron about three feet long free from the fence. Its ends were twisted and unnatural, making it look like a miscast crowbar. As the spoke broke free of the fence, the metal firmed in my hand, returning to its natural state as I released my grasp on it. The bar fell to the ground, clanging against a rock. Solid.

"Wow," Willa whispered.

"Um, yeah," I said.

"Are you super strong now or something?"

"Did you see that thing stretch? That wasn't brute force."

"You just... pulled it off?"

"I... I dunno. I softened it," I said, the words sounding ridiculous even as I said them. "So, I guess?"

"Wow," she said again. She took a deep breath and blew it out. "How much time?"

"Not much," I said without checking my watch. I'd need to pull at least two more bars from the fence to make a hole big enough for me to fit through, although Willa could probably get through the hole I'd just made. I got to work. A few short–albeit bizarre–moments later, three cold iron bars lay on the ground at our feet. The ends of each were long and fibrous, like the end of a piece of taffy that was stretched past the point of breaking.

"I'm sorry, but that's nuts," Willa said, smiling for the first time. For just a moment, her intense focus had wavered, allowing at least a little pressure to release, pressure that had been penned up for long enough. She took a few breaths and shook her head in disbelief. "All right," she said finally. "Want me to go first?"

"I'll go first," I said, checking my watch again. Time to spare.

I grabbed the fence rails at the top of the opening and lifted myself through. The hole was about two feet off the ground and about three feet square, leaving just enough room to stand on the other side, pinned between the newly mangled fence and the thick hedge. Willa followed me through and stood at my side, her cold focus back in full force.

"How much time?" she asked, again.

I checked my watch. "Not much, if this thing is right."

From where we stood behind the thick netting of green, I couldn't see much, so I dug my arms into the bush and began pulling aside the short chunky branches in hopes of getting a clear view. In a moment, I had it.

The brick mansion that I'd gotten to know so well through its floor plan was even more impressive in person. Three stories rose up to a fourth that fit in just beneath a grand, peaked roof. Long chimney stems rose at regular intervals across the black slate rooftop. The east and west ends of the house extended outward like weights at either end of a barbell; linking them on the front of the house was a wide veranda that hung across the front façade just above the main entrance. A long portico extended off the front of the building at the broad double-door main entrance. Similar porticos also stood on each face of the wide rectangular structure, making four in all. Willa and I would be entering the west portico while Gil and Finch would hopefully be busting into the east. If everything went as planned, that was.

I lifted my watch just as the lights across the compound died, dropping the wide expanse of Bluebeard HQ into darkness. It was the first and last thing to go according to plan.

"Now," I said, grabbing Willa's arm and pulling her through the hedges with me. My training kicked in, and I ran across the wide expanse of the yard in a half-crouch, perhaps expecting gunfire. None came. I'd chosen well, we were perfectly lined up with the west portico. After a short fifty-yard dash over slate patios and through lush flowerbeds, we were at the west entrance.

Willa crouched at my side, breathing quickly. From the folds of her black coat, she pulled a small pouch. She unzipped it and passed it to me. "Good luck doing *this* without a light," she said.

It was a lock picking kit, a little skill I'd picked up in the army as a novelty. I'd impress the guys by using a filed Allen wrench and a paperclip to open padlocks on footlockers. This wasn't going to be anything like that. The door before me was a heavy oak number with a pin and tumbler lock probably older than I was. From the kit I pulled a small tension wrench that looked like it was the right size to give me the room I'd need. I grabbed the handle to readjust myself on my haunches when I figured it out.

"It's open," I said.

"What?"

"The door," I turned to her, slipping the small tension wrench into my pocket. "It's not even locked."

Returning the lock picking kit to her coat, Willa scowled. "Why would it be unlocked?"

It's a trap, of course, was the first thing that came to mind, but I bit back the impulse to say it aloud. I shrugged instead. Willa's scowl turned into a glare.

"All right, all right," I said. "It's weird, I know."

"People only leave doors unlocked for one reason," she said. "To let people in."

"Don't read too much into it," I muttered. "The only rich guy I know is Gil, and I can't begin to account for how he acts."

She swallowed hard but nodded her head anyway. "Fair point," she whispered.

From the batter's bag over my shoulder, I pulled my trusty short sword. I found the weight a great comfort in my hand. From Willa's bag, I saw her pull an aluminum baseball bat, apparently the only one of us not to co-opt the baseball bag as a weapons carryall.

"I played softball," she explained with a shrug. I smiled for the last time that day.

"Ready?" I asked. She nodded. I pushed the door open and glanced inside. A dark hallway lead into a wide expanse of a room, plush and well-furnished. I couldn't hear anything except the distant hum of insects in the woods behind me. Somewhere in the house, Bluebeard was probably waiting for us. The thought had occurred to me that we should turn back. Trap or no trap, this whole thing stank to high heaven. At the same time, I knew Willa would not give up. She believed her husband was inside, and if he wasn't, the man responsible for everything most assuredly *was*. It was hard to argue with that.

Willa and I stepped inside.

We fell straight down, into a twisting nest of fire.

CHAPTER 36. OUT OF THE FRYING PAN

Fire, lots and lots of it.

We hit the ground in a rank black cloud. I'm pretty sure that the firestorm took my eyebrows with it, and maybe a little of my shattered confidence. As quickly as we hit the ground, the fire was gone in a swell of wet sulfuric breath. I stumbled to my feet, empty-handed.

"Willa?"

I felt her before I saw her, at my side. The fire was gone, but I couldn't see anything except black smoke. Between coughs, I tried aloud to formulate a coherent game plan. It sounded a bit like this:

"What happened? Where are we? What the holy hell is going on?"

She pulled me somewhere to my left, and I followed, stumbling across uneven, rocky ground that felt like hot pavement beneath my feet. In a minute, we were out of the cloud, the fetid blasts of moist air behind us. I opened my eyes and my jaw dropped.

We were outside. A sun was high above us, a bright *red* sun, bathing us in an intense heat and an unnatural scarlet light. Wherever we were, it was damn desolate. Black rock as far as the eye could see. It was like an onyx version of Ireland's Burren without the added luxury of moss. The rock was jagged and strangely geometric, like broken pieces of onyx glass or volcanic rock, rising and falling like frozen swells of an ocean. It led off into the distance in every direction.

"What the–"

"I don't know Dylan, I don't know so hold on, just hold on a second," Willa shouted, bent at the waist and struggling to catch her breath. "Did you see that...?" She lifted her shaking hand and pointed back behind me at the rolling hills of stone. "Did you see it?"

"See what?"

As I turned, I felt a genuine T-rex tremor pass through the ground. From around a high rise of volcanic rock, a beast emerged, and it wasn't a T-rex. Black scaled and angry, the beast stood about fifteen or twenty feet, supported on four meaty legs that each ended in massive talon-like claws that ripped chunks from the black rock with each step. From its thick body, a long neck extended, on the end waited an angry face with a gaping mouth, filled with row upon row of teeth, each bigger than a shot glass. Two leathery wings were folded on the creature's back. Behind the monster swung a tail that ended with a huge stone ball reminiscent of Finch's mace. Every few paces, the ball of bone cracked against the ground, sending those telltale tremors up my shaking legs.

"Oh," I said. "That."

The beast opened and closed its jaws, a pair of tongues flapping from either side of its mouth. From two small nostrils above the maw, wisps of smoke curled like long strands of a mustache. Yes, really.

"You've got to be kidding me," Willa mumbled, taking a step back.

"Is that a…"

"…dragon?"

"So I guess it was a trap," I said, taking her arm and pulling her into the shadows of a small rise of stone. We collapsed to the ground as a column of fire passed through the air just over our heads. I kicked my legs, struggling to push myself back, the soles of my shoes softening to the heat.

"Get back," I said, pulling her with me.

The ground vibrated again, the dragon was moving. Pebbles trickled downward, falling from the top of the stone hill and raining down on our heads.

"Where's your sword?" Willa shouted over the roar of fire.

"I don't know! Where's the goddamn *house*?"

She pulled me to my feet. We rounded the hill, and peeked over an outcropping of jagged stone at the beast. "I don't know, I was hoping you'd have some bright ideas."

"Hey, I'm new, too, remember?"

The dragon had withdrawn the way it had come, which was a bad sign as it turned out. As I surveyed the barren terrain, I noticed one thing other than the dragon: a door. It was familiar, a heavy oak job, and it hung in mid-air about twelve feet off the ground. That was our exit.

I pointed at it. "We came from there. The good news is, it's still there. The bad news is, it's *up there*. And we're down here. I'm big, but I'm not that big. Oh, also? There's a dragon standing between us and the way out. I *think* that's the way out, anyway."

"You're sure?"

"Am I sure? Of course I'm not sure! We were in the middle of a midnight raid on Bluebeard's secret election campaign mansion when we fell through some kind of gateway portal into a dragon's lair in an alternate reality. Am I sure? I'm not sure of very much right now."

"Yeah, well I like the plan of going through that door there. As long as it gets us out of here."

"All right, but before one of us says 'you go distract it,' we're gonna have to think of a *better* way to get that thing to move," I said, pointing at the monster that stood underneath the door.

"You go distract it," Willa said.

"That's nice."

"No, seriously. And you don't really need to *go* anywhere, magic man. Do some mojo. Can't you conjure a stick to make it fetch or something?"

"I'm not exactly a dragon wrangler, Willa."

"Well, then conjure a honey-baked ham, we need it to *move!*"

As she finished speaking, a pair of doors not unlike ours appeared and snapped open about a hundred yards further past the dragon. From the air tumbled Finch and Gil, arms and legs pin-wheeling as they fell. We watched them hit the ground with the same panache we had as the beast turned and opened its jaws to douse them in flame.

"There's your distraction," I said.

"We have to do something," Willa shouted, rising over the stony outcropping and running across the bare stone opening at full tilt.

"Willa, wait!" I hollered as I followed. My feet pounded on the flattened stone as I ran after her. Our shouting and footfalls caught the beast's attention enough to get it to turn towards us and redirect its fire at us instead. I caught up to Willa in time to tackle her as the fire passed over me, beginning to ignite my clothes.

"Owww oww *owwwww shit*," I growled as I rolled over, choking out the flames on my back. Willa stumbled to her feet and bolted to her left, the dragon's eyes following her every step. I sat up in a smoking heap as the dragon unleashed another breath in Willa's direction. "Watch out!"

The column of flame missed her, but only just. She made it behind another hill in time, but her ponytail may have been a few inches shorter when she did. She gave me the thumbs up over the rock as I crawled behind some cover of my own.

Well, Finch and Gil were here, so they weren't going to come rescue us. No one short of Ron and Archimedes the angry pigeon were going to save us, and I wasn't holding out much hope for that. I watched the sky, waiting for them to make their entrance via skylight. It didn't happen. As it stood, it was the four of us against a dragon. And weaponless, too. At some point during our miraculous transport to Mars from hell, our weapons had been seized. The odds were not good.

I peeked over my cover at the monster. Rather than follow after Gil and Finch, it seemed content to stand equidistant between the pair of doorways, its big head roving back and forth between the two, eyes aglow for any motion. A few times it unleashed waves of fire in the direction of Gil and Finch, but other than that, it was pretty quiet.

"It's just waiting," I mumbled. "Pretty patient for a man-eating lizard of legend."

"Dylan!"

I turned to see the rest of my team reunited behind Willa's big rock hill. Gil and Finch looked to be pretty winded from the long dash past the dragon. Gil looked a little sooty, and he'd dumped his black jacket (which I imagined was on fire somewhere). I waved them over and watched as they crossed the wide expanse unmolested. Apparently if you were moving away from the doors, the dragon couldn't seem to care less.

"Hi guys," I said.

"What the hell happened?" Gil sputtered. "We opened the east door and WHAM, outta the sky we fell."

"Yeah, same thing here," I said. "What took you two so long?"

"Smarty pants here had some trouble with the fence," Gil said.

"It did turn out to be more difficult than I had first imagined," Finch said with a scowl. "But after a few minor alterations the spell proved itself to be more than adequate."

"We got in, no problem. But the question is, where the hell have we gotten? And what the hell is going on?"

"As I feared, this was a trap," Finch said, turning a disapproving eye to Gil. "The doorways were gated, as you can see, and linked with this dreadful place."

"Gated?" Willa and I said in tandem.

"Yeah, it's kinda like a portal," Gil said. "If a doorway is gated, it's like putting a teleporting passageway over it, so that by stepping through the door you inadvertently move through the passage too."

"I do not know where we are, but we were lucky to enter through two different doorways," Finch said, pointing to each offhandedly. "It's effectively doubled our chances of escape."

"I'm pretty sure if you double the odds it's a bad thing," I muttered.

"With our combined wits, I believe we'll make it," Finch said.

"We need a distraction!" Gil said, clapping his hands. "After that, it's easy."

"Easy? We'll still need to get *up* to that doorway," Willa pointed out.

"I'm sure our magic man can figure that one out." Gil smiled and elbowed my ribs.

I groaned. "I guess I could try something..."

"Atta boy," he smiled. "Now, about that distraction."

I admit I wasn't too surprised when all eyes turned to me.

***

The first thing I tried was my old standby: fire. But I was dealing with a dragon here, so guess how that worked out? The thing wasn't even tickled. My own junior sized pillar of fire hit the thing's midsection, just behind its front leg, sending wisps of flame firing off in all directions. The main thrust of fire, though, was basically absorbed. After I'd quit, the beast turned a lazy eye toward us and yawned. Great.

The second thing I tried was some kind of electricity. I didn't think I'd be able to conjure lightning, but I gave it my best shot anyway. I almost managed to summon a thick black cloud, but the exertion was too much. After a minute I had to stop. My muscles were screaming and my hands were shaking badly. I took a moment to catch my breath before trying on a smaller scale. I searched the ground and the atmosphere for some kind of electrical charge, anything at all, a charge big enough to shock a kid's hand on a doorknob would have been a success.

Nothing.

Feeling a bit drained and more than a little stressed, I moved on to Plan C: I picked up a rock and threw it at the damn thing. I missed. It was then that Gil stopped me.

"That's all you got?"

"Hey, man, I may have power but I don't know how to control it; how many times do I have to tell you that? I can do *nothing*. I'm like a circus freak who can levitate a pebble or light a candle. So if you're looking for me to make a hurricane appear and knock that thing on its ass, you're gonna be waiting for a while."

Gil nodded. "Point taken. Remind me to invest in some classes or something when we get back." Taking a deep breath, he stepped clear of our stone cover, raising a hand to block the sun from his face. "All right, no more foolin' around, friends, I'll get us out of this."

He pulled his deerstalker cap from his back pants pocket and straightened his bright yellow Hawaiian Tiki shirt. He unrolled the cap and pulled it over his mangy head of hair. "Too bad I don't have my pipe," he said after a moment. He cracked his knuckles and bent at the waist, touching his toes, grunting with exertion. Finally he turned to us and smiled. "Gimme about thirty seconds, then get goin'."

"Okay," I said. "Get going where?"

"The door," he said, pointing. "Duh."

He smiled again before setting off across the wide expanse of black rock. Gil's footsteps began slow, his shoes tapping against the igneous stone. In the distance, the monster's eyes turned to face Gil, slowly following his progress across the plain. After a few paces, he began to speed up. First power walking, then jogging, until he was finally sprinting across the stone. Gil moved pretty good for an old guy. The beast rose from its haunches and let its mouth open slowly, the whispers of smoke beginning to flow from its nostrils.

"Finch..." I said softly.

"He knows what he's doing," Finch said.

"Is that thirty seconds yet?" Willa asked.

"Just about," I said.

Gil sprinted towards the beast, picking up speed as the monster began approaching him at its lumbering gait. About twenty yards from the first doorway, Gil took a sharp left and began to run parallel to both the exit and the beast. The monster pursued for a few paces before slowing and lowering its head to unleash a gale of fire.

"Now," Finch said.

The three of us broke across the plain towards the dragon at a full run. The beast stopped mid-breath and turned from Gil back to us. With Finch in the lead, we did not slow; Finch led us straight towards the monster's gullet at full speed. I could see a wide valve opening and closing at the back of the gaping dragon's throat, the bright light of fire flickering beyond it with each opening. The dragon opened its yellow eyes wide and took a deep breath, preparing to douse us.

"Hey, Smaug! Or Puff! Or whatever your name is!" Gil shouted. The monster shifted focus, turning its massive body to Gil's screeching voice. From the ground, Gil lifted a bona fide shield, blackened and charred. It was small, but I imagined it would get the job done. He smiled at the monster, not exactly intimidating with the yellow Tiki shirt and Sherlock Holmes hat. Giving a valiant cheer, he charged the beast head on.

The dragon let go a terrible roar as a spiraling ball of fire erupted from its throat and launched across the open plain towards Gil's charging form. Gil ground to a halt and lowered himself to one knee. Tucking his body behind the shield as best he could, he took the hit head on. The fireball knocked him backwards, but the shield held, and it was a glancing blow, at best. The fireball broke apart, dissipating into smaller puffs of ash and smoke as Gil collected himself. With a shake of his head, he resumed his charge.

That's when it happened; my instincts took over. I'd been afraid and I'd been disoriented, but it didn't matter anymore. Gil was in real trouble, and we had to get out of there. Behind Finch and Willa, I shouted, "Keep going!" before turning off course and making a beeline straight for Gil. The dragon was closing on him, its claws leaving a ragged trail behind it, and I wasn't sure how Gil was hoping to walk away from this one.

I raised my hand in the direction of where I'd entered the dragon's lair, opening my fingers and extending my will towards what I knew lay somewhere near the entrance. I called my sword. It seemed not only natural, but *right*. From the shadows beyond the doorway, I saw my trusty short sword rise and rocket through the air like the pointed quarrel of an archer. As it neared me, it spun, the grip rotating to face me. The dragon neared, though it still faced away, unleashing fireball after fireball at Gil. The dragon was only a few paces away when I leapt, caught the short sword, and fell onto its leathery back.

It let out a terrible shriek. I think it was about as surprised as I.

"What the hell are you doing?" Gil shouted from the ground.

I tried to yell "I don't know, run!" but nothing but wordless hollering escaped me.

Lowering the sword, I shot a pulse of energy through it, bringing the blue fire to bear as I turned the point against the dragon's scaly hide and jammed the blade into the beast. The monster began swinging side to side in an effort to throw me free. I had to hang onto the sword for dear life. On the ground beneath me, Gil ran towards the distracted beast and swung his shield, the edge taking a hearty chunk out of the dragon's leg. As the scales were broken, black blood sprayed from the fresh wound like a jet of water from a fractured pipe. Gil screamed and jumped back, shaking his long hair from his face.

I pulled my sword from the dragon's back and rose unsteadily to my feet. Inching along the jagged vertebrae, I moved up the beast's spine towards its neck. The monster had slowed, but even as I approached its head, I could feel its chest swell as it drew another breath, preparing to roast Gil alive.

"Get down!" I shouted as I swung my flaming sword into the monster's neck.

I'd hoped beyond hope that my supercharged blade would cut through the dragon's spine like butter, but it didn't. My sword hit the bone and bounced off, slicing through little more than the skin. The beast screamed again and began to toss its head back and forth. Black blood covered me as I was forced to wrap my arms around its long neck just keep from being thrown.

On the ground, I could see Gil take the creature on again. He lifted his shield and went to ram the sharpened edge into the monster's chest. Instead, he was met with a swinging forearm across the chin, sending his body flying to the ground.

"Finch!" I screamed. "Get Gil! We gotta get outta here!"

It didn't take a theoretical physicist to realize that our odds were bad and getting worse by the second. Each hit just pissed the dragon off further, and now Gil was out cold. We needed to make an exit.

The dragon turned its head and opened its jaws, struggling to gets its teeth into me. I slid down the neck, coming to rest between the animal's massive shoulder blades. Sword still in hand, I lowered the blade to the base of the neck to take aim when a flurry of motion caught my eye. I turned to see Ron swooping from the doorway to my right.

"Get them!" I pointed at Willa and Finch. "I'll take care of this!" Ron halted his progress mid-air and turned, dropping to the ground. Archimedes floated above him, circling in a hail of feathers indecisively before honing in on me.

I hacked against the dragon's neck, drawing nothing but black blood from the surface wounds. The beast's huge jaws swung down and ripped shreds from my clothing with each lunge it made for me. I parried to avoid the huge mouth. It may have been a lethargic dragon, but now it was a pissed off dragon.

Archie came to a stop above me, hovering in mid-air. I heard angry quips being tossed about, the words lost amid the dragon's huge growls. I looked up to see the tiny bird hover near the dragon's thrashing head and slash its beak at the monster's huge yellow eyes. A high-pitched shriek escaped the dragon's throat as something above me was punctured. Hot wet goo rained on me in sickening droplets as Archimedes cheered his victory.

Ron finally appeared before me, making an unceremonial crash-landing in front of the dragon. He looked up at me and gave a hurried thumbs up before lifting Gil's body in his arms. As he was lifted, Gil opened his eyes and blinked, looking terribly confused as Ron flapped his wings and took flight.

I was the last, and I was dead set on not letting the dragon get the best of me. Taking firm hold of the monster's neck, I lowered the blade again, aiming for the base of the dragon's neck. The beast flailed violently, struggling to throw me free as I aimed for its heart (it was a guess, what do I know about dragon anatomy?). With a desperate swing of its head, the monster extended its neck back enough to close its jaws around the nape of my black commando jacket, its three-inch long teeth ripping through the material like paper. With a desperate moan, I pushed the sword into the dragon's chest.

The blade probably missed the heart, but it wasn't stopped by any bones as my blue fire-enshrouded steel disappeared to the hilt. The jaws on my coat opened to release me as the monster took a few drunken steps before falling to its knees. I felt a hand on my shoulder as I turned to see Ron with me on the beast's back.

"Time to go!" he shouted.

I pulled the sword free as a blast of fire erupted from the smoking wound. I hadn't hit its heart, I'd hit something way worse. Jets of flames spewed from the gash, coursing over the volcanic landscape, turning rock formations to molten glass before my eyes. Ron slipped his hands beneath my arms and lifted me with a flap of his wings. Beneath us, I saw the dragon list to the left, the fire pouring from the wound in its chest like an uncontrollable river. Finally, the beast collapsed to the ground as we landed inside the doorway. I looked back to see a great fire envelope the creature's body, sure to leave nothing but ashes and bones in its wake.

Ron pulled me back into our world and slammed the door behind us.

CHAPTER 37. THINGS FALL APART

"That went well," Gil said, his eyes wide.

"You all right?" I asked.

"Yeah, I guess." He was leaning against a marble pillar that supported the portico. Finch and Willa were crouched on either side of him. Ron stood against the closed doors, panting.

"Dragons aren't as cool as I'd hoped," he muttered. Archimedes nodded in agreement from Ron's sweaty shoulder.

"You know, Gil," I said. "I figured you had a better plan than playing chicken with a dragon when you said 'Hey, I've got an idea!'"

"Come on, man, you know I just make it up as I go," Gil muttered, struggling to sit upright. A goose egg was blooming on his head from one of the hits he'd taken.

"And I figured *you* would be more on top of the whole thing," I said, scolding Finch.

"Well, even I didn't think he was going to do that."

"Desperate times, mis amigos," Gil said with a wink. "Help get me up, will you, darlin'?" He tugged on Willa's arm.

"Why? What's your rush?"

"Them," Gil said, pointing.

I looked up as a car door slammed. A phalanx of men in magnificent suits marched towards me, matching briefcases in hands. If the Gestapo had a legal team, this was it. The combined cost of their wardrobe would probably impress even Gil, not to mention their shoes, which were polished well enough to reflect light during an eclipse. One man, however, was not dressed like an evil movie star. He led the way, thin and wiry, his suit a rumpled grey affair with a faded paisley tie. A tell-tale earpiece peeked from his right ear.

Altimerach.

Without a word, Ron and Archimedes launched from beneath the portico and up into the dark night sky in a flurry of wings. That's team solidarity, there.

Altimerach signaled his men, and their hands collectively moved towards unseen shoulder holsters. He said, "Let them go. We have the one we want." Never an encouraging thing to hear.

"Hey there, you sack of monkey shit," Gil said as Willa hauled him to his feet. "*Who* is it exactly that you want again?"

"Let me worry about that, Mr. Abercrombie," Altimerach said, flashing a tight-lipped smile. "Although I must admit, the sight of you and your rabble is truly enough to turn my stomach."

I smiled and gave him the finger. "We're called the Zeros," I said. "If you're gonna deride us, get it right." Willa and Finch remained silent.

Gil continued. "I must say, I'm pretty surprised to see you here, Timmy. What brings you to this fair mansion in the wee small hours?"

The thin man checked his watch. "It's 9:30," he said. "Although, I understand that it's past your bedtime. We're not all doddering old men like yourself."

Before Gil could respond, Altimerach snapped his fingers and a young suit appeared at his elbow, briefcase in hand. With a nod, the case snapped open and the suit withdrew a manila file folder. Altimerach snatched it from the young aide's hand and opened it before him like a hymnal.

"Enough banter," he said. "I'm here to inform you that you're trespassing, and my men are here to apprehend you. My security agents will take you into custody and transport you into the waiting arms of the Philadelphia Police Department. The client I represent intends to press full charges." He smiled again, as tight-lipped as always.

"Your client?" Gil scoffed. "Come on, you're just pissed your dragon isn't working us through his large intestine right now."

Altimerach's face was granite. After a brief pause he continued. "I hope you understand that this is not only private property, but also the property of a civil servant in pursuit of further advancement of public office, government office, to be more precise. Also, you are armed with deadly weapons, making your trespassing on a government official's private residence even more dire." He paused for effect. "My team of lawyers informs me that you are in quite a spot of trouble."

"Yeah, well my team of lawyers can beat up your team of lawyers," Gil said. "Go Team Lawyer."

"Doubtful," Altimerach said. He raised an arm and snapped his fingers again.

From behind him, further car doors opened. Looming shapes that looked all too familiar began approaching, the ominous tapping of claw on pavement ringing through the distant hum of insects. A chill passed through my body and my hand wandered to my side, the dwindling reminder of the last time I'd had the pleasure of such company. Dog soldiers. What a night.

"These are the trespassers," Altimerach said with a tip of his head. "Restrain them and transport them to headquarters. Make sure one of your... better-tempered cohorts conducts the actual exchange with the authorities." With that, Altimerach turned and walked back to his car. "Remember which one we want," he said over his shoulder.

With that, he smiled, a wide, wicked open-mouthed grin that showed off his crooked yellow teeth. As the smile grew, I saw them: two empty sockets at the front corners of Altimerach's upper jaw. His canines, or where his canines should have been. I may have been new to the business, but I understood enough about canines to understand their vampiric significance. Either he was bad about scheduling visits with his dentist, or he was a vampire–"was" being the operative word. He'd been *fixed*.

The clicking of the claws on pavement sounded again, reminding me that the dogs had just been set on us. Willa put a hand on my arm and took an unconscious step back, helping snap me out of whatever trance I'd slipped into. My eyes met the last parked car in Altimerach's caravan as an uneven grin found my lips. The last vehicle was a black minivan, perfect for transporting prisoners, surely our ride. I'd done it once before, I could do it again. I only needed to drag a simple thought across my mind to bring it to fruition. So I did.

Easy as pie, the minivan exploded.

The shredded car was engulfed in flames as the gas tank erupted, launching the wreck into the air before it spun and fell, crushing a pair of dog soldiers. The Zeros jumped on the opportunity, sprinting from the portico straight for the fence, Willa in the lead with me as the caboose. Behind us, chaos reigned, but Altimerach's men were collecting

292

themselves in short order under the direction of his shouts.

"Into the woods!" Gil hollered, pointing at the shrubs as we crossed the expansive lawn. "Where'd you come in?" he asked breathlessly. "Where's the hole you punched through? Can you remember?"

"I do," Willa said, also short of breath as we neared the hedges. Behind us, gunfire cracked through the night as the vamp and his dogs collected themselves. I heard car engines turn over before the harsh beams of headlights came to life and honed in on us.

"Keep your heads down!" I yelled as I heard the *ping* of a bullet striking metal. Sparks leapt from the fence as bullets from Altimerach's goons met the iron in an endless volley. The growling of car engines approached.

Willa's memory was perfect. Behind the Boxwood hedge was the uneven square I'd cleared with my own two hands. She slipped between two large bushes, directly into the gap in the rails. In no more than a moment, she had scrambled through and stumbled into the darkened woods. Finch and Gil followed. I was last, disappearing just as a pair of sedans slid to a halt in the grass, a few yards from the fence. Beyond them, I could hear Altimerach's shouts ringing across Bluebeard's compound. Harsh reports of dogs barking were the only responses.

On the other side of the fence, I turned and grasped the remaining iron spokes, sending hot beams of heat up my forearms and softening the iron in my hands. With a few tugs, the bar stretched. I pulled the top few spokes down and the bottom few up, finally meeting in the middle in a fierce knot of twisted metal.

"That should hold them for a minute," I mumbled.

"Holy cow, did you just do that?" Gil asked.

"Which way?" Willa interrupted.

"Uh, south," Gil said, pointing. "That way. We need to get to the Tank before they get–"

He stopped midsentence at the crack of a pistol. It was close. We turned to the fence in unison in time to see the huge body of a Doberman drop gracefully to the ground on our side of the fence, a Glock 9mm pistol clutched in one massive hand. I opened my palms and pushed with enough raw energy to launch the dog soldier into the iron fence like a catapult. Ripples passed through the air and hit the Doberman at full speed, lifting it from its feet like a feather. The beast's heavy skull cracked against the iron. It collapsed to the ground in a wash of blood and didn't move again.

"Yeah," I said, breathlessly. "We gotta move."

"Oh," Gil muttered. He collapsed into a small tangle of ferns. In a moment, Finch was at his side, a wide blossom of blood spreading across Gil's yellow Hawaiian shirt. His hands were closed over the wound, drops of blood seeping between his fingers.

"Oh my God," Willa murmured. "Oh my God."

"Finch," I said, crouching. "We have to get him up. We have to get him up and get him out of here. If we don't, he's dead and so are we." Even as I spoke, I heard the hungry growls of dogs as they began clawing at the fence, slowly clawing their ways up and over.

"Help me," Finch said.

I grabbed his shoulders and Finch got his legs. Together we lifted his limp body. Already, his eyes had closed. The once vibrant shirtfront was turning black in the dim light, the bright colors swallowed by the heavy flow of blood. Behind us, Altimerach's screeches cut through the night like shattering glass.

"Come on," I said, urging Finch forward. Willa stood at the head of our group, eyes wide and staring out into the woods blindly.

"Where do we go?" she asked.

"That way," I cocked my head, "Just like Gil said. Hurry, Goddamnit."

Gunshots were coming faster now. Around us, the ground was coming to life as errant bullets ripped into the dirt. Willa led us up a steep hill and down a rocky path, heading deeper into the woods, leaving the estate behind. As we moved, the growling of huge dogs seemed to close in. We just weren't going fast enough, and Gil was becoming very heavy. The frantic clawing of dogs was surrounding us, black pelts masking their shapes all too effectively in the darkness.

We slipped down a short slope and fell into a dry creek bed. Finch dropped Gil's legs and pushed Willa and me back into the cover of darkness beneath the shape of a twisted willow tree. The heavy crunching of footsteps on gravel approached, accompanied by the deep sniffing of a beast's muzzle. Our weapons were gone, and we were cornered in a small hollow. Finch herded Willa and me behind him as the dog soldier approached.

I couldn't see much in the darkness, but the dog had no problem with its night vision. It stepped straight up to us, clear as day, raised a heavy pistol, and fired. The bullet hit Finch center mass, but didn't slow him at all. My partner pulled a long knife from inside his black coat and leapt at the dog, a lanky bloodhound with flashes of scarlet on its cheeks. In the dull light, I saw Finch's blade glint before it disappeared into the mutt's soft underbelly. There was a whimper and a second gunshot. A spray of blood exploded into the moonlight. Still, Finch clung to the knife, pushing it deeper and deeper as his free hand struggled with the mercenary's mouth, grasping at the jaw, hoping to stifle any desperate sounds. Barely a whisper escaped the bloodhound's jaws before it collapsed to the ground. When Finch pulled his blade free and turned to face us, the dog's blood covered his arm up to his elbow, and he sported a pair of ragged holes in his chest.

"Get the gun," he said to Willa. She nodded, stunned, before picking up the pistol. "Save your bullets," he said. "Make them last." She nodded again.

Finch nodded and we lifted Gil from the ground again. Every move Finch made was slower and more labored. His eyes looked glassy, but he was persistent. "Come on," he said, his voice weak.

"Are you okay?" I asked.

"Better than the Boss, so come on. Let's go."

We continued into the forest. We'd gone perhaps a dozen paces or so before they were on us. There were at least four of them; big muscled sons of bitches that made Finch's Bloodhound look like a pup. They all carried pistols and unnatural canine grins.

"Drop the old man," the leader–a fat Rottweiler–grunted. Slowly, I complied. It took Finch an extra moment, but soon he followed.

"And you," it growled at Willa. "Drop the pistol." She exhaled heavily before tossing it to the bare earth.

"All right. And now–"

The fat Rottweiler was blown backwards, launching a spurt of arterial blood into the air as a shotgun blast silenced him. Willa and I collapsed to the ground as Finch charged one of the dog soldiers. A second blast echoed through the woods, then a third, each shot interrupted by the frantic racking of the shotgun. All around us, bodies were falling as the ground grew wet with blood.

"What the hell's going on?" Willa shouted. "Who is firing?"

"No idea!" I said. "But let 'em kill each other. Just stay down!"

I stumbled a few feet to Finch's aid. He was standing, tangled with a thick-chested Doberman a foot taller than he was. I hit the two of them, sending all three of us rolling down a small hill and away from the gunfire, depositing us back into the creek bed we'd just escaped. Their hands were clenched around Finch's knife, the blade hovering somewhere between their two bodies, the tip of the blade leveled at the dog soldier's sternum. They rolled and twisted over the rocks as they fought for the blade. Without thinking, I ran to them and jammed my hands between their bodies, finding enough purchase to close my fists over the knife's front bolster just below the blade. I pushed with Finch, trying to twist the steel into the beast heart, but the amount of torque on the knife was staggering. Our nest of hands shook violently as the three of us all fought for control.

Willa followed us down the hill on unsteady feet, calling my name. "Dylan," Willa said, her voice shaking. I could hear approaching footsteps.

"Hold... on..." I struggled to say, as my arms quivered under the strain.

"Dylan," she said again, louder.

Together, Finch and I twisted against the Doberman's grip, pushing the blade towards its chest, the tip just touching a patch of dark fur. The dog had gritted its teeth in a fierce snarl, drool dripping in long strands from its muzzle.

"Dylan!" she shouted finally, grabbing my attention. I spared one glance over my shoulder as another mercenary approached, this one a thick-necked bulldog, a pump action shotgun in one hand. Willa stood, hands raised.

"Oh shit," I grunted. "That's not good."

From the air above him, a dark shape fell from the trees, a wide pair of wings spiraling as the shape twisted and hit the bulldog across the shoulders, knocking the huge dog to the ground. As he stepped through a small patch of light, I saw Ron's leathery skin lift the shotgun from the leafy floor and swing it like an ax. I ducked as the butt of the gun *whooshed* over my head and collided with the Doberman's temple. Immediately, its muscles went slack. Finch and I pried the blade from its huge, limp hands and stood. Finch was breathing in short desperate gasps; he was soaked in blood. Every muscle in my body was burning from exertion. My hand moved to the stitch in my side from where the dog soldier had hit me in Cally's Den; it was aching.

"Here you go," Ron said, handing over the pump action shotgun. I took the gun gingerly, its weight almost enough to topple me.

"Thanks, man. Thanks for coming back."

"I didn't leave you," he said. "I wouldn't do that."

I nodded, trying to catch my breath.

"Where's Gil?" he asked.

I pointed. "Back that way. He's... he's in a bad way."

Together we stumbled back towards where we'd left Gil's prone body on the ground. I had the sour taste of adrenaline in my mouth, and the mad rush beginning to fade, my hands had begun shaking badly. Finch double-checked the unconscious Doberman and Ron's shotgun happy bulldog before we turned our backs on them.

"What happened with that shooting?" Willa asked. "Did one of them shoot the rest?"

Finch nodded. "I believe so."

"Why?"

"No bloody idea."

Gil was lying where we'd left him. The bleeding had slowed, but not stopped. Without so much as a grunt, Ron lifted him in his arms. "Where'd you guys park?" he asked. "We need to get him to the Doc Hanas ASAP."

"Back that way," I said, my breathing finally slowing.

"We need to be careful," Finch said, wincing. His bleeding had not stopped. "There's a good chance Altimerach's men have seized our transportation."

"Then what do we do with no car?" Willa asked.

"Use his," a small voice whispered. It was Gil.

We closed in on Ron and the limp body in his arms. Gil had opened his eyes, but they were fuzzy. His face was disturbingly pale.

"Whose car, Boss?"

A shaking finger rose and pointed over our shoulders.

The shotgun toting bulldog stood behind us, empty-handed, a line of blood trickling from a gash on its temple.

I racked the shotgun and spun, ready to fire.

"Stop," Gil said, as loud as he could muster. "I may not have been able to pay off Cally, but I still do have enough money to manage a merc." There was a trademarked Gil smile in his voice, and it somehow lifted my spirits. But he was slipping away.

The bulldog nodded, wiping the blood from a tawny patch of fur. "The name's Carver. Walt Carver," it said.

"You're on Gil's payroll?" I asked.

The beast nodded. "I am now."

"Okay, Walt. Great." I handed over the shotgun before I collapsed. "Where's your damn car? We could use a ride."

***

It was a shitty red pickup truck about four hundred yards further southwest through the woods, tucked into a clearing just like the Tank. By the time we saw the truck, even Ron was winded, beads of sweat dotting his thick hide.

"Does that piece of shit even run?" Archimedes asked from Ron's quickly rising and falling shoulder.

"It'll get the job done," Carver growled as he opened the driver's side door. "Hurry up, get your boss in, the others are bound to find us soon enough."

"The rest?" Willa asked. "I thought you killed the others."

On cue, the truck's rear window exploded, raining glass down into the pickup's bed and onto the pavement. The bulldog tossed his shotgun back to me as he squeezed into the cab. Beside me, Willa opened fire.

The gunshots were coming from a short string of dark figures at the treeline no more than twenty or thirty yards away. The muzzle flashes were bright enough to illuminate the angry faces of dog mercenaries as they opened fire. Bullets slammed into the truck's thin body, tossing sparks across the blacktop and sending shots ricocheting back into the woods. I pumped the shotgun and sent a blast into the forest, taking out at least one of the soldiers as Finch helped Ron slide Gil's limp body into the pickup's cab.

"Get in!" Carver shouted from the cab as an errant bullet ripped his sideview mirror free. Between gunshots I could hear him wrestle with the ignition, the slovenly truck's engine turning over, but failing to start.

"You're gonna flood it!" I hollered as I fired again.

There was a tap on my shoulder as Finch waved me into the truck. "Her first," I said, nodding to Willa.

Beside me, she was holding her own. Legs spread wide, she held the mercenary's pistol with two hands, her arms locked straight out in front of her, a perfect shooter's stance. She took her time aiming before firing single shots into the darkness. I couldn't tell if she was hitting anything, but she was at least keeping them at bay.

"What do you do for a living again?" I asked.

She shrugged and took another shot. "Get in," she said. "I've got more bullets left than you."

I racked the shotgun and pulled the trigger. It clicked empty. Shit. Behind me, Finch pulled up the tailgate and slammed it shut. I lifted myself into the small bed on shaky arms, feeling the truck's shocks groan under our collected weight. "Come on!" I shouted as I turned back to Willa.

In the cab, Carver was growling as he struggled with the engine, his canine paws repeatedly slamming down on the wheel. In the distance, I could hear the angry rumblings of car engines, a lot of them. Willa still stood in the street, firing shots into the woods, the only return fire we could muster. "Come on!" I shouted again.

I heard Carver scream victoriously as the truck's engine caught, coming to life with a desperate cough. A few hundred yards down the road and back towards Bluebeard's mansion, an army of black sedans rounded a curve, full speed and on our tail. I swore and leaned forward, snagging one arm under Willa's. "All right, Annie Oakley," I said, "That's it. Time to go!" She pulled the trigger one last time, her pistol finally clicking empty.

Beside me, Finch leaned from the truck, grabbing Willa by the belt just as Carver hit the gas. Willa dangled out over the back of the truck, the pavement flying beneath her feet as we struggled to pull her up into the truck. Bullets were hitting the pavement below, ricocheting up into the truck's metal undercarriage as the shooters struggled to take out our tires. Behind us, Ron wrapped one arm around my waist so I wouldn't pitch off the back of the truck as I leaned farther out, grappling for a firm hold on Willa. With a groan, Finch extended a second hand to Willa's arm as we struggled to get her up over the tailgate and into the bed.

That was when it happened.

In the midst of the symphony of gunshots, one caught Finch, his third bullet of the night. I learned later that it hit him in the throat, an inch to the left of his Adam's apple, and passed straight through his neck, exiting out the back in a spray beside his spine. What I felt was a hot jet of blood from Finch splash against me as he collapsed, his hands going limp as he dropped Willa's weight solely on me.

Willa wasn't heavy, but once my arms were extended out away from my body, her meager weight became back-breaking. She slipped downward, her sneakers dragging on the pavement as Ron struggled to keep me in the truck. The Glock fell from her hands, clattering to the road as her arms rose, struggling to grab onto me.

She turned her eyes upward, wide open with fear, as I tried to close my shaking second hand around her belt. I leaned forward, shifting, gritting my teeth as I put her full weight on my one side. The torque was too much. I twisted and felt a muscle in my side tear under the strain. The damage I'd taken at Cally's Casino went through me like a knife as I cried out and Willa slipped from my grasp. She fell, tumbling to the pavement, her body rolling wildly against the roadway.

I collapsed against the tailgate, fresh blood seeping from the once closed line of stitches on my side, the sight of Willa's fearful eyes burned into my brain. I shouted to stop, but behind me in the cab, Carver didn't slow. Willa receded in the distance as the black sedans surrounded her. Slowly, she propped herself up on one elbow. Before any of us could react, a ring of dog soldiers closed in, swallowing her.

CHAPTER 38. THE NEED FOR RESILIENCE

Dr. Hanas had Gil in surgery, and they'd been in there for nearly three hours. It was as good a sign as any, I guess. He wasn't dead yet. Finch was in another room under another doctor's care. I'd been alone in Hanas' subpar waiting room alone; even Carver the bulldog had abandoned me. He'd left to scrub Boss' blood out of his junker. Ron and Archimedes were gone, offering that the sun was soon to rise and they couldn't afford to have Ron turn to stone in some back alley. I didn't have it in me to point out that they had at least six hours of night left.

Willa was gone. Maybe dead. For sure she was in worse shape than me or Finch, maybe even Gil. If she was alive, she was currently being dragged kicking and screaming by a squad of mercenary dog soldiers back to the clutches of known lady-killer Bluebeard. Oh yeah, and she'd fallen off the back of a moving pickup truck, which probably didn't help matters. The thoughts were spinning around my head like a lesson in Worst Case Scenario 101.

For the first hour or so, I'd paced, very nearly carving a trench in the tile floor. Terrible revenge sagas ran through my mind and I savored every imaginary thrust of my sword. Soon, I tired. Somewhere between the night raid and the dragon, the car chase and the shootout, exhaustion caught up with me. The second hour I spent watching a rebroadcast of a baseball game and zoning out. I felt like a zombie.

At nearly 2:00AM, a pale-faced orderly with wire-frame glasses waved me into Finch's room without a word.

He was pale, but not as pale as the last time I'd seen him. From just below his chin downward, his entire body seemed wrapped in gauze, Bubba Ho-Tep style. His eyes were lucid, but slowed by painkillers. When I stepped through the doorway, a weak smile cracked his lips.

"Dylan," he said, his voice low.

"How are you feeling?"

"Reasonably well, considering."

I nodded. I felt like shit, but who was I to complain?

"What happened?" he croaked.

"Gil's in the operating room with Hanas," I said. "They've been in there for a while."

"No, I mean before. What happened?" His glassy eyes moved around the room sluggishly. "Where is Willa? And Ron and Archie. And Carver?"

"Ron and Archie and Carver split," I said, shrugging. "Can't deal with the hospital, I guess."

"And Willa?"

He couldn't remember. That last bullet must've taken a lot out of him. "We lost her," I said.

He remained stoic, Finch to the core. "Dead?"

"I don't know. She fell out of the truck. If she's not dead, they have her."

His eyes lowered as he mulled over my words. I opened my mouth to continue, but he cut me off.

"They will do everything in their power to keep her alive."

"Why?"

"She is the only ace they have left."

"I don't follow."

"The one thing they want and can't get," he said. "What is it?"

It took me a minute. "Her husband. The real Bascombe."

He nodded. "She is the only way to draw him in."

It made enough sense to leave me feeling sick. "Bait," I said.

He nodded again, cringing in pain.

"What can I do?"

Finch was silent, his eyes blank. After a moment, he looked up, his gaze resting on a clock hanging on the wall.

"Nothing now," he said. "Give me a few hours. I'll be back at the office tomorrow morning. We'll make our next move then."

After all the time pacing and stuck in the waiting room, some dam burst. I couldn't do *nothing* anymore. I wanted to act. "What am I supposed to do now? Go to fucking Wendy's? Catch a movie?"

"Get some rest. I told you, I'll be at the office come business hours."

"You're not gonna be on your feet in six hours or sixty," I said, my brain-dead temper rising for the first time in hours. "You'll be lucky if you're back on your feet in a week. Damn lucky."

He shook his head, the foggy look momentarily evaporating from his eyes. "I am not a normal man, Dylan. You have to remember that."

I bit down on my lip. What did he want me to do? Go to sleep? Nice fantasy. Trying to sleep wouldn't be any more productive than the zone-out time I'd had back at Hanas' clinic.

"I haven't forgotten that you're an undead superman or whatever, but we need to act now," I growled, my voice rising. "*Right* now. We need to get her back."

Finch swallowed with a grimace. "I told you, Bluebeard's men will take care of her until Bascombe surfaces. For the moment she is as safe with them as she is with us. We just need to find Bascombe first."

"How do you propose we do that?" I asked, my lip shaking in anger. "A Goddamned classified ad?"

"There is one final option I have," he said, his voice falling to near a whisper. "It is... a last resort, but it is reliable. I have hope. And so should you."

I could tell his strength was waning, so I didn't push. Trying to take your anger out on Finch was as satisfying as taking your anger out on a brick wall, perhaps even less so. Not only could you not make Finch angry, you couldn't break him, either.

"All right," I conceded. "I'll be at the office in the morning, first thing. I'll be waiting for you."

He nodded weakly.

"You'll be there?"

He nodded again.

Without another word, I walked out.

***

I took a cab home even though it would have been easier to walk back to Gil's penthouse. The thought of the two wineglasses left out

303

from a few nights back make my heart hurt, but my couch would remind me of her more than Gil's bachelor pad. It was a hard memory, but one I embraced nonetheless. But when I got home, there was no home.

Instead of the well-loved and lived-in split-level where I'd spent the last few decades of my life, there was nothing, just a pile of smoldering rubble.

I'd been gone for a long while; who knows how long the cops waited for the unlucky tenant to return. Now a ribbon of caution tape outlined what had once been my childhood home. Inside the cordoned off area, long blackened beams that once held the frame together lay amassed in a charred and ashen pile. It was all that remained of the house I'd lived in for thirty years or more. Gone were the family pictures my mother had meticulously salvaged from every dead relative's attic, gone were her flowerbeds, gone were my father's favorite pots and pans, gone was the family china. I had to resist the urge to walk through, searching the rubble for memories that had miraculously survived. If you've ever lived through a fire, you know better. Nothing survives. And if there's anything left, it's far from what you remember.

On a bent and broken shutter lying in what remained of one of my mother's flowerbeds, something caught my eye. I took a few steps into the ruin, just enough to pull the shutter free, and then retreated to the other side of the caution tape, coughing. Scratched deep across the wood's surface were thick letters. The writing had been done quickly by a flurry of knives, or perhaps a claw. It said **CHEAT**. Apparently Cally had come by for a visit. I could imagine him corralling his crew of dog soldier mercenary bullies and giving them the proud okay to torch the house. All over a stupid roulette game. Suddenly I was very sorry I'd missed him. I threw the shutter into the heart of the smoking rubble before returning to the cab and riding away, leaving it all behind me.

***

That's the low point, right there. Pretty much.

It's times like that where you find yourself saying, "At least I have my health." Well, yeah, I did. But my two new–and not to mention *only*–friends did not, with both currently residing in a supernatural health specialist's private facility wrapped with enough gauze to toilet paper the Eiffel Tower. Add Willa's situation to the mix and I found myself ready to lay down on some train tracks.

But I didn't. Instead, I went back to Gil's penthouse and took a shower. I stood under the water and let it wash away all the blood and dirt. With it, I hoped the stream would carry away that which threatened to carry *me* away: hopelessness. There's no room for it at times like that. After the shower, I got dressed in a colorful Tiki shirt from Gil's substantial closet, heated up a pair of microwavable burritos from his freezer, and sat at the kitchen table to eat. They were terrible, and I didn't care.

As I ate, I made plans. By the time I saw the first rays of the morning sun breaking over the horizon, everything had come together.

***

I was at the office first thing, as promised. I had a bag of bagels ready when Dottie opened the door at 7:30AM.

"Where is Mr. Abercrombie?" she asked. "And Mr. Finch?"

"Mr. Abercrombie is currently under the care of Dr. Hanas," I said. "I believe Finch will be along shortly."

She nodded once and that was that. In a few minutes the lights were all on and the coffee was brewing. I waited in my office, staring out over the streets below as the traffic thickened. By the time the sun was up over the skyline, the avenues that surrounded the office building were packed. Dottie appeared with a cup of coffee a few minutes later. She handed it to me gingerly with a smile, a smile both warmer and friendlier than I'd ever seen from her. Her smile spoke volumes. Without a word, she stepped out, closing my door quietly behind her.

At 9:00AM, Finch arrived. He passed my door walking slowly, his gait tentative but not terribly labored. Most of the bandages were gone save for the band wrapped around his throat. The color had returned to his face and he looked as frosty as ever.

"Good morning," he said, nodding.

"Hi."

"How did you sleep?" he asked.

"I didn't."

He walked into my office and took a seat. His eyes moved over me with a quiet air of suspicion. "Why not?"

"I couldn't sleep. So I put together some ideas for what we can do."

I didn't even mention the house. I didn't want to.

"And what exactly did you come up with?"

"Plan B," I said. "The plan Willa and I put together originally. We–"

"Stop," he said, raising a hand. His brow had furrowed and his gaze had sharpened. I was not saying what he wanted to hear.

"What?"

"The Boss was right, you know. That is a dangerous plan, a terribly dangerous plan, and we are going to pursue other options."

"Why? What else is there to do?"

"There are plenty of other avenues yet to be explored," he said.

"Like what? Give me *one*."

Finch stood, his eyes resolute. "Not now, I have more pressing matters."

"*More pressing*? Are you kidding me? Willa's life is on the line here and–"

"There is a great deal more than just Willa Bascombe's life on the line, Dylan, I hope you understand that. If we cannot find her husband, a great deal of this city is in danger, not to mention that both Willa and Alfred Bascombe will certainly be dead. If this city falls into Bluebeard's hands, we will have a great deal more to worry about than lost love, my friend."

"Well, what are we supposed to do next?"

"I *told* you last night: We must find Alfred Bascombe. He is the key."

"I must've forgotten to pack my Bascombe Detector this morning, and I'll be in a real tight spot without it."

"Let me handle that," he said. "I want you to get some rest. You're no good to me dead on your feet, acting as rash as I've learned you are prone to do."

"What's that supposed to mean?"

Finch sighed; all of a sudden he was an annoyed schoolteacher. "It means get some sleep, Dylan. I need you clearheaded and sharp, neither of which you are at the moment. The next few hours are going to be hard enough as it is."

With that, he turned and left, pulling my office door closed behind him. I sat at the desk, fuming, sleep perhaps the farthest thing from my mind. What I really wanted to do was strangle Finch and then get all commando on Bluebeard's ass. It was unrealistic, but I enjoyed the thought anyway.

What Finch didn't know was that Plan B was happening with or without him. It just so happened that he'd opted out. In that case, I was going it alone. I said goodbye to Dottie and headed out.

***

The headquarters for the Department of Sanitation was just as ugly a building as I remembered. The mere sight of it brought a bad taste to my mouth.

I took the elevator up along with three or four well-dressed businessmen sporting suits that were probably made around the time cable TV was invented. One by one, they exited onto ugly floors with uglier pictures hanging on the walls. I was the last passenger, the only passenger to exit on the top floor. Dramatic lighting poured into the elevator as the doors opened, a black hallway branching out endlessly on my right and my left. My memory was sharp enough, and before I knew it, I was knocking on a thick black door.

When it opened, the pale and dead-eyed Arthur Greely stared at me with a contemptible look on his face.

"What in high heavens are you doing here? Back to play more hero? Let me warn you first, we vampires don't cringe at harsh language, either."

My right hand shot out, open and palm down. The fleshy part of my hand between my thumb and index finger hit him dead in the Adam's apple. Spit fired from his lips as he broke out in a fit of coughing and reeled backwards, one hand clasped around his throat. I stepped into the office and shut the door behind me.

Greely had stumbled back into his desk, gagging and choking as he struggled to get his breath. Before he could move, I hit him again, my fist catching him just below the solar plexus. Without another word, he collapsed in a heap on the floor, spasms sweeping through his body as he clutched at his throat.

"I don't have time for your mouth," I said, bending over. His wide and frightened eyes turned up in my direction. "And before you speak again, I remember exactly what you said. You're 'through' with us,

307

right? Yes, I believe that was it. Well, listen up, you sack of shit, *I'm* not through with *you*."

I grabbed his collar and lifted his limp body from the ground. He groped at my hands, struggling uselessly to free himself as I lifted him from the floor and slammed him onto the desktop, scattering papers and pens across the floor. Holding his throat tightly to pin him to the blotter, I raised my right hand up high, sending bolts of power coursing up my forearm to my quivering fist. I didn't have to look, I knew that my signature blue fire had engulfed my hand.

"Now listen closely," I said. "I want you to take me to the Battery. You know, that secret vampire congress that does all your dirty dealing. Understand? I know they're probably way above your measly station, Greely, but you're going to do this for me or I'm going to throw your body out that window." I tilted an eye at the wide window above me.

Somehow, even more color drained from his ghostly face. Despite my hand on his throat, he shook his head vehemently. I tightened my grip.

"What's wrong? Van Helsing got your tongue?"

With a grunt, I lifted his body from the desk blotter and pounded it back against the window. The row of wooden blinds crashed back against the window, smashing through the glass and sending a storm of shards raining onto the street below. I pushed harder and the blinds fell with a sharp snap, tumbling out the window and disappearing from sight. Greely's eyes widened as his torso moved out from the ledge and hung over a great expanse of nothing. His mouth moved frantically like a fish trapped on dry land.

"Speak now, Greely, or I'm moving to the next office to try this all over again with somebody else." Readjusting my grip, I seized hold of his collar, twisting it in a fist and giving him a good shake for emphasis.

His throat free, he sucked a few frantic breaths before letting loose a desperate gasp. "Don't kill me!" he howled, his eyes wide.

I slapped him across the face once with an open hand. "You wanna play ball now?"

He shook his head again. "I don't know what you're talking about," he whispered.

I extended my arm out further, the muscles in my bicep shaking violently as Greely clawed at my skin. "You're getting heavy, Arthur. And I'm getting mighty curious about what'll happen to your body when you hit the pavement from this height."

I loosened my grip for a moment and he slid a few inches. A scream escaped his lips as he turned his wide eyes to the busy streets below. Somewhere behind me, there was a pounding on a door.

"Talk, goddamnit!" I shouted.

He was shaking, teeth biting into his lip and his eyes clenched shut. Through his hands closed around my wrist, I could feel a terrible tremor. Finally, he nodded.

"All right! All right! Just bring me inside. Bring me inside and I'll tell you. I'll tell you everything."

"You'll *tell* me about the Battery?" I asked. "No. You'll *take* me. Do you understand? You'll take me!"

There was a hesitation, but only for a moment. He nodded again. "Yes, I'll take you!" he screamed. "I'll take you! Just bring me back inside. Please!"

"Okay," I said, dragging his flailing body back over the ledge and dropping him onto the glass-strewn floor. "We're leaving. Right now."

CHAPTER 39. BUSINESS LUNCH

Greely drove a black BMW (of course). Behind the wheel, he was silent. I'm pretty sure he expected me to turn to him at any moment and rip his arms off.

When we pulled up outside one of those office supply stores, he gripped the wheel with two hands and squeezed, trying to mask the tremors that were passing up and down his arms.

"Why are we here?" I asked. It was a local chain, the kind that looks more like a grocery store than a place you'd go to buy post-it notes or printer cartridges. Everyone inside wears red aprons and treats reams of printer paper like gold bullion.

"This is the only place I know," he said.

"You're kidding."

"They own it."

"*Roy's Office Superland, Where the* Real *Office Maven Lives*," I read. "Are you messing with me?"

"No," Greely raised his hands, palms out. "Just go inside and talk to the manager, tell him–"

"Nope." I reached over and pulled the keys from the ignition. "We're going together, remember Arthur?" I said, opening my door.

Greely wilted. "Yes. I remember."

I was right; inside the place was all crappy uniforms and fluorescent lighting. I followed Greely to an associate who was putting together a floor model of a cheap particle-board desk. He was on his hands and knees when Greely cleared his throat.

"Can I help you fellas?"

"I want to speak to your manager," Greely said.

"What seems to be the problem?" He stood with some effort and smiled. His name tag said Elton. "I'm shift supervisor right now. What can I do for you gents?"

"We want to speak to your manager."

"Well, is there–"

"Now," I growled.

Elton shifted his gaze from Greely to me. It was enough. Slowly, he nodded his head. "This way," he said.

He led us up a stairwell to a watchtower-like office that overlooked the warehouse floor. The office was stuffy and cluttered with papers and a few computers that had probably been standard when I was in high school. The red aprons were gone, replaced by one guy sitting behind a particularly messy desk. He wore a short-sleeve white button down and an ugly tie with a matching Roy's Office Superland name tag. Elton passed us off with little ceremony. This boob's name was Leonard.

"What can I do for you two?"

"We need to speak with the home office," Greely said. "Or at least your rep."

Leonard cringed and leaned back, his hand moving soothingly to his sternum as if he'd just swallowed a thumbtack. "And you are?"

Greely pulled a card from his jacket pocket. "I'll take responsibility," he said. "Or he will, at least," he said, nodding at me. "Just make the call."

Leonard read over the card carefully before lifting a rotary phone at his elbow and dialing.

"This is crazy," I mumbled. "It can't be real."

"Listen," Greely said, under his breath. "There's a way this works. Not just anybody can call... *them*, and you picked me. I'm not exactly a regional manager, here. And this is all a business, remember? A business. In this case, Mr. Dylan, you're going to have to go to the mountain."

I grunted some response. But by the way Greely was fidgeting beside me, I could tell *something* was happening. Behind the desk, Leonard had turned his back and was talking in hushed tones into the phone. Occasionally he glanced behind him, his color growing paler by the minute. Another good sign.

When he hung up, he swallowed again, grimacing.

"You're in luck." He said it the way a doctor tells a patient they have cancer. "There happens to be a business lunch ready to begin next door. A rather prestigious one."

"Next door?" I asked.

Leonard nodded.

"At the TGI Fridays?"

He nodded again. "The way high-ups are gonna be there."

"Big wigs, eh?" I said.

He nodded ominously, although it was hard for me to take anything related to TGI Fridays as ominous. Except maybe sodium levels.

"Maybe even Roy himself," I said with a smirk. "Mr. Office Superland in the flesh."

Leonard's eyes widened. He nodded solemnly. "Maybe," he said.

"Let's go," Greely said, suddenly in a hurry. "I'll get you in the door, and then I'm gone. I said I'd get you *to* the meeting, and I'm going to do that, nothing more." We pulled the office door closed behind us and clambered down the flight of stairs to the warehouse floor. "That's all I agreed to."

I patted his car keys in my pocket. "I'm pretty sure you're gonna stick with me until I let you go, Arthur."

The TGI Fridays wasn't quite next door. It was a standalone island of a building, floating in the center of the strip mall's parking lot. Time had not been kind to the structure. The brick was beginning to fade and the small shrubs that grew in the gravel flowerbed were browning. I checked my watch. Lunch hour was steadily approaching, but there weren't many cars around the restaurant itself. Inside I could see nothing but empty tables.

"This better not be bullshit," I growled as we crossed an empty stretch of parking lot.

Greely turned to me. "We're a bit out of my depths at this point, Mr. Dylan. Quite frankly, I don't know who is waiting inside this building."

An electronic bell rang when we pulled the door open. Despite the empty lot, there seemed to be a quiet hum of conversation buzzing through the restaurant. A hostess met us at the door with a pair of menus.

"Welcome to TGI Fridays, gentlemen. Just the two of you today?"

"Actually, we're here to meet someone," I ventured. Suddenly the fact that I didn't have anyone's name became quite apparent.

"Mr. Dylan?" the young woman asked.

"Uh, yes?"

"Your friend's waitin' for you right this way." She stepped back with a smile, dropping one of the menus back onto her podium.

"Well, my friend—"

"*Just* you, Mr. Dylan," she said, casting a brief glance on Greely.

I shrugged. "Okay," I said, tossing Greely his car keys.

Greely looked incredibly relieved as he slithered out the door without another word. Through the windows, I saw him dash back to his BMW and peel out. Looks like I'd be calling a cab.

I followed the hostess not to a table or a booth, but to the bar area, which was fairly crowded. An unbroken line of men occupied every seat at the bar but one. Their suits were as I'd come to expect from this crowd: perfect. Complexions ran the gamut from milk white to marble grey, not exactly a diverse group. They spoke in measured tones to each other, a few gesticulating as they spoke. As the hostess and I approached, they turned, an act accomplished almost as one, and I felt an army of cold eyes on me.

Only one man turned around completely, if he was a man at all. Despite his sickly color, his eyes were strong and—dare I say—kind. Crows feet were etched into his skin at the corner of his eyes. Thick-chested without being fat, wizened without being old, and intimidating without being scary, he seemed a man of contradictions. When he swiveled on his stool, the men around him returned to their frosted mugs and the conversations died. He stood and extended one hand to me.

"Mr. Dylan," he said as I took his hand and shook it. His grasp was like stone. Room-temperature stone. "My name is Roy Roach."

"Roy Roach? Seriously?"

"Yes, Mr. Roach, to you." He grinned, a tight, fierce show, just barely brandishing the tips of the fangs that hugged the corners of his mouth. "What can I do for you, young man?"

"Is that your office superland, Roy?" I asked.

He nodded proudly. His already huge chest may have puffed out a little further. "That and the other thirteen locations throughout the tri-state area."

"Neat. Well are you the head or king or whatever of this... Battery?"

On cue, every pale-faced expensive suit-wearing lackey surrounding Roy Roach and me at the TGI Fridays' bar erupted in a perfect chorus of laughter, Mr. Roach's own private laugh track, apparently. Roach himself mock-laughed, his plump body rising and falling without making a sound.

"I believe you mean CEO, Mr. Dylan. CEO. And no, I'm not the CEO. But I am authorized to speak on his behalf," he added quickly as I'd turned to leave. "I understand we have a problem."

I opened my mouth to respond, but Roach stopped me.

"Where are my manners, one moment, please." He lifted his drink from the bar, a red liquid bobbing in the stemmed glass. A Bloody Mary. Of course. He signaled a waitress.

"Colleen, Mr. Dylan and I will be adjourning to a table, my dear."

The young woman clutched two menus in her hands, ready. "Table thirteen, Mr. Roach," she said with a smile.

Roach nodded. "Thank you, darling."

The girl disappeared with the menus. "Do you own this place too?" I joked.

"Yes," he said. "This way, please."

Good host he was, Roach led me to a booth in a corner, overlooking his spacious parking lot like a proud ranch owner. He let me sit first as he turned and surveyed the restaurant's interior. Shoddy knickknacks, bric-a-brac, and antique junk decorated the walls. The carpets were faded and there were scratches on a few barren stretches of wall. Despite all this, Roach smiled and sighed as if overlooking a magnificent vista. Finally, he took a seat across from me.

"Would you like a drink, Mr. Dylan?"

"Manhattan," I said. "On the rocks. Extra cherries." I always felt like a child adding that last bit, but I didn't care enough not to do it.

"A fine choice," Roach said, tapping a fingernail on his own glass. A moment later, a fresh drink appeared in front of me.

It was a little early in the day for me, but what the hell. I sipped the drink and waited, meeting Roach's bright eyes head on, but he seemed in no hurry to do anything. He fished cherries from his drink one by one, pulling them from their stems and chewing them leisurely. After a moment I realized he was waiting for me and would be happy to wait all day.

"I needed to meet with someone in regards to... to making a deal." I took another sip.

"A deal? Are we talking an investment? Or are you looking to get into real estate?"

"No, nothing like that. It has more to do with... with what's been going on recently? With the upcoming mayoral elections?" I babbled on, praying he'd step in. He didn't. Instead, his eyebrows began to rise.

"I don't know what you're referring to, Mr. Dylan."

It wasn't much, but it pissed me off. Today was not the day to give me a bureaucratic runaround. "This is why I need to speak with *your* boss," I growled. "I need someone who knows what's going on. Not some third rate office store owner."

"Excuse me," he said, leaning forward, his smile evaporating. "Be thankful you're getting a meeting at all. Do you know what generally happens to people who do what you did?" He didn't answer his own question at first, instead letting my imagination fill in gaps. The answers I came up with were equal parts threatening and boring. At the moment, I couldn't care less.

"Then why am I sitting at this table?"

"My boss makes a point of not stepping on your boss' toes when possible. Follow?"

There it was. Gil. He had a lot of money and a temper almost as short as mine. Almost. I could see how they'd want to keep him out of their business whenever possible.

"So what if you don't like what I have to say?" I asked.

Roach's smile returned a little too quickly. "Well, I have two options. One, you get thrown out of here on your ass to walk home. Or two, I give the signal and my men will tear you open and show you what your insides look like." He spoke with all the candor and gentleness of a grandparent speaking to a child, but I believed him. "I'd choose your next words wisely."

I took a deep breath and took a heavy swig from my drink. "Well, I'm not here to make an investment."

He nodded.

"I'm here because I need something."

This time, Roach didn't nod. He just waited, staring at me.

"I need the Battery to take care of Bluebeard for me."

"That's enough," Roach intervened. "Unless you have something that the Battery needs *desperately*, then there is nothing you can offer that will make us do anything for you, let alone remove Bluebeard. You have to understand that the people that I work for, they don't do things for other people; *we* don't do things for other people. We are businessmen; we have our own interests, which we hold above all others. We make our own solutions for the problems that we encounter. We do *not* fix other people's problems unless those problems are *our* problems. Make no mistake, Mr. Dylan, we may be new to this capitalist system you have here, but we've taken to it quite well."

"If this problem isn't handled, it *will be* your problem because I will make it your problem," I said, my teeth barred. "Do you hear that, Mr. Roach?"

Roach leaned forward and barred his own teeth, his unnatural vampire canines looking especially nasty up close. "You do not want to threaten me, Mr. Dylan. Nor do you want to threaten the Battery. Do you know what happens when a man like yourself threatens *us*?"

"I don't know, but you'll probably crush my head or something–"

"No, the Battery is not in the habit of going easy on pests like you. We're more likely to kill your family, kill your friends, kill your friends' pets, seize your assets, infect you with a rare and debilitating disease and throw you into the streets like a beggar. Essentially do our damnedest to turn you into a crushed worm. When you're past your lowest, past caring or even pretending to care, that's when we'll kill you. Merely to save you the trouble of doing it yourself."

"Then what are my options here, Roach?"

"I'd say that unless you want someone to break your kneecaps, there's very little I'm willing to do for you. The best advice I can offer is that you crawl into some corner and shrivel up."

"So what the hell was the point of this meeting if you were prepared to offer me nothing?"

Roach smiled. "I have to say, I was more than a little curious. But to answer your question? Common courtesy between enemies. We know you're new here, and we know you don't know what you're doing, so take this meeting as a warning. If you try to cross us again to sell Girl Scout Cookies or ask us for spare change, *don't*. The next time you make contact with us will be the last."

"You won't be able to kill me," I said, the anger bubbling up from my gut like lava. "You don't know who I am."

"What? The son of a gardener whose house was just burned down by an underground gambling kingpin? You're nothing, Mr. Dylan, to me or anyone else. And you have nothing to offer."

"You've been watching me? There must be interest, then. What will it take for you to get Bluebeard out of the picture? Name the price."

"The price?" he smiled. "It will take a *miracle* to get us involved in that capacity. The price is more than you can begin to fathom. And of course we've been watching you, you're part of Gil's crew. He's a player in this game, too, whether he knows it or not."

"What about me? Tell me what you want." All I could think of was Willa slipping away. "I know your boss could use me. I'm damn valuable."

Roach laughed, a deep sickly laugh that made my hair stand on end. He sat back, his mouth wide, and continued, slamming a hand down onto the table.

"What the hell's so funny?"

"Two things. One, what on earth makes you think we need you? And two, if you knew what you were offering, you wouldn't dare do it."

I slapped my hand down on the center of the table, palm down, and spread my fingers wide. Channeling the anger from the pit of my stomach, I sent a wave of fire down my arm to my palm and straight into the table. For a moment my hand glowed a crimson red before the plastic of the table gave way beneath it and I pushed my hand straight through the melted material, leaving a perfect handprint-shaped hold in the center of the booth.

"You don't know what I'm capable of," I said.

Roach grabbed my wrist as I pulled it free and held it over the still smoldering hole. "Cheap parlor tricks aren't enough to convince me of anything."

I stared him straight in the eye as I sent a second breath of fire down my arm, through my wrist and straight into his hand. I heard the sizzle of skin like bacon in a frying pan. Roach hissed and released me.

"I suggest you leave before paramedics have to carry you out," he growled.

"I'm not leaving without a deal, do you understand me?"

"You're a foolish, hot-headed brute with all the sense of an angry six-year old. You're not an asset, you're a liability. You're a blunt knife, Dylan, a stupid man with all the reliability and wherewithal of a child who's found his father's gun. We don't need you on our staff and we don't want you."

"If the price is right," I said through gritted teeth. "You'll take me."

"I said no. Not for my life."

I stood, hitting the table and overturning our glasses. I grabbed Roach's lapels and pulled him to his feet. "You drive a hard bargain, Roach, but I think I can manage." Blue fire engulfed my hands before it began to spread, beginning to cover my whole body. In a moment, I was a blue Human Torch, my clothes perfectly untouched beneath the fire. Roach's eyes grew wide as the flames touched him, blackening his crisp suit.

As his eyes lowered to the fire burning brightly on either side of his face, he could only mutter one question. "How much power... do you have?"

"Wanna find out?" I pulled back one first, preparing to put it through his head. "I figure if I kill enough of you bastards I'll eventually get to one who's willing to listen."

"Wait, wait," he begged, his eyes frozen wide open. "Perhaps we can make a deal."

I dropped him back into an adjacent booth, his eyes a mixture of fear and awe. The blue fire thing had gotten a bit tiresome to me, but it still had the desired effect on guys like Roach. I took a seat across from him.

He swept soot from his collar, struggling to maintain his composure as he cleared his throat. "What is it you want exactly?"

"I don't know if your people are backing Bluebeard or not, but I want him taken care of."

"Let's be specific, Mr. Dylan, we are making a contract after all."

"Kill him if you can, if not, I can take care of it. I want him out of the mayoral race, and I want his backing removed. Right now, he's too well insulated for either me or my associates to so much as touch him."

Roach nodded, calming. "Hostile takeovers are fairly routine in our line of work, Mr. Dylan. We should have no problem taking care of it. And in exchange? I caution you now that you should choose your words wisely. I admit I'd rather have you kill me for being uncooperative than my bosses kill me for making a shoddy deal."

"You get me," I said simply.

He smiled. "And what you possess; your unique... talents. The term?"

"Limited to time. After one year, it expires and I'm free to go."

Roach laughed, the bitter sound making me feel nauseous even as I realized what I was agreeing to.

"Don't be foolish," he said. "Time-based contracts are worthless. We prefer to keep our employees as contractors on a case by case obligation. On retainer, as it were."

"What the hell does that mean?"

"It means we contract you for X number of assignments. At the conclusion of said assignments, you are free to go, but only at the conclusion of the set number of assignments. And *we* assign them to you, you cannot choose."

"A contractor?"

"That's correct."

If anything, the vael would be my safety net, even if they didn't know it. Any job they gave me couldn't be *too* bad, on risk of the vael leaving me just as it had the djinn. Not the best failsafe, but it would have to do.

"Three jobs," I said.

Roach laughed. "Don't insult me. Ten."

I felt sweat begin to form on my brow and top lip. "Five."

He smiled, proudly showing off his fangs. "Nine."

"Seven," I said. "And that's as high as I'll go. Seven assignments and I'm out."

Roach chewed his lip and mulled over my offer, his eyes unfocusing as he stared down at his hands on the tabletop.

"In a contract like this, do you know what damages would be?" he asked after a moment.

"What either of us gets in the event the contract is breached?" I shrugged. "I don't know."

"Death," Roach said, smiling. "Simply death. So the contract is...?"

"Seven assignments or death?" I said, every drop of blood in my body turning to ice as I said the words aloud. "*Seven assignments or death.*"

Roach nodded, extending his hand. "It's a deal," he said. "Per fas et nefas."

I grasped his hand and shook it, his palm feeling even less human than I remembered. "What the hell does that mean?" I asked.

He smiled. "It means 'through good and evil.'"

"Sounds about right," I said. "Seven assignments or death, by hook or by crook."

Roach laughed again. I felt sick.

CHAPTER 40. CONTRACTORS

I was bumping along in a cab, the images of my signature on the contract spinning around my head like a sinking ship in a whirlpool. *It'll be done by the end of business hours today*, Roach had said. *That will be when your contract will take effect.* The words were echoing through my skull like the empty cavern it apparently was.

Stupid, that's what it was. Stupid and impulsive. Two things I was becoming increasingly known for. All of a sudden, I was meeting everyone's meathead expectations perfectly. I was now officially a contractor for the Battery. I was working for the vampires. I didn't really know what that entailed, or even meant, but it solved my problems for the moment. Bluebeard would no longer be a problem. Now all I had to do was wait, right?

Yeah, that was stupid, too. Did I expect the Battery to drop Willa off at my door like the newspaper? The cab twisted through the early afternoon traffic, heading back into town and the empty office. Wretched thoughts of Willa in various states of dead ran through my mind for the duration of the ride.

The office was just as I'd left it: empty. Except for Dottie, of course. She had a cup of black coffee ready for me when I walked through the door. Finch's office door was open, but the room was empty. Not that I would have wanted to say anything. He was coldly pragmatic, but still loyal as hell. Was I loyal? I was now working for Gil's archnemeses. I pushed the thought from my head because I couldn't stand to even think about it.

Instead, I tried to busy myself paging through the library that was left behind in my office by the guy I'd replaced. What had his name been? Parker? I imagined a big brawny man with forearms like tree trunks, brilliant self-control, and a wit to match. He probably died protecting Finch and Gil, putting his body in front of them at the last moment, dying in the line of duty, fighting evil. I'm a champ when it comes to guilt and self-loathing. It's the Irish Catholic blood in me.

At a certain point, all the words quieted in my head. I read about magic and the great war that Finch and Gil were always referencing. The moment in history when things had changed and magic had been officially written off and pushed into the closet. Gil's parents hadn't even been born yet, but Finch was alive. I wondered if he'd fought in it, if he'd known men and women who'd died in it. The thought that I'd entered a world with its own history—a world that had been around for hundreds and hundreds of years—made me feel like I'd just woken to find that I was living a completely different life. I felt small and stupid.

By the time the sun began to lower in the sky, the remains of my patience were gone. No word from Finch, no word from the Battery, and sure as hell no word from Willa. I called and checked in with Dr. Hanas, who told me that Gil was awake, but hadn't spoken. "Things look much better," he said. Not from where I stood.

The sun was a fierce orange in the late afternoon sky when I took the elevator down to the garage to find the Tank waiting in Gil's reserved parking space. Once again, it had been miraculously fixed from the various wrecks we'd managed over the past few days, repaired back up to its usual state of ruin. I found a certain comfort at the cough and sputter of the old engine coming back to life.

My hands worked on their own, guiding the Tank and me through the thickening traffic, deeper into Center City, towards City Hall. All around me, commuters struggled to get out and get back home, leaving the dark grime of downtown behind. I drove against the flow like a madman ignoring an evacuation. It kind of felt like that too.

When I arrived at the Prava Center, there were emergency vehicles everywhere. A roadblock about a hundred yards from the wide glass entryway stopped me dead in the street. I pulled the Tank over and parked. My eyes moved up the length of the building to where I'd first met Bluebeard in his offices; to where I'd fought the djinn and been thrown from the window. It felt like a lifetime ago. How quickly things change.

The building was wreathed in a veil of black smoke. Through the twisting smog, I could make out broken windows and the dim flicker of fire from one floor in particular. Around me on the street, emergency workers gave oxygen to men and women in soot-stained business suits. I felt my jaw slowly drop open. It didn't take a rocket scientist to make any assumptions as to what happened. *So these are the fruits of my labor*, I thought. Great job, Dylan. Down on street level, a few paramedics pulled stretchers from the lobby. Some held struggling bodies bearing scorched, blackened skin, scalded by the fire. More than a few were pushed towards ambulances under white sheets. Those EMTs were in no hurry. I knew what that meant.

Local news vans took up most of the free space that was available. I saw camera crews setting up makeshift lights as reporters spoke hurriedly into cell phones and fixed their make-up. Through the din of voices and sirens, a few ominous words leaked my way, including "*shooting,*" "*disaster,*" and "*nineteen dead.*" I put the Tank in gear and turned it around, struggling to get as far away from the destruction as possible. The words *nineteen dead* were cloying, sticking to me like a foul stink. I did this, I realized again. I did this.

I pulled away, trying to leave it behind me. A light turned red. I stopped, angling the rearview mirror downward so I wouldn't have to see the reflection of the chaos. My mind began floating away, up into the smoky sky as I imagined who those nineteen had been, if they'd been human at all, if they'd deserved what they'd gotten.

There was a knock on the window. I looked up. Standing at the window, his face a stark display of stoicism, Finch stared in at me. I opened the door and he slipped inside as the light turned green.

"What are you doing here, Dylan?" he asked.

"I... I heard about this on the news. It was all over the news," I said. The words were clunky and false in my mouth. I felt like I was trying to speak a foreign language.

"I thought I told you to get some rest."

"I... I couldn't sleep. What happened here?"

"I don't know. Something terrible," he said, turning to look out the window. "Take us back to the office."

I drove. "What are *you* doing here?"

"Same thing" he said. "Heard it on the radio."

"And what did you hear?"

"There was a shooting and a fire in the campaign offices. Certain high ranking officials were killed."

"Which offices?" I asked needlessly. I already knew the answer.

"Bascombe's."

"You mean Bluebeard's?"

"Yes."

"Who was killed?"

He didn't speak at first, just sat staring vacantly out the window. The traffic was thinning as the sun touched the horizon, casting long shadows across the pavement. Behind us, the moon began rising, a full round shape of pale white.

"Only the people who deserved it."

His words carried a certain electric current, and I shivered. Should they have comforted me? Perhaps. But they didn't. I could tell myself the good people were spared. It may have been true, but it didn't change how I felt.

"It was you," I said. "Wasn't it?"

He didn't speak, but nodded. There was black soot on his hands that he was trying to rub off on his black jeans.

"It needed to be done," he said. "And now it is done. Bluebeard won't be a problem in this election. I have no difficulty believing that the mayor will run again, that he will win. Everything will be back to normal." His voice sounded hollow and vacant. "Everything is okay now."

"What about Bluebeard?" I asked. "And Willa? Did you find Willa?"

He shook his head. "No Bluebeard, no Willa. But I did what was required of me. One more assignment finished."

He said the last sentence low, just under his breath. I don't think he expected me to hear, but I did. After a moment, he looked over at me and met my gaze for the first time. His eyes were cold and empty, and they spoke volumes. He was a contractor, just like me. *One more assignment finished.* Roach hadn't even had one of his own people take care of Bluebeard; he'd farmed the job out. *Contracted* it out. To Finch.

That's when it really sank in that I had caused it, I had directly caused it all. The destruction, the ruins, the pile of dead. And it made me sick.

When we pulled into the garage and parked, I stepped out and vomited between two cars. Finch stayed in the Tank, sitting silently.

When I was finished, I got back in and sat down. He looked at me after a moment.

"I can't explain everything to you, Dylan, and you don't want me to, trust me. Just understand that I had to do something today, something I didn't want to do, but I *had* to do. Believe me when I say that I spared all that I could. I spared the innocent. Do you believe me?"

I met his gaze. His gaze didn't lie. I believed him, for good or for bad. So I nodded.

"Remember earlier today when I told you that I had one more connection who could hopefully find Bascombe for us? I met with... with *them* earlier. They gave me what I wanted, but also gave me a job. You see, I... I am indebted to them in a way. I owe them. This job I just did works towards settling my debt. I *had* to do it. And now we'll have Bascombe again, and I believe I know where Bluebeard is. With Bascombe, we'll be able to get Willa back, believe me."

I nodded, but Finch's words all sounded like distant buzzing to me now. I couldn't tell him that it was my contract they'd passed on to him; it was my job. He didn't know, and he didn't have to know.

"This is going to end tonight, all right? We're going to finish this. Together."

I nodded. "All right."

"Just..." he trailed off. After a moment, he took a breath, choosing his words more carefully. "Please, don't ever get in debt to someone, Dylan. All right? Not like this. Believe me."

I closed my eyes, struggling to swallow Finch's tough pill of advice. Too little, too late, unfortunately. "Yeah," I croaked after a minute. "Okay."

We left the Tank in the garage and took the elevator upstairs. Dottie greeted us and directed us to Finch's office where we found Alfred Bascombe waiting, docile and confused.

Somehow, I wasn't fazed at all. It was getting harder and harder to surprise me.

CHAPTER 41. THE RETURN OF MR. BASCOMBE

His eyes were red and cloudy, and when you looked into them, he seemed lost. He sat in the visitor's chair across from Finch's desk, legs stretched out in front of him, his arms crossed. Dottie stood in the doorway behind us.

"I went out to get some dinner and he was here when I returned," she explained. "He is rather... confused." She paused, searching for words. After a moment, she shrugged and stepped out, pulling the door closed behind her.

"Mr. Bascombe?" Finch ventured. "Mr. Bascombe, can you hear me?"

"I thought your friends were going to tell you where he was?" I said.

"They are far from my friends, Dylan. And I was under that impression as well. Yet it seems that they did one better, doesn't it?"

I pulled the second visitor's chair up to face Bascombe while Finch rounded his desk and took a seat, paging through a mound of notes.

"Where am I?" Bascombe creaked, his voice dry as a bone.

"You're with friends, Alfred," I said. His skin was sallow, and he looked even worse than the last time I'd seen him. He'd certainly lost weight, and his hair was patchy in spots. Long bruises ran from his jaw line downward, eventually disappearing beneath his collar. Similar bruises spotted his bare forearms. He'd been manhandled. There was blood and dirt beneath his fingernails. "Are you all right?"

He moved, slowly at first, turning his head about the office, trying to acquaint himself with his surroundings like a main coming out of anesthesia. Each movement brought a groan to his lips as the life slowly returned to him.

"He's been locked up," I said, lifting his emaciated hands for Finch to see. "Look at his nails, he's been clawing at something. You think Bluebeard's guys did it? Dropped him in a hole and forgot about him."

Finch squinted at Bascombe. "Perhaps."

"Where's my wife?" Bascombe moaned, his breathing quickening. "Where's Willa?"

"She's... um," I trailed off, looking to Finch for some help.

"She's well, don't worry," Finch said. "Alfred, I need you to try and wake up. All right? We need you to try and speak." He turned to me. "We need him lucid. Have Dottie get him a cup of cof–"

The door opened, cutting him off, and Dottie entered carrying a big, steaming mug. She handed it to me before withdrawing once again. I pressed the mug into Bascombe's wavering hands and he took a sip.

The hot coffee probably burnt his mouth, but he gave no sign. After a moment, his breathing began to normalize and the drugged-out clouds evaporated from his eyes. He blinked and shook his head, casting out the cobwebs. He took another deep draught from the mug. After a minute, he said, "Where am I exactly?"

"In an office building a few blocks west of City Hall," Finch said. "My name is Alistair Finch. You are with friends, Alfred, let me assure you."

"My name is Dylan," I said as Bascombe's eyes found me. "You're safe now."

"You both seem to know me," he muttered, hitting the mug again.

"Yes, Mr. Bascombe. We are friends with your wife. You have had a rough few weeks, I imagine," Finch said.

"Where have you been?" I asked. "We've been searching for you."

"Locked up." He knocked back the coffee and handed me the empty mug. "Locked up underground somewhere. I... I got out once, but just for a moment." He rubbed his face. "I feel like I've been drugged."

"I would believe that you have been, sir," Finch said. "Do you have any idea who has been holding you? Or where?"

He shook his head. "No, but..." he turned to me, his brow furrowing. "What I saw was me...but not me, and then I do remember seeing *you*," he said, pointing at me. "When I escaped... I saw *me*... and then I saw you."

"Wait, *that* was when you broke out?"

"Like I said, I was underground. There were pipes. And steam. It was dark, I broke the ropes and ran. There were long hallways and it was wet. That's when I saw you."

"Jesus, he was at the Waterworks all along," I said. "The gun, you had a gun, do you remember? You fired it at... uh, yourself?"

He nodded.

"That man," he said. "He was... me. I thought I'd gone crazy, I thought I was insane. Seeing myself. A man with a gun tried to stop me. So I hit him and took it. When I saw... *me*, I... I shot... him. Or it. He was with Willa..." Tears bloomed in the corners of his eyes, breaking free and running down his gaunt face. "Willa," he said again. "My wife. Where is my Willa?"

"She's going to be all right," I said. "She will be. We just need to get her back."

"From that *thing*. That thing that was... me. It took her, didn't it?"

"Yes, it did," Finch said. "We need to get her back, and we need you to come with us."

"What?" I said. "Finch, are you crazy? He can barely stand upright."

"We need him, Dylan."

"Why?"

"I believe we will need his help," Finch said. "There are legends, Dylan, legends about Bluebeard not being able to be killed. Legends that he cannot die," he said softly. "I'll explain later." He turned and raised his voice again. "Mr. Bascombe, how are you feeling? Can you walk?"

With each passing moment, Bascombe's eyes seemed to clear, the flicker of life growing to a glimmer, growing to a dim flame. With a deep sigh, he leaned forward and pulled himself upright. "I can walk." With a creaking of joints and bones, Bascombe clambered unsteadily to his feet. "What's next?" he asked.

From behind us we heard the heavy *thuds* of approaching footsteps. A moment later, the door to Finch's office popped open as Ron appeared, dutiful Archie perched on his shoulder. Ron smiled.

"Sorry I'm late, had to wait for the the sun to slip below the horizon and all. I like that broken window in the conference room, it's pretty easy access. No need to squeeze into the elevator."

"What the hell is that?" Bascombe asked.

"That?" Finch said. "That is our back-up."

***

"So this... Bluebeard fellow has my wife?"

"He does indeed."

"Where is he?"

"Well, we now have reason to believe he is at the Waterworks, sir."

"The Waterworks? Why?"

"That was where you were held," Finch explained.

We were sitting in one of the office's countless conference rooms, trying to get Bascombe up to speed. It was Finch's logic that he had a right to know. In the meantime, I was walking in and out, trying to get some semblance of an arsenal ready to go.

"We were at a fundraiser for, well, you, when we encountered the real you," Finch began, "Does this make sense?"

"That's when I ran into Dylan, here," Bascombe said, nodding in my direction as I piled swords on the floor by the doorway.

"Precisely," Finch said.

"I don't understand how or why all of this is happening," he said.

"Power, Mr. Bascombe. There are many men who want the office of mayor and the power that comes with it."

"I'm not even in the *running* for mayor, damnit."

"You'd be surprised to learn that not only are you in the race, you're the frontrunner by a long shot, bub," Archie chimed in from Ron's shoulder.

"Did that pigeon just talk to me?"

"I'm sorry, I know this must be quite overwhelming for you, Mr. Bascombe," Finch said. "But trust me when I say that we're on your side."

"I just want to find my wife," he said, stricken. "I don't care if the tables and chairs talk, I just want my wife back. Can you do that?"

"You'll need to come with us, Mr. Bascombe. We need the extra manpower."

329

"I wouldn't have it any other way," he said, standing. "When can we leave?"

"The sooner the better," I grunted as I slipped a sheath up and over my shoulder like a bandolier.

"First we need the information," Finch said, raising his hands to stop us. "Remember what happened the last time we rushed into something," he said to me.

The mansion and the dragon and Gil getting shot and Willa getting kidnapped and all that jazz. No, I hadn't forgotten. I probably wouldn't ever forget.

"Point taken," I said.

"Your head is clearing," Finch began, "So please, Mr. Bascombe, tell us what you can remember."

"I think they came for me during the last week in February. It was at night, I remember. There were men in suits; they came on a night when Willa was working late. I was in my study, reviewing the district's budget." His eyes were sliding out of focus as he racked whatever was left of his memory. "They tied me up and dragged me out of the room. I remember a black bag getting pulled over my head. I only saw the suits and the hands that did the work. When the bag was removed, I was tied to thick pipes in the dark. The only light I had came through a barred window somewhere above me. They fed me once every few days. The only water I had was condensation that dripped from the pipes. It tasted like metal."

He shook his head, his eyes darkening. "I could only think of her, of what they were doing to her. She was alone. I didn't care what happened to me after a while, I just wanted to see her, safe. When I broke out and saw that... that *thing* being me, and I saw it with her, I thought I'd die. I thought..." He shook his head. "I wanted to kill it. And I'm not that kind of man. I'm not."

Alfred closed his eyes and another tear ran down his cheek. He'd learned just how much he'd been willing to do for that woman, and it was a startling revelation. A lesson I could empathize with. It could be a shock when you learned *exactly* how far you were willing to go for someone.

"It'll be all right," I said. "We're going to get her."

"You didn't get an idea of how many men or where they were?" Finch persisted.

Bascombe shook his head.

"I don't know what else we can do," Finch said finally. "So let's get ready."

***

When Finch disappeared to get his own gear, I took my leave, giving Ron and Archie the go-ahead to comfort Bascombe as best as a talking bird and gargoyle could. I went into my office and closed the door.

It was silent, and I was alone. I didn't realize it until then, but I'd really needed a minute to myself. I was exhausted and sore and feeling about as low as I could, but there was one more fight left. Through the grand windows overlooking Philadelphia, I saw the city lights stretching endlessly out into the distance. I thought about the deal I'd made and the people who had died because of it. It was all too possible that Willa would join them. For all I knew, she was dead already. Finch had told me that despite everything that had happened, things were *better* now. The election was safe and the city was back on track, at least for the time being. "It was worth it," he'd explained. It may have been. But at the moment, I cared for nothing more than the safety of the woman we'd lost; the safety and well-being of *one* woman. I knew that, despite the politics, Alfred Bascombe felt the same. We'd both learned the hard way exactly what we'd been willing to sacrifice for someone.

I hoped it wasn't all in vain.

CHAPTER 42. INTO THE STORM

On the way to the Waterworks, I'd made an impromptu stop at Hanas' clinic despite Finch's protests. Everyone else waited in the car. I couldn't explain why I stopped, but the honest answer was that I felt like I had to; I had to see the Boss. Inside, I found the good doctor sitting in a weary heap in his office, dark circles beneath his eyes.

"You fellows are certainly making me earn my pay," he moaned.

"How is Gil?"

"Alive, but unconscious again. You can go see him if you want. He is in there." He pointed.

Gil looked bad, pale and sleeping in a bed, his arms at his sides. If I didn't know better, I would've said he was dead. At his side sat Mrs. Robbes-Grillet. She was dabbing tears from her wrinkled cheek when I walked in.

"Hello, young man," she said.

"Good evening, Mrs. Robbes-Grillet."

"The good doctor called me when you and Finch brought Giles in. I've asked Dr. Hanas to contact me whenever this happens. I've been here far too many times over the years."

"Is he all right?"

"Giles?" she asked. "He'll survive. Although I don't know how many more times he can be saved, brought back from the brink. Not after so many scares. This was particularly awful."

"I'm sorry. Things... got out of hand."

"They often do," she said with a resigned shrug. "I've pleaded with Giles so often, begging him to retire. Leave the business to Alistair. He won't listen, of course. He never will. He loves it too much." She shook her head.

"It'll be all right," I said.

She smiled. "It usually is. Giles has a resilience I've never seen before. It's just... difficult, being here so terribly often."

I nodded. "Finch and I are going to take care of it all now."

"I spoke with Dr. Hanas," she said. "Are you two going to get back that young lady friend of yours? And her husband?"

"Yes, m'am," I said with forced certainty. "We are."

"Good." She looked back at Gil's sleeping form, her smile sobering. "She was very sweet, that Mrs. Bascombe. Just be careful," she said. "Please. Come back in one piece. All of you."

I did my best to smile. "We will."

I looked down at Gil and wished he was coming with us. I knew that somehow it would be easier with him at our side. We needed the Boss' steadying hand.

***

When we pulled up outside of the darkened Waterworks, the mood in the Tank was pretty somber. The structure's spread was larger than I remembered, and in the dark it was difficult to get a sense of true size. The colorful lanterns that had hung from chains and lit the compound on the night of the fundraiser were gone. Without them, the Waterworks looked more like an abandoned factory under the pall of night. We all could have gone for some of the Boss' wit at the moment. Or at least one of his stupid bathroom jokes. Or even just an ugly Hawaiian shirt. Anything, really.

To make matters worse, a ball-busting summer storm had been moving in from the south, and sometime during our drive it had arrived. Thunder heavy enough to rattle the Tank roared through the sky every few minutes, intermittently spaced with long twisted bolts of lightning that turned the night to day for seconds at a time. Rain followed, and soon the roads were becoming rivers, the fat drops sounding like a round applause when they hit the Tank's hood and windshield. Cue the "It was a dark and stormy night..."

So it didn't surprise me when we all hesitated to exit the car in front of the Waterworks. Even Alfred Bascombe, who was really chomping at the bit, had to gather himself. None of us knew what waited for us.

333

Maybe nothing. Maybe the end.

"We're going to split up," Finch said from the passenger's seat.

"Famous last words," I muttered.

He ignored me. "Mr. Bascombe," Finch said, "you will come with me. Ron, you will go with Dylan. The bird too."

"Is there any good goddamn reason we're splitting up?" Archie barked from the back seat.

"Based on what I read about this structure back at the office, the Waterworks is large enough for a team of Navy SEALs to get lost in for a week."

"But I figure we have a narrow area to search, right?" I asked. "Alfred popped out of a maintenance corridor not far from the main outdoor patio where the fundraiser took place."

"Can you begin to fathom how many maintenance corridors are located in this structure? Also, I read that the renovations have not yet been completed. Large sections of the building are still under significant construction."

"Oh, fantastic," I mumbled as a crash of thunder hit. "Well, no use in waiting." I turned and looked into the backseat. "Ron? Bird?" Archie muttered something offensive in cockney under his breath. I ignored him. " Ready?"

The gargoyle nodded. "I don't mind the rain," he said. "I'm pretty outdoorsy, remember?" From his fanny pack he pulled a Ziploc back that had a strategically placed hole cut in one corner. With Archie grumbling, Ron pulled the bag over the bird until his head poked from the tiny hole–a makeshift poncho. "*Somebody* hates the rain."

"You're goddamn right," the bird squawked. "Who likes getting wet? Are you deranged?"

"Let's go," I said.

We piled out, a host of medieval weapons shared between us, and ran across the parking lot to the main entrance. I got there first, my short sword in hand, and pulled the blade back to smash through the glass when I saw it was already in pieces. Slipping my arm through, I checked the deadbolt and found it open. With that, I pushed the grand double doors open. Soaked through after only a few seconds in the rain, we slogged inside.

Most of the lights were off, and despite a quick search, we couldn't find a set of switches anywhere. The only lights in sight were the illuminated **EXIT** signs mounted above doorways and electric lamps mounted at the base of each stairway that lead up to the second level gantries.

"Flashlights," I said as I pulled one from my bag. "It's gonna be dark in here."

A crash of lightning wrecked my point, sending harsh rays of crystal white light pouring down through the countless skylights that peppered the ceiling. Through the gantry walkways, pipes, and hanging flowers, unnatural shadows were everywhere.

"This is gonna be fun," I said as Finch and Bascombe began stalking off.

"I think that's a steamin' pile," Archie piped in.

"If we stay on the main path, it should lead us back to the patio of the fundraiser," Finch said. "Unfortunately, the main path forks here at the entrance." He pointed. "Alfred and I will take the left fork. They each wind through separate rooms and buildings, but I think they meet at the end, near the main patio. You gentlemen take the right fork and we will meet at the patio doors. If you see anything, do not engage. We will join up again at the patio and then backtrack to take on whatever we find together. Agreed?"

"Yeah, sure," I said as Ron, Archie, and I started down our fork. I didn't like Finch's plan of splitting up, but it was hard to argue with the logic. It was a huge complex and we'd need to split up if we hoped to see even half of it.

A few twists and turns down the path, and I felt lost already. Ron followed at my heels, the constant pattering of water from his wings making me ever paranoid. The long narrow beam of the flashlight seemed useless in the huge expanse of the Waterworks. The lights were off, but the fans were not, and in the dark everything was moving. My eyes moved from one minuscule movement to another, trying to see everything. But after a few hundred yards, I realized that was impossible.

We stopped at a second juncture. On my left was a stairway heading up into the overhead rafters that connected to a series of gangplanks originally designed as service walks to repair piping. To the right was the twisting path that led deeper into the dark shadows of the Waterworks. At the juncture, I aimed the flashlight beam up the stairs and over the gangplanks, searching for motion or any sign of clues.

"What are you looking for?" Ron asked after a moment.

"A trap. We seem damn good at finding them."

"Up there?"

"I'd rather look than not."

"I get that."

"Can't you make the bird do it?" I asked.

"Do it yourself, dickhead," Archie said with a snap of his beak.

A few bolts of lightning sent enough light through the skylights to make me pretty comfortable about the vacant state of the second level. Without another word, we continued into the next building, following the curved pathway deeper into the thickening gardens.

The first body we found looked human. I didn't get close enough to check his teeth, but he wasn't as pale as I'd expect from a vamp, especially considering the back of his head had been caved in. Gore was splattered across the brick walkway in a violent splash of red. Ron covered his mouth and turned away at the sight. I'd seen worse overseas, but it was pretty gruesome.

"What the hell happened to that goon?" Archie asked.

"Something busted the hell out of his head," I murmured. "A hammer maybe. Or something. Multiple hits, too."

"Is he dead?" Ron asked.

"Do you really need to ask that?"

We continued, and we found more. They were spread along the path and began appearing at an alarming rate. Crushed chests, violent gashes, sliced throats; blood was spilled everywhere. The farther we moved into the darkness, the worse it became. The last body was simple: it had no head, merely a long splash of blood that had spouted across the brick, leading into the dense foliage. The bodies had started to get to me, and I was pretty freaked. But when the flashlight began to flicker, the last of my bravery made way for the nearest exit.

"What was that?" Ron asked.

"The light," I said. "The light just flickered, it's okay."

A flash of lightning filled the room, and my neck snapped to the corner as I followed a quick sprint of movement.

"No, that sound," Ron persisted. "What was that *sound*?"

"Did you see that?" I asked, turning the flashlight into the corner and moving its dying beam across a wide array of fern leaves that twisted in the breeze of the ceiling fans.

"See what? I didn't see anything," Ron said. "I *heard* something."

A drop of water dripped on my head, bringing my heart into my mouth for a moment. Somewhere behind us, I heard the slow groaning of pipes as water surged through them. The hanging gangway creaked.

"What the hell's going on?" Ron whispered.

"Watering going through the pipes?" I ventured. "To water the plants?"

"That wasn't water," Archie squeaked. "That was from something heavy pressing down on the pipes."

More water dripped on my head. "Shit," I said.

"Did you hear that?" Ron asked again.

"Shut up, Ron, all I hear is *you*," I said as I wiped the beads of water off my head. I flicked my wrist to toss the beads into the grass, but the water was heavy and it stuck. I lifted my hand into the light and ran my fingers over the liquid.

It was too viscous to be water, and it wasn't blood. It was too thick, too much like mucous.

"Oh shit," I whispered.

Ron leaned over me. "What's that?"

"I think it's... drool."

From above came a bestial roar and the crackling snap of metal as a copper pipe broke like straw, bringing the djinn's hulking shape down on top of us. I pushed Ron backwards into a flowerbed as the monster turned the bricks on the path into dust. A crash of lightning illuminated the tattooed monster as it stalked across the path and stepped into the gardens, its twisted yellow chain dangling from its emerald hand.

"Get down!" I shouted as the djinn wound up and took a swing.

Behind it, Ron hit the deck as the chain did a full 360, swinging over Ron's head and continuing over the djinn's before coming back down at me. With a roll, I slipped through a tangle of rosebushes as the chain passed through the thin trunk of a flowering dogwood tree, toppling the budding tree's upper half to the ground. Fire erupted from whatever the chain touched, casting bright, flickering light through the otherwise dark room.

The djinn screamed as it stalked me, swinging its chain like a machete, quickly turning the once-lush flowerbed into a conflagration.

Behind the beast, Ron charged it, hitting the monster between the shoulder blades and knocking it to its knees.

"Catch," I yelled as I threw Ron a sword from the bag on my shoulder. The hilt nipped his hand but flew off into the darkness and clattered to the floor. Ron let out his own roar in frustration as he leapt to follow it.

The djinn swung the chain at the gargoyle, missing Ron by inches as he twisted and rolled down the path. From his shoulder, Archie abandoned his Ziploc slicker and took off, disappearing into the dark eaves above.

With the djinn's attention diverted, I lowered the short sword and charged, hitting the monster just above the waist. The sword passed straight through, breaking through the other side as I crashed into the monster's back. The djinn bellowed in pain, and I gave the blade a tug, but couldn't remove it from the beast's back.

The next moment, I saw stars as the djinn reared back and planted its elbow flush on my jaw. I released the sword and stumbled backwards into a nest of fire, feeling the rattle of a busted tooth moving freely in my mouth. I spit a pair of them out without a second thought. Reeling, I pulled myself from the burning garden, my fire-scalded skin screaming. The djinn turned to face me, the amber chain swinging menacingly in its hand, apparently unhampered by the sword buried in its midriff.

I twisted away, swatting at fires that had come to life on my clothing as the djinn lumbered towards me. Empty-handed, I tried to conjure some power from deep within. I waited for the blue fire to erupt so I could swing, but nothing came. Nothing but that damned amber chain.

It sliced through the air over my head as I rolled to my left and found myself going face-first into a shallow stream. The burns on my arms and back steamed in the cool water as I struggled to get back on my feet. The fire in the flowerbed was growing, spreading to wooden planking on the walls and following the few flammable building materials around the room. From somewhere above, I heard glass explode from the heat.

With a great flapping of wings, Ron lifted himself from the ground up into the dark rafters of the room as a crackle of lightning finally illuminated the djinn fully. The point of my sword was jutting from its belly, and long streams of black blood poured from the jagged wound. With a screech, it stomped through the flaming garden and leveled the chain at my face.

From above, Ron dive-bombed, slamming his shoulder into the crown of the djinn's skull with a crash of thunder, sending the two careening to the ground. The djinn recovered first as I screamed for the vael to give me some help. Blue fire, columns of electricity, waves of force, *anything*. And I managed to conjure... not a thing. Weaponless, I charged the djinn as it seized Ron by the ankle, dragging the half-conscious gargoyle off the ground and spinning him over his head like a lasso. Before I could do anything, Ron's spinning body hit me, sending us flying backwards into the trunk of a weeping willow. My field of vision turned into a wave of blurry fire as my head cracked against the tree.

After hitting me, Ron went spiraling into the building's stone wall. Over the slow growing roar of the fire, I could hear a desperate scream from the rafters above me. I lifted my aching body and charged. From above, Archie fell from the darkness, launching himself straight at the djinn's face in a flurry of pecking and scratching. The beast raised a sluggish paw and swung it ineffectually at the tiny bird. Empty-handed but undeterred, I crashed headlong into the djinn's midsection, toppling the monster into a flowerbed of fire.

When it hit the ground, my sword got pushed completely through the beast's stomach until it clattered to the ground. Finally free, I lifted the bloody sword and swung it at the monster, opening a wide gash across its chest. The monster rallied by swinging the chain at my head again. I parried the blow with the my short sword, but couldn't move the blade fast enough to block the monster's fist as it struck me across the head.

I fell backwards, collapsing onto a stairwell. I was cornered. The fire was rising around me, so I pushed myself backwards. With a groan, the djinn began pursuing, a fountain of gore pouring from its midsection and leaving a horrific black trail behind it.

I scrambled backwards up the stairs, swinging the sword as I went, meeting the djinn's amber yellow chain with each mad swing. As we climbed, I could feel the heat as fire overtook the lower level room. Ron was lost in the billowing clouds of smoke somewhere below me.

At the top of the stairs, I stepped onto the gantry way and stumbled as the djinn's chain hit my sword with a resounding crash. The djinn swung and sliced through the metal handrail of the gantry like butter. The walkway shifted beneath us as the djinn stepped onto the gangplank.

"Careful, monster thing," I shouted as the gangplank began to swing under our weight. "Careful!"

I stood stooped over, gripping the grill flooring as I pushed myself backwards. The djinn followed, swinging its chain at me, oblivious to the disintegrating integrity of the suspended walkway as the chain turned the steel to dust. I clambered upright and backpedaled. Beneath us, the shredded steel groaned and began separating, tearing itself apart and spreading like a zipper being pulled open.

With the ground under my feet literally being torn in two, I turned and hauled ass. At the end of the walkway, a passage led through a small doorway and continued into a dark room. It was my only chance. Beneath me was nothing but a raging inferno.

I leapt through the doorway as the walkway collapsed behind me in a shriek of metal. Twisted into the sound of destruction was the scream of the djinn as it plummeted with the gantry.

I collapsed onto a rough, unfinished plywood sheet, the temporary floor suspended above another garden. I couldn't tell if the fire beneath me was spreading, but the wood under my hands was hot and in some places it was smoking. I took that as a yes.

I pulled myself to my feet, nothing but the bloody sword in my hand. Behind me, flames were still growing, threatening to follow me through the doorway. I didn't see Ron anywhere, and his asshole bird buddy had abandoned us. To top it off, the vael had failed me. Turns out magic was a righteously fickle element, a lesson learned at a shitty time. And the night was still young.

I ran towards the stairwell in the distant corner and heard a horrible sound roaring up to meet me from behind. At the opposite end of the room was the doorway that once met with the gantry. It now stood empty since the gantry had fallen. The sound was a fearsome growl accompanied by the cracking of stone. I turned and saw the bloodied claw of the djinn rise above the fiery lip of the stone wall and rip a handhold into the makeshift plywood floor. With a mighty tug, it pulled its body up over the wall and rolled into the room.

Its black and green skin was not just black, its tattoos marred now by smoking burns from the flames below. Blood poured from a dozen injuries, following the beast with every ragged step. Its shoulders rose and fell in gasps as it struggled for air.

"You've got to be kidding me," I groaned. "You're holding your guts in with your hand!"

From its teeth, the monster pulled the amber yellow chain. The length of chain reached across the floor and brought flames to the plywood in a wide swath. "Come to me," the beast growled, its voice anything but human.

I held the short sword out in front of me, clasped tightly in two hands and advanced slowly. The djinn met me head on, swinging its chain like a lasso, meeting my sword repeatedly with a crash of sparks. We battled across the plywood floor as the small fire began to spread.

Beneath my feet, the plywood planks shifted and buckled as they weakened under the flames. With each shifting of the ground, my balance wavered. In one misstep, I moved into the path of the beast, catching one swing of the djinn's claws across my face. I felt the ragged claws tear through my skin. Blood coursed down my face as I toppled over backwards.

The djinn stood over me, giving the chain a wild swing that caught my sword just above the hilt, a link of chain catching on the cross-guard and ripping the blade from my hands. The monster gasped a few jagged breaths as it raised the amber yellow chain for a killing blow.

I took a deep breath and looked deep into the monster's black lifeless eyes, feeling no fear, only regret at failing Willa and Alfred Bascombe, if either was still alive. I cursed my weakness, my temper, and my impetuousness as the monster swung the chain downward, straight for my heart.

Before I could think, the power of the vael exploded in my chest like a firecracker, sending unending waves of power up my arms to my hands. Reaching out, I caught the chain in my two hands. When the burning yellow metal touched my skin, an explosion of white light launched flames across the floor. With a twist of my wrist, I pulled the chain free from the monster's hand and tossed it to the floor.

With both of us empty-handed, the monster charged. I didn't think twice; I swung. I caught the beast on its chin with my bloody fist, tongues of blue fire scorching the beast's skin, setting it aflame and revealing the bone beneath.

The monster screamed and stepped back, its leg punching a hole through the flaming plywood floor. Stumbling, it fell, sending jagged shards of broken plywood plummeting downward into the fires below. In the corner, a wide section of floor became disconnected from the wall and fell, disappearing. I backpedaled as a second shudder followed the first, breaking off broad sections of floor and sending them falling, creating a precarious patchwork. The djinn dragged itself towards me as another chunk of flooring collapsed just behind it.

I crawled backwards as smoke filled the room, careful not to step on a piece of missing floor. After a moment, I hit the rear wall, backed into a corner again. Beside me on the ground lay my trusty short sword. I picked it up and rose to my feet, blade in hand as the djinn stepped from a wall of smoke only a few feet away, jaws hanging open.

Finally, I realized the sword in my hand would not be enough. The djinn was just too much, I couldn't kill it, not before it ripped me apart. As far as I was concerned, there was only one option: get rid of the damned thing. Finch's words about the multiverse raced across my mind like a comet as the djinn charged me at full tilt, its bloody claws swinging for my throat.

I rolled away as the floor began to give way beneath me. I focused all of my will on the power of the vael, realizing it was all I had left. The djinn followed me, its movements desperately sluggish. I sharpened my mind's eye as finely as I could, imagining the end result as best I could. As the floor beneath the djinn gave way, it leapt. I swung the sword horizontally across the air between us, the blade changing from blue to firebrand red as the ground beneath me broke away.

The tip of my sword literally cut *through* the air in a lancing arc, opening a seam in space like a hole punctured in a movie screen. The two halves flapped in the smoldering air before the djinn hit the gap at full speed. The hole shredded momentarily, widening enough to swallow the entire beast into the nothingness beyond as I plummeted down into the flames.

I waved my hand as I fell, like I was remembering an old trick from long ago, and the seam closed with a wisp of smoke. The djinn was gone, effectively erased. And I knew this time it was for good.

Clasping the sword tightly in hand, I fell the twenty-some feet to the raging firestorm. I closed my eyes, preparing for the bone-crushing impact of the ground when I was hit from below. With a ragged tug, my body was pulled upwards. I opened my eyes to see Ron, bloody and exhausted, carrying me. Together, we crashed through the skylight above and launched up into the rain. His flapping ceased as he passed out, bringing us falling down to the rooftop. Unfortunately, there was no rooftop. Only skylight.

An explosion of thunder sounded through the entire structure as Ron and I hurtled through a second skylight and fell back down into the darkness of the Waterworks and what lay waiting.

Oh, it was Bluebeard, by the way.

CHAPTER 43. THIS IS THE END

Talk about some shit luck. Or bizarrely good luck, if I was feeling positive (not that I was). Hey, at least I'd found Bluebeard.

Ron and I hurtled through the skylight and to the ground like a bat out of hell, broken glass spiraling around us like snowflakes. We crashed in a dense clump of holly bushes beside a canary yellow sassafras tree. It could have been worse, we could have hit the brick patio five feet away. The others in the room had not been so lucky.

Slowly, I stood. From my vantage, I could see Willa sitting near the far wall, gagged and tied to a chair, her face a mixture of bruises, long jagged scratches, and raw skin, perhaps injuries from when she'd fallen off the truck. Bluebeard stood over her, facing me, a crowbar in hand and a wicked grin on his face. Drops of blood fell from one end of the bar.

Finch had collapsed not far from where I stood, looking not much more than a mess of red streaked across the concrete. Alfred Bascombe stood at his side, blood dripping from his face, a sword dangling from one hand.

"And look what gravity dragged in!" Bluebeard shouted.

On the ground at my feet, Ron was unmoving. The fall had done a number on him, and he looked to have a respectable collection of broken bones, including one or two that breached his skin. I lifted my sword from the ground and limped to Bascombe's side.

"You all right, Alfred?" I gasped.

He shrugged, his breath whistling through his lips with unmasked desperation. "Could. Be. Better," he said.

Blood pattered to the ground around me from a hundred fresh cuts that one skylight or another had opened. I lifted the sword in my hand, suddenly finding the weight incredibly heavy.

"You two children couldn't stop me with a goddamned army," Bluebeard howled, his massive laugh echoing through the chamber. "You can't kill me."

"I... don't know what else we can do," Bascombe gasped. "Finch hit him... a dozen times or more with that sword, straight on, running him through with that blade. The bastard's not even slowed." He bent over, resting his hands on his knees. Sweat trickled down his face in thick drops, mixing soot stains and blood. "He's invincible or something. He's right," he said softly. "I don't think we can kill him."

"My ass," I said, taking a few excruciating steps forward. As I got closer, I could see that Finch had certainly gotten his shots in. Bluebeard was a mess. Long lacerations cut through his once enviable suit, opening deep gashes across his chest and belly. But other than some nasty stains, he seemed okay. His spirits hadn't even dampened. Over his head, a great window looked into an adjacent building and the fire beyond. As I watched, the heat became too much and the window exploded, showering glass down on us. It only made Bluebeard laugh harder.

"All this trouble," he shouted. "You have made such a mess. And it's all over a mistake. A *mistake*. I never wanted this. Any of this." He took a step towards me and swung the crowbar. I raised the sword in time to parry the swing. The impact of the crowbar on the blade was deafening, the metal on metal collision sending terrible spasms up through my arms. I staggered backwards.

"It had all been so simple," Bluebeard said. "Run for mayor, and we will take over this town. You know, it wasn't even my idea!" He swung again, hitting dead on with a fierce *clang*. I managed a riposte, but only just, a feeble lunge that ripped a shred from Bluebeard's left arm. Blood bloomed from the wound and ran down the suit jacket. I followed immediately with a kick to the groin. The big man twisted and caught the kick on his thigh before slamming his elbow down onto the bridge of my nose. He followed up with a crowbar to my right arm.

I heard each bone crack. Hot blood gushed down my face. I tipped backwards and fell flat on my back, the impact exploding the air from my lungs. Bluebeard stepped forward, raising one massive boot and lowering it straight at my face. I rolled, feeling broken bones grinding as Bluebeard's boot slammed to the ground I'd just cleared. With a grunt of pain, I pulled myself to my feet.

"And now I'm stuck fighting a boy," Bluebeard said, glaring at me. "A weak child who is not fit to scrub my underwear." He laughed as he swung again, a sweeping arc that passed over my head as I ducked. I shifted the short sword from one hand to another, my injured arm tucking against my chest automatically. With the blade in my bad hand, each attack was weaker, each thrust swatted away easier. My strength dwindled, and I could do nothing as Bluebeard backed me into a corner.

"Now I must kill my original—my host, the real Bascombe, and start over, choosing a new host and a new life to live. I won't even get to taste this lovely lady you see here. She will be... wasted," he said, waving the bloody crowbar at Willa, huddled behind him.

With a shout, Alfred Bascombe lunged and crosschecked Bluebeard across the shoulder blades with the flat of his sword. The big man pitched forward, his chin slamming into the pavement, blood spewing from his lips.

I lunged, swinging my blade downward as Bluebeard rolled. The tip of my sword passed through his shoulder, slicing through the muscle and biting into the concrete floor with a flash of sparks. With barely a flick of his wrist, Bluebeard swung and hit me just above the belt with the bent corner of the crowbar. I stumbled backwards and slammed into a wall, a sharp pain running through my belly like a knife. A hot stain of blood spread on my shirt.

Bluebeard rolled to his feet and turned to face Alfred Bascombe, who had knelt at his wife's side. With an awkward slice of the blade, Alfred cut through the thick cords that bound Willa to the chair. She struggled, tearing the bonds free. She rose and pulled the gag from her mouth, the chair overturning behind her.

She grabbed her husband and pulled him back with her. "Dylan!" she shouted, "Let's go! Let's get out of there!"

I fell to one knee, struggling to draw power from the vael. I focused on fire, on Finch's instruction, on *anything*. Bluebeard approached me slowly, taking his time.

"I wanted none of this," I said. "I just wanted the taste of a young woman, just a *taste*. They used that to get me, do you understand? Exploiting my weakness. *Tssk tssk tssk*." He swung the crowbar and I caught the blow across my fingers. I swore and dropped my sword. Numbly, I closed my hand around the hilt and struggled to raise it.

"Manipulation," he said. "That's what it was. *Manipulation*. It is disgusting. They manipulate everyone as they see FIT!" He swung again, this time for my face. I parried and slipped away as he leveled a second swing for my chest. Instead it hit the stone wall with another *clang*. An uneven jag opened in the stone, dust fluttering to the bloody floor.

I lunged, angling the tip of my sword at Bluebeard's heart, but he knocked the blade aside easily. My boot connected with his shin, momentarily hobbling him as I raised my elbow and slammed it across his face. He bellowed and reeled backwards.

Summoning whatever strength the vael had left, I lunged forward, slashing the crowbar from Bluebeard's hand with my first thrust before jamming the length of the sword through his heart with my second. His eyes widened and he stumbled backwards. I heard a yelp of surprise escape Willa's lips. Sword buried in his chest to the guard, I released the blade and collapsed to the ground.

He stood, frozen, with my sword buried deep in his ribcage.

"You got him!" Alfred shouted. "You got him!"

Bluebeard's face contorted as he closed a hand around the hilt of my sword and pulled it slowly from his cracked chest. A dark river of blood pattered to the brick patio, visible wisps of steam rising from the hot red pool. With a terrible grunt, Bluebeard liberated the end of the sword from his chest. Blood had filled his mouth, staining his teeth red, but his smile was unmistakably satisfied.

He bent over and reached for me. I felt his hand close over my throat as he lifted me to my feet.

"I am not a man," he said as he stared into my eyes. "I am a fucking *legend*. I cannot be killed by you."

He plunged my own sword deep into my chest.

He released me, and I collapsed to the ground. The tip of my sword, bursting from my back, clattered against the brick. I tasted blood in my mouth, a strong, bitter flavor of iron. "Oh," I said. *I'm dying*.

Willa screamed as Bluebeard turned to her and Alfred. He smiled again as he bent and picked up the crowbar from the floor. He patted it in his open hand. "Next?"

Standing with his sword in hand and his horrified wife at his side, Alfred Bascombe forgot himself. From where I lay on the ground, I could see his eyes, and in them I saw something change. He forgot the frightening mundanity of his old life, and he left behind the whipped and beaten man he'd become. He simply raised the sword in his two hands and charged. It was no longer about honor or courage or madness, it was simply what needed to be done.

With the last breath of strength, he attacked, his errant lunges and blows repeatedly clanging against Bluebeard's crowbar. Bluebeard laughed with each impact, meeting each of Bascombe's attacks with a careless block, slowly pushing Alfred back using his size and strength.

Catching Bascombe with a knee to the ribs and following it with a bone-crushing elbow to the jaw, Bluebeard dropped Alfred to his knees and raised the crowbar high, holding it high over the crown of the defeated man's head. Desperate and helpless, I howled. This could not be the end. *It couldn't be.*

Bascombe's sword moved in an unnatural blur, crossing the space between them and burying itself in Bluebeard's jugular. The nicked and bent blade hit the bone and kept on going, passing through his throat and spine with only a whisper.

Bluebeard's head hit the ground, parting ways with his body. Alfred Bascombe dropped his sword to the ground and fell to his knees. Willa ran to him.

I closed my eyes and died.

CHAPTER 44. ALL NEGOTIATION

"You were not dead," Finch said. "Despite your flair for the dramatic, we only believed you to be dead."

"No way, brother bear," Gil said. "We didn't *think* you were dead, you *were* dead as Dillinger."

The fire in the grill grew and there was the sizzle of fat dropping into a flame. Given my recent turn with fire, it made me a little uneasy. Gil was standing over my new grill–his house-warming gift, doing his best not to burn the hamburgers. It wasn't working, at least two looked like hockey pucks.

"I can't believe I missed it," he said, taking a draw from his pipe. "Can't friggin' believe it! That damn Hanas wouldn't let me go. I think I was awake. I think. Eleanor was there, she was yellin' at me. Somebody could have pushed me in a wheelchair. I am *formidable*. We are gonna need to have a full debriefing, you guys. I gotta get the full story down in my book, my grimoire."

"And why is that?" I asked, remembering that old leather-bound book I'd seen the first night we'd met.

"You gotta have a record!" he said with a smile. "For the future, to look back on. Always need a good, solid reference, you know?"

"Regardless, Boss," Finch said. "I don't believe you could offer a great deal of help from two wheels," Finch said, resting his hand on the wheelchair's armrest. He nearly grinned as he took a sip from a bottle of Dogfish Head IPA, beer bitter enough to curl your hair.

"You know me, dude. A wheelchair wouldn't slow me a lick. I coulda beat that Bluebeard bastard in my sleep. I'm super strong and super skilled and–"

"You're burning the burgers, man," I interrupted.

"Damn it all!"

We were in my backyard, my *new* backyard. In the days following the melee at the Waterworks, I'd spent most of it in a bed at Hanas' clinic, dreaming of my own bed. By the time I remembered that my bed was a pile of ash, I was healthy enough to have Willa and Alfred push me around in a wheelchair. The first thing I'd done was get out of the city. Thirty-some years in Philadelphia were enough. They drove me south to the 'burbs. I'd cashed Gil's first paycheck, and a few hours later I was writing a check to a very nice woman in the quaint borough of Ridley Park. The check cleared, and it was mine: a small but not too small cottage buried in the heart of a thick wood. It was the kitchen that sold it for me, really, the kitchen and the wide gardens that surrounded it. I gave them a nice incentive to move out quickly and by the time I'd gotten out of the wheelchair, I was moving into my new house.

In this case, "moving in" meant carrying a pair of cardboard boxes into a mostly-empty house. Mostly-empty, yes, but I couldn't have cared less; it was mine. It had a beautiful kitchen and endless flowerbeds that would have made my parents smile. I wished Dad was still around to see it. He would have had a ball setting up the gardens the way he wanted. Before I knew what was happening, a great celebration had been planned. Or at least a welcome home cookout.

"No, I'm not gonna eat chicken," Archie hollered from Ron's shoulder. "I am a bird–*a bird*–do you know how *weird* that would be?"

I smiled and took a sip of my Yuengling beer–or just lager if you're from Philly. Despite Hanas' pleadings, I had to have at least one beer at my welcome home party. I'd done my best to be a host for the first half, showing people around, but by now I was exhausted. Deep into the expanse of the backyard, I'd hobbled over to a slate patio and collapsed into half of Mr. and Mrs. Bascombe's house-warming gift: one of a pair of brand new walnut-stained cedar adirondack chairs.

Willa found me there. "How does it feel?" she asked.

"It's nice." I leaned back, basking in the sunshine. "It is very, very nice. Good to be alive. Thank you again."

"I don't think you ever need to thank me," she said earnestly. "How are you feeling?"

"I am tired," I said honestly. "Very tired."

"I bet."

Hanas had corroborated what everyone else told me: I *was* dead when they brought me in, my own sword sticking from my chest. Hanas had done his resuscitation magic at first, but claimed he had nothing to do with getting my heart beating again. He had described it as "miraculous."

Willa took a seat in the adirondack beside mine and sipped a glass of white wine. Together, we watched the birds. It had been years since I'd lived out of the city, spending almost my whole life squeezed into the cramped and smoggy confines of Philadelphia. I had forgotten how quiet it was away from the city.

"It's me who should be thanking you," she said. "I don't think I ever said thank you, Dylan. For anything." She smiled, the bruises and scrapes on her face almost completely healed. "I wanted to say thank you face to face; it meant a lot to me that I did that."

I shook my head. "You don't need to thank me for anything," I said. "I wanted to do it." I shrugged.

"I know, I just really wanted to say that." She looked back towards the house at the grill and the cluster of men around it. "You saved me and you saved my husband. I will forever be indebted to you for it."

"It wasn't me," I said. "It was us. The Zeros. We all did it together."

She smiled and stood. "I know, but I wanted you to know. And I'm going to be there for you guys. I won't soon forget what you all did for me and Alfred." Without another word, she kissed my cheek and smiled before returning to her husband. From where I sat I could hear her voice, talking and laughing with him. I turned and saw him wrap his arm around her waist. She looked beautiful in a white flowered summer dress. I felt myself smiling despite the sadness. I didn't care. I felt good. Things were good. I was happy.

For the moment, at least.

***

All the time in a hospital bed had given me an opportunity to think, and I did. My first few quiet nights in Ridley Park really got me backtracking, going over the old links and rereading Willa's old file of documents; everything that had led us from the Zeros headquarters to Bluebeard's mansion. Bank statements, deposit slips, paperwork from

Keats' office. The more I searched for, the less I found. At first, it was maddening. By the end, a frightening pattern had begun to emerge.

A few days after that welcome home cookout, I took the Tank out for a ride, driving from Gil's office to the now wearisome sanitation department in the heart of the city. I was unarmed, hoping only to learn that I was wrong so I could move on with things. *Please, let me be wrong.*

The moment I pushed open Arthur Greely's office door, I knew I was right. I was right about everything, and it made me feel sick. Roy Roach sat behind the desk, his feet crossed over Greely's blotter.

"Took you long enough," he said.

I limped inside and pushed the door closed behind me. "What are you doing here?"

"Waiting for you. It's really hard to make these kind of fortuitous appearances work. I've had to come to this shitty office everyday for a week and a half, waiting for you to figure it out. It took you *this* long? Really?"

I shrugged, trying to look nonchalant. "I've been busy."

He smiled again. "Moving into a new house," he nodded. "So I've heard. Please, have a seat."

I didn't move.

"Have a seat before you fall down."

Okay, I was still in pain. With a groan, I lowered myself into the chair opposite him. He lowered his feet and stared at me.

"What do you want, Roy?"

"My name isn't Roy," he said.

"What?"

"I said my name isn't Roy. That was bullshit. That whole thing. I don't own that awful office supplier or that restaurant. My name's not Roy," he said, "and *no one* is my boss."

It took me a minute. I'm the brawn, remember? "Of course. You're the CEO."

He nodded. "I am an expert negotiator," he said. "Expert. And you and Bluebeard proved much easier marks than I'd originally imagined. You should take some lessons from that djinn bastard; he was a real bear."

I felt a cold pit opened in the bottom of my stomach. "How much of it was faked?" I asked.

"How much of it?" he laughed. "It was *all* faked. But you still don't get it," he smiled. "You don't understand the scope; you don't know *why*."

"Tell me. I think I deserve at least that."

"Certainly," he said. From Greely's desk drawer he pulled a bottle of whiskey and a pair of glasses. "I came prepared," he smiled. "Care for a drink?"

I took a deep breath. "Yes."

He nodded and poured, handing me a generously filled tumbler.

"So I'm a big picture kind of guy, all right? In the last fiscal year, we lost nine contractors mid-assignment; that is a twelve-year high. We'd never had as bad a year as we did last year. Our contractors are incredibly valuable when it comes to the welfare of the company. Without a strong pool, we struggle to meet our goals. So, a few months back I took measures to change that, moving to employ a high powered contractor to broker the hardest of deals and settle the worst of debts."

"The djinn."

"That's correct," he smiled. "But not completely. You see, we put out an offer to the djinn to get him interested, but there was a catch. We would hire him for huge sums of money and power, but only if he was able to capture a vael and bring it to us in the form of himself–and he did. But the stupid bastard had to put ripples in the water, drawing unnecessary attention to himself, unable to resist experimenting with the vael's capabilities."

"The revenants."

"Correct again. It turns out that the djinn was inexperienced in our world's magic, so on his first night on this plain of the multiverse, he decided to stick his toe in the water. What's the worst that could happen? Well, in this case, he drew the attention of Gil's gang of losers."

"So we messed up your plan, huh?"

He smiled. "No. You see, that's the brilliant part of my plan. I know djinn, I've dealt with them for decades. They are stupid and evil and incredibly illogical, and it's their illogic that becomes so predictable. I knew from the beginning that he would draw Abercrombie's attention. In fact, I *counted* on it. However, I didn't count on *you*, Mr. Dylan."

I threw back the glass of whiskey in one toss, a cold sweat beginning to seep into my clothes.

"I didn't want to deal with you," Roach said. "I didn't lie when I said that you are stupid and rash and out of control. You *are* a liability. I didn't want you. You see, I never saw you coming. Let's rewind, shall we? After I'd killed Gil's other associate, the man Parker, I expected Gil and Finch to take months finding a replacement–as it usually does, but you were hired in a matter of only a few weeks. Because of that, *you* were not a part of my plan. I had expected Finch and Gil to fight the djinn alone, and for the vael to move into Finch, a young man who already happens to *be* one of my acting contractors. Why hire outside the company when you can promote from within?"

"Why would the vael choose Finch over Gil?"

He smiled. "It would, trust me. I know Gil much better than you."

I swallowed and took a deep breath. "But it chose me."

He nodded. "Yes, it chose you, instead. Because of that, I had to alter my plans. Certain associates of mine had already begun to back that oaf Bluebeard, but the bastard was a hard sell when it came to political aspirations. A few checks with my name on them were enough to change that. He was even easier than you were. Like the djinn, I knew Bluebeard would draw your attention like a blinking neon sign."

"So this was all about the vael?" I muttered, my mind spinning.

"Of course it was," he said. "The power of the vael is incredible. You have only just begun to learn."

"You never answered my first question. How much of it was faked?"

"None of it was truly fake, but *all of it* was orchestrated. I needed you to think everything was your doing, your choice. Altimerach was my man on the inside for most of it, guiding you along, watching you, keeping in touch with me. And do you think Finch is the only good man under my thumb?" He smiled. "You'd be surprised what someone is willing to do to stay alive. Like Mrs. Burton," he said. "My friend in Michigan."

"What about Talus Fox and the mansion?"

"That was a trap, certainly. I'd hoped Mr. Abercrombie's impetuousness would have brought him to the mansion alone and removed him from the equation, but alas."

I wondered if Gil had realized it was a trap even before we had, and if this was why he had never spoken of it again.

Roach gave me a sickening smile. "I still got what I wanted at the end of the day."

I leaned over and closed my eyes. The entire thing was a long con, done solely to get me to sign a contract.

"Careful now, don't puke on the rug." He kicked a trashcan in my direction. "There were some wild cards, of course, like that gambler Cally and the subnormal Keats, and of course the ever perseverant Mrs. Bascombe herself, but it all worked out in the end. By the way, I got Cally off your back for the moment. No need to thank me, I'm just protecting my investment."

"And this was all to get me to agree to a damn contract?"

He nodded. "Of course. The easiest way to steal someone's soul is to get them to sell it to you cheap."

"Bluebeard was your agent."

He shrugged. "Not officially, but the Battery were funding him. When you made the deal with me, we essentially fired him. We didn't even kill him. I let you guys do the dirty work yourself."

There was a terrible logic to it. The more I turned over Roach's words in my head, the worse I felt. After a moment, I looked up at him, suddenly exhausted. "Is there anything else? I want to leave."

"Yes, as a matter of fact," he said, standing. "Mr. Greely will be your handler. He will contact you when he has your first assignment. I expect prompt deliverance of all contracts assigned to you, do you understand?"

I nodded.

"This is the last time you'll see me. You will not be contacting me or anyone else in the Battery again. You work for us now, not the other way around."

He rounded the desk and strode past me, opening the office door. "I expect you can see yourself out."

"Wait," I said. "What's your name?"

He stopped in the doorway. "I forgot a long time ago, so I chose my own. You can call me Carrion. I like for my reputation to precede me." He turned and smiled over his shoulder, baring long vampire canines in a ferocious grin. With that, he left.

A few minutes later, I hobbled downstairs, for a moment seriously contemplating running into traffic. What's it like to get conned? Terrible, and I hadn't *just* gotten conned, I felt like I'd taken a beating for nine rounds. Now I just wanted to go home and lay down in my new bed in my new house, put a new album on my new stereo and hope everything would be better tomorrow.

Outside, Finch sat in the Tank's passenger seat, waiting for me. I wasn't surprised. Like I said, it's getting pretty hard to surprise me. Although Carrion had managed in spades.

I slipped into the driver's seat.

"Are you all right?" he asked.

I shook my head. "Not really. How did you figure it out?"

"It took me a little while, but it was something that Carrion had said to me once that came back to me. Also, the fact that you turned up at the Prava Center that afternoon when I busted up his office was strange." He shook his head. "All I had to do then was watch you and wait. And now I know."

"Are you here to scold me? Or fire me? Rip me a new asshole and then tell Gil?"

He shook his head. "No. Gil doesn't know about me, and he won't know about you, either." He took a deep breath and watched the traffic creep past City Hall. "It is terrible at first," he admitted. "The contract is a yoke around your neck."

"Does it get easier?" I asked.

He shrugged. "I believe it does, yes. Humans are very adaptable creatures."

I didn't say anything.

"I went to the Battery about ten years ago," he said. "I was tired and desperate and I went to them to try and get my soul back. I jumped through hoop after hoop after hoop. At the end of the story, I got nothing, and they got my signature." He shook his head. "I wanted so badly to be a man again. I gave up the last thing I had."

"Have I?" I asked.

He turned to me and smiled, perhaps the first genuine smile I'd ever seen on his face. "No," he said. "It will be easier now, much easier, because we are in this together. Also, do you remember what Dr. Hanas told you?"

"When?"

"When you first woke up."

"He said that I should be dead."

"That's right. You should be."

"I don't follow."

"The vael, Dylan, the vael brought you back to life. Call it what you want, faith or destiny or whatever, but the vael would not let you die. You are a good man, and you are supposed to do good things. Otherwise, you would be dead right now."

"So what does that mean?" I asked after a long moment.

Finch smiled. "The vael saved you *after* you made the deal with the Battery. At the very least, the vael believes you to be inherently good." He nodded. "That means all we need is time. In time, we will break the Battery; you, me, and Gil. Together. I have no doubt in my mind. All we need is time."

"Time."

He nodded. "Yes, time."

"And until we bust up the Battery?"

"Until then, we keep up hope."

"Hope," I said. "Hope for what?"

"Hope of... possibility. It is hope that gives me the strength to tie my shoes in the morning. A life lived without hope is a dungeon."

I didn't respond.

"We can make it work," Finch said. "Carrion is right when he says it is all just a negotiation. Everything is negotiation. With hope and a bit of perseverance, we can make it work."

"Hope," I said. He nodded once more.

I looked around me. Kids walked by, laughing, having just gotten out of school. An old man held hands with an old woman, smiling as a radio hanging from his wrist played a late afternoon Phillies game. From the small speaker, I heard the crowd cheer. Down in South Philly, the Phillies were winning. Above me, the sun was perfect on the cloudless blue sky.

"Hope," I said again.

Finch watched me. "Why are you smiling?"

I started the car. "An old Abercrombian saying comes to mind. 'The only way out of a storm is through it.' Isn't that right?"

"That is right," he said with the barest hint of a grin.

"Well, okay then," I nodded and put the Tank in gear. "Let's get back to work."

ABOUT THE AUTHOR

Eric Bonkowski lives in Delaware. He is inspired daily by Saturday afternoon cliffhanger serials, classic comics and comic strips, and horror films of the '30s and '40s–to say nothing of mystery, fantasy, and science fiction pulp writings of every age.

He spends his time reading, watching campy movies, and writing, supported all the while by his remarkable wife and family. During the rare quieter moments, he can be found listening to jazz and falling asleep well before bedtime.

He is the author of the *Gil's Grimoire* series and the *Brick Brannigan* series.

Visit him at:

http://www.gilsgrimoire.com

http://www.brickbrannigan.com